PARAMOUNT PICTURES PRESENTS
A HOWARD W. KOCH, JR./GENE KIRKWOOD
PRODUCTION

A MICHAEL MANN
FILM
THE KEEP

SCOTT GLENN
JÜRGEN PROCHNOW
ROBERT PROSKY
AND IAN McKELLEN

MUSIC SCORE BY
TANGERINE DREAM

EXECUTIVE PRODUCER
COLIN M. BREWER

BASED ON THE NOVEL BY
F. PAUL WILSON

SCREENPLAY BY
MICHAEL MANN

PRODUCED BY
GENE KIRKWOOD AND HOWARD W. KOCH, JR.

DIRECTED BY
MICHAEL MANN

A PARAMOUNT PICTURE

F. PAUL WILSON

BERKLEY BOOKS, NEW YORK

This Berkley book contains the complete
text of the original hardcover edition.
It has been completely reset in a typeface
designed for easy reading, and was printed
from new film.

THE KEEP

A Berkley Book / published by arrangement with
William Morrow and Company, Inc.

PRINTING HISTORY
William Morrow and Company edition published 1981
Berkley edition / October 1982
Fifth printing / December 1983

ISBN: 0-425-06440-9

A BERKLEY BOOK ® TM 757,375
Berkley Books are published by The Berkley Publishing Group,
200 Madison Avenue, New York, New York 10016.
The name "BERKLEY" and the stylized "B" with design
are trademarks belonging to Berkley Publishing Corporation.
PRINTED IN THE UNITED STATES OF AMERICA

ACKNOWLEDGMENTS

The author would like to thank Rado L. Lencek, professor of Slavic languages at Columbia University, for his prompt and enthusiastic response to a very odd request from a stranger.

The author also wishes to acknowledge an obvious debt to Howard Phillips Lovecraft, Robert Ervin Howard, and Clark Ashton Smith.

F. PAUL WILSON
April, 1979—January, 1981

to Al Zuckerman

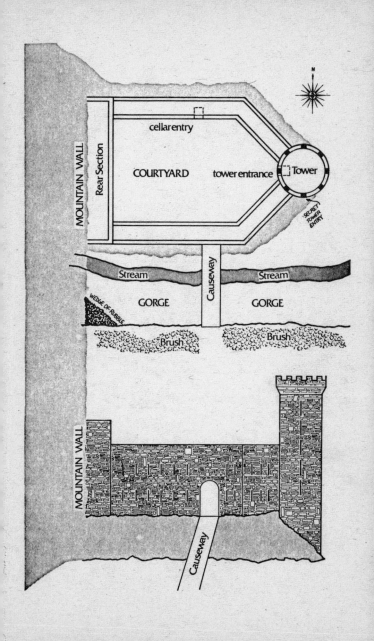

PROLOGUE

A year and a half ago there had been another name on the door, a Polish name, and no doubt a title and the name of a department or bureau in the Polish government. But Poland no longer belonged to the Poles, and the name had been crudely obliterated with thick, heavy strokes of black paint. Erich Kaempffer paused outside the door and tried to remember the name. Not that he cared. It was merely an exercise in memory. A mahogany plaque now covered the spot, but smears of black showed around its edges. It read:

SS-Oberführer W. Hossbach
RSHA——Division of Race and Resettlement
Warsaw District

He paused to compose himself. What did Hossbach want of him? Why the early morning summons? He was

1

angry with himself for letting this get to him, but no one in the SS, no matter how secure his position, even an officer rising as rapidly as he, could be summoned to report "immediately" to a superior's office without experiencing a spasm of apprehension.

Kaempffer took one last deep breath, masked his anxiety, and pushed through the door. The corporal who acted as General Hossbach's secretary snapped to attention. The man was new and Kaempffer could see that the soldier didn't recognize him. It was understandable —Kaempffer had been at Auschwitz for the past year.

"Sturmbannführer Kaempffer," was all he said, allowing the youngster to take it from there. The corporal pivoted and strode through to the inner office. He returned immediately.

"Oberführer Hossbach will see you now, Herr Major."

Kaempffer breezed past the corporal and stepped into Hossbach's office to find him sitting on the edge of his desk.

"Ah, Erich! Good morning!" Hossbach said with uncharacteristic joviality. "Coffee?"

"No thank you, Willhelm." He had craved a cup until this very moment, but Hossbach's smile had immediately put him on guard. Now there was a knot where an empty stomach had been.

"Very well, then. But take off your coat and get comfortable."

The calendar said April, but it was still cold in Warsaw. Kaempffer wore his overlong SS greatcoat. He removed it and his officer's cap slowly and hung them on the wall rack with great care, forcing Hossbach to watch him and, perhaps, to dwell on their physical differences. Hossbach was portly, balding, in his early fifties. Kaempffer was a decade younger, with a tightly muscled frame and a full head of boyishly blond hair. And Erich Kaempffer was on his way *up*.

"Congratulations, by the way, on your promotion and on your new assignment. The Ploiesti position is quite a plum."

"Yes." Kaempffer maintained a neutral tone. "I just

hope I can live up to Berlin's confidence in me."

"I'm sure you will."

Kaempffer knew that Hossbach's good wishes were as hollow as the promises of resettlement he made to the Polish Jews. Hossbach had wanted Ploiesti for himself—every SS officer wanted it. The opportunities for advancement and for personal profit in being commandant of the major camp in Romania were enormous. In the relentless pursuit of position within the huge bureaucracy created by Heinrich Himmler, where one eye was always fixed on the vulnerable back of the man ahead of you, and the other eye ever watchful over your shoulder at the man behind you, there was no such thing as a sincere wish for success.

In the uncomfortable silence that followed, Kaempffer scanned the walls and repressed a sneer as he noted more lightly colored squares and rectangles where degrees and citations had been hung by the previous occupant. Hossbach had not redecorated. Typical of the man to try to give the impression that he was much too busy with SS matters to bother with trifles such as having the walls painted. It was so obviously an act. Kaempffer did not need to put on a show of his devotion to the SS. His every waking hour was devoted to furthering his position in the organization.

He pretended to study the large map of Poland on the wall, its face studded with colored pins representing concentrations of undesirables. It had been a busy year for Hossbach's RSHA office; it was through here that Poland's Jewish population was being directed toward the "resettlement center" near the rail nexus of Auschwitz. Kaempffer imagined his own office-to-be in Ploiesti, with a map of Romania on the wall, studded with his own pins. Ploiesti . . . there could be no doubt that Hossbach's cheery manner boded ill. Something had gone wrong somewhere and Hossbach was going to make full use of his last few days as superior officer to rub Kaempffer's nose in it.

"Is there some way I might be of service to you?" Kaempffer finally asked.

"Not to me, per se, but to the High Command. There

is a little problem in Romania at the moment. An inconvenience, really."

"Oh?"

"Yes. A small regular army detachment stationed in the Alps north of Ploiesti has been suffering some losses—apparently due to local partisan activity—and the officer wishes to abandon his position."

"That's an army matter." Major Kaempffer didn't like this one bit. "It has nothing to do with the SS."

"But it does." Hossbach reached behind him and plucked a piece of paper off his desk top. "The High Command passed this on to Obergruppenführer Heydrich's office. I think it is rather fitting that I pass it on to you."

"Why fitting?"

"The officer in question is Captain Klaus Woermann, the one you brought to my attention a year or so ago because of his refusal to join the Party."

Kaempffer allowed himself an instant of guarded relief. "And since I'll be in Romania, this is to be dumped in my lap."

"Precisely. Your year's tutelage at Auschwitz should not only have taught you how to run an efficient camp, but how to deal with partisan locals as well. I'm sure you'll solve the matter quickly."

"May I see the paper?"

"Certainly."

Kaempffer took the proffered slip of paper and read the two lines. Then he read them again.

"Was this decoded properly?"

"Yes. I thought the wording rather odd myself, so I had it double-checked. It's accurate."

Kaempffer read the message again:

> *Request immediate relocation.*
> *Something is murdering my men.*

A disturbing message. He had known Woermann in the Great War and would always remember him as one of the stubbornest men alive. And now, in a new war, as an officer in the Reichswehr, Woermann had repeatedly refused to join the Party despite relentless pressure. Not a man to abandon a position, strategic or otherwise, once he had assumed it. Something must be very wrong for him to request relocation.

But what bothered Kaempffer even more was the choice of words. Woermann was intelligent and precise. He knew his message would pass through a number of hands along the transcription and decoding route and had been trying to get something across to the High Command without going into detail.

But what? The word "murder" implied a purposeful human agent. Why then had he preceded it with "something"? A thing—an animal, a toxin, a natural disaster —could kill but it could not murder.

"I'm sure I don't have to tell you," Hossbach was saying, "that since Romania is an ally state rather than an occupied territory, a certain amount of finesse will be required."

"I'm quite well aware of that."

A certain amount of finesse would be required in handling Woermann, too. Kaempffer had an old score to settle with him.

Hossbach tried to smile, but the attempt looked more like a leer to Kaempffer. "All of us at RSHA, all the way up to General Heydrich, will be most interested to see how you fare in this . . . before you move on to the major task at Ploiesti."

The emphasis on the word "before," and the slight pause preceding it were not lost on Kaempffer. Hossbach was going to turn this little side trip to the Alps into a trial by fire. Kaempffer was due in Ploiesti in one week; if he could not handle Woermann's problem with sufficient dispatch, then it might be said of him that perhaps he was not the man to set up the resettlement camp at Ploiesti. There would be no shortage of candidates to take his place.

Spurred by a sudden sense of urgency, he rose and put on his coat and cap. "I foresee no problems. I'll leave at once with two squads of *einsatzkommandos*. If air transport can be arranged and proper rail connections made, we can be there by this evening."

"Excellent!" Hossbach said, returning Kaempffer's salute.

"Two squads should be sufficient to take care of a few guerrillas." He turned and stepped to the door.

"More than sufficient, I'm sure."

SS-Sturmbannführer Kaempffer did not hear his superior's parting remark. Other words filled his mind: *"Something is murdering my men."*

DINU PASS, ROMANIA
28 April 1941
1322 hours

Captain Klaus Woermann stepped to the south window of his room in the keep's tower and spat a stream of white into the open air.

Goat's milk—*gah*! For cheese, maybe, but not for drinking.

As he watched the liquid dissipate into a cloud of pale droplets plummeting the hundred feet or so to the rocks below, Woermann wished for a brimming stein of good German beer. The only thing he wanted more than the beer was to be gone from this antechamber to Hell.

But that was not to be. Not yet, anyway. He straightened his shoulders in a typically Prussian gesture. He was taller than average and had a large frame that had once supported more muscle but was now tending toward flab. His dark brown hair was cropped close; he had wide-set eyes, equally brown; a slightly crooked nose, broken in his youth; and a full mouth capable of a toothy grin when appropriate. His gray tunic was open to the waist, allowing his small paunch to protrude. He patted it. Too much sausage. When frustrated or dissatisfied, he tended to nibble between meals, usually at a sausage. The more frustrated and dissatisfied, the more he nibbled. He was getting fat.

Woermann's gaze came to rest on the tiny Romanian village across the gorge, basking in the afternoon sunlight, peaceful, a world away. Pulling himself from the window, he turned and walked across the room, a room lined with stone blocks, many of them inlaid with peculiar brass-and-nickel crosses. Forty-nine crosses in this room to be exact. He knew. He had counted them numerous times in the last three or four days. He walked past an easel holding a nearly finished painting, past a cluttered makeshift desk to the opposite window, the one that looked down on the keep's small courtyard.

Below, the off-duty men of his command stood in small groups, some talking in low tones, most sullen and silent, all avoiding the lengthening shadows. Another night was coming. Another of their number would die.

One man sat alone in a corner, whittling feverishly. Woermann squinted down at the piece of wood taking shape in the carver's hands—a crude cross. As if there weren't enough crosses around!

The men were afraid. And so was he. Quite a turn-around in less than a week. He remembered marching them through the gates of the keep as proud soldiers of the Wehrmacht, an army that had conquered Poland, Denmark, Norway, Holland, and Belgium; and then, after sweeping the remnants of the British Army into the sea at Dunkirk, had gone on to finish off France in thirty-nine days. And just this month, Yugoslavia had been overrun in twelve days, Greece in a mere twenty-one as of yesterday. Nothing could stand against them. Born victors.

But that had been last week. Amazing what six horrible deaths could do to the conquerors of the world. It worried him. During the past week the world had constricted until nothing existed for him and for his men beyond this undersized castle, this tomb of stone. They had run up against something that defied all their efforts to stop it, that killed and faded away, only to return to kill again. The heart was going out of them.

They . . . Woermann realized that he had not included himself among them for some time. The fight had gone out of his own heart back in Poland, near the town of Posnan . . . after the SS had moved in and he had seen firsthand the fate of those "undesirables" left in the wake of the victorious Wehrmacht. He had protested. As a result, he had seen no further combat since then. Just as well. He had lost all pride that day in thinking of himself as one of the conquerors of the world.

He left the window and returned to the desk. He stood at its edge, oblivious to the framed photographs of his wife and his two sons, and stared down at the decoded message there.

> *SS-Sturmbannführer Kaempffer arriving today with detachment einsatzkommandos. Maintain present position.*

Why an SS major? This was a regular army position. The SS had nothing to do with him, with the keep, or with Romania as far as he knew. But then there were so many things he failed to understand about this war. And Kaempffer, of all people! A rotten soldier, but no doubt an exemplary SS man. Why here? And why with einsatzkommandos? They were extermination squads. Death's Head Troopers. Concentration camp muscle. Specialists in killing unarmed civilians. It was their work he had witnessed outside Posnan. Why were they coming here?

Unarmed civilians . . . the words lingered . . . and as they did, a smile crept slowly into the corners of his mouth, leaving his eyes untouched.

Let the SS come. Woermann was now convinced there was an unarmed civilian of sorts at the root of all the deaths in the keep. But not the helpless cringing sort the SS was used to. Let them come. Let them taste the fear they so dearly loved to spread. Let them learn to believe in the unbelievable.

Woermann believed. A week ago he would have laughed at the thought. But now, the nearer the sun to the horizon, the more firmly he believed . . . and feared.

All within a week. There had been unanswered questions when they had first arrived at the keep, but no fear. A week. Was that all? It seemed ages ago that he had first laid eyes on the keep . . .

ONE

IN SUMMATION: The refining complex at Ploiesti has relatively good natural protection to the north. The Dinu Pass through the Transylvanian Alps offers the only overland threat, and that a minor one. As detailed elsewhere in the report, the sparse population and spring weather conditions in the pass make it theoretically possible for a sizable armored force to make its way undetected from the southwest Russian steppes, over the southern Carpathian foothills, and through the Dinu Pass to emerge from the mountains a scant twenty miles northwest of Ploiesti with only flat plains between it and the oil fields.

Because of the crucial nature of the petrol supplied by Ploiesti, it is recommended that until Operation Barbarossa is fully under way, a small watch force be set up within the Dinu Pass. As mentioned in the body of the report, there is an old fortification midway along the pass which should serve adequately as a sentry base.

DEFENSE ANALYSIS FOR PLOIESTI, ROMANIA
Submitted to Reichswehr High Command 1 April 1941

Dinu Pass, Romania
Tuesday, 22 April
1208 hours

No such thing as a long day here, no matter what the
time of year, thought Woermann as he looked up the
sheer mountain walls, an easy thousand feet high on
either side of the pass. The sun had to climb a 30-degree
arc before it could peek over the eastern wall and could
travel only 90 degrees across the sky before it was again
out of sight.

The sides of the Dinu Pass were impossibly steep, as
close to vertical as mountain wall could be without over-
balancing and crashing down; a bleak expanse of stark,
jagged slabs with narrow ledges and precipitous drops,
relieved occasionally by conical collections of crumbling
shale. Brown and gray, clay and granite, these were the
colors, interspersed with snatches of green. Stunted
trees, bare now in the early spring, their trunks gnarled
and twisted by the wind, hung precariously by tenacious
roots that had somehow found weak spots in the rock.
They clung like exhausted mountaineers, too tired to
move up or down.

Close behind his command car Woermann could hear
the rumble of the two lorries carrying his men, and
behind them the reassuring rattle of the supply truck
with their food and weapons. All four vehicles were
crawling in line along the west wall of the pass where for
ages a natural shelf of rock had been used as a road. The
Dinu was narrow as mountain passes go, averaging only
half a mile across the floor along most of its serpentine
course through the Transylvanian Alps—the least explored area of Europe. Woermann looked longingly at
the floor of the pass, fifty feet below to his right; it was
smooth and green and pathed along its center. It would
have been a smoother, shorter trip down there, but his

orders warned that their destination was inaccessible to wheeled vehicles from the floor of the pass. They had to keep to the ridge road.

Road? Woermann snorted. This was no road. He would have classed it as a trail or, more appropriately, a ledge. A road it was not. The Romanians hereabouts apparently did not believe in the internal combustion engine and had made no provisions for the passage of vehicles using it.

The sun disappeared suddenly; there was a rumble, a flash of lightning, and then it was raining again. Woermann cursed. Another storm. The weather here was maddening. Squalls repeatedly swooped down between the walls of the pass, spearing lightning in all directions, threatening to bring the mountains down with their thunder, dumping rain in torrents as if trying to lose ballast so they could rise over the peaks and escape. And then they would be gone as abruptly as they had arrived. Like this one.

Why would anyone want to live here? he wondered. Crops grew poorly, yielding enough for subsistence and little more. Goats and sheep seemed to do well enough, thriving on the tough grasses below and the clear water off the peaks. But why choose a place like this to live?

Woermann had his first look at the keep as the column passed through a small flock of goats clustered at a particularly sharp turn in the path. He immediately sensed something strange about it, but it was a benign strangeness. Castlelike in design, it was not classified a castle because of its small size. So it was called a *keep*. It had no name, and that was peculiar. It was supposedly centuries old, yet it looked as if the last stone had been slipped into place only yesterday. In fact, his initial reaction was that they had made a wrong turn some where. This could not possibly be the deserted 500-year-old fortification they were to occupy.

Halting the column, he checked the map and confirmed that this indeed was to be his new command post. He looked at the structure again, studying it.

Ages ago a huge flat slab of rock had thrust itself out from the western wall of the pass. Around it ran a deep gorge through which flowed an icy stream that appeared to spring from within the mountain. The keep sat on that slab. Its walls were sleek, perhaps forty feet high, made of granite block, melting seamlessly into the granite of the mountainside at its rear—the work of man somehow at one with the work of nature. But the most striking feature of the small fortress was the solitary tower that formed its leading edge: flat-topped, jutting out toward the center of the pass, at least 150 feet from its notched parapet to the rocky gorge below. That was the keep. A holdover from a different age. A welcome sight in that it assured dry living quarters during their watch over the pass.

But strange the way it looked so new.

Woermann nodded to the man next to him in the car and began folding the map. His name was Oster, a sergeant; the only sergeant in Woermann's command. He doubled as a driver. Oster signaled with his left hand and the car moved forward with the other three vehicles following. The road—or trail, rather—widened as they swung farther around the bend, and came to rest in a tiny village nestled against the mountainside south of the keep, just across the gorge from it.

As they followed the trail into the center of the village, Woermann decided to reclassify that as well. This was no village in the German sense; this was a collection of stucco-walled, shake-roofed huts, all single-story affairs except for the one at the northernmost end. This stood to the right, had a second floor and a sign out front. He didn't read Romanian but had a feeling it was an inn of sorts. Woermann couldn't imagine the need for an inn—who would ever come here?

A few hundred feet or so beyond the village, the trail ended at the edge of the gorge. From there a timbered causeway supported by stone columns spanned the 200 feet or so across the rocky gorge, providing the keep's sole link to the world. The only other possible means of entry were to scale its sheer stone walls from below, or to slide and rope-hop down a thousand feet of equally sheer mountainside from above.

Woermann's practiced military eye immediately assessed the strategic values of the keep. An excellent watchpost. This entire stretch of the Dinu Pass would be in plain view from the tower; and from the keep's walls fifty good men could hold off an entire battalion of Russians. Not that Russians would ever be coming through the Dinu Pass, but who was he to question High Command?

There was another eye within Woermann, and it was assessing the keep in its own way. An artist's eye, a landscape lover's . . . to use water colors, or to trust oil pigment to catch that hint of brooding watchfulness? The only way to find out would be to try them both. He would have plenty of free time during the coming months.

"Well, Sergeant," he said to Oster as they halted at the edge of the causeway, "what do you think of your new home?"

"Not much, sir."

"Get used to it. You'll probably be spending the rest of the war here."

"Yes, sir."

Noting an uncharacteristic stiffness in Oster's replies, Woermann glanced at his sergeant, a slim, dark man only slightly more than half Woermann's age.

"Not much war left anyway, Sergeant. Word came as we set out that Yugoslavia has surrendered."

"Sir, you should have told us! It would have lifted our spirits!"

"Do they need lifting so badly?"

"We'd all prefer to be in Greece at the moment, sir."

"Nothing but thick liquor, tough meat, and strange dancing there. You wouldn't like it."

"For the *fighting*, sir."

"Oh, that."

Woermann had noticed the facetious turn of his mind moving closer and closer to the surface during the past year. It was not an enviable trait in any German officer and could be dangerous to one who had never become a Nazi. But it was his only defense against his mounting frustration at the course of the war and of his career. Sergeant Oster had not been with him long enough to realize this. He'd learn in time, though.

"By the time you got there, Sergeant, the fighting would be over. I expect surrender within the week."

"Still, we all feel we could be doing more for the Führer there than in these mountains."

"You shouldn't forget that it is your Führer's will that we be stationed here." He noted with satisfaction that the "your" slipped right by Oster.

"But why, sir? What purpose do we serve?"

Woermann began his recitation: "High Command considers the Dinu Pass a direct link from the steppes of Russia to all those oil fields we passed at Ploiesti. Should relations between Russia and the Reich ever deteriorate, the Russians might decide to launch a sneak attack at Ploiesti. And without that petrol, the Wehrmacht's mobility would be seriously impaired."

Oster listened patiently despite the fact that he had heard the explanation a dozen times before and had himself given a version of the same story to the men in the detachment. Yet Woermann knew he remained unconvinced. Not that he blamed him. Any reasonably intelligent soldier would have questions. Oster had been in the army long enough to know that it was highly irregular to place a seasoned veteran officer at the head of four infantry squads with no second officer, and then to assign the entire detachment to an isolated pass in the mountains of an ally state. It was a job for a green lieutenant.

"But the Russians have plenty of their own oil, sir, and we have a treaty with them."

"Of course! How stupid of me to forget! A treaty. No one breaks treaties anymore."

"You don't think Stalin would dare betray the Führer, do you?"

Woermann bit back the reply that leaped to mind:

Not if your Führer can betray him first. Oster wouldn't understand. Like most members of the post-war generation, he had come to equate the best interests of the German people with the will of Adolf Hitler. He had been inspired, inflamed by the man. Woermann had found himself far too old for such infatuation. He had celebrated his forty-first birthday last month. He had watched Hitler move from beer halls, to the Chancellory, to godhood. He had never liked him.

True, Hitler had united the country and had started it on the road to victory and self-respect again, something for which no loyal German could fault him. But Woermann had never trusted Hitler, an Austrian who surrounded himself with all those Bavarians—all southerners. No Prussian could trust a bunch of southerners like that. Something ugly about them. What Woermann had witnessed at Posnan had shown him just how ugly.

"Tell the men to get out and stretch," he said, ignoring Oster's last question. It had been rhetorical, anyway. "Inspect the causeway to see if it will support the vehicles while I go over and take a look inside."

As he walked the length of the causeway, Woermann thought its timbers looked sturdy enough. He glanced over the edge at the rocks and gurgling water below. A long way down—sixty feet at least. Best to have the lorries and the supply truck empty but for their drivers, and to bring them across one at a time.

The heavy wooden gates in the keep's entrance arch were wide open, as were the shutters on most of the windows in the walls and in the tower. The keep seemed to be airing out. Woermann strolled through the gates and into the cobblestone courtyard. It was cool and quiet. He noticed that there was a rear section to the keep, apparently carved into the mountain, that he hadn't seen from the causeway.

He turned around slowly. The tower loomed over him; gray walls surrounded him on every side. He felt as if he were standing within the arms of a huge slumbering beast, one he dared not awaken.

Then he saw the crosses. The inner walls of the courtyard were studded with hundreds of them . . . thousands of them. All the same size and shape, all the same unusual design: The upright was a good ten inches high, squared at the top and lipped at the base; the crosspiece measured about eight inches and had a slight upward angle at each end. But the odd part was the height on the uprights at which the crosspiece was set—any higher and the cross would have become an upper-case "T."

Woermann found them vaguely disturbing . . . something wrong about them. He stepped over to the nearest cross and ran his hand over its smooth surface. The upright was brass and the crosspiece nickel, all skillfully inlaid into the surface of the stone block.

He looked around again. Something else bothered him. Something was missing. Then it hit him—birds. There were no pigeons on the walls. Castles in Germany had flocks of pigeons about them, nesting in every nook and cranny. There wasn't a single bird to be seen anywhere on the walls, the windows, or the tower.

He heard a sound behind him and whirled, unsnapping the flap on his holster and resting his palm on the butt of his Luger. The Romanian government might be an ally of the Reich, but Woermann was well aware that there were groups within its borders that were not. The National Peasant Party, for instance, was fanatically anti-German; it was out of power now but still active. There might be violent splinter groups here in the Alps, hiding, waiting for a chance to kill a few Germans.

The sound was repeated, louder now. Footsteps, relaxed, with no attempt at stealth. They came from a doorway in the rear section of the keep, and as Woermann watched, a thirtyish man in a sheepskin *cojoc* stepped through the opening. He didn't see Woermann. There was a mortar-filled palette in his hand, and he squatted with his back to Woermann and began to patch some crumbling stucco around the doorframe.

"What are you doing here?" Woermann barked. His orders had implied that the keep was deserted.

Startled, the mason leaped up and spun around, the anger in his face dying abruptly as he recognized the uniform and realized that he had been addressed in German. He gibbered something unintelligible—something in Romanian, no doubt. Woermann realized with annoyance that he'd have to either find an interpreter or learn some of the language if he was going to spend any time here.

"Speak German! What are you doing here?"

The man shook his head in a mixture of fear and indecision. He held up an index finger, a signal to wait, then shouted something that sounded like "Papa!"

There was a clatter above as an older man with a woolly *caciula* on his head pushed open the shutters of one of the tower windows and looked down. Woermann's grip tightened on the butt of his Luger as the two Romanians carried on a brief exchange. Then the older one called down in German:

"I'll be right down, sir."

Woermann nodded and relaxed. He went again to one of the crosses and examined it. Brass and nickel . . . almost looked like gold and silver.

"There are sixteen thousand eight hundred and seven such crosses imbedded in the walls of this keep," said a voice behind him. The accent was thick, the words practiced.

Woermann turned. "You've counted them?" He judged the man to be in his mid-fifties. There was a strong family resemblance between him and the younger mason he had startled. Both were dressed in identical peasant shirts and breeches except for the older man's woolly hat. "Or is that just something you tell your tour customers?"

"I am Alexandru," he said stiffly, bowing slightly at the waist. "My sons and I work here. And we take no one on tours."

"That will change in a moment. But right now: I was led to believe the keep was unoccupied."

"It is when we go home at night. We live in the village."

"Where's the owner?"

Alexandru shrugged. "I have no idea."

"Who is he?"

Another shrug. "I don't know."

"Who pays you, then?" This was getting exasperating. Didn't this man know how to do anything other than shrug and say he didn't know?

"The innkeeper. Someone brings money to him twice a year, inspects the keep, makes notes, then leaves. The innkeeper pays us monthly."

"Who tells you what to do?" Woermann waited for another shrug but it did not come.

"No one." Alexandru stood straight and spoke with quiet dignity. "We do everything. Our instructions are to maintain the keep as new. That's all we need to know. Whatever needs doing, we do. My father spent his life doing it, and his father before him, and so on. My sons will continue after me."

"You spend your entire lives maintaining this building? I can't believe that!"

"It's bigger than it looks. The walls you see around you have rooms within them. There are corridors of rooms below us in the cellar and carved into the mountainside behind us. Always something to be done."

Woermann's gaze roamed up the sullen walls, half in shadow, and down to the courtyard again, also deep in shadow despite the fact that it was early afternoon. Who had built the keep? And who was paying to have it maintained in such perfect condition? It didn't make sense. He stared at the shadows and it occurred to him that had he been the keep's builder he would have placed it on the other side of the pass where there was a better southern and western exposure to the light and the warmth of the sun. As it was situated, night must always come early to the keep.

"Very well," he told Alexandru. "You may continue your maintenance tasks after we settle in. But you and your sons must check with the sentries when you enter and leave." He saw the older man shaking his head. "What's wrong?"

"You cannot stay here."

"And why not?"

"It is forbidden."

"Who forbids?"

Alexandru shrugged. "It's always been that way. We are to maintain the keep and see to it that no one trespasses."

"And of course, you're always successful." The old man's gravity amused him.

"No. Not always. There have been times when travelers have stayed against our wishes. We do not resist them—we have not been hired to fight. But they never stay more than one night. Most not even that long."

Woermann smiled. He had been waiting for this. A deserted castle, even a pocket-sized one such as this, had to be haunted. If nothing else, it would give the men something to talk about.

"What drives them away? Moaning? Chain-rattling spectres?"

"No . . . no ghosts here, sir."

"Deaths then? Gruesome murders? Suicides?" Woermann was enjoying himself. "We have more than our share of castles in Germany, and there's not a one that doesn't have some fireside scare story connected with it."

Alexandru shook his head. "No one's ever died here. Not that I know of."

"Then what? What drives trespassers out after only one night?"

"Dreams, sir. Bad dreams. And always the same, from what I can gather . . . something about being trapped in a tiny room with no door and no windows and no lights . . . utter darkness . . . and cold . . . very cold . . . and something in the dark with you . . . colder than the dark . . . and hungry."

Woermann felt a hint of a chill across his shoulders and down his back as he listened. It had been on his mind to ask Alexandru if he himself had ever spent a night in the keep, but the look in the Romanian's eyes as he spoke was answer enough. Yes, Alexandru had spent a night in the keep. But only once.

"I want you to wait here until my men are across the causeway," he said, shaking off the chill. "Then you can give me a tour."

Alexandru's face was a study in helpless frustration. "It is my duty, Herr Captain," he said with stern dignity, "to inform you that no lodgers are allowed here in the keep."

Woermann smiled, but with neither derision nor condescension. He understood duty and respected this man's sense of it.

"Your warning has been delivered. You are faced with the German Army, a force beyond your power to resist, and so you must step aside. Consider your duty faithfully discharged."

This said, Woermann turned and moved toward the gate.

He still had seen no birds. Did birds have dreams? Did they, too, nest here for one night and never return?

The command car and the three unloaded trucks were driven across the causeway and parked in the courtyard without incident. The men followed on foot, carrying their own gear, then returned to the other side of the gorge to begin bringing over the contents of the supply truck—food, generators, antitank weapons—by hand.

While Sergeant Oster took charge of the work details, Woermann followed Alexandru on a quick tour of the keep. The number of identical brass-and-nickel crosses inlaid at regular intervals in the stones of every corridor, every room, every wall, continued to amaze him. And the rooms . . . they seemed to be everywhere: within the walls girding the courtyard, under the courtyard, in the rear section, in the watchtower. Most of them were small; all were unfurnished.

"Forty-nine rooms in all, counting the suites in the tower," Alexandru said.

"An odd number, don't you think? Why not round it off to fifty?"

Alexandru shrugged. "Who is to say?"

Woermann ground his teeth. *If he shrugs once more* . . .

They walked along one of the rampart walls that ran out diagonally from the tower then angled straight back to the mountain. He noted that there were crosses imbedded in the breast-high parapet, too. A question rose in his mind: "I don't recall seeing any crosses in the outer aspect of the wall."

"There aren't any. Only on the inside. And look at the blocks here. See how perfectly they fit. Not a speck of mortar is used to hold them together. All the walls in the keep are constructed this way. It's a lost art."

Woermann didn't care about stone blocks. He indicated the rampart beneath their feet. "You say there are rooms below us here?"

"Two tiers of them within each wall, each with a slit window through the outer wall, and a door to a corridor leading to the courtyard."

"Excellent. They'll do nicely for barracks. Now to the tower."

The watchtower was of unusual design. It had five levels, each consisting of a two-room suite that took up all of the level save the space required for a door onto a small exposed landing. A stone stairway climbed the inner surface of the tower's northern wall in a steep zigzag.

Breathing hard after the climb, Woermann leaned over the parapet that rimmed the tower roof and scanned the long stretch of the Dinu Pass commanded by the keep. He could now see the best placements for his antitank rifles. He had little faith in the effectiveness of the 7.92mm Panzerbuchse 38s he had been given, but then he didn't expect to have to use them. Nor the mortars. But he would set them up anyway.

"Not much can go by unnoticed from up here," he said, speaking to himself.

Alexandru replied unexpectedly. "Except in the

spring fog. The whole pass gets filled with heavy fog every night during the spring.''

Woermann made a mental note of that. Those on watch duty would have to keep their ears open as well as their eyes.

"Where are all the birds?" he asked. It bothered him that he hadn't seen any yet.

"I've never seen a bird in the keep," Alexandru said. "Ever."

"Doesn't that strike you as odd?"

"The keep itself is odd, Herr Major, what with its crosses and all. I stopped trying to explain it when I was ten years old. It's just here."

"Who built it?" Woermann asked, and turned away so he wouldn't have to see the shrug he knew was coming.

"Ask five people and you will get five answers. All different. Some say it was one of the old lords of Wallachia, some say it was a defiant Turk, and there are even a few who believe it was built by one of the Popes. Who knows for sure? Truth can shrink and fancy can grow much in five centuries.''

"You really think it takes that long?" Woermann said, taking in a final survey of the pass before he turned away. *It can happen in a matter of a few years.*

As they reached courtyard level, the sound of hammering drew Alexandru toward the corridor that ran along the inner wall of the south rampart. Woermann followed. When Alexandru saw men hammering at the walls, he ran ahead for a closer look, then scurried back to Woermann.

"Herr Captain, they're driving spikes between the stones!" he cried, his hands twisting together as he spoke. "Stop them! They're ruining the walls!"

"Nonsense! Those 'spikes' are common nails, and there's one being placed only every ten feet or so. We have two generators and the men are stringing up lights. The German Army does not live by torchlight."

As they progressed down the corridor, they came upon a soldier kneeling on the floor and stabbing at one

of the blocks in the wall with his bayonet. Alexandru
became even more agitated.

"And him?" the Romanian said in a harsh whisper.
"Is he stringing lights?"

Woermann moved swiftly and silently to a position
directly behind the preoccupied private. As he watched
the man pry at one of the inlaid crosses with the point of
his heavy blade, Woermann felt himself tremble and
break out in a cold sweat.

"Who assigned you to this duty, soldier?"

The private started in surprise and dropped his
bayonet. His pinched face paled as he turned to see his
commanding officer standing over him. He scrambled
to his feet.

"Answer me!" Woermann shouted.

"No one, sir." He stood at attention, eyes straight
ahead.

"What was your assignment?"

"To help string the lights, sir."

"And why aren't you?"

"No excuse, sir."

"I'm not your drill sergeant, soldier. I want to know
what you had in mind when you decided to act like a
common vandal rather than a German soldier. Answer
me!"

"Gold, sir," the private said sheepishly. It sounded
lame and he evidently knew it. "There's been talk that
this castle was built to hide papal treasure. And all these
crosses, sir . . . they look like gold and silver. I was
just—"

"You were neglecting your duty, soldier. What's your
name?"

"Lutz, sir."

"Well, Private Lutz, it's been a profitable day for
you. You've not only learned that the crosses are made
of brass and nickel rather than gold and silver, but
you've earned yourself a place on the first watch all
week as well. Report to Sergeant Oster when you've
finished with the lights."

As Lutz sheathed his fallen bayonet and marched

away, Woermann turned to Alexandru to find him white-faced and trembling.

"The crosses must never be touched!" the Romanian said. "Never!"

"And why not?"

"Because it's always been that way. Nothing in the keep is to be changed. That is why we work. That is why you must not stay here!"

"Good day, Alexandru," Woermann said in a tone he hoped would signal the end of the discussion. He sympathized with the older man's predicament, but his own duty took precedence.

As he turned away he heard Alexandru's plaintive voice behind him.

"Please, Herr Captain! Tell them not to touch the crosses! Not to touch the crosses!"

Woermann resolved to do just that. Not for Alexandru's sake, but because he could not explain the nameless fear that had crept over him as he had watched Lutz pry at that cross with his bayonet. It had not been a simple stab of unease, but rather a cold, sick dread that had coiled about his stomach and squeezed. And he could not imagine why.

Wednesday, 23 April
0320 hours

It was late by the time Woermann gratefully settled into his bedroll on the floor of his quarters. He had chosen the third floor of the tower for himself; it stood above the walls and was not too hard a climb. The front room would serve as an office, the smaller rear room as a personal billet. The two front windows—glassless rectangular openings in the outer wall flanked by wooden shutters—gave him a good view of most of the pass, and the village as well; through the pair of windows to the rear he was able to keep an eye on the courtyard.

The shutters were all open to the night. He had turned off his lights and spent a quiet moment at the front windows. The gorge was obscured by a gently undulating layer of fog. With the passing of the sun, cold air had begun to slip down from the mountain peaks, mixing with the moist air along the floor of the pass, which still retained some heat from the day. A white drifting river of mist was the result. The scene was lit only by starlight, but such an incredible array of stars as seen only in the mountains. He could stare at them and almost understand the delirious motion in Van Gogh's *Starry Night*. The silence was broken only by the low hum of the generators situated in a far corner of the courtyard. A timeless scene, and Woermann lingered over it until he felt himself nodding off.

Once in the bedroll, however, he found sleep elusive despite his fatigue, his mind scattering thoughts in all directions: cold tonight, but not cold enough for the fireplaces . . . no wood for them anyway . . . heat wouldn't be a problem with summer coming on . . . neither would water since they had found cisterns full of it in the cellar floor, fed continuously by an underground stream . . . sanitation always a problem . . . how long were they going to be here anyway? . . . should he let the men sleep in tomorrow after the long day they had just finished? . . . maybe get Alexandru and his boys to fashion some cots for the men and himself to get them off these cold stone floors . . . especially if they would be here into the fall and winter months . . . if the war lasted that long . . .

The war . . . it seemed so far away now. The thought of resigning his commission drifted across his mind again. During the day he could escape it, but here in the dark where he was alone with himself it crept up and crouched on his chest, demanding attention.

He couldn't resign now, not while his country was still at war. Especially not while he was stationed in these desolate mountains at the whim of the soldier-politicians in Berlin. That would be playing directly into their hands. He knew what was on their minds: Join the Party or we'll keep you out of the fight; join the Party or we'll disgrace you with assignments like watchdog duty in the Transylvanian Alps; join the Party or resign.

Perhaps he'd resign after the war. This spring marked his twenty-fifth year in the army. And with the way things were going, perhaps a quarter century was enough. It would be good to be home every day with Helga, spend some time with the boys, and hone his painting skills on Prussian landscapes.

Still . . . the army had been home for so long, and he could not help but believe that the German Army would somehow outlast these Nazis. If he could just hang on long enough . . .

He opened his eyes and looked into the darkness. Although the wall opposite him was lost in shadow, he could almost sense the crosses inlaid in the stone blocks there. He was not a religious man, but there was unaccountable comfort to be found in their presence.

Which brought to mind the incident in the corridor this afternoon. Try as he might, Woermann could not completely shake off the dread that had gripped him as he had watched that private—what was his name? Lutz?—gouging that cross.

Lutz . . . Private Lutz . . . that man was trouble . . . better have Oster keep an eye on him . . .

He drifted into sleep wondering if Alexandru's nightmare awaited him.

TWO

Private Hans Lutz squatted under a naked low-wattage bulb, a lone figure perched on an island of light midstream in a river of darkness, pulling deeply on a cigarette, his back against the cold stone of the keep's cellar walls. His helmet was off, revealing blond hair and a youthful face marred by the hard set of his eyes and mouth. Lutz ached all over. He was tired. He wanted nothing more than to climb into his bedroll for a few hours of oblivion. In fact, if it were just a bit warmer down here in the cellar he would doze off right where he was.

But he could not allow that to happen. Getting first watch for the entire week was bad enough—God knows what would happen if he got caught sleeping on duty. And it was not beyond Captain Woermann to come strolling down the very corridor where Lutz was sitting, just to check up on him. He had to stay awake.

Just his luck for the captain to come by this afternoon. Lutz had been eyeing those funny-looking crosses since he first set foot in the courtyard. Finally, after an hour of his being near them, the temptation had been too great. They had looked like gold and silver, yet it seemed impossible they would be. He'd had to find out, and now he was in trouble.

Well, at least he had satisfied his curiosity: no gold or silver. The knowledge hardly seemed worth a week of first watch, though.

He cupped his hands around the pulsating glow of his cigarette tip to warm them. *Gott*, it was cold! Colder down here than in the open air up on the rampart where Ernst and Otto were patrolling. Lutz had come down to the cellar knowing it was cold. Ostensibly, he hoped the lower temperature would refresh him and help keep him awake; actually, he wanted a chance for a private reconnaissance.

For Lutz had yet to be dissuaded from his belief that there was papal treasure here. There were too many indications—in fact, everything pointed to it. The crosses were the first and most obvious clue; they weren't good, strong, symmetrical Maltese crosses, but they were crosses nonetheless. And they did look like gold and silver. Further, none of the rooms was furnished, which meant that no one was intended to live here. But far more striking was the constant maintenance: Some organization had been paying the upkeep of this place for centuries without interruption. *Centuries!* He knew of only one organization with the power, the resources, and the continuity for that—the Catholic Church.

As far as Lutz was concerned, the keep was being maintained for only one purpose: to safeguard Vatican loot.

It was here somewhere—behind the walls or under the floors—and he'd find it.

Lutz stared at the stone wall across the corridor from him. The crosses were particularly numerous down here in the cellar, and as usual they all looked the same—

—except perhaps for that one off to the left there, the one in the stone on the bottom row at the edge of the light . . . something different about the way the wan illumination glanced off its surface. A trick of the light? A different finish?

Or a different metal?

Lutz took his Schmeisser automatic from its resting place across his knees and leaned it against the wall. He unsheathed his bayonet as he crawled across the corridor on his hands and knees. The instant the point touched the yellow metal of the cross's upright he knew he was on to something: The metal was soft . . . soft and yellow as only solid gold can be.

His hands began to tremble as he dug the tip of the blade into the interface of cross and stone, wedging it deeper and deeper until he felt it grate against stone. Despite increasing pressure, he could advance the blade no farther. He had penetrated to the rear of the inlaid cross. With a little work he was sure he could pop the entire thing out of the stone in one piece. Leaning against the handle of the knife, Lutz applied steadily increasing pressure. He felt something give and stopped to look.

Damn! The tempered steel of the bayonet was tearing through the gold. He tried to adjust the vector of force more directly outward from the stone, but the metal continued to bulge, to stretch—

—the stone moved.

Lutz withdrew the bayonet and studied the block. Nothing special about it: two feet wide, about a foot and a half high, and probably a foot deep. It was unmortared like the rest of the blocks in the wall, only now it stood a full quarter inch out from its fellows. He rose and paced the distance down to the doorway on the left; entering the room there, he paced the distance back to the wall within. He repeated the procedure on the other side in the room to the right of the loose stone. Simple addition and subtraction revealed a significant discrepancy. The number of steps didn't match.

There was a large dead space behind the wall.

With a tight thrill tingling in his chest, Lutz fairly fell upon the loose block, prying frantically at its edge. Despite his best efforts, however, he could not move it any farther out of the wall. He hated the thought, but finally had to admit that he couldn't do it alone. He would have to bring someone else in on this.

Otto Grunstadt, patrolling the wall at this moment, was the obvious choice. He was always looking for a way to pick up a few quick and easy marks. And there were more than a few involved here. Behind that loose stone waited millions in papal gold. Lutz was sure of it. He could almost taste it.

Leaving his Schmeisser and bayonet behind, he ran for the stairs.

"Hurry, Otto!"

"I still don't know about this," Grunstadt said, trotting to keep up. He was heavier, darker than Lutz, and sweating despite the cold. "I'm supposed to be on duty above. If I'm caught—"

"This will only take a minute or two. It's right over here," Lutz said.

After helping himself to a kerosene lamp from the supply room, he had literally pulled Grunstadt from his post, talking all the while of treasure and of being rich for life, of never having to work again. Like a moth catching sight of a light, Grunstadt had followed.

"See?" Lutz said, standing over the stone and pointing. "See how it's out of line?"

Grunstadt knelt to examine the warped and lacerated border of the stone's inlaid cross. He picked up Lutz's bayonet and pressed the cutting edge against the yellow metal of the upright. It cut easily.

"Gold, all right," he said softly. Lutz wanted to kick him, tell him to hurry up, but he had to let Grunstadt make up his own mind. He watched him try the bayonet point on all the other crosses within reach. "All the other uprights are brass. This is the only one that's worth anything."

"And the stone that it's in is loose," Lutz added

quickly. "And there's a dead space behind it six feet wide and who knows how deep."

Grunstadt looked up and grinned. The conclusion was inescapable. "Let's get started."

Working in concert they made progress, but not quickly enough to satisfy Lutz. The stone block canted infinitesimally to the left, then to the right, and after fifteen minutes of backbreaking labor it stood less than an inch out from the wall.

"Wait," Lutz panted. "This thing is a foot deep. It'll take all night like this. We'll never finish before the next watch. Let's see if we can bend the center of the cross out a little more. I've got an idea."

Using both bayonets, they managed to bulge the gold upright out of its groove at a point just below the silver crosspiece, leaving enough space behind it to slip Lutz's belt through between the metal and the stone.

"Now we can pull straight out!"

Grunstadt returned the smile, but weakly. He seemed uneasy about being away from his post for so long. "Then let's get to it".

They put their feet on the wall above and beside the block, each with both hands on the belt, then threw their aching backs, legs, and arms into extracting the stubborn stone. With a high-pitched scrape of protest, it began to move, shimmying, shuddering, sliding. Then it was out. They pushed it to the side and Lutz fumbled for a match.

"Ready to be rich?" He lit the kerosene lamp and held it to the opening. Nothing but darkness within.

"Always," Grunstadt replied. "When do I start counting?"

"Soon as I get back." He adjusted the flame, then began to belly-crawl through the opening, pushing the lamp ahead of him. He found himself in a narrow stone shaft, angled slightly downward . . . and only four feet long. The shaft ended at another stone block, identical to the one they had just struggled so long and so hard to move. Lutz held the lamp close to it. This cross looked like gold and silver, too.

"Give me the bayonet," he said, reaching his hand back to Grunstadt.

Grunstadt placed the handle of the bayonet into the waiting palm. "What's the matter?"

"Roadblock."

For a moment, Lutz felt defeated. With barely room for one man in the narrow shaft, it would be impossible to remove the second stone that faced him. The whole wall would have to be broken through, and that was more than he and Grunstadt could hope to accomplish on their own, no matter how many nights they worked at it. He didn't know what to do next, but he had to satisfy his curiosity as to the metals in the inlaid cross before him. If the upright was gold, he would at least be sure that he was on the right track.

Grunting as he twisted within the confinement of the shaft, Lutz dug the point of the bayonet into the cross. It sank easily. But more, the stone began to swing backward, as if hinged on its left side. Ecstatic, Lutz pushed at it with his free hand and found that it was only a façade no more than an inch thick. It moved easily at his touch, releasing a waft of cold, fetid air from the darkness beyond it. Something in that air caused the hair on his arms and at the base of his neck to stand on end.

Cold, he thought, as he felt himself shiver involuntarily, but not *that* cold.

He stifled a growing unease and crawled forward, sliding the lamp ahead of him along the stone floor of the shaft. As he passed it through the new opening, the flame began to die. It neither flickered nor sputtered within its glass chimney, so the blame could not be laid on any turbulence in the cold air that continued to drift past him. The flame merely began to waste away, to wither on its wick. The possibility of a noxious gas crossed his mind, but Lutz could smell nothing and felt no shortness of breath, no eye or nasal irritation.

Perhaps the kerosene was low. As he pulled the lamp back to him to check, the flame returned to its former size and brightness. He shook the base and felt the liquid slosh around within. Plenty of kerosene. Puzzled, he pushed the lamp forward again, and again the flame began to shrink. The farther into the chamber he pushed it, the smaller it became, illuminating absolutely nothing. Something was wrong here.

"Otto!" he called over his shoulder. "Tie the belt around one of my ankles and hold on. I'm going further down."

"Why don't we wait until tomorrow . . . when it's light?"

"Are you mad? The whole detail will know then! They'll all want a share—and the captain will probably take most of it! We'll have done all the work and we'll wind up with nothing!"

Grunstadt's voice wavered. "I don't like this anymore."

"Something wrong, Otto?"

"I'm not sure. I just don't want to be down here anymore."

"Stop talking like an old woman!" Lutz snapped. He didn't need Grunstadt going soft on him now. He felt uneasy himself, but there was a fortune just inches away and he wasn't going to let anything stop him from claiming it. "Tie that belt and hold on! If this shaft gets any steeper, I don't want to slip down."

"All right," came the reluctant reply from behind him. "But hurry."

Lutz waited until he felt the belt cinch tight around his left ankle, then began to crawl forward into the dark chamber, the lamp ahead of him. He was seized by a sense of urgency. He moved as quickly as the confined space would allow. By the time his head and shoulders were through the opening, the lamp's flame had dimmed to a tiny blue-white flicker . . . as if the light were unwelcome, as if the darkness had sent the flame back into its wick.

As Lutz advanced the lamp a few more inches, the flame died. With its passing he realized he was not alone.

Something as dark and as cold as the chamber he had

entered was awake and hungry and beside him. He began to shake uncontrollably. Terror ripped through his bowels. He tried to retreat, to pull his shoulders and head back but he was caught. It was as if the shaft had closed upon him, holding him helpless in a darkness so complete there was no up or down. Cold engulfed him, and so did fear—a combined embrace that threatened to drive him mad. He opened his mouth to call for Otto to pull him back. The cold entered him as his voice rose in an agony of terror.

Outside, the belt Grunstadt held in his hands began to whip back and forth as Lutz's legs writhed and kicked and thrashed about in the shaft. There was a sound like a human voice, but so full of horror and despair, and sounding so far away, that Grunstadt could not believe it came from his friend. The sound came to an abrupt gurgling halt that was awful to hear. And as it ceased, so did Lutz's frantic movements.

"Hans?"

No answer.

Thoroughly frightened, Grunstadt hauled back on the belt until Lutz's feet were within reach. He then gripped both boots and pulled Lutz back into the corridor.

When he saw what he had delivered from the shaft, Grunstadt began to scream. The sound echoed up and down the cellar corridor, reverberating and growing in volume until the very walls began to shake.

Cowed by the amplified sound of his own terror, Grunstadt stood transfixed as the wall into which his friend had crawled bulged outward, minute cracks appearing along the edges of the heavy granite blocks. A wide crevice jagged up from the space left by the stone they had removed. The few puny lights strung along the corridor began to dim, and when they were nearly out, the wall burst open with a final convulsive tremor, showering Grunstadt with shards of shattered stone and releasing something inconceivably black that leaped out and enveloped him with a single smooth swift flowing motion.

The horror had begun.

THREE

Tavira, Portugal
Wednesday, 23 April
0235 hours (Greenwich Mean Time)

The red-haired man suddenly found himself awake. Sleep had dropped away like a loosened cloak and at first he did not know why. It had been a hard day of fouled nets and rough seas; after turning in at his usual hour, he should have slept through until first light. Yet now, after only a few hours, he was awake and alert. Why?

And then he knew.

Grim faced, he pounded his fist once, twice, into the cool sand around the low wooden frame of his bed. There was anger in his movements, and a certain resignation. He had hoped this moment would never come, had told himself time and again that it never would. But now that it was here, he realized it had been inevitable all along.

He rose from the bed and, clad only in a pair of undershorts, began to roam the room. He had smooth, even features, but the olive tint of his skin clashed with the red of his hair; his scarred shoulders were broad, his waist narrow. He moved with feline grace about the interior of the tiny shack, snatching items of clothing from hooks on the walls, personal articles from the table beside the door, all the while mentally planning his route of travel to Romania. When he had gathered up what he wanted, he tossed everything onto the bed and rolled it up in the bed blanket, tied the roll with string at both ends.

After pulling on a jacket and loose pants, he slung the rolled blanket across his shoulder, grabbed a short shovel and stepped out into the night air, cool, salty, moonless. Over the dunes, the Atlantic hissed and rumbled against the shore. He walked to the landward side of the dune nearest his hut and began to dig. Four feet down the shovel scraped against something solid. The red-haired man knelt and began to dig with his hands. A few quick, fierce movements brought him to a long, narrow, oilskin-wrapped case which he tugged and wrested from the hole. It measured five feet or so in length, was perhaps ten inches wide and only an inch deep. He paused, his shoulders slumping as he held the case in his hands. He had almost come to believe that he would never have to open it again. Putting it aside, he dug farther and came up with an unusually heavy money belt, also wrapped in oilskin.

The belt went under his shirt and around his waist, the long, flat case under his arm. With the onshore breeze ruffling his hair, he walked over the dune to where Sanchez kept his boat, high on the sand and tied to a piling as proof against the unlikely possibility of its drifting away in a freak tide. A careful man, Sanchez. A good boss. The red-haired man had enjoyed working for him.

Rummaging in the boat's forward compartment, he pulled out the nets and threw them on the sand. Next came the wooden box for tools and tackle. This joined the nets on the sand, but not before he had extricated a hammer and nail from its jumbled contents. He walked toward Sanchez's piling, drawing four Austrian hundred-kronen gold pieces from his money belt. There were many other gold coins in the belt, different sizes from different countries: Russian ten-ruble chevronets, Austrian hundred-shilling pieces, Czech ten-ducats, U.S. double eagles, and more. He would have to depend heavily on the universal acceptance of gold in order to travel the length of the Mediterranean in wartime.

With two swift, powerful strokes of the hammer, he pierced the four coins with a nail, fixing them to the piling. They'd buy Sanchez a new boat. A better one.

He untied the rope from the piling, dragged the boat into the quiet surf, hopped in, and grabbed the oars. When he had rowed past the breakers and had pulled the single sail to the top of its mast, he turned the prow east toward Gibraltar, not far away, and allowed himself a final look at the tiny starlit fishing village at the southern tip of Portugal that had been his home for the past few years. It hadn't been easy to work his way into their trust. These villagers had never accepted him as one of their own, and never would; but they had accepted him as a good worker. They respected that. The work had accomplished its purpose, leaving him lean and tight-muscled again after too many years of soft city-living. He had made friends, but no close ones. None he could not walk away from.

It was a hard life here, yet he would gladly work twice as hard and stay rather than go where he must and face what he must. His hands clenched and unclenched tensely at the thought of the confrontation that awaited him. But there was no one else to go. Only him.

He could not allow delay. He had to reach Romania as quickly as possible and had to travel the entire 2,300-mile length of the Mediterranean Sea to get there.

In the recently disturbed corner of his mind was the realization that he might not get there in time. That he might already be too late . . . a possibility too awful to contemplate.

FOUR

Woermann awoke trembling and sweating at the same instant as everyone else in the keep. It was not Grunstadt's prolonged and repeated howling that had done it, for Woermann was out of earshot of the sound. Something else had ripped him gasping with terror from his sleep . . . the feeling that something had gone terribly wrong.

After a moment of confusion, Woermann shrugged into his tunic and trousers and ran down the steps to the base of the tower. The men were beginning to trickle out of their rooms and into the courtyard as he arrived, to gather in tense, muttering groups listening to the eerie howl that seemed to come from everywhere. He directed three of the men toward the arch that led to the cellar stairs. He had just reached the top of the stairs himself when two of them reappeared, white faced, tight lipped, and trembling.

"There's a dead man down there!" one said.

"Who is it?" Woermann asked as he pushed between them and started down the steps.

"I think it's Lutz, but I'm not sure. His head's gone!"

A uniformed corpse awaited him in the central corridor. It lay on its belly, half covered with stony rubble. Headless. But the head had not been sliced off, as with a guillotine, or hacked off—it had been *torn* off, leaving stumps of arteries and a twisted vertebra protruding within the ragged edge of the skin of the neck. The soldier had been a private, and that was all he could tell at first glance. A second private sat nearby, his wide, blank, staring eyes fixed on the hole in the wall before him. As Woermann watched, the second soldier shuddered and emitted a loud, long, wavering ululation that raised the fine hairs along Woermann's nape.

"What happened here, Private?" Woermann asked, but the soldier did not react. Woermann grabbed his shoulder and shook him but there was no sign in the eyes that he even knew his commanding officer was there. He seemed to have crawled into himself and blocked out the rest of the world.

The rest of the men were inching down the corridor to see what had happened. Steeling himself, Woermann leaned over the headless figure and went through its pockets. The wallet held an identity card for Private Hans Lutz. He had seen dead men before, victims of war, but this was different. This sickened him in a way the others had not. Battlefield deaths were mostly impersonal; this was not. This was horrible, mutilating death for its own sake. And in the back of his mind was the question: Is this what happens when you deface a cross here in the keep?

Oster arrived with a lamp. When it was lit, Woermann held it before him and gingerly stepped through the large hole in the wall. The light bounced off blank walls. His breath puffed white in the air and drifted away behind him. It was cold, colder than it should be, with a musty odor, and something more . . . a hint of putrescence that made him want to back away. But the men were watching.

He followed the cool draught of air to its source: a large, ragged hole in the floor. The stone of the floor had apparently fallen in when the wall collapsed. There was inky blackness below. Woermann held the lamp over the opening. Stone steps, strewn with rubble from the collapsed floor, led downward. One particular piece of rubble looked more spherical than the others. He lowered the lamp for a better look and stifled a cry when he saw what it was. The head of Private Hans Lutz, open eyed and bloody mouthed, stared back at him.

FIVE

It did not occur to Magda to question her actions until she heard her father's voice calling her.

"Magda!"

She looked up and saw her face in the mirror over her dresser. Her hair was down, a glossy cascade of dark brown that splashed against her shoulders and flowed down her back. She was unaccustomed to seeing herself so. Usually, her hair was tightly coiled up under her kerchief, all but a few stubborn strands tucked safely out of sight. She never let it down during the day.

An instant's confusion: What day was it? And what time? Magda glanced at the clock. Five minutes to five. Impossible! She had already been up for fifteen or twenty minutes. It must have stopped during the night. Yet when she picked it up she could feel the mechanism ticking away within. Strange . . .

Two quick steps took her to the window on the other side of the dresser. A peek behind the heavy shade revealed a dark and quiet Bucharest, still asleep.

Magda looked down at herself and saw she was still in her nightgown, the blue flannel one, tight at the throat and sleeves and loose all the way down to the floor. Her breasts, although not large, jutted out shamelessly under the soft, warm, heavy fabric, free of the tight undergarments that imprisoned them during the day. She quickly folded her arms over them.

Magda was a mystery to the community. Despite her soft, even features, her smooth, pale skin and wide brown eyes, at thirty-one she remained unmarried. Magda the scholar, the devoted daughter, the nursemaid. Magda the spinster. Yet many a younger woman who was married would have envied the shape and texture of those breasts: fresh, unmarred, unsuckled, untouched by any hand but her own. Magda felt no desire to alter that.

Her father's voice broke through her reverie.

"Magda! What are you doing?"

She glanced at the half-filled suitcase on the bed and the words sprang unbidden to her mind. "Packing us some warm clothes, Papa!"

After a brief pause her father said, "Come in here so I don't wake up the rest of the building with my shouting."

Magda made her way quickly through the dark to where her father lay. It took but a few steps. Their street-level apartment consisted of four rooms—two bedrooms side by side, a tiny kitchen with a wood-burning stove, and a slightly larger front room that served as foyer, living room, dining room, and study. She sorely missed their old house, but they had had to move in here six months ago to make the most of their savings, selling off the furniture that didn't fit. They had affixed the family mezuzah to the inside of the apartment's doorpost instead of the outside. Considering the temper of the times, that seemed wise.

One of her father's Gypsy friends had carved a small

patrin circle on the outer surface of the door. It meant "friend."

The tiny lamp on the nightstand to the right of her father's bed was lit; a high-backed wooden wheelchair sat empty to the left. Pressed between the white covers of his bed like a wilted flower folded into the pages of a scrapbook lay her father. He raised a twisted hand, gloved in cotton as always, and beckoned, wincing at the pain the simple gesture caused him. Magda grasped the hand as she sat down beside him, massaging the fingers, hiding her own pain at seeing him fade away a little each day.

"What's this about packing?" he asked, his eyes bright in the tight, sallow glow of his face. He squinted at her. His glasses lay on the nightstand and he was virtually blind without them. "You never told me about leaving."

"We're both going," she replied, smiling.

"Where?"

Magda felt her smile falter as confusion came over her again. Where *were* they going? She realized she had no firm idea, only a vague impression of snowy peaks and chill winds.

"The Alps, Papa."

Her father's lips parted in a toothy smile that threatened to crack the parchment-like skin stretched so tightly over his facial bones.

"You must have been dreaming, my dear. We're going nowhere. *I* certainly won't be traveling far—ever again. It was a dream. A nice dream, but that's all. Forget it and go back to sleep."

Magda frowned at the crushed resignation in her father's voice. He had always been such a fighter. His illness was sapping more than his strength. But now was no time to argue with him. She patted the back of his hand and reached for the string on the bedside lamp.

"I guess you're right. It was a dream." She kissed him on the forehead and turned out the light, leaving him in darkness.

Back in her room, Magda studied the partially packed

suitcase waiting on the bed. Of course it had been a dream that had made her think they were going somewhere. What else could it be? A trip anywhere was out of the question.

Yet the feeling remained . . . such a dead certainty that they were going somewhere north, and soon. Dreams weren't supposed to leave such definite impressions. It gave her an odd, uncomfortable feeling . . . like tiny cold fingers running lightly along the skin of her arms.

She couldn't shake the certainty. And so she closed the suitcase and shoved it under the bed, leaving the straps unfastened and the clothes inside . . . warm clothes . . . it was still cold in the Alps this time of year.

SIX

It was hours before Woermann could sit with Sergeant Oster and have a cup of coffee in the mess. Private Grunstadt had been carried to a room and left alone there. He had been placed in his bedroll after being stripped and washed by two of his fellow privates. He had apparently wet and soiled his clothes before going into his delirium.

"As near as I can figure it," Oster was saying, "the wall collapsed and one of those big blocks of stone must have landed on the back of his neck and torn his head off."

Woermann sensed that Oster was trying to sound very calm and analytical, but inside was as confused and shocked as everybody else.

"As good an explanation as any, I suppose, barring a

46

medical examination. But it still doesn't tell us what they were up to down there, and it doesn't explain Grunstadt's condition."

"Shock."

Woermann shook his head. "That man has been through battle. I know he's seen worse. I can't accept shock as the whole answer. There's something else."

He had arrived at his own reconstruction of the events of the preceding night. The stone block with its vandalized cross of gold and silver, the belt around Lutz's ankle, the shaft into the wall . . . it all indicated that Lutz had crawled into the shaft expecting to find more gold and silver at its end. But all that was there was a small, empty, blind cubicle . . . like a tiny prison cell . . . or hiding place. He could think of no good reason why there should be any space there at all.

"They must have upset the balance of the stones in the wall by removing that one at the bottom," Oster said. "That's what caused the collapse."

"I doubt that," Woermann replied, sipping his coffee for warmth as well as for stimulation. "The cellar floor, yes: That weakened and fell into the subcellar. But the corridor wall . . ." He remembered the way the stones had been scattered about the corridor, as if blown out by an explosion. He could not explain that. He set his coffee cup down. Explanations would have to wait.

"Come. Work to do." He headed for his quarters while Oster went to make the twice daily radio call to the Ploiesti defense garrison. The sergeant was instructed to report the casualty as an accidental death.

The sky was light as Woermann stood at the rear window of his quarters and looked down on the courtyard, still in shadow. The keep had changed. There was an unease about it. Yesterday the keep had been nothing more than an old stone building. Now it was more. Each shadow seemed deeper and darker than before, and sinister in some unfathomable way.

He blamed it on predawn malaise and on the shock of death so near at hand. Yet as the sun finally conquered the mountaintops on the far side of the pass, chasing the shadows and warming the stone walls of the keep, Woermann had the feeling that the light could not banish what was wrong. It could only drive it beneath the surface for a while.

The men felt it, too. He could see that. But he was determined to keep their spirits up. When Alexandru arrived this morning, he would send him back immediately for a cartload of lumber. There were cots and tables to be made. Soon the keep would be filled with the healthy sound of hammers in strong hands driving good nails into seasoned wood. He walked to the window facing the causeway. Yes, there was Alexandru and his two boys now. Everything was going to be all right.

He lifted his gaze to the tiny village, transected by the sunlight pouring over the mountaintops—its upper half aglow, its lower half still in shadow. And he knew he would have to paint the village just as he saw it now. He stepped back: The village, framed in the drab gray of the wall, shone like a jewel. That would be it . . . the village seen through the window in the wall. The contrasts appealed to him. He had an urge to set up a canvas and start immediately. He painted best under stress and most loved to paint then, losing himself in perspective and composition, light and shadow, tint and texture.

The rest of the day went quickly. Woermann oversaw the placement of Lutz's body in the subcellar. It and the severed head were carried down through the opening in the cellar floor and covered with a sheet on the dirt floor of the cavern below. The temperature down there felt close to freezing. There was no sign of vermin about and it seemed the best place to store the cadaver until later in the week when arrangements could be made for shipment home.

Under normal circumstances, Woermann would have been tempted to explore the subcellar—the subterranean cavern with its glistening walls and inky recesses might have sparked an interesting painting. But not this time. He told himself it was too cold, that he would wait until summer and do a proper job of it. But that wasn't true. Something about this cavern urged him to be gone from it as soon as possible.

It became apparent as the day progressed that Grunstadt was going to be a problem. There was no sign of improvement. He lay in whatever position he was placed and stared into space. Every so often he would shudder and moan; occasionally, he would howl at the top of his lungs. He soiled himself again. At this rate, with no intake of food or fluid and without skilled nursing care, he would not survive the week. Grunstadt would have to be shipped out with Lutz's remains if he didn't snap out of it.

Woermann kept close watch on the mood of the men during the day and was satisfied with their response to the physical tasks he set for them. They worked well despite their lack of sleep and despite Lutz's death. They had all known Lutz, known what a schemer and a plotter he was, that he rarely carried his full share of the load. It seemed to be the consensus that he had brought on the very accident that had killed him.

Woermann saw to it that there was no time for mourning or brooding, even for those few so inclined. A latrine system had to be organized, lumber commandeered from the village, tables and chairs made. By the time the evening mess was cleared, there were few in the detachment willing to stay up for even an after-dinner cigarette. To a man, except for those on watch, they headed for their bedrolls.

Woermann allowed an alteration in the watch so that the courtyard guard would cover the corridor that led to Grunstadt's room. Because of his cries and moans, no one would spend the night within a hundred feet of him; but Otto had always been well liked by the men and they felt an obligation to see that he did himself no harm.

Near midnight, Woermann found himself still wide awake despite a desperate desire to sleep. With the dark had come a sense of foreboding that refused to let him relax. He finally gave in to a restless urge to be up and about and decided to tour the guard posts to be sure those on sentry duty were awake.

His tour took him down Grunstadt's corridor and he decided to look in on him. He tried to imagine what could have driven the man into himself like that. He peeked through the door. A kerosene lamp had been left burning with a low flame in a far corner of the room. The private was in one of his quiet phases, breathing rapidly, sweating and whimpering. The whimpering was followed regularly by a prolonged howl. Woermann wanted to be far down the hall when that occurred. It was unnerving to hear a human voice make a sound like that . . . the voice so near and the mind so far away.

He was at the end of the corridor and about to step into the courtyard again when it came. Only this wasn't like the others. This was a shriek, as if Grunstadt had suddenly awakened and found himself on fire, or pierced by a thousand knives—there was physical as well as emotional agony in the sound this time. And then it cut off, like pulling the plug on a radio in mid-song.

Woermann froze for an instant, his nerves and muscles unwilling to respond to his commands; with intense effort he forced himself to turn and run back down the corridor. He burst into the room. It was cold, colder than a minute ago, and the kerosene lamp was out. He fumbled for a match to relight it, then turned to Grunstadt.

Dead. The man's eyes were open, bulging toward the ceiling; the mouth was agape, the lips drawn back over the teeth as if frozen in the middle of a scream of horror. And his neck—the throat had been ripped open. There was blood all over the bed and splattered on the walls.

Woermann's reflexes took over. Before he even knew what he was doing, his hand had clawed his Luger from its holster and his eyes were searching the corners of the room for whoever had done this. But he could see no one. He ran to the narrow window, stuck his head through, and looked up and down the walls. There was no rope, no sign of anyone making an escape. He jerked

his head back into the room and looked around again.
Impossible! No one had come down the corridor, and
no one had gone out the window. And yet Grunstadt
had been murdered.

The sound of running feet cut off further thought—
the guards had heard the shriek and were coming to investigate. Good . . . Woermann had to admit to himself
that he was terrified. He couldn't bear to be alone in this
room much longer.

Thursday, 24 April

After seeing to it that Grunstadt's body was placed
next to Lutz's, Woermann made sure the men were
again kept busy all day building cots and tables. He
fostered the belief that there was an anti-German partisan group at work in the area. But he found it impossible to convince himself; for he had been on the
corridor when the murder had occurred and knew there
was no way the killer could have got by him without
being seen—unless he could fly or walk through walls.
So what was the answer?

He announced that the sentries would be doubled
tonight, with extra men posted in and around the
barracks to safeguard those who were sleeping.

With the sound of insistent hammering rising from
the courtyard below, Woermann took time out in the afternoon to set up one of his canvases. He began to
paint. He had to do something to get that awful look on
Grunstadt's face out of his mind; it helped to concentrate on mixing his pigments until their color ap-
proximated that of the wall in his room. He decided to
place the window to the right of center, then spent the
better part of two hours in the late afternoon blending
the paint and smoothing it onto the canvas, leaving a
white area for the village as seen through the window.

That night he slept. After interrupted slumber the first night, and none on the second, his exhausted body fairly collapsed onto his bedroll.

Private Rudy Schreck walked his patrol cautiously and diligently, keeping an eye on Wehner on the far side of the courtyard. Earlier in the evening, two men for this tiny area had seemed a bit much, but as darkness had grown and consolidated its hold on the keep, Schreck found himself glad to have someone within earshot. He and Wehner had worked out a routine: Both would walk the perimeter of the courtyard within an arm's length of the wall, both going clockwise at opposite sides. It kept them always apart, but it meant better surveillance.

Rudy Schreck was not afraid for his life. Uneasy, yes, but not afraid. He was awake, alert; he had a rapid-fire weapon slung over his shoulder and knew how to use it—whoever had killed Otto last night was not going to have a chance against him. Still, he wished for more light in the courtyard. The scattered bulbs spilling stark pools of brightness here and there along the periphery did nothing to dispel the overall gloom. The two rear corners of the courtyard were especially dark wells of blackness.

The night was chilly. To make matters worse, fog had seeped in through the barred gate and hung in the air around him, sheening the metal surface of his helmet with droplets of moisture. Schreck rubbed a hand across his eyes. Mostly he was tired. Tired of everything that had to do with the army. War wasn't what he had thought it would be. When he had joined up two years ago he had been eighteen with a head full of dreams of sound and fury, of great battles and noble victories, of huge armies clashing on fields of honor. That was the way it had always been in the history books. But real war hadn't turned out that way. Real war was mostly waiting. And the waiting was usually dirty, cold, nasty, and wet. Rudy Schreck had had his fill of war. He wanted to be home in Treysa. His parents were there, and so was a girl named Eva who hadn't been writing as often as she used to. He wanted his own life back again, a life in which there were no uniforms and no inspections, no drills, no sergeants, and no officers. And no watch duty.

He was coming to the rear corner of the courtyard on the northern side. The shadows looked deeper than ever there . . . much deeper than on his last turn. Schreck slowed his pace as he approached. This is silly, he thought. Just a trick of the light. Nothing to be afraid of.

And yet . . . he didn't want to go in there. He wanted to skirt this particular corner. He'd go into all the other corners, but not this one.

Squaring his shoulders, Schreck forced himself forward. It was only shadow.

He was a grown man, too old to be afraid of the dark. He continued straight ahead, maintaining an arm's length from the wall, into the shadowed corner—

—and suddenly he was lost. Cold, sucking blackness closed in on him. He spun around to go back the way he had come but found only more blackness. It was as though the rest of the world had disappeared. Schreck pulled the Schmeisser off his shoulder and held it ready to fire. He was shivering with cold yet sweating profusely. He wanted to believe this was all a trick, that Wehner had somehow turned off all the lights at the instant he had entered the shadow. But Schreck's senses dashed that hope. The darkness was too complete—it pressed against his eyes and wormed its way into his courage.

There was someone approaching. Schreck could neither see nor hear him, but someone was there. Coming closer.

"Wehner?" he said softly, hoping his terror didn't show in his voice. "Is that you, Wehner?"

But it wasn't Wehner. Schreck realized that as the

presence neared. It was someone—thing—else. What felt like a length of heavy rope suddenly coiled around his ankles. As he was yanked off his feet, Private Rudy Schreck began screaming and firing wildly until the darkness ended the war for him.

Woermann was jolted awake by a short sputtering burst from a Schmeisser. He sprang to the window overlooking the courtyard. One of the guards was running toward the rear. Where was the other? Damn! He had posted *two* guards in the courtyard! He was just about to turn and run for the stairs when he saw something on the wall. A pale lump . . . it almost looked like . . .

It was a body . . . upside down . . . a naked body hanging from a rope tied to its feet. Even from his tower window Woermann could see the blood that had run down from the throat over the face. One of his soldiers, fully armed and on patrol, had been slaughtered and stripped and hung up like a chicken in a butcher's window.

The fear that had so far only been nibbling at Woermann now asserted an icy, viselike grip on him.

Friday, 25 April

Three dead men in the subcellar. Defense command at Ploiesti had been notified of the latest mortality but no comment had been radioed back.

There was much activity in the courtyard during the day, but little accomplished. Woermann decided to pair the guards tonight. It seemed incredible that a partisan guerrilla could take an alert, seasoned soldier by surprise at his post, but it had happened. It would not happen with a pair of sentries.

In the afternoon he returned to his canvas and found a bit of relief from the atmosphere of doom that had settled on the keep. He began adding blotches of shadow to the blank gray of the wall, and then detail to the edges of the window. He had decided to leave out the crosses since they would be a distraction from the village, which he wanted to be the focus. He worked like an automaton, narrowing his world to the brushstrokes on the canvas, shutting away the terror around him.

Night came quietly. Woermann kept getting up from his bedroll and going to the window overlooking the courtyard, a useless routine but a compulsion, as if he could keep everyone alive by maintaining a personal watch on the keep. On one of his trips to the window, he noticed the courtyard sentry walking his tour alone. Rather than call down and cause a disturbance, he decided to investigate personally.

"Where's your partner?" he asked the lone sentry when he reached the courtyard.

The soldier whirled, then began to stammer. "He was tired, sir. I let him take a rest."

An uneasy feeling clawed at Woermann's belly. "I gave orders for all sentries to travel in pairs! Where is he?"

"In the cab of the first lorry, sir."

Woermann quickly crossed to the parked vehicle and pulled open the door. The soldier within did not move. Woermann poked at his arm.

"Wake up."

The soldier began to lean toward him, slowly at first, then with greater momentum until he was actually falling toward his commanding officer. Woermann caught him and then almost dropped him. For as he fell, his head angled back to reveal an open, mangled throat. Woermann eased the body to the ground, then stepped back, clamping his jaw against a scream of fright and horror.

Saturday, 26 April

Woermann had Alexandru and his sons turned away
at the gate in the morning. Not that he suspected them
of complicity in the deaths, but Sergeant Oster had
warned him that the men were edgy about their inability
to maintain security. Woermann thought it best to avoid
a potentially ugly incident.

He soon learned that the men were edgy about more
than security. Late in the morning a brawl broke out in
the courtyard. A corporal tried to pull rank on a private
to make him give up a specially blessed crucifix. The
private refused and a fight between two men escalated
into a brawl involving a dozen. It seemed there had been
small talk about vampires after the first death; it had
been ridiculed then. But with each new baffling death
the idea had gained credence until believers now outnumbered nonbelievers. This was, after all, Romania,
the Transylvanian Alps.

Woermann knew he had to nip this in the bud. He
gathered the men in the courtyard and spoke to them for
half an hour. He told them of their duty as German
soldiers to remain brave in the face of danger, to remain
true to their cause, and not to let fear turn them against
one another, for that would surely lead to defeat.

"And finally," he said, noticing his audience becoming restive, "you must all put aside fear of the supernatural. There is a human agent at work in these deaths
and we will find him or them. It is now plain that there
must be a number of secret passages within the keep that
allows the killer to enter and leave without being seen.
We'll spend the rest of the day searching for those passages. And I am assigning half of you to guard duty
tonight. We are going to put a stop to this once and for
all!"

The men's spirits seemed to be lifted by his words. In
fact, he had almost convinced himself.

He moved about the keep constantly during the rest
of the day, encouraging the men, watching them
measure floors and walls in search of dead spaces, tap-

ping the walls for hollow sounds. But they found nothing. He personally made a quick reconnaissance of the cavern in the subcellar. It appeared to recede into the heart of the mountain; he decided to leave it unexplored for now. There was no time, and no signs of disturbance in the dirt of the cavern floor to indicate that anyone had passed this way in ages. He left orders, however, to place four men on guard at the opening to the subcellar in the unlikely event that someone might try to gain entrance through the cavern below.

Woermann managed to sneak off for an hour during the late afternoon to sketch in the outline of the village. It was his only respite from the growing tension that pressed in on him from all sides. As he worked with the charcoal pencil, he could feel the unease begin to slip away, almost as if the canvas were drawing it out of him. He would have to take some time tomorrow morning to add color, for it was the village as it looked in the early light that he wished to capture.

As the sun sank and the fading light forced him to quit, he felt all the dread and foreboding filter back. With the sun overhead he could easily believe it was a human agent killing his men; he could laugh at talk of vampires. But in the growing darkness, the gnawing fear returned along with the memory of the bloody, sodden weight of that dead soldier in his arms last night.

One safe night. One night without a death, and maybe I can beat this thing. With half of the men guarding the other half tonight, I ought to be able to turn this around and start gaining ground tomorrow.

One night. Just one deathless night.

Sunday, 27 April

The morning came as Sunday mornings should—bright and sunny. Woermann had fallen asleep in his

chair; he found himself awake at first light, stiff and
sore. It took a moment before he realized that his
night's sleep had gone uninterrupted by screams or gun-
shots. He pulled on his boots and hurried to the courtyard to assure himself that there were as many men alive
this morning as there had been last night. A quick check
with one of the sentries confirmed it: No deaths had
been reported.

Woermann felt ten years younger. He had done it!
There was a way to foil this killer after all! But the ten
years began to creep back on him as he saw the worried
face of a private who was hurrying across the courtyard
toward him.

"Sir!" the man said as he approached. "There's
something wrong with Franz—I mean Private Ghent.
He's not awake."

Woermann's limbs suddenly felt very weak and
heavy, as if all their strength had suddenly been si-
phoned away. "Did you check him?"

"No, sir. I—I'm—"

"Lead the way."

He followed the private to the barracks within the
south wall. The soldier in question was in his bedroll in
a newly made cot with his back to the door.

"Franz!" called his roommate as they entered. "The
captain's here!"

Ghent did not stir.

Please, God, let him be sick or even dead of a heart
seizure, Woermann thought as he stepped to the bed.
But please don't let his throat be torn. Anything but
that.

"Private Ghent!" he said. There was no evidence of
movement, not even the easy rise and fall of the covers
over a sleeping man. Dreading what he would see,
Woermann leaned over the cot.

The bedroll flap was pulled to Ghent's chin. Woermann did not pull it down. He did not have to. The
glassy eyes, sallow skin, and drying red stain soaking
through the fabric told him what he would find.

T

"The men are on the verge of panic, sir," Sergeant Oster was saying.

Woermann daubed color onto the canvas in short, quick, furious jabs. The morning light was right where he wanted it on the village and he had to make the most of the moment. He was sure Oster thought he had gone mad, and maybe he had. Despite the carnage around him, the painting had become an obsession.

"I don't blame them. I suppose they want to go into the village and shoot a few of the locals. But that won't—"

"Begging your pardon, sir, but that's not what they're thinking."

Woermann lowered his brush. "Oh? What, then?"

"They think that the men who've been killed didn't bleed as much as they should have. They also think Lutz's death was no accident . . . that he was killed the same as the others."

"Didn't bleed . . . ? Oh, I see. Vampire talk again."

Oster nodded. "Yessir. And they think Lutz let it out when he opened that shaft into the dead space in the cellar."

"I happen to disagree," Woermann said, hiding his expression as he turned back to the painting. He had to be the steadying influence, the anchor for his men. He had to hold fast to the real and the natural. "I happen to think Lutz was killed by falling stone. I happen to think that the four subsequent deaths had nothing to do with Lutz. And I happen to believe they bled quite profusely. There is nothing around here drinking anyone's blood, Sergeant!"

"But the throats . . ."

Woermann paused. Yes, the throats. They hadn't been cut—no knife or garroting wire had been used. They had been torn open. Viciously. But by what? Teeth?

"Whoever the killer is, he's trying to scare us. And he's succeeding. So here's what we'll do: I'm putting every single man in the detachment on guard duty tonight, including myself. Everyone will travel in pairs. We'll have this keep so thickly patrolled that a moth won't be able to fly through unnoticed!"

"But we can't do that every night, sir!"

"No, but we can do it tonight, and tomorrow night if need be. And then we'll catch whoever it is."

Oster brightened. "Yessir!"

"Tell me something, Sergeant," Woermann said as Oster saluted and turned to go.

"Sir?"

"Had any nightmares since we moved into the keep?"

The younger man frowned. "No, sir. Can't say that I have."

"Any of the men mention any?"

"None. You having nightmares, Captain?"

"No." Woermann shook his head in a way that told Oster he was through with him for now. No nightmares, he thought. But the days have certainly become a bad dream.

"I'll radio Ploiesti now," Oster said as he went out the door.

Woermann wondered if a fifth death would get a rise out of the Ploiesti defense command. Oster had been reporting a death a day, yet no reaction. No offer of help, no order to abandon the keep. Obviously they didn't care too much what happened here as long as somebody was keeping watch on the pass. Woermann would have to make a decision about the bodies soon. But he wanted desperately to get through one night without a death before shipping them out. Just one.

He turned back to the painting, but found the light had changed. He cleaned his brushes. He had no real hope of capturing the killer tonight, but still it might be the turning point. With everyone on guard and paired, maybe they'd all survive. And that would do wonders for morale. Then an ugly thought struck him as he placed his tubes of pigment into their case: What if one of his own men were the killer?

T

Monday, 28 April

Midnight had come and gone, and so far so good. Sergeant Oster had set up a checkpoint in the center of the courtyard and as yet there was no one unaccounted for. The extra lights in the courtyard and atop the tower bolstered the men's confidence despite the long shadows they cast. Keeping all the men up all night had been a drastic measure, but it was going to work.

Woermann leaned out one of his windows overlooking the courtyard. He could see Oster at his table, see the men walking in pairs along the perimeter and atop the walls. The generators chugged away over by the parked vehicles. Extra spotlights had been trained on the craggy surface of the mountainside that formed the rear wall of the keep to prevent anyone from sneaking in from above. The men on the ramparts were keeping a careful eye on the outer walls to see that no one scaled them. The front gates were locked, and there was a squad guarding the break into the subcellar.

The keep was secure.

As he stood there, Woermann realized that he was the only man in the entire structure who was alone and unguarded. It made him hesitate to look behind him into the shadowy corners of his room. But that was the price of being an officer.

Keeping his head out the window slot, he looked down and noticed a deepening of the shadow at the juncture of the tower and the south wall. As he watched, the bulb there grew dimmer and dimmer until it was out. His immediate thought was that something had broken the line, but he had to discard that notion when he saw all the other bulbs still glowing. A bad bulb, then. That was all. But what a strange way for a bulb to go dead. Usually they flared blue-white first, then went out. This one just seemed to fade away.

One of the guards down there on the south wall had noticed it too and was coming over to him to investigate. Woermann was tempted to call down to him to take his partner with him but decided against it. The second man was standing in clear view by the parapet. It was a dead-end corner down there anyway. No possible danger.

He looked on as the soldier disappeared into the shadow—a peculiarly deep shadow. After perhaps fifteen seconds, Woermann looked away, but then was drawn back by a choked gurgle from below, followed by the clatter of wood and steel on stone—a dropped weapon.

He jumped at the sound, feeling his palms grow slick against the stone windowsill as he peered below. And still he could see nothing within the shadow.

The other guard, the first's partner, must have heard it too, for he started over to see what was wrong.

Woermann saw a dull, red spark begin to glow within the shadow. As it slowly brightened, he realized that it was the bulb coming back to life. Then he saw the first soldier. He lay on his back, arms akimbo, legs folded under him, his throat a bloody ruin. Sightless eyes stared up at Woermann, accusing him. There was nothing else, no one else in the corner.

As the other soldier began shouting for help, Woermann pulled himself back into the room and leaned against the wall, choking back bile as it surged up from his stomach. He could not move, could not speak. *My God, my God!*

He staggered over to the table that had been made for him only two days ago and grabbed a pencil. He had to get his men out of here—out of the keep, out of the Dinu Pass if necessary. There was no defense against what he had just witnessed. And he would not contact Ploiesti. This message would go straight to High Command.

But what to say? He looked at the mocking crosses

for inspiration but none came. How to make High Command understand without sounding like a madman? How to tell them that he and his men must leave the keep, that something uncanny threatened them, something immune to German military power.

He began to jot down phrases, crossing each out as he thought of a better one. He despised the thought of surrendering any position, but it would be inviting disaster to spend another night here. The men would be nearly uncontrollable now. And at the present death rate, he would be an officer without a command if he stayed much longer.

Command . . . his mouth twisted sardonically at the word. He was no longer in command of the keep. Something dark and awful had taken over.

SEVEN

They were halfway through the strait when he sensed the boatman beginning to make his move.

It had not been an easy journey. The red-haired man had sailed past Gibraltar in the dark to Marbella where he had chartered the thirty-foot motor launch that now pulsed around him. It was sleek and low with two over-sized engines. Its owner was no weekend captain. The red-haired man knew a smuggler when he saw one.

The owner had haggled fiercely over the fee until he learned he was to be paid in gold U.S. double eagles: half on departure, the rest upon their safe arrival on the northern shore of the Sea of Marmara. To traverse the length of the Mediterranean the owner had insisted on taking a crew. The red-haired man had disagreed; he would be crew enough.

They had run for six days straight, each man taking

the helm for eight hours at a stretch, then resting for the next eight, keeping the boat at a steady twenty knots, twenty-four hours a day. They had stopped only at secluded coves where the owner's face seemed well known, and only long enough to fill the tanks with fuel. The red-haired man paid all expenses.

And now, alerted by the slowing of the boat, he waited for the owner, Carlos, to come below and try to kill him. Carlos had had his eye out for such a chance ever since they had left Marbella, but there had been none. Now, nearing the end of their journey, Carlos had only tonight left to get the money belt. The red-haired man knew that was what he was after. He had felt Carlos brush against him repeatedly to assure himself that his passenger still wore it. Carlos knew there was gold there; and it was plain by its bulk that there was a lot. He also appeared to be consumed with curiosity about the long, flat case his passenger always kept at his side.

It was a shame. Carlos had been a good companion the past six days. A good sailor, too. He drank a bit too much, ate more than a bit too much, and apparently did not bathe anywhere near enough. The red-haired man gave a mental shrug. He had smelled worse in his day. Much worse.

The door to the rear deck opened, letting in a breath of cool air; Carlos was framed briefly in starlight before closing the door behind him.

Too bad, the red-haired man thought, as he heard the faint scrape of steel being withdrawn from a leather sheath. A good journey was coming to a sad end. Carlos had expertly guided them past Sardinia, sped them across the clear, painfully blue water between the northern tip of Tunisia and Sicily, then north of Crete and up through the Cyclades into the Aegean. They were presently threading the Dardanelles, the narrow channel connecting the Aegean with the Sea of Marmara.

Too bad.

He saw the light flash off the blade as it was raised

over his chest. His left hand shot out and gripped the wrist before the knife could descend; his right hand gripped Carlos's other hand.

"Why, Carlos?"

"Give me the gold!" The words were snapped out.

"I might have given you more if you'd asked me. Why try to kill me?"

Carlos, gauging the strength of the hands holding him, tried a different tack. "I was only going to cut the belt off. I wasn't going to hurt you."

"The belt is around my waist. Your knife is over my chest."

"It's dark in here."

"Not that dark. But all right . . ." He loosened his grip on the wrists. "How much more do you want?"

Carlos ripped his knife hand free and plunged it downward, growling, "All of it!"

The red-haired man again caught the wrist before the blade could strike. "I wish you hadn't done that, Carlos."

With steady, inexorable deliberateness, the red-haired man bent his assailant's knife hand inward toward his own chest. Joints and ligaments popped and cracked in protest as they were stretched to the limit. Carlos groaned in pain and fear as his tendons ruptured and the popping was replaced by the sickening crunch of breaking bones. The point of his knife was now directly over the left side of his chest.

"No! Please . . . *no!*"

"I gave you a chance, Carlos." His own voice sounded hard, flat, and alien in his ears. "You threw it away."

Carlos's voice rose to a scream that ended abruptly as his fist was rammed against his ribs, driving the blade into his heart. His body went rigid, then limp. The red-haired man let him slip to the floor.

He lay still for a moment and listened to his heart beat. He tried to feel remorse but there was none. It had been a long time since he had killed someone. He ought to feel *something*. There was nothing. Carlos was a cold-blooded murderer. He had been dealt what he had intended to deal. There was no room for remorse in the red-haired man, only a desperate urgency to get to Romania.

Rising, he picked up the long, flat case, stepped up through the door to the rear deck, and took the helm. The engines were idling. He pushed them to full throttle.

The Dardanelles. He had been through here before, but never during a war, and never at full speed in the dark. The starlit water was a gray expanse ahead of him, the coast a dark smudge to the left and right. He was in one of the narrowest sections of the strait where it funneled down to a mile across. Even at its widest it never exceeded four miles. He traveled by compass and by instinct, without running lights, in a limbo of darkness.

There was no telling what he might run into in these waters. The radio said Greece had fallen; that might or might not be true. There could be Germans in the Dardanelles now, or British or Russians. He had to avoid them all. This journey had not been planned; he had no papers to explain his presence. And time was against him. He needed every knot the engines could put out.

Once into the wider Sea of Marmara twenty miles ahead, he'd have maneuvering room and would run as far as his fuel would take him. When that got low, he would beach the boat and move overland to the Black Sea. It would cost him precious time, but there was no other way. Even if he had the fuel, he could not risk running the Bosporus. There the Russians would be thick as flies around a corpse.

He pushed on the throttles to see if he could coax any more speed from the engines. He couldn't.

He wished he had wings.

EIGHT

Magda held her mandolin with practiced ease, the pick oscillating rapidly in her right hand, the fingers of her left traveling up and down the neck, hopping from string to string, from fret to fret. Her eyes concentrated on a sheet of handwritten music: one of the prettiest Gypsy melodies she had yet committed to paper.

She sat within a brightly painted wagon on the outskirts of Bucharest. The interior was cramped, the living space further reduced by shelves full of exotic herbs and spices on every wall, by brightly colored pillows stuffed into every corner, by lamps and strings of garlic hanging from the low ceiling. Her legs were crossed to support the mandolin, but even then her gray woolen skirt barely cleared her ankles. A bulky gray sweater that buttoned in the front covered a simple white blouse. A tattered scarf hid the brown of her hair. But the drabness of her clothing could not steal the shine from her eyes, or the color from her cheeks.

Magda let herself drift into the music. It took her away for a while, away from a world that became increasingly hostile to her with each new day. *They* were out there: the ones who hated Jews. They had robbed her father of his position at the university, ordered the two of them out of their lifelong home, removed her king—not that King Carol had ever deserved her loyalty, but still, he had been the king—and replaced him with General Antonescu and the Iron Guard. But no one could take away her music.

"Is that right?" she asked when the last note had echoed away, leaving the interior of the wagon quiet again.

The old woman sitting on the far side of the tiny, round, oak table smiled, crinkling up the dark skin around her black Gypsy eyes. "Almost. But the middle goes like this."

The woman placed a well-shuffled deck of checker-backed cards on the table and picked up a wooden *naiou*. Looking like a wizened Pan as she placed the pipes to her lips, she began to blow. Magda played along until she heard her own notes go sour, then she changed the notations on her sheet.

"That's it, I guess," she said, gathering her papers into a pile with a small sense of satisfaction. "Thank you so much, Josefa."

The old woman held out her hand. "Here. Let me see."

Magda handed her the sheet and watched as the old woman's gaze darted back and forth across the page. Josefa was the *phuri dai*, the wise woman of this particular tribe of Gypsies. Papa had often spoken of how beautiful she had once been; but her skin was weathered now, her raven hair thickly streaked with silver, her body shrunken. Nothing wrong with her mind, though.

"So this is my song." Josefa did not read music.

"Yes. Preserved forever."

The old woman handed it back. "But I won't play it

this way forever. This is the way I like to play it now. Next month I may decide to change something. I've already changed it many times over the years.''

Magda nodded as she placed the sheet with the others in her folder. She had known Gypsy music to be largely improvisational before she had started her collection. That was to be expected—Gypsy *life* was largely improvisational, with no home other than a wagon, no written language, nothing at all to pin them down. Perhaps that was what drove her to try to capture some of their vitality and cage it on a music staff, to preserve it for the future.

"It will do for now," Magda replied. "Maybe next year I'll see what you've added."

"Won't the book be published by then?"

Magda felt a pang. "I'm afraid not."

"Why not?"

Magda busied herself with putting her mandolin away, not wishing to answer but unable to dodge the question gracefully. She did not look up as she spoke. "I have to find a new publisher."

"What happened to the old one?"

Magda kept her eyes down. She was embarrassed. It had been one of the most painful moments in her life, learning that her publisher was reneging on their agreement. She still stung from it.

"He changed his mind. Said this was not the right time for a compendium of Romanian Gypsy music."

"Especially by a Jewess," Josefa added.

Magda looked up sharply, then down again. *How true*. "Perhaps." She felt a lump form in her throat. She didn't want to talk about this. "How's business?"

"Terrible." Josefa shrugged as she set the *naiou* aside and picked up her tarot deck again. She was dressed in the mismatched, cast-off clothes common to Gypsies: flowered blouse, striped skirt, calico kerchief. A dizzying array of colors and patterns. Her fingers, as if acting of their own volition, began shuffling the deck. "I only see a few of the old regulars for readings these days. No new trade since they made me take the sign down.''

Magda had noted that this morning as she had approached the wagon. The sign over the rear door that had read "Doamna Josefa: Fortunes Told" was gone, as was the palmar diagram in the left window and the cabalistic symbol in the right. She had heard that all Gypsy tribes had been ordered by the Iron Guard to stay right where they were and to "deal no fraud" to the citizens.

"So, Gypsies are out of favor, too?"

"We Rom are always out of favor, no matter the time or place. We are used to it. But you Jews . . ." She clucked and shook her head. "We hear things . . . terrible things from Poland."

"We hear them, too," Magda said, suppressing a shudder. "But we are also used to being out of favor." *At least some of us are.* Not her. She would never get used to it.

"Going to get worse, I fear," Josefa said.

"The Rom may fare no better." Magda realized she was being hostile but couldn't help it. The world had become a frightening place and her only defense of late had been denial. The things she had heard couldn't be true, not about the Jews, or about what was happening to Gypsies in the rural regions—tales of round-ups by the Iron Guard, forced sterilizations, then slave labor. It had to be wild rumor, scare stories. And yet, with all the terrible things that had indeed been happening . . .

"I do not worry," Josefa said. "Cut a Gypsy into ten pieces and you have not killed him; you have only made ten Gypsies."

Magda was quite certain that under similar circumstances you would only be left with a dead Jew. Again she tried to change the subject.

"Is that a tarot deck?" She knew perfectly well it was.

Josefa nodded. "You wish a fortune?"

"No. I really don't believe in any of that."

"To tell the truth, many times I do not believe in it either. Mostly the cards say nothing because there is really nothing to say. So we improvise, just as we do in

music. And what harm is there in it? I don't do the
hokkane baro; I just tell the *gadjě* girls that they are
going to find a wonderful man soon, and the *gadjě* men
that their business ventures will soon be bearing fruit.
No harm."

"And no fortune."

Josefa lifted her narrow shoulders. "Sometimes the
tarot reveals. Want to try?"

"No. Thank you, but no." She didn't want to know
what the future held. She had a feeling it could only be
bad.

"Please. A gift from me."

Magda hesitated. She didn't want to offend Josefa.
And after all, hadn't the old woman just told her that
the deck usually told nothing? Maybe she would make
up a nice fantasy for her.

"Oh, all right."

Josefa extended the pack of cards across the table.
"Cut."

Magda separated the top half and lifted it off. Josefa
slipped this under the remainder of the deck and began
to deal, talking as her hands worked.

"How is your father?"

"Not well, I'm afraid. He can hardly stand now."

"Such a shame. Not often you can find a *gadjě* who
knows how to *rokker*. Yoska's bear did not help his
rheumatism?"

Magda shook her head. "No. And it's not just
rheumatism he has. It's much worse." Papa had tried
anything and everything to halt the progressive twisting
and gnarling of his limbs, even going so far as to allow
Josefa's grandson's trained bear to walk on his back, a
venerable Gypsy therapy that had proven as useless as
all the latest "miracles" of modern medicine.

"A good man," Josefa said, clucking. "It's wrong
that a man who knows so much about this land must . . .
be kept . . . from seeing it . . . anymore . . ." She
frowned as her voice trailed off.

"What's the matter?" Magda asked. Josefa's
troubled expression as she looked down at the cards

spread out on the table made Magda uneasy. "Are you all right?"

"Hmmm? Oh, yes. I'm fine. It's just these cards . . ."

"Something wrong?" Magda refused to believe that cards could tell the future any more than could the entrails of a dead bird; yet under her sternum was a pocket of tense anticipation.

"It's the way they divide. I've never seen anything like it. The neutral cards are scattered, but the cards that can be read as good are all on the right here"—she moved her hand over the area in question—"and the bad or evil cards are all over on the left. Odd."

"What does it mean?"

"I don't know. Let me ask Yoska." She called her grandson's name over her shoulder, then turned back to Magda. "Yoska is very good with the tarot. He's watched me since he was a boy."

A darkly handsome young man in his mid-twenties with a porcelain smile and a muscular build stepped in from the front room of the wagon and nodded to Magda, his black eyes lingering on her. Magda looked away, feeling naked despite her heavy clothing. He was younger than she, but that had never intimidated him. He had made his desires known on a number of occasions in the past. She had rebuffed him.

He looked down at the table, where his grandmother was pointing. Deep furrows formed slowly in his smooth brow as he studied the cards. He was quiet a long time, then appeared to come to a decision.

"Shuffle, cut, and deal again," he said.

Josefa nodded agreement and the routine was repeated. This time with no small talk. Despite her skepticism, Magda found herself leaning forward and watching the cards as they were placed on the table one by one. She knew nothing of tarot and would have to rely solely on the interpretation of her hostess and her grandson. When she looked up at their faces, she knew something was not right.

"What do you think, Yoska?" the old woman said in a low voice.

"I don't know . . . such a concentration of good and evil . . . and such a clear division between them."

Magda swallowed. Her mouth was dry. "You mean it came out the same? Twice in a row?"

"Yes," Josefa said. "Except that the sides are different. The good is now on the left and the evil is on the right." She looked up. "That would indicate a choice. A grave choice."

Anger suddenly drove out Magda's growing unease. They were playing some sort of a game with her. She refused to be anyone's fool. "I think I'd better go." She grabbed her folder and mandolin case and rose to her feet. "I'm not some naive *gadjé* girl you can have fun with."

"No! Please, once more!" The old Gypsy woman reached for her hand.

"Sorry, but I really must be going."

She hurried for the rear door of the wagon, realizing she wasn't being fair to Josefa, but leaving all the same. Those grotesque cards with their strange figures, and the awed, puzzled expression on the faces of the two Gypsies filled her with a desperate urge to be out of the wagon. She wanted to be back in Bucharest, back to sharp, clear lines and firm pavements.

NINE

The snakes had arrived.

SS men, especially officers, reminded Woermann of snakes. SS-Sturmbannführer Erich Kaempffer was no exception.

Woermann would always remember an evening a few years before the war when a local *Hohere SS-und Polizeiführer*—the high-sounding name for a local chief of state police—held a reception in the Rathenow district. Captain Woermann, as a decorated officer in the German Army and a prominent local citizen, had been invited. He hadn't wanted to go, but Helga so seldom had a chance to attend a fancy official reception and she glowed so when she dressed up, that he hadn't had the heart to refuse.

Against one wall of the reception hall had stood a glass terrarium in which a three-foot snake coiled and

75

uncoiled incessantly. It was the host's favorite pet. He kept it hungry. On three separate occasions during the evening he invited all the guests to watch as he threw a toad to the snake. A passing glance during the first feeding had sufficed for Woermann—he saw the toad halfway along its slow, head-first journey down the snake's gullet, still alive, its legs kicking frantically in a vain attempt to free itself.

The sight had served to make a dull evening grim. When he and Helga had passed the tank on their way out, Woermann saw that the snake was still hungry, still winding around the inside of the cage, looking for a fourth toad despite the three swellings along its length.

He thought of that snake as he watched Kaempffer wind around the front room of Woermann's quarters, from the door, around the easel, around the desk, to the window, then back again. Except for his brown shirt, Kaempffer was clad entirely in black—black jacket, black breeches, black tie, black leather belt, black holster, and black jackboots. The silver Death's Head insignia, the SS paired thunderbolts, and his officer's pins were the only bright spots on his uniform . . . glittering scales on a poisonous, blond-headed serpent.

He noticed that Kaempffer had aged somewhat since their chance meeting in Berlin two years ago. *But not as much as I*, Woermann thought grimly. The SS major, although two years older than Woermann, was slimmer and therefore looked younger. Kaempffer's blond hair was full and straight and still unmarred by gray. A picture of Aryan perfection.

"I noticed you only brought one squad with you," Woermann said. "The message said two. Personally, I'd have thought you'd bring a regiment."

"No, Klaus," Kaempffer said in a condescending tone as he wound about the room. "A single squad would be more than enough to handle this so-called problem of yours. My einsatzkommandos are rather proficient in taking care of this sort of thing. I brought two squads because this is merely a stop along my way."

"Where's the other squad? Picking daisies?"

"In a manner of speaking, yes." Kaempffer's smile was not a nice thing to see.

"What's that supposed to mean?" Woermann asked.

Removing his cap and coat, Kaempffer threw them on Woermann's desk, then went to the window overlooking the village. "In a minute, you shall see."

Reluctantly, Woermann joined the SS man at the window. Kaempffer had arrived only twenty minutes ago and already was usurping command. With his extermination squad in tow, he had driven across the causeway without a second's hesitation. Woermann had found himself wishing the supports had weakened during the past week. No such luck. The major's jeep and the truck behind it had made it safely across. After debarking and telling Sergeant Oster—Woermann's Sergeant Oster—to see that the einsatzkommandos were well quartered immediately, he had paraded into Woermann's suite with his right arm flailing a "Heil Hitler" and the attitude of a messiah.

"Seems you've come quite a way since the Great War," Woermann said as they watched the quiet, darkened village together. "The SS seems to suit you."

"I prefer the SS to the regular army, if that's what you're implying. Far more efficient."

"So I've heard."

"I'll show you how efficiency solves problems, Klaus. And solving problems eventually wins wars." He pointed out the window. "Look."

Woermann saw nothing at first, then noticed some movement at the edge of the village. A group of people. As they approached the causeway, the group lengthened into a parade: ten village locals stumbling before the proddings of the second squad of einsatzkommandos.

Woermann found himself shocked and dismayed, even though he should have expected something like this.

"Are you insane? Those are Romanian citizens! We're in an ally state!"

"German soldiers have been killed by one or more Romanian citizens. And it's highly unlikely General Antonescu will raise much of a fuss with the Reich over the deaths of a few country bumpkins.''

"Killing them will accomplish nothing!''

"Oh, I've no intention of killing them right away. But they'll make excellent hostages. Word has been spread through the village that if one more German soldier dies, all those ten locals will be shot immediately. And ten more will be shot every time another German is killed. This will continue until either the murders stop or we run out of villagers.''

Woermann turned away from the window. So this was the New Order, the New Germany, the ethic of the Master Race. This was how the war was to be won.

"It won't work,'' he said.

"Of course it will.'' Kaempffer's smugness was unbearable. "It always has and always will. These partisans feed on the backslapping they get from their drinking companions. They play the hero and milk the role for all it's worth—until their friends start dying, or until their wives and children are marched off. Then they become good little peasants again.''

Woermann searched for a way to save those villagers. He knew they'd had nothing to do with the killings. "This time is different.''

"I hardly think so. I do believe, Klaus, that I've had far more experience with this sort of thing than you.''

"Yes . . . Auschwitz, wasn't it?''

"I learned much from Commandant Hoess.''

"You like learning?'' Woermann snatched the major's hat from the desk and tossed it to him. "I'll show you something *new*! Come with me!''

Moving swiftly and giving Kaempffer no time to ask questions, Woermann led him down the tower stairs to the courtyard, then across to another stairway leading down to the cellar. He stopped at the rupture in the wall and lit a lamp, then led Kaempffer down a mossy stairway into the cavernous subcellar.

"Cold down here,'' Kaempffer said, his breath misting in the lamplight as he rubbed his hands together.

"It's where we keep the bodies. All six of them.''

"You haven't shipped any back?"

"I didn't think it wise to ship them out one at a time . . . might cause talk among the Romanians along the way . . . not good for German prestige. I had planned to take them all with me when I left today. But as you know, my request for relocation was denied."

He stopped before the six sheet-covered figures on the hard-packed earth, noting with annoyance that the sheets over the bodies were in disarray. It was a minor thing, but he felt the least that could be done for these men before their final burial was to treat their remains with respect. If they had to wait before being returned to their homeland, they ought to wait in clean uniforms and a neatly arranged shroud.

He went first to the man most recently killed and pulled back the sheet to expose the head and shoulders.

"This is Private Remer. Look at his throat."

Kaempffer did so, his face impassive.

Woermann replaced the sheet, then lifted the next, holding the lamp up so Kaempffer could get a good look at the ruined flesh of another throat. He then continued down the line, saving the most gruesome for last.

"And now—Private Lutz."

Finally, a reaction from Kaempffer: a tiny gasp. But Woermann gasped, too. Lutz's face stared back at them upside down. The top of his head had been set against the empty spot between his shoulders; his chin and the mangled stump of his neck were angled away from his body toward the empty darkness.

Quickly, gingerly, Woermann swiveled the head until it sat properly, vowing to find the man who had been so careless with the remains of a fallen comrade, and to make him regret it. He carefully rearranged all the sheets, then turned to Kaempffer.

"Do you understand now why I tell you hostages won't make a bit of difference?"

The major didn't reply immediately. Instead, he turned and headed for the stairs and warmer air. Woermann sensed that Kaempffer had been shaken more than he had shown.

"Those men were not just killed," Kaempffer said finally. "They were mutilated!"

"Exactly! Whoever or *whatever* is doing this is utterly mad! The lives of ten villagers won't mean a thing."

"Why do you say 'whatever'?"

Woermann held Kaempffer's gaze. "I'm not sure. All I know is that the killer comes and goes at will. Nothing we do, no security measure we try, seems to matter."

"Security doesn't work," Kaempffer said, regaining his former bravado as they re-entered the light and the warmth of Woermann's quarters, "because security isn't the answer. *Fear* is the answer. Make the killer *afraid* to kill. Make him fear the price others are going to have to pay for his action. Fear is your best security, always."

"And what if the killer is someone like you? What if he doesn't give a damn about the villagers?"

Kaempffer didn't answer.

Woermann decided to press the point. "Your brand of fear fails to work when you run up against your own kind. Take that back to Auschwitz when you go."

"I'll not be returning to Poland, Klaus. When I finish up here—and that should only take me a day or two—I'll be heading south to Ploiesti."

"I can't see any use for you there—no synagogues to burn, only oil refineries."

"Continue making your snide little comments, Klaus," Kaempffer said, nodding his head ever so slightly as he spoke through tight lips. "Enjoy them now. For once I get my Ploiesti project under way, you will not dare to speak to me so."

Woermann sat down behind his rickety desk. He was growing weary of Kaempffer. His eyes were drawn to the picture of his younger son, Fritz, the fifteen-year-old.

"I still fail to see what attraction Ploiesti could hold for the likes of you."

"Not the refineries, I assure you—I leave them to the High Command to worry about."

"Gracious of you."

Kaempffer did not appear to hear. "No, my concern is the railways."

Woermann continued staring at the photo of his son. He echoed Kaempffer: "Railways."

"Yes! The greatest railway nexus in Romania is to be found at Ploiesti, making it the perfect place for a resettlement camp."

Woermann snapped out of his trance and lifted his head. "You mean like Auschwitz?"

"Exactly! That's why the Auschwitz camp is where it is. A good rail network is crucial to efficient transportation of the lesser races to the camps. Petroleum leaves Ploiesti by rail for every part of Romania." He had spread his arms wide; he began to bring them together again. "And from every corner of Romania trains will return with carloads of Jews and Gypsies and all the other human garbage abroad in this land."

"But this isn't occupied territory! You can't—"

"The Führer does not want the undesirables of Romania to be neglected. It's true that Antonescu and the Iron Guard are removing the Jews from positions of influence, but the Führer has a more vigorous plan. It has come to be known in the SS as 'The Romanian Solution.' To implement it, Reichsführer Himmler has arranged with General Antonescu for the SS to show the Romanians how it is done. *I* have been chosen for that mission. I will be commandant of Camp Ploiesti."

Appalled, Woermann found himself unable to reply as Kaempffer warmed to his subject.

"Do you know how many Jews there are in Romania, Klaus? Seven hundred and fifty thousand at last count. Perhaps a million! No one knows for sure, but once I start an efficient record system, we'll know exactly. But that's not the worst of it—the country is absolutely crawling with Gypsies and Freemasons. And worse yet: Muslims! Two million undesirables in all!"

"If only I had known!" Woermann said, rolling his eyes and pressing his hands against the side of his face. "I never would have set foot in this sinkhole of a country!"

Kaempffer heard him this time. "Laugh if you wish, Klaus, but Ploiesti will be most important. Right now we are transferring Jews all the way from Hungary to Auschwitz at a great waste of time, manpower, and fuel. Once Camp Ploiesti is functioning, I foresee many of them being shipped to Romania. And as commandant, I shall become one of the most important men in the SS . . . in the Third Reich! Then it shall be my turn to laugh."

Woermann remained silent. He had not laughed . . . he found the whole idea sickening. Facetiousness was his only defense against a world coming under the control of madmen, against the realization that he was an officer in the army that was enabling them to achieve that control. He watched Kaempffer begin to coil back and forth about the room again.

"I didn't know you were a painter," the major said, stopping before the easel as if seeing it for the first time. He studied it a moment in silence. "Perhaps if you had spent as much time ferreting out the killer as you obviously have on this morbid little painting, some of your men might—"

"Morbid! There's nothing at all morbid about that painting!"

"The shadow of a corpse hanging from a noose—is that cheerful?"

Woermann was on his feet, approaching the canvas. "What are you talking about?"

Kaempffer pointed. "Right there . . . on the wall."

Woermann stared. At first he saw nothing. The shadows on the wall were the same mottled gray he had painted days ago. There was nothing that even faintly resembled . . . no, wait. He caught his breath. To the left of the window in which the village sat gleaming in the sunrise . . . a thin vertical line connecting to a larger dark shape below it. It *could* be seen as a hunched corpse hanging from a rope. He vaguely remembered painting the line and the shape, but in no way had he intended to add this gruesome touch to the work. He could not bear, however, to give Kaempffer the satisfaction of hearing him admit that he saw it, too.

"Morbidity, like beauty, is in the eye of the beholder."

But Kaempffer's mind was already moving elsewhere. "It's lucky for you the painting's finished, Klaus. After I've moved in, I'll be much too busy to allow you to come up here and fiddle with it. But you can resume after I'm on my way to Ploiesti."

Woermann had been waiting for this, and was ready for it. "You're not moving into my quarters."

"Correction: *my* quarters. You seem to forget that I outrank you, *Captain*."

Woermann sneered. "SS rank! Worthless! Worse than meaningless. My sergeant is four times the soldier you are! Four times the man, too!"

"Be careful, Captain. That Iron Cross you received in the last war will carry you only so far!"

Woermann felt something snap inside him. He pulled the black-enameled, silver-bordered Maltese cross from his tunic and held it out to Kaempffer. "*You* don't have one! And you never will! At least not a real one—one like this, without a nasty little swastika at its center!"

"Enough!"

"No, not enough! Your SS kills helpless civilians— women, children! I earned this medal fighting men who were able to shoot back. And we both know," Woermann said, his voice dropping to a fierce whisper, "how much you dislike an enemy who shoots back!"

Kaempffer leaned forward until his nose was barely an inch from Woermann's. His blue eyes gleamed in the white fury of his face. "The Great War . . . that is all past. *This* is the Great War—*my* war. The old war was your war, and it's dead and gone and forgotten!"

Woermann smiled, delighted that he had finally penetrated Kaempffer's loathsome hide. "Not forgotten. Never forgotten. Especially your bravery at Verdun!"

"I'm warning you," Kaempffer said. "I'll have you —" And then he closed his mouth with an audible snap.

For Woermann was moving forward. He had

stomached all he could of this strutting thug who
discussed the "liquidation" of millions of defenseless
lives as matter-of-factly as he might discuss what he was
going to have for dinner. Woermann made no overtly
threatening gesture, yet Kaempffer took an involuntary
step backward at his approach. Woermann merely
walked past him and opened the door.

"Get out."

"You can't do this!"

"Out."

They stared at each other for a long time. For a
moment he thought Kaempffer might actually challenge
him. Woermann knew the major was in better condition
and physically stronger—but only physically. Finally,
Kaempffer's gaze wavered and he turned away. They
both knew the truth about SS-Sturmbannführer
Kaempffer. Without a word, he picked up his black
greatcoat and stormed out of the room. Woermann
closed the door quietly behind him.

He stood still for a moment. He had let Kaempffer
get to him. His control used to be better. He walked
over to the easel and stared at his canvas. The more he
looked at the shadow he had painted on the wall, the
more it looked like a hanging corpse. It gave him a
queasy feeling and annoyed him as well. He had meant
for the sunlit village to be the focus of the painting, but
all he could see now was that damned shadow.

He tore himself away and returned to his desk, staring
again at the photograph of Fritz. The more he saw of
men like Kaempffer, the more he worried about Fritz.
He hadn't worried this much when Kurt, the older boy,
had been in combat in France last year. Kurt was
nineteen, a corporal already. A man now.

But Fritz—they were doing things to Fritz, those
Nazis. The boy had somehow been induced to join the
local *Jugendführer*, the Hitler Youth. When Woermann
had been home on his last leave, he had been hurt and
dismayed to hear his son's fourteen-year-old mouth
regurgitating that Aryan Master Race garbage, and
speaking of "Der Führer" with an awed reverence that

had once been reserved for God alone. The Nazis were stealing his son from him right under his nose, turning the boy into a snake like Kaempffer. And there did not seem to be a thing Woermann could do about it.

There didn't seem to be anything he could do about Kaempffer either. He had no control over the SS officer. If Kaempffer decided to shoot Romanian peasants, there was no way to stop him, other than to arrest him. And he could not do that. Kaempffer was here by authority of the High Command. To arrest him would be insubordination, an act of brazen defiance. His Prussian heritage rebelled at the thought. The army was his career, his home . . . it had been good to him for a quarter century. To challenge it now . . .

Helpless. That was how he felt. It brought him back to a clearing outside Posnan, Poland, a year and a half ago, shortly after the fighting had ended. His men had been setting up bivouac when the sound of automatic gunfire came from over the next rise, about a mile away. He had gone to investigate. Einsatzkommandos were lining up Jews—men and women of all ages, children —and systematically slaughtering them with fusillades of bullets. After the bodies had been rolled into the ditch behind them, more were lined up and shot. The ground had turned muddy with blood and the air had been full of the reek of cordite and the cries of those who were still alive and in agony, and to whom no one would bother to administer a *coup de grâce*.

He had been helpless then, and he was helpless now. Helpless to make this war into one of soldier against soldier, helpless to stop the thing that was killing his men, helpless to stop Kaempffer from slaughtering those Romanian villagers.

He slumped into the chair. What was the use? Why even try anymore? Everything was changing for the worse. He had been born with the century, a century of hope and promise. Yet he was fighting in his second war, a war he could not understand.

And yet he had wanted this war. He had yearned for a chance to strike back at the vultures who had settled upon the Fatherland after the last war, saddling it with impossible reparations, grinding its face into the dirt year after year after year. His chance had come, and he had participated in some of the great German victories. The Wehrmacht was unstoppable.

Why, then, did he feel such malaise? It seemed wrong for him to want to be out of it all and back in Rathenow with Helga. It seemed wrong to be glad that his father, also a career officer, had died in the Great War and could not see what atrocities were being done today in the name of the Fatherland.

And still, with everything so wrong, he held on to his commission. Why? The answer to that one, he told himself for the hundredth—possibly the thousandth—time, was that in his heart he believed the German Army would outlast the Nazis. Politicians came and went, but the army would always be the army. If he could just hold on, the German Army would be victorious, and Hitler and his gangsters would fade from power. He believed that. He had to.

Against all reason, he prayed that Kaempffer's threat against the villagers would have the desired effect—that there would be no more deaths. But if it didn't work . . . if another German was to die tonight, Woermann knew whom he wanted it to be.

TEN

Major Kaempffer lay awake in his bedroll, still rankling at Woermann's contemptuous insubordination. Sergeant Oster, at least, had been helpful. Like most regular army men, he responded with fearful obedience to the black uniform and the Death's Head insignia—something to which Oster's commanding officer seemed quite immune. But then, Kaempffer and Woermann had known each other long before there was an SS.

The sergeant had readily found quarters for the two squads of einsatzkommandos and had suggested a dead-end corridor at the rear of the keep as a compound for the prisoners from the village. An excellent choice: The corridor had been carved into the stone of the mountain itself and provided entry to four large rooms. Sole access to the retention area was through another long corridor running at an angle directly out to the courtyard. Kaempffer assumed that the section originally had been

87

designed as a storage area since the ventilation was poor and there were no fireplaces in the rooms. The sergeant had seen to it that the entire length of both corridors, from the courtyard to the blank stone wall at the very end, was well lit by a new string of light bulbs, making it virtually impossible for anyone to surprise the einsatzkommandos who would be on guard in pairs at all times.

For Major Kaempffer himself, Sergeant Oster had found a large, double-sized room on the second level within the rear section of the keep. He had suggested the tower, but Kaempffer had refused; to have moved into the first or second level would have been convenient but would have meant being *below* Woermann. The fourth tower level involved too many steps to be taken too many times a day. The rear section of the keep was better. He had a window overlooking the courtyard, a bedframe commandeered from one of Woermann's enlisted men, and an unusually heavy oak door with a secure latch. His bedroll was now supported by the newly made frame, and the major lay within it, a battery lamp on the floor beside him.

His eyes came to rest on the crosses in the walls. They seemed to be everywhere. Curious. He had wanted to ask the sergeant about them but had not wanted to detract from his posture of knowing everything. This was an important part of the SS mystique and he had to maintain it. Perhaps he would ask Woermann—when he could bring himself to speak to him again.

Woermann . . . he couldn't get the man off his mind. The irony of it all was that Woermann was the last person in the world Kaempffer would have wished to be billeted with. With Woermann around he could not be the type of SS officer he wished to be. Woermann could fix his gaze on him and pierce right through the SS uniform, through the veneer of power, and see a terrified eighteen-year-old. That day in Verdun had been a turning point in both their lives . . .

. . . *the British breaking through the German line in a surprise counterattack, the fire pinning down Kaempffer and Woermann and their whole company, men dying on all sides, the machine gunner hit and down, the British charging . . . pull back and regroup, the only sane thing to do, but no word from the company commander . . . probably dead . . . Private Kaempffer seeing no one in his entire squad left alive except a new recruit, a green volunteer named Woermann sixteen years old, too young to fight . . . motioning to the kid to start moving back with him . . . Woermann shaking his head and crawling up to the machine gun emplacement . . . firing skittishly, erratically at first, then with greater confidence . . . Kaempffer crawling away, knowing the British would be burying the kid later that day.*

But Woermann had not been buried that day. He had held off the enemy long enough for the line to be reinforced. He was promoted, decorated with the Iron Cross. And when the Great War ended he was *Fahnenjunker*, an officer candidate, and managed to remain with the minuscule remnant of the army that was left after the Versailles debacle.

Kaempffer, on the other hand, the son of a clerk from Augsburg, found himself on the street after the war. He had been afraid and penniless, one of many thousands of veterans of a lost war and a defeated army. They were not heroes—they were an embarrassment. He wound up joining the nihilistic *Freikorps Oberland*, and from there it was not far to the Nazi Party in 1927; after proving his *volkisch*, his pure German pedigree, he joined the SS in 1931. From then on, the SS became Kaempffer's home. He had lost his home after the first war and had sworn he would never be homeless again.

In the SS he learned the techniques of terror and pain; he also learned the techniques of survival: how to keep an eye out for weaknesses in his superiors, and how to hide his own weaknesses from the aggressive men below him. Eventually, he maneuvered himself into the position of first assistant to Rudolf Hoess, the most efficient of all the liquidators of Jewry.

Again, he learned so well that he was elevated to the rank of Sturmbannführer and assigned the task of setting up the resettlement camp at Ploiesti.

He ached to get to Ploiesti and begin. Only the unseen killers of Woermann's men stood in his way. They had to be disposed of first. Not a problem, merely an annoyance. He wanted it taken care of quickly, not only to allow him to move on, but also to make Woermann look like the bumbler he was. A quick solution and he would be on his way in triumph, leaving Klaus Woermann behind, an impotent has-been.

A quick solution would also defuse anything Woermann might ever say about the incident at Verdun. If Woermann should ever decide to accuse him of cowardice in the face of the enemy, Kaempffer would need only point out that the accuser was an embittered, frustrated man striking out viciously at one who had succeeded where he had failed.

He turned off the lamp on the floor. Yes . . . he needed a quick solution. So much to do, so many more important matters awaiting his attention.

The only thing that bothered him about all this was the unsettling, inescapable fact that Woermann was afraid. Truly afraid. And Woermann did not frighten easily.

He closed his eyes and tried to doze. After a while he felt sleep begin to slip over him like a warm, gentle blanket. He was almost completely covered when he felt it brutally snatched away. He found himself wide awake, his skin suddenly clammy and crawling with fear. Something was outside the door to his room. He heard nothing, saw nothing. Yet he knew it was there. Something with such a powerful aura of evil, of cold hate, of sheer malevolence, that he could sense its presence through the wood and the stone that separated it from him. It was out there, moving along the corridor, passing the door, and moving away. Away. . . .

His heart slowed, his skin began to dry. It took a few moments, but he was eventually able to convince himself that it had been a nightmare, a particularly vivid one, the kind that shakes you from the early stages of sleep.

Major Kaempffer arose from his bedroll and gingerly

began removing his long underwear. His bladder had involuntarily emptied during the nightmare.

Privates Friedrich Waltz and Karl Flick, members of the first Death's Head unit under Major Kaempffer, stood in their black uniforms, their gleaming black helmets, and shivered. They were bored, cold, and tired. This was not the sort of night duty they were accustomed to. Back at Auschwitz they had had warm, comfortable guardhouses and watchtowers where they could sit and drink coffee and play cards while the prisoners cowered in their drafty shacks. Only occasionally had they been required to do gate duty and march the perimeter in the open air.

True, here they were inside, but their conditions were as cold and as damp as the prisoners'. That wasn't right.

Private Flick slung his Schmeisser behind his back and rubbed his hands together. The fingertips were numb despite his gloves. He stood beside Waltz who was leaning against the wall at the angle of the two corridors. From this vantage point they could watch the entire length of the entry corridor to their left, all the way to the black square of night that was the courtyard, and at the same time keep watch on the prison block to their right.

"I'm going crazy, Karl," Waltz said. "Let's do something."

"Like what?"

"How about making them fall out for a little *Sachsengruss*?"

"They aren't Jews."

"They aren't Germans, either."

Flick considered this. The *Sachsengruss*, or Saxon greeting, had been his favorite method of breaking down new arrivals at Auschwitz. For hours on end he would make them perform the exercise: deep knee bends with arms raised and hands behind the head. Even a man in top condition would be in agony within half an hour. Flick had always found it exhilarating to watch the expressions on the prisoners' faces as they felt their bodies begin to betray them, as their joints and muscles cried out in anguish. And the fear in their faces. For those who fell from exhaustion were either shot on the spot or kicked until they resumed the exercise. He and Waltz couldn't shoot any of the Romanians tonight, but at least they could have some fun with them. But it might be hazardous.

"Better forget it," Flick said. "There's only two of us. What if one of them tries to be a hero?"

"We'll only take a couple out of the room at a time. Come on, Karl! It'll be fun!"

Flick smiled. "Oh, all right."

It wouldn't be as challenging as the game they used to play at Auschwitz, where he and Waltz held contests to see how many of a prisoner's bones they could break and still keep him working. But at least a little *Sachsengruss* would be diverting.

Flick began fishing out the key to the padlock that had transformed the last room on the corridor into a prison cell. There were four rooms available and they could have divided the villagers up; instead, they had crowded all ten into a single chamber. He was anticipating the look on their faces when he opened the door —the wincing, lip-quivering fear when they saw his smile and realized they would never receive any mercy from him. It gave him a certain feeling inside, something indescribable, wonderful, something so addictive that he craved more and more of it.

He was halfway to the door when Waltz's voice stopped him.

"Just a minute, Karl."

He turned. Waltz was squinting down the corridor toward the courtyard, a puzzled expression on his face. "What is it?" Flick asked.

"Something's wrong with one of the bulbs down there. The first one—it's going out."

"So?"

"It's fading out." He glanced at Flick and then back down the corridor. "Now the second one's fading!" His voice rose half an octave as he lifted his Schmeisser and cocked it. "Get over here!"

Flick dropped the key, swung his own weapon to the ready position, and ran to join his companion. By the time he reached the juncture of the two corridors, the third light had faded out. He tried but could make out no details of the corridor behind the dead bulbs. It was as if the area had been swallowed by impenetrable darkness.

"I don't like this," Waltz said.

"Neither do I. But I don't see a soul. Maybe it's the generator. Or a bad wire." Flick knew he didn't believe this any more than Waltz did. But he had had to say something to hide his growing fear. Einsatzkommandos were supposed to arouse fear, not feel it.

The fourth bulb began to die. The dark was only a dozen feet away.

"Let's move into here," Flick said, backing into the well-lit recess of the rear corridor. He could hear the prisoners muttering in the last room behind them. Though they could not see the dying bulbs, they sensed something was wrong.

Crouched behind Waltz, Flick shivered in the growing cold as he watched the illumination in the outer corridor continue to fade. He wanted something to shoot at but could see only blackness.

And then the blackness was upon him, freezing his joints and dimming his vision. For an instant that seemed to stretch to a lifetime, Private Karl Flick became a victim of the soulless terror he so loved to inspire in others, felt the deep, gut-tearing pain he so loved to inflict on others. Then he felt nothing.

T

Slowly the illumination returned to the corridors, first to the rear, then to the access passage. The only sounds came from the villagers trapped in their cell: whimpering from the women, relieved sobs from the men as they all felt themselves released from the panic that had seized them. One man tentatively approached the door to peer through a tiny space between two boards. His field of vision was limited to a section of floor and part of the rear wall of the corridor.

He could see no movement. The floor was bare except for a splattering of blood, still red, still wet, still steaming in the cold. And on the rear wall there was more blood, but this was smeared instead of splattered. The smears seemed to form a pattern, like letters from an alphabet he almost recognized, forming words that hovered just over the far edge of recognition. Words like dogs howling in the night, naggingly present, but ever out of reach.

The man turned away from the door and rejoined his fellow villagers huddled in the far corner of the room.

There was someone at the door.

Kaempffer's eyes snapped open; he feared that the earlier nightmare was going to repeat itself. But no. He could sense no dark, malevolent presence on the other side of the wall this time. The agent here seemed human. And clumsy. If stealth were the intruder's aim, he was failing miserably. But to be on the safe side, Kaempffer pulled his Luger from the holster coiled at his elbow.

"Who's there?"

No reply.

The rattle of a fumbling hand working the latch continued. Kaempffer could see breaks in the strip of light along the bottom of the door, but they gave no clue as to who might be out there. He considered turning on the lamp, but thought better of it. The dark room gave him an advantage—an intruder would be silhouetted against the light from the hall.

"Identify yourself!"

The fumbling at the latch stopped, to be replaced by a faint creaking and cracking, as if some huge weight were leaning against the door, trying to get through it. Kaempffer couldn't be sure in the dark, but he thought he saw the door bulge inward. That was two-inch oak! It would take massive weight to do that! As the creaking of the wood grew louder, he found himself trembling and sweating. There was nowhere to go. And now there was another sound, as if something were *clawing* at the door to get in. The noises assailed him, growing louder, paralyzing him. The wood was cracking so that it seemed it must break into a thousand fragments; the hinges cried out as their metal fastenings were tortured from the stone. Something had to give! He knew he should be chambering a shell into his Luger but he could not move.

The latch suddenly screeched and gave way, the door bursting open and slamming against the wall. Two figures stood outlined in the light from the hall. By their helmets, Kaempffer knew them to be German soldiers, and by their jackboots he knew them to be two of the einsatzkommandos he had brought with him. He should have relaxed at the sight of them, but for some reason he did not. What were they doing breaking into his room?

"Who is it?" he demanded.

They made no reply. Instead, they stepped forward in unison toward where he lay frozen in his bedroll. There was something wrong with their gait—not a gross disorder, but a subtle grotesquery. For one disconcerting moment, Major Kaempffer thought the two soldiers would march right over him. But they stopped at the edge of his bed, simultaneously, as if on command. Neither said a word. Nor did they salute.

"What do you want?" He should have been furious, but the anger did not come. Only fear. Against his wishes, his body was shrinking into the bedroll, trying to hide.

"Speak to me!" It was a plea.

No reply. He reached down with his left hand and

found the battery lamp on the floor beside his bed, all the while keeping the Luger in his right trained on the silent pair looming over him. When his questing fingers found the toggle switch, he hesitated, listening to his own rasping respirations. He had to see who they were and what they wanted, but a deep part of him warned against turning on the light.

Finally, he could stand it no longer. With a groan, he flicked the toggle and held the lamp up.

Privates Flick and Waltz stood over him, faces white and contorted, eyes glazed. A gaping crescent of torn and bloodied flesh grinned down at him from the place where each man's throat had been. No one moved . . . the two dead soldiers wouldn't, Kaempffer couldn't. For a long, heart-stopping moment, Kaempffer lay paralyzed, the lamp held aloft in his hand, his mouth working spasmodically around a scream of fear that could not pass his locked throat.

Then there was motion. Silently, almost gracefully, the two soldiers leaned forward and fell onto their commanding officer, pinning him in his bedroll under hundreds of pounds of limp dead flesh.

As Kaempffer struggled frantically to pull himself out from under the two corpses, he heard a far-off voice begin to wail in mortal panic. An isolated part of his brain focused on the sound until he had identified it.

The voice was his own.

"*Now* do you believe?"

"Believe what?" Kaempffer refused to look up at Woermann. Instead, he concentrated on the glass of kummel pressed between both palms. He had downed the first half in one gulp and now sipped steadily at the rest. By slow, painful degrees he was beginning to feel that he had himself under control again. It helped that he was in Woermann's quarters and not his own.

"That SS methods will not solve this problem."

"SS methods *always* work."

"Not this time."

"I've only begun! No villagers have died yet!"

Even as he spoke, Kaempffer admitted to himself that he had run up against a situation completely beyond the experience of anyone in the SS. There were no precedents, no one he could turn to for advice. There was something in the keep beyond fear, beyond coercion. Something magnificently adept at using fear as its own weapon. This was no guerrilla group, no fanatic arm of the National Peasant Party. This was something beyond war, beyond nationality, beyond race.

Yet the village prisoners would have to die at dawn. He could not let them go—to do so would be to admit defeat, and he and the SS would lose face. He must never allow that to happen. It made no difference that their deaths would have no effect on the . . . *thing* that was killing the men. They had to die.

"And they won't die," Woermann said.

"What?" Kaempffer finally looked up from the glass of kummel

"The villagers—I let them go."

"How dare you!" Anger—he began to feel alive again. He rose from his chair.

"You'll thank me later on when you don't have the systematic murder of an entire Romanian village to explain. And that's what it would come to. I know your kind. Once started on a course, no matter how futile, no matter how many you hurt, you keep going rather than admit you've made a mistake. So I'm keeping you from getting started. Now you can blame your failure on me. I will accept the blame and we can all find a safer place to quarter ourselves."

Kaempffer sat down again, mentally conceding that Woermann's move had given him an out. But he was trapped. He could not report failure back to the SS. That would mean the end of his career.

"I'm not giving up," he told Woermann, trying to appear stubbornly courageous.

"What else can you do? You can't fight this!"

"I *will* fight it!"

"How?" Woermann leaned back and folded his hands over his small paunch. "You don't even know what you're fighting, so how can you fight it?"

"With guns! With fire! With—" Kaempffer shrank away as Woermann leaned toward him, cursing himself for cringing, but helpless against the reflex.

"Listen to me, *Herr* Sturmbannführer: Those men were dead when they walked into your room tonight. Dead! We found their blood in the rear corridor. They died in your makeshift prison. Yet they walked off the corridor, up to your room, broke through the door, marched up to your bed, and fell on you. How are you going to fight something like that?"

Kaempffer shuddered at the memory. "They didn't die until they got to my room! Out of loyalty they came to report to me despite their mortal wounds!" He didn't believe a word of it. The explanation came automatically.

"They were dead, my friend," Woermann said without the slightest trace of friendship in his tone. "You didn't examine their bodies—you were too busy cleaning the crap out of your pants. But I did. I examined them just as I have examined every man who has died in this godforsaken keep. And believe me, those two died on the spot. All the major blood vessels in their necks were torn through. So were their windpipes. Even if you were Himmler himself, they couldn't have reported to you."

"Then they were carried!" Despite what he had seen with his own eyes he pressed for another explanation. The dead didn't walk. They couldn't!

Woermann leaned back and stared at him with such disdain that Kaempffer felt small and naked.

"Do they also teach you to lie to yourself in the SS?"

Kaempffer made no reply. He needed no physical examination of the corpses to know that they had been dead when they had walked into his room. He had known that the instant the light from his lamp had shone on their faces.

Woermann rose and strode toward the door. "I'll tell the men we leave at first light."

"NO!" The word passed his lips louder and shriller than he wished.

"You don't really intend to stay here, do you?" Woermann asked, his expression incredulous.

"I must complete this mission!"

"But you can't! You'll lose! Surely you see that now!"

"I see only that I shall have to change my methods."

"Only a madman would stay!"

I don't want to stay! Kaempffer thought. *I want to leave as much as anyone!* Under any other circumstances he would be giving the order to move out himself. But that was not one of his options here. He had to settle the matter of the keep—settle it once and for all—before he could leave for Ploiesti. If he bungled this job, there were dozens of his fellow SS officers lusting after the Ploiesti project, watching and waiting to leap at the first sign of weakness and wrest the prize away from him. He had to succeed here. If he could not, he would be left behind, forgotten in some rear office as others in the SS took over management of the world.

And he needed Woermann's help. He had to win him over for just a few days, until they could find a solution. Then he would have him court-martialed for freeing the villagers.

"What do you think it is, Klaus?" he asked softly.

"What do I think *what* is?" Woermann's tone was annoyed, frustrated, his words clipped brutally short.

"The killing—who or what do you think is doing it?"

Woermann sat down again, his face troubled. "I don't know. And at this point, I don't care to know. There are now eight corpses in the subcellar and we must see to it that there aren't any more."

"Come now, Klaus. You've been here a week . . . you must have formed an idea." Keep talking, he told himself. The longer you talk, the longer before you've got to return to that room.

"The men think it's a vampire."

A vampire! This was not the kind of talk he needed, but he fought to keep his voice low, his expression friendly.

"Do you agree?"

"Last week—God, even three days ago—I'd have said no. Now, I'm not so sure. I'm no longer sure of anything. If it *is* a vampire, it's not like the ones you read about in horror stories. Or see in the movies. The only thing I'm sure of is that the killer is not human."

Kaempffer tried to recall what he knew about vampire lore. Was the thing that killed the men drinking their blood? Who could tell? Their throats were such a ruin, and there was so much spilled on their clothes, it would take a medical laboratory to determine whether some of the blood was missing. He had once seen a pirated print of the silent movie, *Nosferatu*, and had watched the American version of *Dracula* with German subtitles. That had been years ago, and at the time the idea of a vampire had seemed as ludicrous as it deserved to be. But now . . . there certainly was no beak-nosed Slav in formal dress slinking around the keep. But there were most certainly eight corpses in the subcellar. Yet he could not see himself arming his men with wooden stakes and hammers.

"I think we shall have to go to the source," he said as his thoughts reached a dead end.

"And where's that?"

"Not where—who. I want to find the owner of the keep. This structure was built for a reason, and it is being maintained in perfect condition. There has to be a reason for that."

"Alexandru and his boys don't know who the owner is."

"So they say."

"Why should they lie?"

"Everybody lies. Somebody has to pay them."

"The money is given to the innkeeper and he dispenses it to Alexandru and his boys."

"Then we'll interrogate the innkeeper."

"You might also ask him to translate the words on the wall."

Kaempffer started. "What words? What wall?"

"Down where your two men died. There's something written on the wall in their blood."

"In Romanian?"

Woermann shrugged. "I don't know. I can't even recognize the letters, let alone the language."

Kaempffer leaped to his feet. Here was something he could handle. "I want that innkeeper!"

⊤

The man's name was Iuliu.

He was grossly overweight, in his late fifties, balding on his upper pate, and mustachioed on his upper lip. His ample jowls, unshaven for at least three days, trembled as he stood in his nightshirt and shivered in the rear corridor where his fellow villagers had been held prisoner.

Almost like the old days, Kaempffer thought, watching from the shadows of one of the rooms. He was starting to feel more like himself again. The man's confused, frightened countenance brought him back to his early years with the SS in Munich, when they would roust the Jew shopkeepers out of their warm beds in the early morning hours, beat them in front of their families, and watch them sweat with terror in the cold before dawn.

But the innkeeper was no Jew.

It really didn't matter. Jew, Freemason, Gypsy, Romanian innkeeper, what really mattered to Kaempffer was the victim's sense of complacency, of self-confidence, of security; the victim's feeling that he had a place in the world and that he was safe—that was what Kaempffer felt he had to smash. They had to learn that there was no safe place when he was around.

He let the innkeeper shiver and blink under the naked bulb for as long as his own patience would allow. Iuliu had been brought to the spot where the two einsatzkommandos had been killed. Anything that had even remotely resembled a ledger or a record book had been taken from the inn and dropped in a pile behind him. His eyes roamed from the bloodstains on the floor, to the bloody scrawl on the rear wall, to the implacable

faces of the four soldiers who had dragged him from
his bed, then back to the bloodstains on the floor.
Kaempffer found it difficult to look at those stains. He
kept remembering the two gashed throats that had supplied the blood, and the two dead men who had stood
over his bed.

When Major Kaempffer began to feel his own fingers
tingle with cold despite his black leather gloves, he
stepped out into the light of the corridor and faced
Iuliu. At the sight of an SS officer in full uniform, Iuliu
took a step backward and almost tripped over his
ledgers.

"Who owns the keep?" Kaempffer asked in a low
voice without preamble.

"I do not know, *Herr* Officer."

The man's German was atrocious, but it was better
than working through an interpreter. He slapped Iuliu
across the face with the back of his gloved hand. He felt
no malice; this was standard procedure.

"Who owns the keep?"

"I don't know!"

He slapped him again. *"Who?"*

The innkeeper spat blood and began to weep.
Good—he was breaking.

"I don't know!" Iuliu cried.

"Who gives you the money to pay the caretakers?"

"A messenger."

"From whom?"

"I don't know. He never says. From a bank, I think.
He comes twice a year."

"You must have to sign a receipt or cash a check.
Whom is it from?"

"I sign a letter. At the top it says The Mediterranean
Bank of Switzerland. In Zurich."

"How does the money come?"

"In gold. In twenty-lei gold pieces. I pay Alexandru
and he pays his sons. It has always been this way."

Kaempffer watched Iuliu wipe his eyes and compose
himself. He had the next link in the chain. He would
have the SS central office investigate the Mediterranean
Bank in Zurich to learn who was sending gold coins to

an innkeeper in the Transylvanian Alps. And from there back to the owner of the account, and from there back to the owner of the keep.

And then what?

He didn't know, but this seemed to be the only way to proceed at the moment. He turned and stared at the words scrawled on the wall behind him. The blood—Flick's and Waltz's blood—with which the words had been written had dried to a reddish brown. Many of the letters were either crudely formed or were not like any letters he had ever seen. Others were recognizable. As a whole, they were incomprehensible. Yet they had to mean something.

ТЪЖИН ОСТАВИТЕ НАШЬ АДМЬ

He gestured to the words. "What does that say?"

"I don't know, *Herr* Officer!" He cringed from the glittering blue of Kaempffer's eyes. "Please . . . I really don't!"

From Iuliu's expression and the sound of his voice, Kaempffer knew the man was telling the truth. But that was not a real consideration—never had been and never would be. The Romanian would have to be pressed to the limit, battered, broken, and sent limping back to his fellow villagers with tales of the merciless treatment he had received at the hands of the officer in the black uniform. And then they would know: They must cooperate, they must crawl over one another in their eagerness to be of service to the SS.

"You lie," he screamed and slammed the back of his hand across Iuliu's face again. "Those words are Romanian! I want to know what they say!"

"They are *like* Romanian, Herr Officer," Iuliu said, cowering in fear and pain, "but they are not. I don't know what they say!"

This tallied with the information Kaempffer had gleaned from his own translating dictionary. He had been studying Romania and its languages since the first

day he had got wind of the Ploiesti project. By now he
knew a little of the Daco-Romanian dialect and expected soon to be passably fluent in it. He did not want
any of the Romanians he would be working with to
think they could slip anything by him by speaking in
their own language.

But there were three other major dialects which varied
significantly from one another. And the words on the
wall, while similar to Romanian, did not appear to
belong to any of them.

Iuliu, the innkeeper—probably the only man in the
village who could read—did not recognize them. Still,
he had to suffer.

Kaempffer turned away from Iuliu and from the four
einsatzkommandos around him. He spoke to no one in
particular, but his meaning was understood.

"Teach him the art of translation."

There was a heartbeat's pause, then a dull thud
followed by a choking groan of agony. He did not have
to watch. He could picture what was happening: One of
the guards had driven the end of his rifle barrel into the
small of Iuliu's back, a sharp, savage blow, sending
Iuliu to his knees. They would now be clustered around
him, preparing to drive the toes and heels of their
polished jackboots into every sensitive area of his body.
And they knew them all.

"That will be enough!" said a voice he instantly
recognized as Woermann's.

Enraged at the intrusion, Kaempffer wheeled to con-
front him. This was insubordination! A direct challenge
to his authority! But as he opened his mouth to repri-
mand Woermann, he noticed that the captain's hand
rested on the butt of his pistol. Surely he wouldn't use
it. And yet . . .

The einsatzkommandos were looking to their major
expectantly, not quite sure of what to do. Kaempffer
longed to tell them to proceed as ordered but found he
could not. Woermann's baleful stare and defiant stance
made him hesitate.

"This local has refused to cooperate," he said lamely.

"And so you think beating him unconscious—or to death, perhaps—will get you what you want? How intelligent!" Woermann moved forward to Iuliu's side, blandly pushing the einsatzkommandos aside as if they were inanimate objects. He glanced down at the groaning innkeeper, then fixed each of the guards with his stare. "Is this how German troops act for the greater glory of the Fatherland? I'll bet your mothers and fathers would love to come and watch you kick an unarmed aging fat man to death. How brave! Why don't you invite them someday? Or did you kick *them* to death the last time you were home on leave?"

"I must warn you, Captain—" Kaempffer began, but Woermann had turned his attention to the innkeeper.

"What can you tell us about the keep that we don't already know?"

"Nothing," Iuliu said from the floor.

"Any wives' tales or scare stories or legends?"

"I've lived here all my life and never heard any."

"No deaths in the keep? Ever?"

"Never."

As Kaempffer watched, he saw the innkeeper's face light with a kind of hope, as if he had thought of a way to survive the night intact.

"But perhaps there is someone who could help you. If I may just get my registration book . . . ?" He indicated the jumbled ledgers on the floor.

When Woermann nodded to him, he crawled across the floor and picked out a worn, stained, cloth-covered volume from the rest. He fumbled through the pages feverishly until he came to the entry he wanted.

"Here it is! He has been here three times in the past ten years, each time sicker than the last, each time with his daughter. He is a great teacher at the University of Bucharest. An expert in the history of this region."

Kaempffer was interested now. "When was the last time?"

"Five years ago." He shrank away from Kaempffer as he replied.

"What do you mean by sick?" Woermann asked.

"He could not walk without two canes last time."

Woermann took the ledger from the innkeeper. "Who is he?"

"Professor Theodor Cuza."

"Let's just hope he's still alive," Woermann said, tossing the ledger to Kaempffer. "I'm sure the SS has contacts in Bucharest who can find him if he is. I suggest you waste no time."

"I never waste time, Captain," Kaempffer said, trying to regain some of the face he knew he had lost with his men. He would never forgive Woermann for that. "As you enter the courtyard you will notice my men already busy prying at the walls, loosening the stones. I expect to see your men helping them as soon as possible. While the Mediterranean Bank in Zurich is being investigated, and while this professor is being sought out, we shall all be busy dismantling this structure stone by stone. For if we should obtain no useful information from the bank or from the professor, we shall already be started toward destroying every possible hiding place within the keep."

Woermann shrugged. "Better than sitting around and waiting to be killed, I suppose. I'll have Sergeant Oster report to you and he can coordinate work details." He turned, pulled Iuliu to his feet, and pushed him down the corridor, saying, "I'll be right behind you to see that the sentry lets you out."

But the innkeeper held back an instant and said something to the captain in a low tone. Woermann began to laugh.

Kaempffer felt his face grow hot as rage welled up within him. They were talking about him, belittling him. He could always tell.

"What is the joke, Captain?"

"This Professor Cuza," Woermann said, his laughter fading but the mocking smile remaining on his lips, "the man who might possibly know something that could keep a few of us alive . . . he's a Jew!"

Renewed laughter echoed from the captain as he walked away.

ELEVEN

The harsh, insistent pounding from without rattled their apartment door on its hinges.

"Open up!"

Magda's voice failed her for an instant, then she quavered out the question to which she already knew the answer. "Who is it?"

"Open immediately!"

Magda, dressed in a bulky sweater and a long skirt, her glossy brown hair undone, was standing by the door. She looked over at her father seated in his wheelchair at the desk.

"Better let them in," he said with a calm she knew was forced. The tight skin of his face allowed little expression, but his eyes were afraid.

Magda turned to the door. With a single motion she undid the latch and jerked back as if fearing it would

bite her. It was fortunate that she did, for the door flew
open and two members of the Iron Guard, the Romanian equivalent of German stormtroopers, lurched in,
helmeted, armed with rifles held at high port.

"This is the Cuza residence," the one toward the rear
said. It was a question but had been uttered as a state-
ment, as if daring anyone listening to disagree.

"Yes," Magda replied, backing away toward her
father. "What do you want?"

"We are looking for Theodor Cuza. Where is he?"
His eyes lingered on Magda's face.

"I am he," Papa said.

Magda was at his side, her hand resting protec-
tively atop the high wooden back of his wheelchair.
She was trembling. She had dreaded this day, had
hoped it would never come. But now it looked as if
they were to be dragged off to some resettlement camp
where her father would not survive the night. They
had long feared that the anti-Semitism of this regime
would become an institutionalized horror similar to
Germany's.

The two guardsmen looked at Papa. The one to the
rear, who seemed to be in charge, stepped forward and
withdrew a piece of paper from his belt. He glanced
down at it, then up again.

"You cannot be Cuza. He's fifty-six. You're too
old!"

"Nevertheless, I am he."

The intruders looked at Magda. "Is this true? This is
Professor Theodor Cuza, formerly of the University of
Bucharest?"

Magda found herself mortally afraid, breathless,
unable to speak, so she nodded.

The two Iron Guards hesitated, obviously at a loss as
to what to do.

"What do you want of me?" Papa asked.

"We are to bring you to the rail station and accompany you to the junction at Campina where you will
be met by representatives of the Third Reich. From
there—"

"Germans? But why?"

"It is not for you to ask! From there—"

"Which means they don't know either," Magda heard her father mutter.

"—you will be escorted to the Dinu Pass."

Papa's face mirrored Magda's surprise at their destination, but he recovered quickly.

"I would love to oblige you, gentlemen," Papa said, spreading his twisted fingers, encased as always in cotton gloves, "for there are few places in the world more fascinating than the Dinu Pass. But as you can plainly see, I'm a bit infirm at the moment."

The two Iron Guards stood silent, indecisive, eyeing the old man in the chair. Magda could sense their reactions. Papa looked like an animated skeleton with his thin, glossy, dead-looking skin, his balding head fringed with wisps of white hair, his stiff fingers looking thick and crooked and gnarled even through the gloves, and his arms and neck so thin there seemed to be no flesh over the bones. He looked frail, fragile, brittle. He looked eighty. Yet their papers said to find a man of fifty-six.

"Still you must come," the leader said.

"He can't!" Magda cried. "He'll die on a trip like that!"

The two intruders glanced at each other. Their thoughts were easy to read: They had been told to find Professor Cuza and see that he got to the Dinu Pass as quickly as possible. And alive, obviously. Yet the man before them did not look as if he would make it to the station.

"If I have the expert services of my daughter along," she heard her father say, "I shall perhaps be all right."

"No, Papa! You can't!" What was he *saying*?

"Magda . . . these men mean to take me. If I am to survive, you must come along with me." He looked up at her, his eyes commanding. "You must."

"Yes, Papa." She could not imagine what he had in mind, but she had to obey. He was her father.

He studied her face. "Do you realize the direction in

which we will be traveling, my dear?''

He was trying to tell her something, trying to key something in her mind. Then she remembered her dream of a week ago, and the half-packed suitcase still sitting under her bed.

"North!"

✝

Their two Iron Guard escorts were seated across the aisle of the passenger car from them, engaged in low conversation when they were not trying to visually pierce Magda's heavy clothing. Papa had the window seat, his hands double gloved, leather over cotton and folded in his lap. Bucharest was sliding away behind them. A fifty-three-mile trip by rail lay ahead—thirty-five miles to Ploiesti and eighteen miles north of there to Campina. After that the going would be rough. She prayed it would not be too much for him.

"Do you know why I had them bring you along?" he said in his dry voice.

"No, Papa. I see no purpose in either of us going. You could have got out of it. All they need do is have their superiors look at you and they'd know you're not fit to travel."

"They wouldn't care. And I'm fitter than I look—not well, by any standard, but certainly not the walking cadaver I appear to be."

"Don't talk like that!"

"I stopped lying to myself long ago, Magda. When they told me I had rheumatoid arthritis, I said they were wrong. And they were: I had something worse. But I've accepted what's happening to me. There's no hope, and there's not that much more time. So I think I should make the best of it."

"You don't have to rush it by allowing them to drag you up to the Dinu Pass!"

"Why not? I've always loved the Dinu Pass. It's as

good a place to die as any. And they were going to take
me no matter what. I'm wanted up there for some
reason and they are intent on getting me there, even in a
hearse." He looked at her closely. "But do you know
why I told them I had to have you along?"

Magda considered the question. Her father was ever
the teacher, ever playing Socrates, asking question after
question, leading his listener to a conclusion. Magda often found it tedious and tried to reach the conclusion as
swiftly as possible. But she was too tense at the moment
for even a halfhearted attempt at playing along.

"To be your nurse, as usual," she snapped. "What
else?" She regretted the words as soon as she uttered
them, but her father seemed not to notice. He was too
intent on what he wanted to say to take offense.

"Yes!" he said, lowering his voice. "That's what I
want them to think. But it's really your chance to get
out of the country! I want you to come to the Dinu Pass
with me, but when you get the chance—at the first opportunity—I want you to run off and hide in the hills!"

"Papa, no!"

"Listen to me!" he said, leaning his face toward her
ear. "This chance will never come again. We've been in
the Alps many times. You know the Dinu Pass well.
Summer's coming. You can hide for a while and then
make your way south."

"To where?"

"I don't know—anywhere! Just get yourself out of
the country. Out of Europe! Go to America! To
Turkey! To Asia! Anywhere, but go!"

"A woman traveling alone in wartime," Magda said,
staring at her father and trying to keep her voice from
sounding scornful. He wasn't thinking clearly. "How
far do you think I'd get?"

"You must try!" His lips trembled.

"Papa, what's wrong?"

He looked out the window for a long time, and when
he finally spoke his voice was barely audible.

"It's all over for us. They're going to wipe us off the
face of the Continent."

"Who?"

"Us! Jews! There's no hope left for us in Europe. Perhaps somewhere else."

"Don't be so—"

"It's true! Greece has just surrendered! Do you realize that since they attacked Poland a year and a half ago they haven't lost a battle? No one has been able to stand up to them for more than six weeks! Nothing can stop them! And that madman who leads them intends to eradicate our kind from the face of the earth! You've heard the tales from Poland—it's soon going to be happening here! The end of Romanian Jewry has been delayed only because that traitor Antonescu and the Iron Guard have been at each other's throats. But it seems they've settled their differences during the past few months, so it won't be long now."

"You're wrong, Papa," Magda said quickly. This kind of talk terrified her. "The Romanian people won't allow it."

He turned on her, his eyes blazing. " 'Won't allow it?' Look at us! Look at what has happened so far! Did anyone protest when the government began the 'Romanianization' of all property and industry in the hands of Jews? Did a single one of my colleagues at the university—trusted friends for decades!—so much as question my dismissal? Not one! *Not one!* And has one of them even stopped by to see how I am?" His voice was beginning to crack. "Not one!"

He turned his face back toward the window and was silent.

Magda wished for something to say to make it easier for him, but no words came. She knew there would have been tears on his cheeks now if his disease had not rendered his eyes incapable of forming them. When he spoke again, he had himself once more under control, but he kept his gaze directed at the flat green farmland rolling by.

"And now we are on this train, under guard of Romanian fascists, on our way to be delivered into the hands of German fascists. We are finished!"

She watched the back of her father's head. How bitter and cynical he had become. But then, why not? He had a disease that was slowly tying his body into knots, distorting his fingers, turning his skin to wax paper, drying his eyes and mouth, making it increasingly hard for him to swallow. As for his career—despite years at the university as an unchallenged authority on Romanian folklore, despite the fact that he was next in line as head of the Department of History, he had been unceremoniously fired. Oh, they said it was because his advancing debility made it necessary, but Papa knew it was because he was a Jew. He had been discarded like so much trash.

And so: His health was failing, he had been removed from the pursuit of Romanian history—the thing he loved most—and now he had been dragged from his home. And above and beyond all that was the knowledge that engines designed for the destruction of his race had been constructed and were already operating with grim efficiency in other countries. Soon it would be Romania's turn.

Of course he's bitter! she thought. *He has every right to be!*

And so do I. It's my race, my heritage, too, they wish to destroy. And soon, no doubt, my life.

No, not her life. That couldn't happen. She could not accept that. But they had certainly destroyed any hope she had held of being something more than secretary and nursemaid to her father. Her music publisher's sudden about-face was proof enough of that.

Magda felt a heaviness in her chest. She had learned the hard way since her mother's death eleven years ago that it was not easy being a woman in this world. It was hard if you were married, and harder still if you were not, for there was no one to cling to, no one to take your side. It was almost impossible for any woman with an ambition outside the home to be taken seriously. If you were married, you should go back home; if you were not, then there was something doubly wrong with you. And if you were Jewish . . .

She glanced quickly to the area where the two Iron Guards sat. *Why am I not permitted the desire to leave my mark on this world? Not a big mark . . . a scratch would do. My book of songs . . . it would never be famous or popular, but perhaps someday a hundred years from now someone would come across a copy and play one of the songs. And when the song is over, the player will close the cover and see my name . . . and I'll still be alive in a way. The player will know that Magda Cuza passed this way.*

She sighed. She wouldn't give up. Not yet. Things were bad and would probably get worse. But it wasn't over. It was never over as long as one could hope.

Hope, she knew, was not enough. There had to be something more; just what that might be she didn't know. But hope was the start.

The train passed an encampment of brightly colored wagons circled around a smoldering central fire. Papa's pursuit of Romanian folklore had led him to befriend the Gypsies, allowing him to tap their mother lode of oral tradition.

"Look!" she said, hoping the sight would lift his spirits. He loved those people so. "Gypsies."

"I see," he said without enthusiasm. "Bid them farewell, for they are as doomed as we are."

"Stop it, Papa!"

"It's true. The Rom are an authoritarian's nightmare, and because of that, they, too, will be eliminated. They are free spirits, drawn to crowds and laughter and idleness. The fascist mentality cannot tolerate their sort; their place of birth was the square of dirt that happened to lie under their parents' wagon on the day of their birth; they have no permanent address, no permanent place of employment. And they don't even use one name with any reliable frequency, for they have three: a public name for the *gadjé*, another for use among their tribe members, and a secret one whispered in their ear at birth by their mother to confuse the Devil, should he come for them. To the fascist mind they are an abomination."

"Perhaps," Magda said. "But what of us? Why are *we* an abomination?"

He turned away from the window at last. "I don't know. I don't think anyone really knows. We are good citizens wherever we go. We are industrious, we promote trade, we pay our taxes. Perhaps it is our lot. I just don't know." He shook his head. "I've tried to make sense out of it, but I cannot. Just as I cannot make sense out of this forced trip to the Dinu Pass. The only thing of interest there is the keep, but that is of interest only to the likes of you and me. Not to Germans." -

He leaned back and closed his eyes. Before long, he was dozing, snoring gently. He slept all the way past the smoking towers and tanks of Ploiesti, awakened briefly as they passed to the east of Floresti, then dozed again. Magda spent the time worrying about what lay ahead for them, and what the Germans could possibly want with her father in the Dinu Pass.

As the plains drifted by outside the window, Magda drifted into a familiar reverie, one in which she was married to a handsome man, loving and intelligent. They would have great wealth, but it would not go for things like jewelry and fine clothes—they were toys to Magda and she could see no use or meaning in owning them—but for books and curios. They would dwell in a house that would resemble a museum, stuffed with artifacts of value only to them. And that house would lie in a far-off land where no one would know or care that they were Jewish. Her husband would be a brilliant scholar and she would be widely known and respected for her musical arrangements. There would be a place for Papa, too, and money enough to get him the best doctors and nurses, giving her time to herself to work on her music.

A small, bitter smile curved Magda's lips. An elaborate fantasy—and that was all it ever would be. It was too late for her. She was thirty-one, well past the age when any eligible man would consider her suitable for a wife and prospective mother of his children. All she was good for now was somebody's mistress. And that, of course, she could never accept.

Once, a dozen years ago, there had been someone . . . Mihail . . . a student of Papa's. They had both been attracted to each other. Something might have come of that. But then Mother had died and Magda had stayed close to Papa—so close that Mihail had been left out. She had had no choice; Papa had been utterly shattered by Mother's death and it was Magda who had held him together.

Magda fingered the slim gold band on her right ring finger. It had been her mother's. How different things would have been if she hadn't died.

Once in a while Magda thought of Mihail. He had married someone else . . . they had three children now. Magda had only Papa.

Everything changed with Mother's death. Magda couldn't explain how it happened, but Papa grew to be the center of her life. Although she had been surrounded by men in those days, she took no notice of them. Their attentions and advances had lain like beads of water on a glass figurine, unappreciated, unabsorbed, leaving not so much as a hazy ring when they evaporated.

She spent the intervening years suspended between a desire to be somehow extraordinary, and a longing for all the very ordinary things that most other women took for granted. And now it was too late. There was really nothing ahead for her—she saw that more clearly every day.

And yet it could have been so different! So much better! If only Mother hadn't died. If only Papa hadn't fallen sick. If only she hadn't been born a Jew. She could never admit the last to Papa. He'd be furious—and crushed—to know she felt that way. But it was true. If they were not Jews, they would not be on this train; Papa would still be at the university and the future would not be a yawning chasm full of darkness and dread with no exit.

The plains gradually turned hilly and the tracks began to slope upward. The sun was sitting atop the Alps as the train climbed the final slope to Campina. As they passed the towers of the smaller Steaua refinery, Magda began to help her father into his sweater. When that was on, she tightened the kerchief over her hair and went to get his wheelchair from an alcove at the rear of the car. The younger of the two Iron Guards followed her back. She had felt his eyes on her all during the trip, probing the folds of her clothes, trying to find the true outline of her body. And the farther the train had moved from Bucharest, the bolder his stares had become.

As Magda bent over the chair to straighten the cushion on the seat, she felt his hands grip her buttocks through the heavy fabric of her skirt. The fingers of his right hand began to try to worm their way between her legs. Her stomach turning with nausea, she straightened up and wheeled toward him, restraining her own hands from clawing at his face.

"I thought you'd like that," he said, and moved closer, sliding his arms around her. "You're not bad-looking for a Jew, and I could tell you were looking for a real man."

Magda looked at him. He was anything but "a real man." He was at most twenty, probably eighteen, his upper lip covered with a fuzzy attempt at a mustache that looked more like dirt than hair. He pressed himself against her, pushing her back toward the door.

"The next car is baggage. Let's go."

Magda kept her face utterly impassive. "No."

He gave her a shove. "Move!"

As she tried to decide what to do, her mind worked furiously against the fear and revulsion that filled her at his touch. She had to say something, but she didn't want to challenge him or make him feel he had to prove himself.

"Can't you find a girl that wants you?" she said, keeping her eyes directly on his.

He blinked. "Of course I can."

"Then why do you feel you must steal from one who doesn't?"

"You'll thank me when it's over," he said, leering.

"Must you?"

He withstood her gaze for a moment, then dropped his eyes. Magda did not know what would come next. She readied herself to put on an unforgettable exhibition of screaming and kicking if he continued to try to force her into the next car.

The train lurched and screeched as the engineer applied the brakes. They were coming into Campina junction.

"There's no time now," he said, stooping to peer out the window as the station ramp slid by. "Too bad."

Saved. Magda said nothing. She wanted to slump with relief but did not.

The young Iron Guardsman straightened and pointed out the window. "I think you would have found me a gentle lover compared to them."

Magda bent and looked through the glass. She saw four men in black military uniforms standing on the station platform and felt weak. She had heard enough about the German SS to recognize its members when she saw them.

TWELVE

The red-haired man stood on the seawall feeling the dying light of the sun warm against his side as it stretched the shadow of the piling beside him far out over the water. The Black Sea. A silly name. It was blue, and it looked like an ocean. All around him, two-story brick-and-stucco houses crowded up to the water's edge, their red tile roofs almost matching the deepening color of the sun.

It had been easy to find a boat. The fishing around here was good more often than not, but the fishermen remained poor no matter how good the catch. They spent their lives struggling to break even.

No sleek, swift, smuggler's launch this time, but a lumbering, salt-encrusted sardine fisher. Not at all what he needed, but the best he could get.

The smuggler's boat had taken him in near Silivri,

west of Constantinople—no, they were calling it Istanbul now, weren't they? He remembered the current regime changing it nearly a decade ago. He'd have to get used to the new name, but old habits were hard to break. He had beached the boat, jumped ashore with his long, flat case under his arm, then pushed the launch back into the Sea of Marmara where it would drift with the corpse of its owner until found by a fisherman or by some ship of whatever government was claiming that particular body of water at that particular time.

From there it had been a twenty-mile trip over the gently undulating moorland of European Turkey. A horse had proved as easy to buy on the south coast as a boat had been to rent here on the north. With governments falling left and right and no one sure whether today's money would be tomorrow's wastepaper, the sight and feel of gold could be counted on to open many doors.

And so now he stood on the rim of the Black Sea, tapping his feet, drumming his fingers on the flat case, waiting for his battered vessel to finish fueling. He resisted the urge to rush over and give the owner a few swift kicks to hurry him up. That would be fruitless. He knew he couldn't rush these people; they lived at their own speed, one much slower than his.

It would be 250 miles due north of here to the Danube Delta, and almost 200 more west from there overland to the Dinu Pass. If not for this idiot war, he could have hired an airplane and been there long before now.

What had happened? Had there been a battle in the pass? The short-wave had said nothing of fighting in Romania. No matter. Something had gone wrong. And he had thought everything permanently settled.

His lips twisted. Permanently? He of all people should have known how rare indeed it was for anything to be permanent.

Still, there remained a chance that events had not progressed beyond the point of no return.

THIRTEEN

THE KEEP
Tuesday, 29 April
1752 hours

"Can't you see he's exhausted?" Magda shouted, her fear gone now, replaced by her anger and her fierce protective instinct.

"I don't care if he's about to breathe his last gasp," the SS officer said, the one called Major Kaempffer. "I want him to tell me everything he knows about the keep."

The ride from Campina to the keep had been a nightmare. They had been unceremoniously trundled into the back of a lorry and watched over by a surly pair of enlisted men while another pair drove. Papa had recognized them as einsatzkommandos and had quickly explained to Magda what their areas of expertise were. Even without the explanation she would have found them repulsive; they treated her and Papa like so much baggage. They spoke no Romanian, using instead a lan-

guage of shoves and prods with rifle barrels. But Magda
soon sensed something else below their casual brutality
—a preoccupation. They seemed to be glad to be out of
the Dinu Pass for a while, and reluctant to return.

The trip was especially hard on her father, who found
it nearly impossible to sit on the bench that ran along
each side of the lorry's payload area. The vehicle tipped
and lurched and bounced violently as it raced along a
road never intended for its passage. Every jolt was
agony for Papa, with Magda watching helplessly as he
winced and gritted his teeth as pain shot through him.
Finally, when the lorry had to stop at a bridge to wait
for a goat cart to move aside, Magda helped him off the
bench and back into his wheelchair. She moved quickly,
unable to see what was going on outside the vehicle, but
knowing that as long as the driver kept banging impatiently on the horn, she could risk moving Papa. After that, it was a matter of holding on to the wheelchair
to keep it from rolling out the back while struggling to
keep herself from sliding off the bench once the lorry
started moving again. Their escort sneered at her plight
and made not the slightest effort to help. She was as
exhausted as her father by the time they reached the
keep.

The keep . . . it had changed. It looked as well kept as
ever in the dusk when they rolled across the causeway,
but as soon as they passed through the gate, she felt
it—an aura of menace, a change in the very air that
weighed on the spirit and touched off chills along the
neck and shoulders.

Papa noticed it, too, for she saw him lift his head and
look around, as if trying to classify the sensation.

The Germans seemed to be in a hurry, and there
seemed to be two kinds of soldiers, some in gray, some
in SS black. Two of the ones in gray opened up the rear
of the lorry as soon as it stopped and began motioning
them out, saying, *"Schnell! Schnell!"*

Magda addressed them in German, which she understood and could speak reasonably well. "He cannot

walk!'' This was true at the moment—Papa was on the verge of physical collapse.

The two in gray did not hesitate to leap into the back of the truck and lift her father down, wheelchair and all, but it was left to her to push him across the courtyard. She felt the shadows crowding against her as she followed the soldiers.

"Something's gone wrong here, Papa!" she whispered in his ear. "Can't you *feel* it?"

A slow nod was his only reply.

She rolled him into the first level of the watchtower. Two German officers awaited them there, one in gray, one in black, standing by a rickety table under a single shaded light bulb hanging from the ceiling.

The evening had only begun.

"Firstly," Papa said, speaking flawless German in reply to Major Kaempffer's demand for information, "this structure isn't a keep. A keep, or donjon as it was called in these parts, was the final inner fortification of a castle, the ultimate stronghold where the lord of the castle stayed with his family and staff. This building"—he made a small gesture with his hands—"is unique. I don't know what you should call it. It's too elaborate and well built for a simple watchpost, and yet it's too small to have been built by any self-respecting feudal lord. It's always been called 'the keep,' probably for lack of a better name. It will do, I suppose."

"I don't care what you *suppose*!" the major snapped. "I want what you *know*! The history of the keep, the legends connected with it—everything!"

"Can't it wait until morning?" Magda said. "My father can't even think straight now. Maybe by then—"

"No! We must know *tonight*!"

Magda looked from the blond-haired major to the other officer, the darker, heavier captain named Woermann who had yet to speak. She looked into their eyes and saw the same thing she had seen in all the German soldiers they had encountered since leaving the train; the common denominator that had eluded her was now clear. These men were afraid. Officers and enlisted men alike, they were all terrified.

"Specifically in reference to what?" Papa said.

Captain Woermann finally spoke. "Professor Cuza, during the week we have been here, eight men have been murdered." The major was glaring at the captain, but the captain kept on speaking, either oblivious to the other officer's displeasure, or ignoring it. "One death a night, except for last night when two throats were slashed."

A reply seemed to form on Papa's lips. Magda prayed he would not say anything that would set the Germans off. He appeared to think better of it. "I have no political connections, and know of no group active in this area. I cannot help you."

"We no longer think there's a political motive here," the captain said.

"Then what? Who?"

The reply seemed almost physically painful for Captain Woermann. "We're not even sure it's a who."

The words hung in the air for an endless moment, then Magda saw her father's mouth form the tiny, toothy oval that had come to pass for a grin lately. It made his face look like death.

"You believe the supernatural to be at work here, gentlemen? A few of your men are killed, and because you can't find the killer, and because you don't want to think that a Romanian partisan might be getting the better of you, you look to the supernatural. If you really want my—"

"*Silence, Jew!*" the SS major said, naked rage on his face as he stepped forward. "The only reason you are here and the only reason I do not have you and your daughter shot at once is the fact that you have traveled this region extensively and are an expert on its folklore. How long you remain alive will depend on how useful you prove to be. So far you have said nothing to convince me that I have not wasted my time bringing you here!"

Magda saw Papa's smile evaporate as he glanced at

her, then back to the major. The threat to her had struck home.

"I will do what I can," he said gravely, "but first you must tell me everything that has happened here. Perhaps I can come up with a more realistic explanation."

"For your sake, I hope so."

Captain Woermann told the story of the two privates who had penetrated the cellar wall where they had found a cross of gold and silver rather than brass and nickel, of the narrow shaft leading down to what appeared to be a blind cell, of the rupture of the wall into the corridor, of the collapse of part of the floor into the subcellar, of the fate of Private Lutz and of those who followed him. The captain also told of the engulfing darkness he had seen on the rampart two nights ago, and of the two SS men who somehow had walked up to Major Kaempffer's room after their throats had been torn out.

The story chilled Magda. Under different circumstances she might have laughed at it. But the atmosphere in the keep tonight, and the grim faces of these two German officers gave it credence. And as the captain spoke, she realized with a start that her dream of traveling north might have occurred at just about the time the first man had died.

But she couldn't dwell on that now. There was Papa to look after. She had watched his face as he had listened; she had seen his mortal fatigue slip away as each new death and each bizarre event was related. By the time Captain Woermann had finished, Papa had metamorphosed from a sick old man slumped in his wheelchair to Professor Theodor Cuza, an expert being challenged in his chosen field. He paused at length before replying.

Finally: "The obvious assumption here is that something was released from that little room in the wall when the first soldier broke into it. To my knowledge, there has never been a single death in the keep before this. But then, there has never before been a foreign army living in the keep. I would have thought the deaths the work of

patriotic"—he emphasized the word—"Romanians but
for the events of the last two nights. There is no natural
explanation I know for the way the light died on the
wall, nor for the animation of ex-sanguinated corpses.
So perhaps we must look outside nature for our explanation."

"That's why you're here, Jew," the major said.

"The simplest solution is to leave."

"Out of the question!"

Papa mulled this. "I do not believe in vampires, gentlemen." Magda caught a quick warning glance from
him—she knew that was not entirely true. "At least not
anymore. Nor werewolves, nor ghosts. But I've always
believed there was something special about the keep. It
has long been an enigma. It is of unique design, yet
there is no record of who built it. It is maintained in perfect condition, yet no one claims ownership. There is no
record of ownership anywhere—I know, for I spent
years trying to learn who built it and who maintains it."

"We are working on that now," Major Kaempffer
said.

"You mean you're contacting the Mediterranean
Bank in Zurich? Don't waste your time, I've already
been there. The money comes from a trust account set
up in the last century when the bank was founded; expenses for maintenance of the keep are paid from interest on the money in the account. And before that, I
believe, it was paid through a similar account in a different bank, possibly in a different country . . . the inn-
keepers' records over the generations leave much to be
desired. But the fact is there is no link anywhere to the
person or persons who opened the account; the money is
to be held and the interest is to be paid *in perpetuum*."

Major Kaempffer slammed his fist down on the table.
"Damn! What good are you, old man!"

"I'm all you have, *Herr* Major. But let me go further
with this: Three years ago I went so far as to petition the
Romanian government—then under King Carol—to
declare the keep a national treasure and take over
ownership. It was my hope that such *de facto*

nationalization would bring out the owners, if any still live. But the petition was refused. The Dinu Pass was considered too remote and inaccessible. Also, since there is no Romanian history specifically connected with the keep, it could not be officially considered a national treasure. And finally, and most importantly, nationalization would require use of government funds for maintenance of the keep. Why should that be wasted when private money is doing such an excellent job?

"I had no defense against those arguments. And so, gentlemen, I gave up. My failing health confined me to Bucharest. I had to be satisfied with having exhausted all research resources, with being the greatest living authority on the keep, knowing more about it than anyone else. Which amounts to absolutely nothing."

Magda bristled at her father's constant use of "I." She had done most of the work for him. She knew as much about the keep as he. But she said nothing. It was not her place to contradict her father, not in the presence of others.

"What about these?" Captain Woermann said, pointing to a motley collection of scrolls and leather-bound books in the corner of the room.

"Books?" Papa's eyebrows lifted.

"We've started dismantling the keep," Major Kaempffer said. "This thing we're after will soon have no place left to hide. We'll eventually have every stone in the place exposed to the light of day. *Then* where will it go?"

Papa shrugged. "A good plan . . . as long as you don't release something worse." Magda watched him casually turn his head toward the pile of books, but not before taking note of Kaempffer's startled expression—that possibility had never occurred to the major. "But where did you find the books? There was never a library in the keep, and the villagers can barely read their names."

"In a hollow spot in one of the walls being dismantled," the captain said.

Papa turned to her. "Go see what they are."

Magda stepped over to the corner and knelt beside the books, grateful for an opportunity to be off her feet even for a few minutes. Papa's wheelchair was the only seat in the room, and no one had offered to get a chair for her. She looked at the pile, smelled the familiar musty odor of old paper; she loved books and loved that smell. There were perhaps a dozen or so there, some partially rotten, one in scroll form. Magda pushed her way through them slowly, allowing the muscles of her back as much time as possible to stretch before she had to rise again. She picked up a random volume. Its title was in English: *The Book of Eibon*. It startled her. It couldn't be . . . it was a joke! She looked at the others, translating their titles from the various languages in which they were written, the awe and disquiet mounting within her. These were genuine! She rose and backed away, nearly tripping over her own feet in her haste.

"What's wrong?" Papa asked when he saw her face.

"Those books!" she said, unable to hide her shock and revulsion. "They're not even supposed to exist!"

Papa wheeled his chair closer to the table. "Bring them over here!"

Magda stooped and gingerly lifted two of them. One was *De Vermis Mysteriis* by Ludwig Prinn; the other, *Cultes des Goules* by Comte d'Erlette. Both were extremely heavy and her skin crawled just to touch them. The curiosity of the two officers had been aroused to such an extent that they, too, bent to the pile and brought the remaining texts to the table.

Trembling with excitement that increased with each article placed on the table, Papa muttered under his breath between calling out the titles as he saw them.

"*The Pnakotic Manuscripts*, in scroll form! The duNord translation of *The Book of Eibon*! *The Seven Cryptical Books of Hsan*! And here—*Unaussprechlichen Kulten* by von Juntz! These books are priceless! They've been universally suppressed and forbidden through the ages, so many copies burned that only whispers of their titles have remained. In some cases, it has been questioned whether they ever existed at all! But here they are, perhaps the last surviving copies!''

"Perhaps they were forbidden for a good reason, Papa,'' Magda said, not liking the light that had begun to shine in his eyes. Finding those books had shaken her. They were purported to describe foul rites and contacts with forces beyond reason and sanity. To learn that they were real, that they and their authors were more than sinister rumors, was profoundly unsettling. It warped the texture of everything.

"Perhaps they were,'' Papa said without looking up. He had pulled off his outer leather gloves with his teeth and was slipping a rubber cap onto his right index fingertip, still gloved in cotton. Adjusting his bifocals, he began leafing through the pages. "But that was in another time. This is the twentieth century. I can't imagine there being anything in these books we couldn't deal with now.''

"What could possibly be so awful?'' Woermann said, pulling the leatherbound, iron-hasped copy of *Unaussprechlichen Kulten* toward him. "Look. This one's in German.'' He opened the cover and flipped through the pages, finally stopping near the middle and reading.

Magda was tempted to warn him but decided against it. She owed these Germans nothing. She saw the captain's face blanch, saw his throat working in spasms as he slammed the book shut.

"What kind of sick, demented mind is responsible for this sort of thing? It's—it's—'' He could not seem to find the words to express what he felt.

"What have you got there?'' Papa said, looking up from a book whose title he had not yet announced. "Oh, the von Juntz book. That was first published privately in Düsseldorf in 1839. An extremely small edition, perhaps only a dozen copies . . .'' His voice trailed off.

"Something wrong?'' Kaempffer said. He had stood apart from the others, showing little curiosity.

"Yes. The keep was built in the fifteenth century . . . that much I know for sure. These books were all written before then, all except that von Juntz book. Which means that as late as the middle of the last century, possibly later, someone visited the keep and deposited this book with the others.''

"I don't see how that helps us now," Kaempffer said.

"It does nothing to prevent another of our men"—he smiled as an idea struck him—"or perhaps even you or your daughter, from being murdered tonight."

"It does cast a new light on the problem, though," Papa said. "These books you see before you have been condemned through the ages as evil. I deny that. I say they are not evil, but are *about* evil. The one in my hands right now is especially feared—the *Al Azif* in the original Arabic."

Magda heard herself gasp. "Oh, no!" That one was the worst of all!

"Yes! I don't know much Arabic, but I know enough to translate the title and the name of the poet responsible for it." He looked from Magda back to Kaempffer. "The answer to your problem may well reside within the pages of these books. I'll start on them tonight. But first I wish to see the corpses."

"Why?" It was Captain Woermann speaking. He had composed himself again after his glance into the von Juntz book.

"I wish to see their wounds. To see if there were any ritual aspects about their deaths."

"We'll take you there immediately." The major called in two of his einsatzkommandos as escort.

Magda didn't want to go—she didn't want to have to look at dead soldiers—but she feared waiting alone for everyone's return, so she took the handles of her father's chair and wheeled him toward the cellar stairs. At the top, she was elbowed aside as the two SS soldiers followed the major's orders and carried her father, chair and all, down the steps. It was cold down there. She wished she hadn't come.

"What about these crosses, Professor?" Captain Woermann asked as they walked along the corridor, Magda again pushing the chair. "What's their significance?"

"I don't know. There's not even a folk tale about them in the region, except in connection with speculation that the keep was built by one of the Popes. But the fifteenth century was a time of crisis for the Holy Roman Empire, and the keep is situated in an area that was under constant threat from the Ottoman Turks. So the papal theory is ridiculous."

"Could the Turks have built it?"

Papa shook his head. "Impossible. It's not their style of architecture, and crosses are certainly not a Turkish motif."

"But what about the *type* of cross?"

The captain seemed to be profoundly interested in the keep, and so Magda answered him before Papa could; the mystery of the crosses had been a personal quest of hers for years.

"No one knows. My father and I searched through countless volumes of Christian history, Roman history, Slavic history, and nowhere have we found a cross resembling these. If we had found a historical precedent to this type of cross, we could have possibly linked its designer with the keep. But we found nothing. They are as unique as the structure which houses them."

She would have continued—it kept her from thinking about what she might have to see in the subcellar—but the captain did not appear to be paying much attention to her. It could have been because they had reached the breach in the wall, but Magda sensed it was because of the source of the information—she was, after all, only a woman. Magda sighed to herself and remained silent. She had encountered the attitude before and knew the signs well. German men apparently had many things in common with Romanian men. She wondered if all men were the same.

"One more question," the captain said to Papa. "Why, do you think, are there never any birds here at the keep?"

"I never noticed their absence, to tell the truth."

Magda realized she had never seen a bird here in all her trips, and it had never occurred to her that their absence was wrong . . . until now.

The rubble outside the broken wall had been neatly stacked. As Magda guided Papa's wheelchair between the orderly piles, she felt a cold draft from the opening in the floor beyond the wall. She reached into the pocket behind the high back of the wheelchair and pulled out Papa's leather gloves.

"Better put these back on," she said, stopping and holding the left one open so he could slip his hand in.

"But he already *has* gloves on!" Kaempffer said, impatient at the delay.

"His hands are very sensitive to cold," Magda said, now holding the right glove open. "It's part of his condition."

"And just what *is* the condition?" Woermann asked.

"It's called scleroderma." Magda saw the expected blank look on their faces.

Papa spoke as he adjusted the gloves on his hands. "I'd never heard of it either until I was diagnosed as having it. As a matter of fact, the first two physicians who examined me missed the diagnosis. I won't go into details beyond saying that it affects more than the hands."

"But *how* does it affect your hands?" Woermann asked.

"Any sudden drop in temperature drastically alters the circulation in my fingers; for all intents and purposes, they temporarily lose their blood supply. I've been told that if I don't take good care of them I could develop gangrene and lose them. So I wear gloves day and night all year round except in the warmest summer months. I even wear a pair to bed." He looked around. "I'm ready when you are."

Magda shivered in the draft from below. "I think it's too cold for you down there, Papa."

"We're certainly not going to bring the bodies up here for his inspection," Kaempffer said. He gestured to the two enlisted SS men who again lifted the chair and carried it and its frail occupant through the hole in the wall. Captain Woermann had picked up a kerosene lamp from the floor and lit it. He led the way. Major Kaempffer brought up the rear with another. Reluctantly, Magda fell in line, staying close behind her father, terrified that one of the soldiers carrying him might slip on the slimy steps and let him fall. Only when the wheels of his chair were safely on the dirt floor of the subcellar did she relax.

One of the enlisted men began pushing Papa's chair behind the two officers as they walked toward eight sheet-covered objects stretched out on the floor thirty feet away. Magda held back, waiting in the pool of the light by the steps. She had no stomach for this.

She noted that Captain Woermann seemed perturbed as he walked around the bodies. He bent and straightened the sheets, adjusting them more evenly around the still forms. A subcellar . . . she and Papa had been to the keep again and again over the years and had never even guessed the existence of a subcellar. She rubbed her hands up and down over her sweatered arms, trying to generate some warmth. Cold.

She glanced around apprehensively, looking for signs of rats in the dark. The new neighborhood they had been forced to move into back in Bucharest had rats in all the cellars; so different from the cozy home they'd had near the university. Magda knew her reaction to rats was exaggerated, but she could not help it. They filled her with loathing . . . the way they moved, their naked tails dragging after them . . . they made her sick.

But she saw no scuttling forms. She turned back and watched the captain begin to lift the sheets one by one, exposing the head and shoulders of each dead man. She was missing what was being said over there, but that was all right. She was glad she could not see what Papa was seeing.

Finally, the men turned back toward Magda and the stairs. Her father's voice became intelligible as he neared.

". . . and I really can't say that there's anything ritualistic about the wounds. Except for the decapitated man, all the deaths seem to have been caused by simple

severing of the major vessels in the neck. There's no sign
of teeth marks, animal or human, yet those wounds are
certainly not the work of any sharp instrument. Those
throats were torn open, *savaged* in some way that I cannot possibly define."

How could Papa sound so clinical about such things?

Major Kaempffer's voice was surly and menacing.
"Once again you've managed to say much yet tell us
nothing!"

"You've given me little to work with. Haven't you
anything else?"

The major stalked ahead without bothering to reply.
Captain Woermann, however, snapped his fingers.

"The words on the wall! Written in blood in a
language nobody knows."

Papa's eyes lit up. "I must see them!"

Again the chair was lifted, and again Magda traveled
behind to the courtyard. Once there she took over the
task of propelling him after the Germans as they headed
for the rear of the keep. Soon they were all at the end of
a blind corridor looking at the ruddy brown letters
scrawled on the wall.

The strokes, Magda noticed, varied in thickness, but
all were of a width consistent with a human finger. She
shuddered at the thought and studied the words. She
recognized the language and knew she could make the
translation if only her mind would concentrate on the
words and not on what their author had used for ink.

ТЪЖИН ОСТАВИТЕ НАЩЬ АДМЪ

"Do you have any idea what it means?" Woermann
asked.

Papa nodded. "Yes," he said, and paused,
mesmerized by the display before him.

"Well?" Kaempffer said.

Magda could tell that he hated to depend on a Jew for
anything, and worse to be kept waiting by one. She

wished her father would be more careful about provoking him.

"It says, *'Strangers, leave my home!'* It's in the imperative form." His voice had an almost mechanical quality as he spoke. He was disturbed by something about the words.

Kaempffer slapped his hand against his holster. "Ah! So the killings *are* politically motivated!"

"Perhaps. But this warning, or demand, or whatever you might wish to call it, is perfectly couched in Old Slavonic, a dead language. As dead as Latin. And those letters are formed just the way they were written back then. I should know. I've seen enough of the old manuscripts."

Now that Papa had identified the language, Magda's mind could focus on the words. She thought she knew what was so disturbing.

"Your killer, gentlemen," he went on, "is either a most erudite scholar, or else he has been frozen for half a millennium."

FOURTEEN

"It appears we have wasted our time," Major Kaempffer said, puffing on a cigarette as he strutted about. The four were again in the lowest level of the watchtower.

In the center of the room, Magda leaned exhaustedly against the back of the wheelchair. She sensed there was some sort of tug-of-war going on between Woermann and Kaempffer, but couldn't understand the rules or the motivations of the players. Of one thing she was certain, however: Papa's life and her own hung on the outcome.

"I disagree," Captain Woermann said. He leaned against the wall by the door, his arms folded across his chest. "As I see it, we know more than we did this morning. Not much, but at least it's progress . . . we haven't been making any on our own."

"It's not enough!" Kaempffer snapped. "Nowhere near enough!"

"Very well, then. Since we have no other sources of information open to us, I think we should abandon the keep immediately."

Kaempffer made no reply; he merely continued puffing and strutting back and forth across the far end of the room.

Papa cleared his throat for attention.

"Stay out of this, Jew!"

"Let's hear what he has to say. That's why we dragged him here, isn't it?"

It was gradually becoming clear to Magda that there was a deep hostility between the two officers. She knew Papa had recognized it, too, and was surely trying to turn it to their advantage.

"I may be able to help." Papa gestured to the pile of books on the table. "As I mentioned before, the answer to your problem may lie in those books. If they do hold the answer, I am the only person who—with the aid of my daughter—can ferret it out. If you wish, I shall try."

Kaempffer stopped pacing and looked at Woermann.

"It's worth a try," Woermann said. "I for one don't have any better ideas. Do you?"

Kaempffer dropped his cigarette butt to the floor and slowly ground it out with his toe. "Three days, Jew. You have three days to come up with something useful." He strode past them and out the door, leaving it open behind him.

Captain Woermann heaved himself away from the wall and turned toward the door, his hands clasped at his back. "I'll have my sergeant arrange for a pair of bedrolls for you two." He glanced at Papa's frail body. "We have no other bedding."

"I will manage, Captain. Thank you."

"Wood," Magda said. "We'll need some wood for a fire."

"It doesn't get that cold at night," he said, shaking his head.

"My father's hands—if they act up on him, he won't even be able to turn the pages."

Woermann sighed. "I'll ask the sergeant to see what he can do—perhaps some scrap lumber." He turned to go, then turned back to them. "Let me tell you two something. The major will snuff you both out with no more thought than he gave to that cigarette he just finished. He has his own reasons for wanting a quick solution to this problem and I have mine: I don't want any more of my men to die. Find a way to get us through a single night without a death and you will have proven your worth. Find a way to defeat this thing and I may be able to get you back to Bucharest and keep you safe there."

"And then again," Magda said, "you may not." She watched his face carefully. Was he really offering them hope?

Captain Woermann's expression was grim as he echoed her words. "And then again, I may not."

After ordering wood brought to the first-level rooms, Woermann stood and thought for a moment. At first he had considered the pair from Bucharest a pitiful couple—the girl bound to her father, the father bound to his wheelchair. But as he had watched them and heard them speak, he had sensed subtle strengths within the two of them. That was good. For they both would need cores of steel to survive this place. If armed men could not defend themselves here, what hope was there for a defenseless female and a cripple?

He suddenly realized he was being watched. He could not say how he knew, but the feeling was definitely there. It was a sensation he would find unsettling in the most pleasant surroundings; but here, with the knowledge of what had been happening during the past week, it was unnerving.

Woermann peered up the steps curving away to his right. No one there. He went to the arch that opened onto the courtyard. All the lights were on out there, the pairs of sentries intent on their patrols.

Still the feeling of being watched.

He turned toward the steps, trying to shrug it off, hoping that if he moved from this spot the feeling would pass. And it did. As he climbed toward his quarters, the sensation evaporated.

But the underlying fear remained with him, the fear he lived with every night in the keep—the certainty that before morning someone was going to die horribly.

T

Major Kaempffer stood within the dark doorway to the rear section of the keep. He watched Woermann pause at the tower entry arch, then turn and start up the steps. Kaempffer felt an impulsive urge to follow him—to hurry back across the courtyard, run up to the third level of the tower, rap on Woermann's door.

He did not want to be alone tonight. Behind him was the stairway up to his own quarters, the place where just last night two dead men had walked in and fallen on him. He dreaded the very thought of going back there.

Woermann was the only one who could possibly be of any use to him tonight. As an officer, Kaempffer could not seek out the company of the enlisted men, and he certainly could not go sit with the Jews.

Woermann was the answer. He was a fellow officer and it was only right that they keep each other company. Kaempffer stepped out of the doorway and started briskly for the tower. But after a few paces he came to a faltering halt. Woermann would never let him through the door, let alone sit and share a glass of schnapps with him. Woermann despised the SS, the Party, and everyone associated with either. Why? Kaempffer found the attitude baffling. Woermann was pure Aryan. He had nothing to fear from the SS. Why, then, did he hate it so?

Kaempffer turned and re-entered the rear structure of the keep. There could be no rapprochement with Woermann. The man was simply too pig-headed and narrow-minded to accept the realities of the New Order. He was doomed. And the farther Kaempffer stayed away, the better.

Still . . . Kaempffer needed a friend tonight. And there was no one.

Hesitantly, fearfully, he began a slow climb to his quarters, wondering if a new horror awaited him.

The fire added more than heat to the room. It added light, a warm glow that the single light bulb under its conical shade could not hope to match. Magda had spread out one of the bedrolls next to the fireplace for her father, but he was not interested. Never in the past few years had she seen him so fired, so animated. Month after month the disease had sapped his strength, burdening him with heavier and heavier fatigue until his waking hours had grown few and his sleeping hours many.

But now he seemed a new man, feverishly poring over the texts before him. Magda knew it couldn't last. His diseased flesh would soon demand rest. He was running on stolen energy. He had no reserves.

Yet Magda hesitated to insist that he rest. Lately, he had lost interest in everything, spending his days seated by the front window, staring out at the streets and seeing nothing. Doctors, when she could get one in to see him, had told her it was melancholia, common in his condition. Nothing to be done for it. Just give him aspirin for the constant ache, and codeine—when available—for the awful pains in every joint.

He had been a living dead man. Now he was showing signs of life. Magda couldn't bring herself to damp them. As she watched, he paused over *De Vermis Mysteriis*, removed his glasses, and rubbed a cotton-gloved hand over his eyes. Now perhaps was the time to pry him away from those awful books and persuade him to rest.

"Why didn't you tell them about your theory?" she asked.

"Eh?" He looked up. "Which one?"

"You told them you don't really believe in vampires, but that's not quite true, is it? Unless you finally gave up on that pet theory of yours."

"No, I still believe there might have been one true vampire—just one—from whom all the Romanian lore has originated. There are solid historical clues, but no proof. And without hard proof I could never publish a paper. For the same reason, I chose not to say anything about it to the Germans."

"Why? They're not scholars."

"True. But right now they think of me as a learned old man who might be of use to them. If I told them my theory they might think I was just a crazy old Jew and useless. And I can think of no one with a shorter life expectancy than a useless Jew in the company of Nazis. Can you?"

Magda shook her head quickly. This was not how she wanted the conversation to go. "But what of the theory? Do you think the keep might have housed . . ."

"A vampire?" Papa made a tiny gesture with his immobile shoulders. "Who can even say what a vampire might really be? There's been so much folklore about them, who can tell where reality leaves off—assuming there was *some* reality involved—and myth begins? But there's so much vampire lore in Transylvania and Moldavia that something around here must have engendered it. At its core, every tall tale has a kernel of truth."

His eyes were alight in the expressionless mask of his face as he paused thoughtfully. "I'm sure I don't have to tell you that there is something uncanny going on here. These books are proof enough that this structure has been connected with deviltry. And that writing on the wall . . . whether the work of a human madman or a sign that we are dealing with one of the *moroi*, the undead, is yet to be seen."

"What do *you* think?" she asked, pressing for some

sort of reassurance. Her flesh crawled at the thought of the undead actually existing. She had never given such tales the slightest bit of credence, and had often wondered if her father had been playing some sort of intellectual game in his talk of them. But now . . .

"I don't think anything right now. But I *feel* we may be on the verge of an answer. It's not rational yet . . . not something I can explain. But the feeling is there. You feel it, too. I can tell."

Magda nodded silently. She felt it. Oh, yes, she felt it.

Papa was rubbing his eyes again. "I can't read anymore, Magda."

"Come, then," she said, shaking off her disquiet and moving toward him. "I'll help you to bed."

"Not yet. I'm too wound up to sleep. Play something for me."

"Papa—"

"You brought your mandolin. I know you did."

"Papa, you know what it does to you."

"Please?"

She smiled. She could never refuse him anything for long. "All right."

She had catty-cornered the mandolin into the larger suitcase before leaving. It had been reflex, really. The mandolin went wherever Magda went. Music had always been central to her life—and since Papa had lost his position at the university, a major part of their livelihood. She had become a music teacher after moving into their tiny apartment, bringing her young students in for mandolin lessons or going to their homes to teach them piano. She and Papa had been forced to sell their own piano before moving.

She seated herself in the chair that had been brought in with the firewood and the bedrolls and made a quick check of the tuning, adjusting the first set of paired strings, which had gone flat during the trip. When she was satisfied, she began a complicated mixture of strumming and bare-fingered picking she had learned from the Gypsies, providing both rhythm and melody. The tune was also from the Gypsies, a typically tragic melody of unrequited love followed by death of a broken heart. As she finished the second verse and moved into the first bridge, she glanced up at her father.

He was leaning back in his chair, eyes closed, the gnarled fingers of his left hand pressing the strings of an imaginary violin through the fabric of his gloves, the right hand and forearm dragging an imaginary bow across those same strings but in only the minute movements his joints would allow. He had been a good violinist in his day, and the two of them had often done duets together on this song, she picking counterpoint to the soaring, tearful, *molto rubato* figures he would coax from his violin.

And although his cheeks were dry, he was crying.

"Oh, Papa, I should have known . . . that was the wrong song." She was furious with herself for not thinking. She knew so many songs, and yet she had picked one that would most remind him that he could no longer play.

She started to rise to go to him and stopped. The room did not seem as well lit as it had a moment ago.

"It's all right, Magda. At least I can remember all the times I played along with you . . . better than never having played at all. I can still hear in my head how my violin used to sound." His eyes were still closed behind his glasses. "Please. Play on."

But Magda did not move. She felt a chill descend upon the room and looked about for a draft. Was it her imagination, or was the light fading?

Papa opened his eyes and saw her expression. "Magda?"

"The fire's going out!"

The flames weren't dying amid smoke and sputter; they were merely wasting away, retreating into the charred wood. And as they waned, so did the bulb strung from the ceiling. The room grew steadily darker, but with a darkness that was more than a mere absence of light. It was almost a physical thing. With the darkness came a penetrating cold, and an odor, a sour acrid aroma of evil that conjured images of corruption and open graves.

"What's happening?"

"He's coming, Magda! Stand over by me!"

Instinctively, she was already moving toward Papa, seeking to shelter him even as she herself sought shelter at his side. Trembling, she wound up in a crouch beside his chair, clutching his gnarled hands in hers.

"What are we going to do?" she said, not knowing why she was whispering.

"I don't know." Papa, too, was trembling.

The shadows grew deeper as the light bulb faded and the fire died to wan glowing embers. The walls were gone, misted in impenetrable darkness. Only the glow from the coals, a dying beacon of warmth and sanity, allowed them to keep their bearings.

They were not alone. Something was moving about in that darkness. Stalking. Something unclean and hungry.

A wind began to blow, rising from a breeze to full gale force in a matter of seconds, howling through the room although the door and the shutters had all been pulled closed.

Magda fought to free herself from the terror that gripped her. She released her father's hands. She could not see the door, but remembered it having been directly opposite the fireplace. With the icy gale whipping at her, she moved around to the front of Papa's wheelchair and began to push it backward to where the door should be. If only she could reach the courtyard, maybe they would be safe. Why, she could not say, but staying in this room seemed like standing in a queue and waiting for death to call their names.

The wheelchair began to roll. Magda pushed it about five feet toward the place where she had last seen the door and then she could push it no farther. Panic rushed over her. Something would not let them pass! Not an invisible wall, hard and unyielding, but almost as if someone or something in the darkness was holding the back of the chair and making a mockery of her best efforts.

And for an instant, in the blackness above and behind the back of the chair, the impression of a pale face looking down at her. Then it was gone.

Magda's heart was thumping and her palms were so wet they were slipping on the chair's oaken armrests. This wasn't really happening! It was all a hallucination! None of it was real . . . that was what her mind told her. But her body *believed*! She looked into her father's face so close to hers and knew his terror reflected her own.

"Don't stop here!" he cried.

"I can't get it to move any farther!"

He tried to crane his neck around to see what blocked them but his joints forbade it. He turned back to her.

"Quick! Over by the fire!"

Magda changed the direction of her efforts, leaning backwards and pulling. As the chair began to roll toward her, she felt something clutch her upper arm in a grip of ice.

A scream clogged in her throat. Only a high-pitched, keening wail escaped. The cold in her arm was a pain, shooting up to her shoulder, lancing toward her heart. She looked down and saw a hand gripping her arm just above the elbow. The fingers were long and thick; short, curly hairs ran along the back of the hand and up the length of the fingers to the dark, overlong nails. The wrist seemed to melt into the darkness.

The sensations spreading over her from that touch, even through the fabric of her sweater and the blouse beneath it, were unspeakably vile, filling her with loathing and revulsion. She searched the air over her shoulder for a face. Finding none, she let go of Papa's chair and struggled to free herself, whimpering in naked fear. Her shoes scraped and slid along the floor as she twisted and pulled away, but she could not break free. And she could not bring herself to touch that hand with her own.

Then the darkness began to change, lighten. A pale, oval shape moved toward her, stopping only inches away. It was a face. One from a nightmare.

He had a broad forehead. Long, lank black hair hung in thick strands on either side of his face, strands like dead snakes attached by their teeth to his scalp. Pale skin, sunken cheeks, and a hooked nose. Thin lips were

drawn back to reveal yellowed teeth, long and almost
canine in quality. But it was the eyes, gripping Magda
more fiercely than the icy hand on her arm, killing off
her wailing cry and stilling her frantic struggles.

The eyes. Large and round, cold and crystalline, the
pupils dark holes into a chaos beyond reason, beyond
reality itself, black as a night sky that had never been
blued by the sun or marred by the light of moon and
stars. The surrounding irises were almost as dark,
dilating as she watched, widening the twin doorways,
drawing her into the madness beyond . . .

. . . madness. The madness was so attractive. It was
safe, it was serene, it was isolated. It would be so good
to pass through and submerge herself in those dark
pools . . . so good . . .

No!

Magda fought the feeling, fought to push herself
away. But . . . why fight? life was nothing but disease
and misery, a struggle that everyone eventually lost.
What was the use? Nothing you did really mattered in
the long run. Why bother?

She felt a swift undertow, almost irresistible, drawing
her toward those eyes. There was lust there, for her, but
a lust that went beyond the mere sexual, a lust for all
that she was. She felt herself turn and lean toward those
twin doorways of black. It would be so easy to let go . . .

. . . she held on, something within her refusing to
surrender, urging her to fight the current. But it was so
strong, and she felt so tired, and what did it all matter,
anyway?

A sound . . . music . . . and yet not music at all. A
sound in her mind, all that music was not . . . non-
melodic, disharmonic, a delirious cacophony of discord
that rattled and shook and sent tiny cracks through the
feeble remainder of her will. The world around her—
everything—began to fade, leaving only the eyes . . .
only the eyes . . .

. . . she wavered, teetering on the edge of forever . . .

. . . then she heard Papa's voice.

Magda clutched at the sound, clung to it like a rope,

pulled herself hand over hand along its length. Papa was not calling to her, was not even speaking in Romanian, but it was his voice, the only familiar thing in the chaos about her.

The eyes turned away. Magda was free. The hand released her.

She stood gasping, perspiring, weak, confused, the gale in the room pulling at her clothes, at the kerchief that bound her hair, stealing her breath. And her terror grew, for the eyes were now turning on her father. He was too weak!

But Papa did not flinch under the gaze. He spoke again as he had before, the words garbled, incomprehensible to her. She saw the awful smile on the white face fade as the lips drew into a thin line. The eyes narrowed to mere slits, as if the mind behind them were considering Papa's words, weighing them.

Magda watched the face, unable to do anything more. She saw the line of the lips curl up infinitesimally at the corners. Then a nod, no more than a jot of movement. A decision.

The wind died as if it had never been. The face receded into the darkness.

All was still.

Motionless, Magda and her father faced each other in the center of the room as the cold and the dark slowly dissipated. A log in the fireplace split lengthwise with a crack like a rifle shot and Magda felt her knees liquefy with the sound. She fell forward and only by luck and desperation was she able to grasp the arm of the wheelchair for support.

"Are you all right?" Papa said, but he wasn't looking at her. He was feeling his fingers through the gloves.

"I will be in a minute." Her mind recoiled at what she had just experienced. "What was it? My God, *what was it*?"

Papa was not listening. "They're gone. I can't feel anything in them." He began to pull the gloves from his fingers.

His plight galvanized Magda. She straightened and

began to push the chair over to the fire, which was springing to life again. She was weak with reaction and fatigue and shock, but that seemed to be of secondary importance. *What about me? Why am I always second? Why do I always have to be strong?* Once . . . just once . . . she would like to be able to collapse and have someone tend to her. She forcibly submerged the thoughts. That was no way for a daughter to think when her father needed her.

"Hold them out, Papa! There's no hot water so we'll have to depend on the fire to warm them up!"

In the flickering light of the flames she saw that his hands had gone dead white, as white as those of that . . . *thing*. Papa's fingers were stubby with coarse, thick skin and curved, ridged nails. There were small punctate depressions in each fingertip, scars left by tiny areas of healed gangrene. They were the hands of a stranger— Magda could remember when his hands had been graceful, animated, with long, mobile, tapering fingers. A scholar's hands. A musician's. They had been living things. Now they were mummified caricatures of life.

She had to get them warmed up, but not too quickly. At home in Bucharest she had always kept a pot of warm water on the stove during the winter months for these episodes. The doctors called it Raynaud's phenomenon; any sudden drop in temperature caused constrictive spasms in the blood vessels of his hands. Nicotine had a similar effect, and so he had been cut off from his beloved cigars. If his tissues were deprived of oxygen too long or too often, gangrene would take root. So far he had been lucky. When gangrene had set in, the areas had been small and he had been able to overcome it. But that would not always be the case.

She watched as he held his hands out to the fire, rotating them back and forth against the warmth as best as his stiff joints would allow. She knew he could feel nothing in them now—too cold and numb. But once circulation returned he would be in agony as his fingers throbbed and tingled and burned as if on fire.

"Look what they've done to you!" she said angrily as the fingers changed from white to blue.

Papa looked up questioningly. "I've had worse."

"I know. But it shouldn't have happened at all! What are they trying to do to us?"

"They?"

"The Nazis! They're toying with us! Experimenting on us! I don't know what just happened here . . . it was very realistic, but it wasn't real! Couldn't have been! They hypnotized us, used drugs, dimmed the lights—"

"It was real, Magda," Papa said, his voice soft with wonder, confirming what she knew in her soul, what she had so wanted him to deny. "Just as those forbidden books are real. I know—"

Breath suddenly hissed through his teeth as blood began to flow into his fingers again, turning them dark red. The starved tissues punished him as they gave up their accumulated toxins. Magda had been through this with him so many times she could almost feel the pain herself.

When the throbbing subsided to an endurable level, he continued, his words coming in gasps.

"I spoke to him in Old Slavonic . . . told him we were not his enemies . . . told him to leave us alone . . . and he left."

He grimaced in pain a moment, then looked at Magda with bright, glittering eyes. His voice was low and hoarse.

"It's him, Magda. I know it! It's *him*!"

Magda said nothing. But she knew it, too.

FIFTEEN

Captain Woermann had tried to stay awake through the night but had failed. He had seated himself at the window overlooking the courtyard with his Luger unholstered in his lap, though he doubted a 9mm parabellum would help against whatever haunted the keep. Too many sleepless nights and too little fitful napping during the days had caught up with him again.

He awoke with a start, disoriented. For a moment he thought he was back in Rathenow, with Helga down in the kitchen cooking eggs and sausage, and the boys already up and out and milking the cows. But he had been dreaming.

When he saw the sky was light, he leaped from the chair. Night was gone and he was still alive. He had survived another night. His elation was short-lived, for he knew that someone else had not survived. Somewhere in the keep he knew a corpse lay still and bloody, awaiting discovery.

He holstered the Luger as he crossed the room and stepped out on the landing. All was quiet. He trotted down the stairs, rubbing his eyes and massaging his stubbled cheeks to full wakefulness. As he reached the lowest level, the doors to the Jews' quarters opened and the daughter came out.

She didn't see him. She carried a metal pot in her hand and wore a vexed look on her face. Deep in thought, she passed through the open door into the courtyard and turned right toward the cellar stairs, completely oblivious to him. She seemed to know exactly where she was going, and that troubled him until he remembered that she had been in the keep a number of times before. She knew of the cellar cisterns, knew there was fresh water there.

Woermann stepped out into the courtyard and watched her move. There was an ethereal quality about the scene: a woman walking across the cobblestones in the dawn light, surrounded by gray stone walls studded with metallic crosses, streamers of fog on the courtyard floor eddying in her wake. Like a dream. She looked to be a fine woman under all those layers of clothing. There was a natural sway to her hips when she walked, an unpracticed grace that was innately appealing to the male in him. Pretty face, too, especially with those wide brown eyes. If she'd only let her hair out from under that kerchief, she could be a beauty.

At another time, in another place, she would have been in grave danger in similar company—five squads of women-starved soldiers. But these soldiers had other things on their minds; these soldiers feared the dark, and the death that unfailingly accompanied it.

He was about to follow her into the cellar to assure himself that she sought no more than fresh water for the pot in her hand, when he spied Sergeant Oster pounding toward him.

"Captain! Captain!!"

Woermann sighed and braced himself for the news. "Whom did we lose?"

"No one!" He held up a clipboard. "I checked on everyone and they're all alive and well!"

Woermann did not allow himself to rejoice—he had been fooled on this score last week—but he did allow himself to hope.

"You're sure? Absolutely sure?"

"Yes, sir. All except for the Major, that is. And the two Jews."

Woermann glanced toward the rear of the keep, to Kaempffer's window. Could it be . . . ?

"I was saving the officers for last," Oster was saying, almost apologetically.

Woermann nodded, only half-listening. Could it be? Could Erich Kaempffer have been last night's victim? It was too much to hope for. Woermann had never imagined he could hate another human being as much as he had come to hate Kaempffer in the last day and a half.

It was with eager anticipation that he began walking toward the rear of the keep. If Kaempffer were dead, not only would the world be a brighter place, but he would again be senior officer and would have his men out of the keep by noon. The einsatzkommandos could come along or stay behind to die until a new SS officer arrived. He had no doubt they would fall in right behind him as he left.

If, however, Kaempffer still lived, it would be a disappointment, but one with a bright side: For the first time since they had arrived, a night would have passed without the death of a German soldier. And that was good. It would boost morale immeasurably. It would mean there was perhaps a slim hope of overcoming the death curse that blanketed them here like a shroud.

As Woermann crossed the courtyard with the sergeant hurrying behind him, Oster said, "Do you think the Jews are responsible?"

"For what?"

"For nobody dying last night."

Woermann paused and glanced between Oster and
Kaempffer's window almost directly overhead. Oster
apparently had no doubt that Kaempffer was still alive.

"Why do you say that, Sergeant? What could they
have done?"

Oster's brow wrinkled. "I don't know. The men
believe it . . . at least my men—I mean *our* men—believe
it. After all, we lost someone every night except last
night. And the Jews arrived last night. Maybe they
found something in those books we dug up."

"Perhaps." He led the way into the rear section of
the keep and ran up the steps to the second level.

Intriguing, but improbable. The old Jew and his
daughter could not have come up with anything so
soon. Old Jew . . . he was beginning to sound like
Kaempffer! Awful.

Woermann was puffing by the time they reached
Kaempffer's room. Too much sausage, he told himself
again. Too many hours sitting and brooding instead of
moving about and burning up that paunch. He was
reaching for the latch on Kaempffer's door when it
swung open and the major himself appeared.

"Ah! Klaus!" he said bluffly. "I thought I heard
someone out here." Kaempffer adjusted the black
leather strap of his officer's belt and holster across his
chest. Satisfied that it was secure, he stepped out into
the hall.

"How nice to see you looking so well," Woermann
said.

Kaempffer, struck by the obvious insincerity, glanced
at him sharply, then at Oster.

"Well, Sergeant, who was it this time?"

"Sir?"

"Dead! Who died last night? One of mine or one of
yours? I want the Jew and his daughter brought over to
the corpse, and I want them to—"

"Pardon, sir," Oster said, "but no one died last
night."

Kaempffer's eyebrows shot up and he turned to
Woermann. "No one? Is this true?"

"If the sergeant says so, that's good enough for me."

"Then we've done it!" he smacked fist into his palm and puffed himself up, gaining an inch of height in the process. "We've *done* it!"

" 'We?' And pray tell, dear Major—just what did 'we' do?"

"Why, we got through a night without a death! I told you if we held on we could beat this thing!"

"That you did," Woermann said, choosing his words carefully. He was enjoying this. "But just tell me: What had the desired effect? Exactly what was it that protected us last night? I want to make sure I have this straight so I can see to it that we repeat the process tonight."

Kaempffer's self-congratulatory elation faded as quickly as it had bloomed. "Let's go see that Jew." He pushed past Oster and Woermann and started for the steps.

"I thought that would occur to you before too long," Woermann said, following at a slower pace.

As they reached the courtyard, Woermann thought he heard the faint sound of a woman's voice coming from the cellar. He could not understand the words, but her distress was evident. The sounds became louder, shriller. The woman was shouting in anger and fear.

He ran over to the cellar entry. The professor's daughter was there—he remembered now that her name was Magda—and she was wedged into the angle formed by the steps and the wall. Her sweater had been torn open, so had the blouse and other garments beneath it, all pulled down over one shoulder, exposing the white globe of a breast. An einsatzkommando had his face buried against that breast while she kicked and raged and beat her fists ineffectively against him.

Woermann recoiled for an instant at the sight, then he was racing down the steps. So intent was the soldier on Magda's breast that he did not seem to hear Woermann's approach. Clenching his teeth, Woermann kicked the soldier in the right flank with all the force he could muster. It felt good—good to hurt one of these bastards. With difficulty he resisted the urge to go on kicking him.

The SS trooper grunted with pain and reared up, ready to charge at whoever had struck the blow. When he saw that he faced an officer, it was still apparent in his eyes that he was debating whether or not to lash out anyway.

For a few heartbeats, Woermann almost wished the private would do just that. He waited for the slightest sign of a forward rush, his hand ready to draw his Luger. He would never have imagined himself capable of shooting another German soldier, but something inside him hungered to kill this man, to strike out through him at everything that was wrong with the Fatherland, the army, his career.

The soldier backed off. Woermann felt himself relax.

What was happening to him? He had never hated before. He had killed in battle, at long range and face to face, but never with hatred. It was an uncomfortable, disorienting sensation, as if a stranger had taken up residence unbidden in his home and he could not find a way to make him leave.

As the soldier stood and straightened his black uniform, Woermann glanced at Magda. She had her clothes closed and rearranged, and was rising from a crouch on the steps. Without a hint of warning, she spun and slapped the palm of her hand across her tormentor's face with stinging force, rocking his head back and sending him reeling off the bottom step in surprise. Only an outflung hand against the stone wall prevented him from going over onto his back.

She spat something in Romanian, her tone and facial expression conveying whatever meaning her words did not, and walked past Woermann, retrieving her half-spilled waterpot as she moved.

It required all of Woermann's Prussian reserve to keep from applauding her. Instead, he turned back to the soldier who was plainly torn between standing at attention in the presence of an officer, and taking reprisal on the girl.

Girl . . . why did he think of her as a girl? She was perhaps a dozen years younger than he, but easily a decade older than his son, Kurt, and he considered Kurt a man. Perhaps it was because of a certain unsullied freshness about her, a certain innocence. Something there that was precious, to be preserved, protected.

"What's your name, soldier?"

"Private Leeb, sir. Einsatzkommandos."

"Is it customary for you to attempt rape while on duty?"

No reply.

"Was what I just saw part of your assigned duties here in the cellar?"

"She's only a Jew, sir."

The man's tone implied that this particular fact was sufficient explanation for anything he might have done to her.

"You did not answer my question, soldier!" His temper was nearing the breaking point. "Was attempted rape part of your duty here?"

"No, sir." The reply was as reluctant as it was defiant.

Woermann stepped down and snatched Private Leeb's Schmeisser from his shoulder. "You are confined to quarters, Private—"

"But sir!"

Woermann noted that the plea was not directed to him but to someone above and behind him. He did not have to turn and look to know who it was, so he continued speaking without missing a beat.

"—for deserting your post. Sergeant Oster will decide on a suitable disciplinary action for you"—he paused and looked up to the head of the stairs, directly into Kaempffer's eyes—"unless, of course, the major has a particular punishment in mind."

It was technically within Kaempffer's rights to interfere at this point, since their commands were separate and they answered to different authority; and

Kaempffer was here at the behest of the High Command
to which all the uniformed forces must ultimately
answer. He was also the senior officer. But Kaempffer
could do nothing here. To let Private Leeb off would be
to condone desertion of an assigned post. No officer
could allow that. Kaempffer was trapped. Woermann
knew it and intended to take full advantage.

The major spoke stiffly. "Take him away, Sergeant. I
will deal with him later."

Woermann tossed the Schmeisser to Oster, who
marched the crestfallen einsatzkommando up the
stairs.

"In the future," Kaempffer said acidly when the
sergeant and the private were out of earshot, "you will
not discipline or give orders to my men. They are not
under your command, they are under *mine*!"

Woermann started up the stairs. When he came
abreast of Kaempffer, he wheeled on him. *"Then keep
them on their leashes!"*

The major paled, startled by the unexpected outburst.

"Listen, *Herr* SS officer," Woermann continued, letting all his anger and disgust rise to the surface, "and
listen well. I don't know what I can say to get this
through to you. I'd try reason but I think you're immune to it. So I'll try to appeal to your instinct for self-
preservation—we both know how well developed that
is. Think: Nobody died last night. And the only thing
different about last night from all the other nights was
the presence of the two Jews from Bucharest. There *has*
to be a connection. Therefore, if for no other reason
than the chance that they may be able to come up with
an answer to the killings and a way to stop them, you
must keep your animals away from them!"

He did not wait for a reply, fearing he might try to
throttle Kaempffer if he did not move away immediately. He turned and walked toward the watchtower.
After a few steps, he heard Kaempffer begin to follow
him. He went to the door of the first-level suite,
knocked, but did not wait for a reply before entering.
Courtesy was one thing, but he intended to maintain an

indisputable position of authority in the eyes of these two civilians.

The professor merely glared at the two Germans as they entered. He was alone in the front room, sipping at water in a tin cup, still seated in his wheelchair before the book-laden table, just as they had left him the night before. Woermann wondered if he had moved at all during the night. His gaze strayed to the books, then darted away. He remembered the excerpt he had seen in one of them last night . . . about preparing sacrifices for some deity whose name was an unpronounceable string of consonants. He shuddered even now at the memory of what was to be sacrificed, and of how it was prepared. How anyone could sit and read that and not get sick . . .

He scanned the rest of the room. The girl wasn't there—probably in the back. This room seemed smaller than his own, two stories up . . . maybe it was just an impression created by the clutter of the books and the luggage.

"Is this morning an example of what we must face to get drinking water?" the waxy masked old man said through his tiny mouth, his voice dry, scaly. "Is my daughter to be assaulted every time she leaves the room?"

"That has been taken care of," Woermann told him. "The man will be punished." He stared at Kaempffer, who had sauntered to the other side of the room. "I can assure you it will not happen again."

"I hope not," Cuza replied. "It is difficult enough trying to find any useful information in these texts under the best conditions. But to labor under the threat of physical abuse at any moment . . . the mind rebels."

"It had better *not* rebel, Jew!" Kaempffer said. "It had better do as it is told!"

"It's just that it's impossible for me to concentrate on these texts when I'm worried about my daughter's safety. That should not be too hard to grasp."

Woermann sensed that the professor was aiming an

appeal at him but he was not sure what it was.

"It's unavoidable, I'm afraid," he told the old man. "She is the only woman on what is essentially an army base. I don't like it any more than you. A woman doesn't belong here. Unless . . ." A thought struck him. He glanced at Kaempffer. "We'll put her up in the inn. She could take a couple of the books with her and study them on her own, and come back to confer with her father."

"Out of the question!" Kaempffer said. "She stays here where we can keep an eye on her." He approached Cuza at the table. "Right now I'm interested in what you learned last night that kept us all alive!"

"I don't understand . . ."

"No one died last night," Woermann said. He watched for reaction in the old man's face; it was difficult, perhaps impossible, to discern a change of expression in that tight, immobile skin. But he thought he saw the eyes widen almost imperceptibly in surprise.

"Magda!" he called. "Come here!"

The door to the rear room opened and the girl appeared. She looked composed after the incident on the cellar steps, but he saw that her hand trembled as it rested on the doorframe.

"Yes, Papa?"

"There were no deaths last night!" Cuza said. "It must have been one of those incantations I was reading!"

"Last night?" the girl's expression betrayed an instant of confusion, and something else: a fleeting horror at the mention of last night. She locked eyes with her father and a signal seemed to pass between them, perhaps the tiniest nod from the old man, then her face lit up.

"Wonderful! I wonder which incantation?"

Incantation? Woermann thought. He would have laughed at this conversation last Monday.

It smacked of a belief in spells and black magic. But now . . . he would accept anything that got them all through the night alive. Anything.

"Let me see this incantation," Kaempffer said, interest lighting his eyes.

"Certainly." Cuza pulled over a weighty tome. "This is *De Vermis Mysteriis* by Ludwig Prinn. It's in Latin." He glanced up. "Do you read Latin, Major?"

A tightening of the lips was Kaempffer's only reply.

"A shame," the professor said. "Then I shall translate for—"

"You're lying to me, aren't you, Jew?" Kaempffer said softly.

But Cuza was not to be intimidated, and Woermann had to admire him for his courage. "The answer is here!" he cried, pointing to the pile of books before him. "Last night proves it. I still don't know what haunts the keep, but with a little time, a little peace, and fewer interruptions, I'm sure I can find out. Now, good day, gentlemen!"

He adjusted his thick glasses and pulled the book closer. Woermann hid a smile at Kaempffer's impotent rage and spoke before the major could do anything rash.

"I think it would be in our best interests to leave the professor to the task he was brought here for, don't you, Major?"

Kaempffer clasped his hands behind him and strode through the door. Woermann took one last look at the professor and his daughter before following. They were hiding something, those two. Whether about the keep itself or the murderous entity that stalked its corridors at night, he could not say. And right now it really didn't matter. As long as no more of his men died in the night, they were welcome to their secret. He was not sure he ever wanted to know. But should the deaths begin again, he would demand a full accounting.

T

Professor Cuza pushed the book away from him as soon as the door closed behind the captain. He rubbed the fingers of his hands one at a time, each in turn.

Mornings were the worst. That was when everything hurt, especially the hands. Each knuckle was like a rusted hinge on the door to an abandoned woodshed, protesting with pain and noise at the slightest disturbance, fiercely resisting any change in position. But it wasn't just his hands. All his joints hurt. Awakening, rising, and getting into the wheelchair that circumscribed his life was a chorus of agony from the hips, the knees, the wrists, the elbows, and the shoulders. Only by midmorning, after two separate doses of aspirin and perhaps some codeine when he had it, did the pain in his inflamed connective tissues subside to a tolerable level. He no longer thought of his body as flesh and blood; he saw it as a piece of clockwork that had been left out in the rain and was now irreparably damaged.

Then there was the dry mouth which never let up. The doctors had told him it was "not uncommon for scleroderma patients to experience a marked decrease in the volume of salivary secretions." They said it so matter-of-factly, but there was nothing matter-of-fact about living with a tongue that always tasted like plaster of Paris. He tried to keep some water at hand at all times; if he didn't sip occasionally his voice began to sound like old shoes dragging across a sandy floor.

Swallowing, too, was a chore. Even the water had trouble going down. And food—he had to chew everything until his jaw muscles cramped and then hope it wouldn't get stuck halfway to his stomach.

It was no way to live, and he had more than once considered putting an end to the whole charade. But he had never made the attempt. Possibly because he lacked the courage; possibly because he still possessed enough courage to face life on whatever terms he was offered. He wasn't sure which.

"You all right, Papa?"

He looked up at Magda. She stood near the fireplace with her arms crossed tightly over her chest, shivering.

It wasn't from the cold. He knew she had been badly
shaken by their visitor last night and had hardly slept.
Neither had he. But then to be assaulted not thirty feet
from her sleeping quarters . . .

Savages! What he would give to see them all dead—
not just the ones here, but every stinking Nazi who
stepped outside his border! And those still inside the
German border as well. He wished for a way to exterminate them before they could exterminate him. But
what could he do? A crippled scholar who looked half
again his real age, who could not even defend his own
daughter—what could he do?

Nothing. He wanted to scream, to break something,
to bring down the walls as Samson had done. He wanted
to cry. He cried too easily of late, despite his lack of
tears. That wasn't manly. But then, he wasn't much of a
man anymore.

"I'm fine, Magda," he said. "No better, no worse
than usual. It's you that worries me. This is no place
for you—no place for any woman."

She sighed. "I know. But there's no way to leave here
until they let us."

"Always the devoted daughter," he said, feeling a
burst of warmth for her. Magda was loving and loyal,
strong-willed yet dutiful. He wondered what he had ever
done to deserve her. "I wasn't talking about *us*. I was
talking about *you*. I want you to leave the keep as soon
as it's dark."

"I'm not too good at scaling walls, Papa." Her smile
was wan. "And I've no intention of trying to seduce the
guard at the gate. I wouldn't know how."

"The escape route lies right below our feet. Remember?"

Her eyes widened. "Oh, yes. I'd forgotten about
that!"

"How could you forget? You found it."

It had happened on their last trip to the pass. He had
still been able to get about on his own then but had
needed two canes to bolster the failing strength in
his legs. Unable to go himself, he had sent Magda down

into the gorge in search of a cornerstone at the base of the keep, or perhaps a stone with an inscription on it . . . anything to give him a clue as to the builders of the keep. There had been no inscription. But Magda had come across a large, flat stone in the wall at the very base of the watchtower; it had moved when she leaned against it. It was hinged on the left and perfectly balanced. Sunlight pouring through the opening had revealed a set of stairs leading upward.

Over his protests she had insisted on exploring the base of the tower in the hope that some old records might have been left within. All she found was a long, steep, winding set of stairs that ended in a seemingly blind niche in the ceiling of the base. But it was not a blind end—the niche was in the very wall that divided the two rooms they now occupied. Within it, Magda discovered another perfectly balanced stone, scored to look like the smaller rectangular blocks that made up the rest of the wall, which swung open into the larger of the two rooms, permitting secret ingress and egress from the bottom suite of the tower.

Cuza had attached no significance to the stairway then—a castle or keep always had a hidden escape route. Now he saw it as Magda's stairway to freedom.

"I want you to take the stairs down to the bottom as soon as it is dark, let yourself out into the gorge, and start walking east. When you get to the Danube, follow it to the Black Sea, and from there to Turkey or—"

"Without you?"

"Of course without me!"

"Put it out of your mind, Papa! Where *you* stay, *I* stay."

"Magda, I'm commanding you as your father to obey me!"

"Don't! I will not desert you. I couldn't live with myself if I did!"

As much as he appreciated the sentiment, it did nothing to lessen his frustration. It was clear that the commanding approach was not going to work this time. He decided to plead. Over the years he had become adept at getting his way with her. By one method or another, by browbeating or twisting her up with guilt, he could usually make her accede to whatever he desired. Sometimes he did not like himself for the way he dominated her life, but she was his daughter, and he, her father. And he had needed her. Yet now that it was time to cut her free so she could save herself, she would not go.

"Please, Magda. As one last favor to a dying old man who would go smiling to his grave if he knew you were safe from the Nazis."

"And me knowing I left you among them? Never!"

"Please listen to me! You can take the *Al Azif* with you. It's bulky I know, but it's probably the last surviving copy in any language. There isn't a country in the world where you couldn't sell it for enough money to keep you comfortable for life."

"No, Papa," she said with a determination in her voice that he could not recall ever hearing before.

She turned away and walked into the rear room, closing the door behind her.

I've taught her too well, he thought. I've bound her so tightly to me I cannot push her away even for her own good. Is that why she never married? Because of me?

Cuza rubbed his itching eyes with cotton-gloved fingers, thinking back over the years. Ever since puberty Magda had been a constant object of male attention. Something in her appealed to different sorts of men in different ways; she rarely left one untouched. She probably would have been married and a mother a number of times over by now—and he, a grandfather—if her mother had not died so suddenly eleven years ago. Magda, only twenty then, had changed, taking on the roles of his companion, secretary, associate, and now nurse. The men about soon found her remote. Magda gradually built up a shell of self-absorption. Cuza knew every weak spot in that shell—and could pierce it at will. To all others she was immune.

But there were more pressing concerns at the moment. Magda faced a very short future unless she escaped the keep. Beyond that, there was the apparition they had encountered last night. Cuza was sure it would return with the passing of the day, and he did not want Magda here when it did. There had been something in its eyes that had caused fear to grip his heart like an icy fist. Such an unspeakable hunger there . . . he wanted Magda far away tonight.

But more than anything else he wanted to stay here by himself and wait for it to return. This was the moment of a lifetime—a dozen lifetimes! To actually come face to face with a myth, with a creature that had been used for centuries to frighten children. Adults, too. To document its existence! He had to speak to this thing again . . . induce it to answer. He had to learn which of the myths surrounding it were true and which, false.

The mere thought of the meeting made his heart race with excitement and anticipation. Strangely, he did not feel terribly threatened by the creature. He knew its language and had even communicated with it last night. It had understood and had left them unharmed. He sensed the possibility of a common ground between them, a place for a meeting of minds. He certainly did not wish to stop it or harm it—Theodor Cuza was not an enemy of anything that reduced the ranks of the German Army.

He looked down at the littered table before him. He was sure he would find nothing threatening to it in these despicable old books. He now understood why the books had been suppressed—they were abominations. But they were useful as props in the little play he was acting out for those two bickering German officers. He had to remain in the keep until he had learned all he could from the being that dwelt here. Then the Germans could do what they wished with him.

But Magda . . . Magda had to be on her way to safety before he could devote his attention to anything else. She would not leave of her own accord . . . what if she were driven out? Captain Woermann might be the key there. He did not seem too happy about having a woman quartered in the keep. Yes, if Woermann could be provoked . . .

Cuza despised himself for what he was about to do.

"Magda!" he called. "Magda!"

She opened the door and looked out. "I hope this is not about my leaving the keep, because—"

"Not the keep; just the room. I'm hungry and the Germans told us they'd feed us from their kitchen."

"Did they bring us any food?"

"No. And I'm sure they won't. You'll have to go get some."

She stiffened. "Across the courtyard? You want me to go back out there after what happened?"

"I'm sure it won't happen again." He hated lying to her, but it was the only way. "The men have been warned by their officers. And besides, you'll not be on any dark cellar stairway. You'll be out in the open."

"But the way they look at me . . ."

"We have to eat."

There was a long pause as his daughter stared at him. Then she nodded. "I suppose we do."

Magda buttoned her sweater all the way to the neck as she crossed the room, saying nothing as she left.

Cuza felt his throat constrict as the door closed behind her. She had courage, and trust in him . . . a trust he was betraying. And yet keeping. He knew what she faced out there, and yet he had knowingly sent her into it. Supposedly for food.

He wasn't the slightest bit hungry.

SIXTEEN

Land was in sight again.

Sixteen unnervingly frustrating hours, each one like an endless day, were finally at an end. The red-haired man stood on the weathered bow and looked shoreward. The sardiner had chugged across the placid expanse of the Black Sea at a steady pace, a good pace, but one made maddeningly slow by the sole passenger's relentless sense of urgency. At least they had not been stopped by either of the two military patrol boats they had passed, one Russian, one Romanian. That could have proved disastrous.

Directly ahead lay the multichanneled delta where the Danube emptied into the Black Sea. The shore was green and swampy, pocked with countless coves. Getting ashore would be easy, but traveling through the bogs to higher, drier land would be time consuming. And there was no time!

He had to find another way.

The red-haired man glanced over his shoulder at the old Turk at the helm, then forward again to the delta. The sardine boat didn't draw much—it could move comfortably in about four feet of water. It was a possibility—take one of these tiny delta tributaries up to the Danube itself, then chug west along the river to a point, say, just east of Galati. They would be traveling against the current but it had to be faster than scrambling on foot through miles of sucking mire.

He dug into his money belt and brought out two Mexican fifty-peso pieces. Together they gave a weight of about two and a half ounces of gold. Turning again, he held them up to the Turk, addressing him in his native tongue.

"Kiamil! Two more coins if you'll take me upstream!"

The fisherman stared at the coins, saying nothing, chewing his lower lip. There was already enough gold in his pocket to make him the richest man in his village. At least for a while. But nothing lasts forever, and soon he would be out on the water again, hauling in his nets. The two extra coins could forestall that. Who knew how many days on the water, how many hand cuts, how many pains in an aging back, how many hauls of fish would have to be unloaded at the cannery to earn an equivalent amount?

The red-haired man watched Kiamil's face as the calculations of risks against profits played across it. And as he watched, he, too, calculated the risks: They would be traveling by day, never far from shore because of the narrowness of the waterway along most of the route, in Romanian waters in a boat of Turkish registry.

It was insane. Even if by some miracle of chance they reached the edge of Galati without being stopped, Kiamil could not expect a similar miracle on the return trip downstream. He would be caught, his boat impounded, and he imprisoned. Conversely, there was little risk to the red-haired man. If they were stopped and brought into port, he was sure he could find a way to escape and continue his trek. But Kiamil at the very least would lose his boat. Possibly his life.

It wasn't worth it. And it wasn't fair. He lowered the coins just as the Turk was about to reach for them.

"Never mind, Kiamil," he said. "I think it might be better if we just keep to our original agreement. Put me ashore anywhere along here."

The old man nodded, relief rather than disappointment showing on his leathery face at the withdrawal of the offer. The sight of the gold coins held out to him had almost turned him into a fool.

As the boat nosed toward shore, the red-haired man slipped the cord that tied the blanket roll with all his possessions over his shoulder and lifted the long, flat case under his arm. Kiamil reversed the engines within a foot or two of the gray mixture of sand and dirt overgrown with rank, wiry grasses that served for a bank here. The red-haired man stepped onto the gunwale and leaped ashore.

He turned to look back at Kiamil. The Turk waved and began to back the boat away from shore.

"Kiamil!" he shouted. "Here!" He tossed the two fifty-peso gold pieces out to the boat one at a time. Each was unerringly snatched from the air by a brown, callused hand.

With loud and profuse thanks in the name of Mohammed and all that was holy in Islam ringing in his ears, the red-haired man turned and began to pick his way across the marsh. Clouds of insects, poisonous snakes, and bottomless holes of quicksand lay directly ahead of him, and beyond that would be units of Iron Guard. They could not stop him, but they could slow him down. As threats to his life they were insignificant compared to what he knew lay half a day's ride due west in the Dinu Pass.

SEVENTEEN

Woermann stood at his window and watched the men in the courtyard. Yesterday they had been intermingled, the black uniforms interspersed with the gray ones. This afternoon they were separated, an invisible line dividing the einsatzkommandos from the regular army men.

Yesterday they had had a common enemy, one who killed regardless of the color of the uniform. But last night the enemy had not killed, and by this afternoon they were all acting like victors, each side claiming credit for the night of safety. It was a natural rivalry. The einsatzkommandos saw themselves as elite troops, SS specialists in a special kind of warfare. The regular army men saw themselves as the real soldiers; although they feared what the black uniform of the SS represented, they looked on the einsatzkommandos as little more than glorified policemen.

Unity had begun to break down at breakfast. It had

been a normal mess period until the girl, Magda, had shown up. There had been some good-natured jostling and elbowing for a place near her as she moved past the food bins, filling a tray for herself and her father. Not an incident really, but her very appearance at morning mess had begun to divide the two groups. The SS contingent automatically assumed that since she was a Jew they had a pre-emptive right to do with her as they wished. The regular army men did not feel anyone had a pre-emptive right to the girl. She was beautiful. Try as she might to cover her hair in that old kerchief and bundle her body in those shapeless clothes, she could not conceal her femininity. It radiated through all her attempts to minimize it. It was there in the softness of her skin, in the smoothness of her throat, the turn of her lips, the tilt of her sparkling brown eyes. She was fair game for anyone as far as the regular army troops were concerned—with the *real* fighting men getting first chance, of course.

Woermann hadn't noticed it at the time but the first cracks in the previous day's solidarity had appeared.

At the noon mess a shoving match between gray uniforms and black ones began, again while the girl was going through the line. Two men slipped and fell on the floor during the minor fracas, and Woermann sent the sergeant over to break it up before any serious blows could be struck. By that time Magda had taken her food and departed.

Shortly after lunch she had wandered about, looking for him. She had told him that her father needed a cross or a crucifix as part of his research into one of the manuscripts. Could the captain lend her one? He could—a little silver cross removed from one of the dead soldiers.

And now the off-duty men sat apart in the courtyard while the rest worked at dismantling the rear of the keep. Woermann was trying to think of ways to avoid certain trouble at the evening mess. Maybe the best thing to do was to have someone load up a tray at each meal and bring it to the old man and his daughter in the tower. The less seen of the girl, the better.

His eyes were drawn to movement directly below him. It was Magda, hesitant at first, and then with straight-backed, high-chinned decisiveness, marching bucket in hand toward the cellar entry. The men followed her at first with their eyes, then they were on their feet, drifting toward her from all corners of the courtyard, like soap bubbles swirling toward an unstoppered drain.

When she came up from the cellar with her bucket of water, they were waiting for her in a thick semicircle, pushing and shoving toward the front for a good close look at her. They were calling to her, moving before, beside, and behind her as she tentatively made her way back to the tower. One of the einsatzkommandos blocked her way but was pushed aside by a regular army man who grabbed her bucket with exaggerated gallantry and carried it ahead of her, a clown footman. But the SS man who had been pushed out of the way snatched at the bucket; he only succeeded in spilling the contents over the legs and the boots of the one who now held it.

As laughter started from the black uniforms, the face of the regular army man turned a bright red. Woermann could see what was coming but was helpless to stop it from his position on the third level of the tower. He watched the soldier in gray swing the bucket at the SS man who had spilled the water on him, saw the bucket connect full force with the head, then Woermann was away from the window and running down the steps as fast as his legs would carry him.

As he reached the bottom landing, he saw the door to the Jews' suite swing shut behind a flash of skirt fabric, then he was out in the courtyard facing a full-scale brawl. He had to fire his pistol twice to get the men's attention and had to threaten to shoot the next one who threw a punch before the fighting actually stopped.

The girl had to go.

As things quieted down, Woermann left his men with
Sergeant Oster and headed directly for the first floor of
the tower. While Kaempffer was busy squaring away the
einsatzkommandos, Woermann would use the opportunity to start the girl on her way out of the keep. If
he could get her across the causeway and into the inn
before Kaempffer was aware of what was happening,
there was a good chance he could keep her out.

He did not bother to knock this time, but pushed the
door open and stepped inside. *"Fräulein* Cuza!"

The old man was still sitting at the table; the girl was
nowhere in sight. "What do you want with her?"

He ignored the father. *"Fräulein* Cuza!"

"Yes?" she said, stepping out of the rear room, her
face anxious.

"I want you packed to leave for the inn immediately.
You have two minutes. No more."

"But I can't leave my father!"

"Two minutes and you are leaving, with or without
your things!"

He would not be swayed, and he hoped his face
showed it. He did not like to separate the girl and her
father—the professor obviously needed care and she obviously was devoted to caring for him—but the men under his command came first, and she was a disruptive influence. The father would have to remain in the keep;
the daughter would have to stay in the inn. There was no
room for argument.

Woermann watched her cast a pleading look at her
father, begging him to say something. But the old man
remained silent. She took a deep breath and turned
toward the back room.

"You now have a minute and a half," Woermann
told her.

"A minute and a half for what?" said a voice behind
him. It was Kaempffer.

Groaning inwardly and readying himself for a battle
of wills, Woermann faced the SS man.

"Your timing is superb as usual, Major," he said. "I
was just telling *Fräulein* Cuza to pack her things and

move herself over to the inn.''

Kaempffer opened his mouth to reply but was cut off by the professor.

"I forbid it!'' he cried in his dry, shrill voice. "I will not permit you to send my daughter away!''

Kaempffer's eyes narrowed as his attention was drawn from Woermann to Cuza. Even Woermann found himself turning in surprise to see what had prompted the outburst.

"You *forbid*, old Jew?'' Kaempffer said in a hoarse voice as he moved past Woermann to the professor. "*You* forbid? Let me tell you something: You forbid nothing around here! *Nothing!*''

The old man bowed his head in resignation.

Satisfied with the result of his vented anger, Kaempffer turned back to Woermann. "See that she's out of here immediately. She's a troublemaker!''

Dazed and bemused, Woermann watched Kaempffer storm out of the room as abruptly as he had arrived. He looked at Cuza whose head was no longer bowed, and who now appeared to be resigned to nothing.

"Why didn't you protest before the major arrived?'' Woermann asked him. "I had the impression you wanted her out of the keep.''

"Perhaps. But I changed my mind.''

"So I noticed—and in a most provocative manner at a most strategic moment. Do you manipulate everyone this way?''

"My dear Captain,'' Cuza said, his tone serious, "no one pays much attention to a cripple. People look at the body and see that it's wrecked by an accident or wasted by illness, and they automatically carry the infirmity to the mind within that body. 'He can't walk, therefore he can't have anything intelligent or useful or interesting to say.' So a cripple like me soon learns how to make other people come up with an idea he has already thought of, and to have them arrive at that idea in such a way that they believe it originated with them. It's not manipulation—it's a form of persuasion.''

As Magda emerged from the rear room, suitcase in hand, Woermann realized with chagrin, and perhaps a touch of admiration, that he, too, had been manipulated—or "persuaded," to give the professor his due. He now knew whose idea it had been for Magda to make those repeated trips to the mess and the cellar. The realization did not bother him too much, though. His own instincts had always been against having a woman in the keep.

"I'm going to leave you at the inn unguarded," he told Magda. "I'm sure you understand that if you run off it will not go well with your father. I'm going to trust in your honor and your devotion to him."

He did not add that it would be courting a riot to decide which soldiers would do guard duty on her—competition for the double benefit of separation from the keep and proximity to an attractive female would further widen the existing rift between the two contingents of soldiers. He had no choice but to trust her.

A look passed between father and daughter.

"Have no fear, Captain," Magda said, glaring at her father. "I have no intention of running off and deserting him."

He watched the professor's hands bunch into two thick, angry fists.

"You'd better take this," Cuza said, pushing one of the books toward her, the one he had called the *Al Azif*. "Study it tonight so we can discuss it tomorrow."

There was a trace of mischief in her smile. "You know I don't read Arabic, Papa." She picked up another, slimmer volume. "I think I'll take this one instead."

They stared at each other across the table. They were at an impasse of wills, and Woermann thought he had a good idea where the conflict lay.

Without warning, Magda stepped around the table and kissed her father on the cheek. She smoothed his sparse white hairs, then straightened up and looked Woermann directly in the eye.

"Take care of my father, Captain. Please. He's all I have."

Woermann heard himself speaking before he could think: "Don't worry. I'll see to everything."

He cursed himself. He shouldn't have said that. It went against all his officer training, all his Prussian rearing. But there was that look in her eyes that made him want to do as she asked. He had no daughter of his own, but if he had he would want her to care about him the way this girl cared about her father.

No . . . he had no need to worry about her running off. But the father—he was a sly one. He would bear watching. Woermann warned himself never to take anything about these two for granted.

T

The red-haired man sent his mount plunging through the foothills toward the southeast entrance to the Dinu Pass. The greening terrain around him went by unnoticed in his haste. As the sun slipped down the sky ahead of him, the hills on each side grew steeper and rockier, closing on him, narrowing until he was confined to a path a scant dozen feet wide. Once through the bottleneck up ahead he would be on the wide floor of the Dinu Pass. From there on it would be an easy trip, even in the dark. He knew the way.

He was about to congratulate himself on avoiding the many military patrols in the area when he spotted two soldiers up ahead blocking his path with ready rifles and fixed bayonets. Rearing his mount to a halt before the pair, he quickly decided on a course of action—he wanted no trouble, so he would play it meek and mild.

"Where to in such a hurry, goatherd?"

It was the older of the two who spoke. He had a thick mustache and a pitted face. The younger man laughed at the word "goatherd." Apparently it held some derogatory meaning for them.

"Up the pass to my village. My father is sick. Please let me by."

"All in good time. How far up do you intend to go?"

"To the keep."

" 'The keep'? Never heard of it. Where is it?"

That answered one question for the red-haired man. If the keep were involved in a military action in the pass, these men at least would have heard of it.

"Why are you stopping me?" he asked them, trying to look puzzled. "Is something wrong?"

"It is not for the likes of you to question the Iron Guard," Mustache said. "Get down from there so we can have a better look at you."

So they weren't just soldiers; they were members of the Iron Guard. Getting through here was going to be tougher than he had thought. The red-haired man dismounted and stood silent, waiting as they scrutinized him.

"You're not from around here," Mustache said. "Let me see your papers."

That was the question the red-haired man had feared throughout his trip. "I don't have them with me, sir," he said in his most deferential manner. "I left in such a hurry that I forgot them. I'll go back and get them if you wish."

A look passed between the two soldiers. A traveler without papers had no legal rights to speak of—his noncompliance with the law gave them a free hand to deal with him in any way they saw fit.

"No *papers*?" Mustache had his rifle at the port position across the front of his chest. As he spoke he emphasized his words with sharp outward thrusts of his rifle, slamming the bolt assembly and the side of the stock against the red-haired man's ribs. "*How* do we *know* you're *not* running *guns* to the *peasants* in the *hills*?"

The red-haired man winced and backed away, showing more pain than he felt; to absorb the blows stoically would only incite Mustache to greater violence.

Always the same, he thought. No matter what the time or place, no matter what the ruling power calls itself, its bullyboys remain the same.

Mustache stepped back and pointed his rifle at the red-haired man. "Search him!" he told his younger partner.

The young one slung his rifle over a shoulder and

began roughly slapping his hands over the traveler's clothes. He stopped when he came to the money belt. With a few deft moves he opened the shirt and removed the belt from beneath. When they saw the gold coins in the pouches, another look passed between them.

"Where'd you *steal* that?" Mustache said, once again slamming the side of his rifle against the red-haired man's ribs.

"It's mine," he told them. "It's all I have. But you can keep it if you'll just let me be on my way." He meant that. He didn't need the gold anymore.

"Oh, we'll keep it all right," Mustache said. "But first we'll see what else you've got." He pointed to the long, flat case strapped to the right flank of the horse. "Open that," he told his companion.

The red-haired man decided then that he had let this go as far as he could. He would not let them open the case.

"Don't touch that!" he said.

They must have sensed menace in his voice, for both soldiers stopped and stared at him. Mustache's lips worked in anger. He stepped forward to slam his rifle against the red-haired man once more.

"Why you—"

Although the red-haired man's next moves looked carefully planned, they were all reflex. As Mustache made to thrust with his rifle, the red-haired man deftly ripped it out of his grasp. While Mustache stared dumbly at his empty hands, the red-haired man swung the butt of the rifle up and cracked the man's jaw; from there all that was needed to crush the larynx was a short jab against the exposed throat. Turning, he saw the other soldier unslinging his weapon. The red-haired man took a single step and drove the bayonet on the other end of his borrowed rifle full length into the younger man's chest. With a sigh, the soldier sagged and died.

The red-haired man viewed the scene dispassionately. Mustache was still alive, but barely. His back was arched, his face tinged with blue as his hands tore at his throat, trying in vain to let some air through to his lungs.

As before, when he had killed Carlos the boatman, the red-haired man felt nothing. No triumph, no regret. He could not see how the world would be poorer for the passing of two members of the Iron Guard, and he knew that if he had waited much longer it might have been him on the ground, wounded or dead.

By the time the red-haired man had replaced the money belt around his waist, Mustache lay as still as his companion. He hid the bodies and the rifles in the rocks on the northern slope and resumed his gallop toward the keep.

⊤

Magda paced about her tiny candlelit room at the inn, anxiously rubbing her hands together, stopping every so often at the window to glance out at the keep. It was dark tonight, with high clouds moving in from the south, and no moon.

The dark frightened her . . . the dark and being alone. She could not remember when she had last been alone like this. It was neither right nor proper for her to be staying unchaperoned at the inn. It helped some to know that Iuliu's wife, Lidia, would be around, but she would be little help if that thing in the keep decided to cross the gorge and come to her.

She had a clear view of the keep from her window—in fact, hers was the only room with a window facing north. She had requested it for that reason. There had been no problem; she was the only guest.

Iuliu had been most gracious, almost obsequious. That puzzled her. He had always been courteous during their previous stays, but in a rather perfunctory way. Now he virtually fawned over her.

From where she stood she could pick out the lit window in the first level of the tower where she knew Papa now sat. There was no sign of movement; that meant he was alone. She had been furious with him earlier when she realized how he had maneuvered her out of the keep. But as the hours passed, her anger gave way to worry. How would he take care of himself?

She turned and leaned back against the sill, looking at the four white stucco walls that confined her. Her room was small: a narrow closet, a single dresser with a beveled mirror above it, a three-legged stool, and a large, too soft bed. Her mandolin lay on the bed, untouched since her arrival. The book too, *Cultes des Goules*, lay untouched in the bottom drawer of the dresser. She had no intention of studying it; she had taken it only for show.

She had to get out for a while. She blew out two of the candles, but left the third burning. She did not want the room to be totally dark. After last night's encounter, she would fear the dark forever.

A polished wood stairway took her down to the first floor. She found the innkeeper hunched on the front stoop, sitting and whittling dejectedly.

"Something wrong, Iuliu?"

He started at the sound of her voice, looked her once in the eye, then returned to his aimless whittling.

"Your father—he is well?"

"For the moment, yes. Why?"

He put down the knife and covered his eyes with both hands; the words came out in a rush. "You're both here because of me. I'm ashamed . . . I'm not a man. But they wanted to know all about the keep and I couldn't tell them what they wanted. And then I thought of your father, who knows all there is to know about the keep. I didn't know how sick he was now, and I never thought they'd bring you, too. But I couldn't help it! They were hurting me!"

Magda experienced a brief flare of anger—Iuliu had no right mentioning Papa to the Germans! And then she admitted that under similar circumstances, she, too, might have told them anything they wanted to know. At least now she knew how they had connected Papa with the keep, and she had an explanation for Iuliu's deferential manner.

His pleading expression touched her as he looked up at her. "Do you hate me?"

Magda leaned over and placed a hand on his round shoulder. "No. You didn't mean us any harm."

He covered her hand with his. "I hope all will go well for you."

"So do I."

She walked slowly along the path to the gorge, the silence broken only by the pebbles crunching underfoot, echoing in the moist air. She stopped and stood in the thick, freshly budded brush to the right of the causeway and hugged her sweater more tightly around her. It was midnight, and cool and damp; but the chill she felt went deeper than any caused by a simple drop in temperature. Behind her the inn was a dim shadow; across the causeway lay the keep, ablaze with light in many of its windows. The fog had risen up from the bottom of the pass, filling the gorge and surrounding the keep. Light from the courtyard filtered up through the fine haze in the air, making a glow like a phosphorescent cloud. The keep looked like an ungainly luxury liner adrift in a phantom sea of fog.

Fear settled over her as she stared at the keep.

Last night . . . considering the mortal threats of the day, it had been easy for her to avoid thinking about last night. But here in the dark it all came back—those eyes, that icy grip on her arm. She ran her hand over the spot near her elbow where the thing had touched her. There was still a mark on the skin there, pale gray. The area looked dead, and she hadn't been able to wash it off. She hadn't told Papa. But it was proof: Last night had not been a dream. The nightmare was a reality. A type of creature she had blithely assumed to be fantasy had become real, and it was over there in that stone building. So was Papa. She knew that right now he was waiting for it. He hadn't told her so, but she knew. Papa hoped to be visited tonight, and she would not be there to help him. The thing had spared them last night, but could Papa count on such luck two nights in a row?

And what if it did not visit Papa tonight? What if it crossed the gorge and came to her? She could not bear the thought of another encounter like last night's!

It was all so unreal! The undead were fiction!

And yet last night . . .

The sound of hoofbeats interrupted her musings. She turned and dimly saw a horse and a rider passing the inn at full gallop. They approached the causeway, apparently with every intention of charging over to the keep, but at the last minute the rider fiercely reined his steed to a halt at its edge. Horse and man stood limned in the glow that filtered across the gorge from the keep. She noted a long, flat box strapped to the horse's right flank. The rider dismounted and took a few tentative steps onto the causeway, then stopped.

Magda crouched in the brush and watched him study the keep. She could not say exactly why she chose to hide herself, but the events of the past few days had made her distrust anyone she did not know.

He was tall, leanly muscular, bare-headed, his hair wind-twisted and reddish, his breathing rapid but unlabored. She could see his head move as his eyes followed the sentries atop the keep walls. He seemed to be counting them. His posture was tense, as if he were forcibly restraining himself from battering his body against the closed gates at the far end of the causeway. He appeared frustrated, angry, and puzzled.

He stood still and quiet for a long time. Magda felt her calves begin to ache from squatting on them for so long, but she dared not move. At last he turned and walked back to his horse. His eyes scanned the edge of the gorge, back and forth, as he moved. He suddenly stopped and stared directly at the spot where Magda crouched. She held her breath as her heart began to pound in alarm.

"You there!" he called. "Come out!" His tone was commanding, his accent hinting at the Meglenitic dialect.

Magda made no move. How could he possibly see her through the dark and the brush?

"Come out or I'll drag you out!"

Magda found a heavy stone near her right hand. Gripping it tightly, she rose quickly and stepped forward. She would take her chances in the open. Neither this man nor anyone else was going to drag her anywhere without a fight. She had been pushed around enough today.

"Why were you hiding in there?"

"Because I don't know who you are." Magda made her voice sound as defiant as she could.

"Fair enough." His head gave a curt nod as he spoke.

Magda could sense the tension coiled within him, yet felt it had nothing to do with her. That eased her mind a little.

He gestured toward the keep. "What's going on in there? Who has the keep lit up like a cheap tourist attraction?"

"German soldiers."

"I thought those helmets looked German. But why here?"

"I don't know. I'm not sure they know, either."

She watched him stare at the keep a moment longer and heard him mutter something under his breath that sounded like "Fools!" But she was not sure. There was a remoteness about him, a feeling that he was not the least bit concerned with her, that the only thing he cared about was the keep. She relaxed her grip on the stone in her hand but did not drop it. Not yet.

"Why are you so interested?" she asked.

He looked at her, his features shadowed. "Just a tourist. I've been this way before and thought I'd stop by the keep on my way through the mountains."

She knew immediately that was a lie. No sightseer rode at night through the Dinu Pass at the speed with which this man had arrived. Not unless he was mad.

Magda took a step backward and started walking toward the inn. She feared to stay in the dark with a man who told patent lies.

"Where are you going?"

"Back to my room. It's chilly out here."

"I'll escort you back."

Uneasy, Magda quickened her pace. "I'll find my own way, thank you."

He did not seem to hear, or if he did he chose to ignore what she had said. He pulled his mount around and came up beside her, matching her stride and leading the horse behind him. Ahead, the inn sat like a large two-story box. She could see dim light in her window from the candle she had left burning.

"You can put that rock down," he said. "You won't need it."

Magda hid her startled reaction. Could this man see in the dark? "I'll be the judge of that."

He had a sour smell, a mixture of man sweat and horse sweat which she found unpleasant. She further quickened her pace to leave him behind.

He did not bother to catch up.

Magda dropped the stone as she reached the front stoop of the inn and went inside. To her right, the tiny dining area was dark and empty. To her left, Iuliu was at the table he used as a front desk, preparing to blow out his candle.

"Better wait," she told him as she hurried past. "I think you have another guest coming."

His face lit up. "Tonight?"

"Immediately."

Beaming, he opened the registration book and un-stoppered the inkwell. The inn had been in Iuliu's family for generations. Some said it had been built to house the masons who had constructed the keep. It was nothing more than a small two-story house, and not by any means an income-producing venture—the number of travelers who stopped at the inn during the course of a year was ludicrously low. But the first floor served as a home for the family and there was always someone about in the rare event that a traveler did appear. The major portion of Iuliu's insubstantial income came from the commission he received for acting as bursar to the workers in the keep. The rest came from wool from the flock of sheep his son tended—those that had not been sacrificed to put a little meat on the family table and clothes on their backs.

Two of the inn's three rooms rented at one time—a bonanza.

Magda ran lightly to the top of the stairs but did not enter her room immediately. She paused to listen to what the stranger would tell Iuliu. She wondered at her interest as she stood there. She had found the man unattractive in the extreme; in addition to his odor and grimy appearance, there was a trace of arrogance and condescension that she found equally offensive.

Why, then, was she eavesdropping? It was not like her.

She heard a heavy tread on the front stoop, and then on the floor as the man entered. His voice echoed up the stairwell.

"Ah, innkeeper! Good! You're still up. Arrange for someone to rub down my horse and stall her for a few days. She's my second mount of the day and I've ridden her hard. I want her well dried before she's put away for the night. Hello? Are you listening?"

"Yes . . . yes, sir." Iuliu's voice sounded hoarse, strained, frightened.

"Can you do it?"

"Yes. I—I'll have my nephew come over right away."

"And a room for myself."

"We have two left. Please sign."

There was a pause. "You can give me the one directly overhead—the one on the north side."

"Uh, pardon, sir, but you must put your surname. 'Glenn' is not enough." Iuliu's voice trembled as he spoke.

"Do you have anyone else named Glenn staying here?"

"No."

"Is there anyone else in the area named Glenn?"

"No, but—"

"Then Glenn alone will do."

"Very well, sir. But I must tell you that the north room is occupied. You may have the east room."

"Whoever it is, tell him to switch rooms. I'll pay extra."

"It's not a him, sir. It's a her, and I don't think she'll move."

How very true, Iuliu, Magda thought.

"Tell her!" It was a command, in a tone not to be denied.

As Magda heard Iuliu's scurrying feet approach the stairs, she ducked into her room and waited. The stranger's attitude infuriated her. And what had he done to frighten Iuliu so?

She opened her door at the first knock and stared at the portly innkeeper, his hands nervously clutching and twisting the fabric of his shirt front, his face pale and beaded, with so much sweat that his mustache had begun to droop. He was terrified.

"Please, *Domnisoara* Cuza," he blurted, "there's a man downstairs who wants this room. Will you please let him have it? Please?"

He was whining. Pleading. Magda felt sorry for him, but she was not going to give up this room.

"Absolutely not!" She began to close the door but he put his hand out.

"But you must!"

"I will *not*, Iuliu. And that's final!"

"Then would you . . . would you tell him. Please?"

"Why are you so afraid of him? Who is he?"

"I don't know who he is. And I'm not really . . ." His voice trailed off. "Won't you please tell him for me?"

Iuliu was actually quivering with fear. Magda's first impulse was to let the innkeeper handle his own affairs, but then it occurred to her that she would derive a certain pleasure from telling the arrogant newcomer that she was keeping her room. For two days now she had been allowed no say in what had happened to her. Standing firm on this small matter would be a welcome change.

"Of course I'll tell him."

She squeezed past Iuliu and hurried down the steps. The man was waiting impassively in the foyer, casually and confidently leaning on the long, flat box she had previously seen strapped to the horse's flank. It was the first time she had seen him in the light and she reconsidered her initial assessment. Yes, he was grimy, and she could smell him from the foot of the stairs, but his features were even, his nose long and straight, his cheek-bones high. She noticed how truly red his hair was, like a dark flame; a bit wild and overlong, perhaps, but that, like his odor, could well be the natural result of a long, hard trip. His eyes held her for a moment, startling in their blueness, their clarity. The only jarring note in his appearance was the olive tone of his skin—out of place in the company of his hair and eyes.

"I thought it might be you."

"I'm keeping my room."

"I require it," he said, straightening up.

"It's mine for now. You're welcome to it when I leave."

He took a step toward her. "It's important that I have a northern exposure. I—"

"I have my own reasons for wanting to keep my eye on the keep," Magda said, cutting him off from another lie, "just as I'm sure you have yours. But mine are of great personal importance. I will not leave."

His eyes blazed suddenly, and for an instant Magda was afraid she had overstepped her bounds. Just as suddenly, he cooled and stepped back, a half-smile playing about the corners of his mouth.

"You're obviously not from around here."

"Bucharest."

"I thought as much." Magda caught a hint of something in his eyes, something akin to grudging respect. But that didn't seem right. Why would he look at her that way when she was blocking him from what he wanted? "You won't reconsider?" he said.

"No."

"Ah, well," he sighed, "an eastern exposure it is, then. Innkeeper! Show me to my room!"

Iuliu came rushing down the stairs, nearly tripping in his haste. "Right away, sir. The room to the right at the top of the stairs is all ready for you. I'll take this—" He reached for the case but Glenn snatched it away.

"I can handle that very well by myself. But there's a blanket roll on the back of my horse that I'll be

needing." He started up the stairs. "And be sure to see
to that horse! She's a good and true beast." With a brief
parting glance at Magda, a glance that stirred an unfamiliar but not unpleasant sensation within her, he
went up the steps two at a time. "And draw me a bath
immediately!"

"Yes, sir!" Iuliu leaned over to Magda and clasped
both her hands in his. "Thank you!" he whispered, still
frightened, but apparently less so. He then rushed out to
the horse.

Magda stood in the middle of the foyer for a moment,
wondering at the evening's strange chain of events.
There were unanswered questions here at the inn but she
couldn't think about them now, not while there were
more fearful questions to be answered at the keep—

The keep! She had forgotten about Papa! She hurried
up the stairs, passing the closed door to Glenn's room
on her way, then pushed into her own room and rushed
to the window. There in the watchtower, Papa's light
burned the same as before.

She sighed with relief and lay back on the bed. A bed
. . . a real bed. Maybe everything would turn out all
right tonight after all. She smiled to herself. No, that
tactic wasn't going to work. Something *was* going to
happen. She closed her eyes against the light of the gut-
tering candle atop the dresser, its glow doubled by the
mirror behind it. She was tired. If for just a minute she
could rest her eyes, she'd be better . . . think about good
things, like Papa being allowed to go back to Bucharest
with her, fleeing the Germans and that hideous
manifestation . . .

The sound of movement out in the hall drew her
thoughts away from the keep. It sounded like that man,
Glenn, going down to the back room for a bath. At least
he wouldn't always smell the way he did tonight. But
why should she care? He did seem concerned about the
welfare of his horse, and that could be read as a sign of
a compassionate man. Or just a practical one. Had he
really said it was his second mount of the day? Could
any man ride two horses into such a lather? She could
not imagine why Iuliu seemed so terrified of the

newcomer. He seemed to know Glenn, and yet had not known his name until he had signed it. It didn't make sense.

Nothing made sense anymore . . . her thoughts drifted . . .

The sound of a door closing startled her awake. It was not her own. It must have been Glenn's. There was a creak on the stair. Magda bolted upright and looked at the candle—it had lost half its length since the last time she looked. She leaped to the window. The light was still on in her father's room.

There was no sound from below, but she could make out the dim shape of a man moving along the path toward the causeway. His movements were catlike. *Silent*. She was sure it was Glenn. As Magda watched, he stepped into the brush to the right of the causeway and stood there, precisely where she had stood earlier. The mist that filled the gorge overflowed and lapped at his feet. Like a sentinel, he watched the keep.

Magda felt a stab of anger. What was he doing out there? That was *her* spot. He had no right to take it. She wished she had the courage to go out there and tell him to leave, but she did not. She did not fear him, actually, but he moved too quickly, too decisively. This Glenn was a dangerous man. But not to her, she felt. To others. To those Germans in the keep, perhaps. And didn't that make him an ally of sorts? Still, she could not go unescorted to him in the dark and tell him to leave and allow her to keep her own vigil.

But she could observe him. She could set herself up behind him and see what he was up to while keeping her eye on Papa's window. Maybe she'd learn why he was here. That was the question that nagged her as she padded down the stairs, through the darkened foyer, and out onto the road. She crept toward a large rock not too far behind him. He would never know she was there.

"Come to reclaim your vantage point?"

Magda jumped at the sound of his voice—he had not even looked around!

"How did you know I was here?"

"I've been listening to your approach ever since you left the inn. You're really rather clumsy."

There it was again—that smug self-assurance.

He turned and gestured to her. "Come up here and tell me why you think the Germans have the keep lit up like that in the wee hours. Don't they ever sleep?"

She held back, then decided to accept his invitation. She would stand at the edge there, but not too close to him. As she neared, she noted he smelled worlds better.

"They're afraid of the dark," she said.

"Afraid of the dark." His tone had gone flat. He did not seem surprised by her reply. "And just why is that?"

"A vampire, they think."

In the dim light filtering across the gorge from the keep, Magda saw his eyebrows rise. "Oh? Is that what they've told you? Do you know someone in there?"

"I've been in there myself. And my father's in there right now." She pointed to the keep. "The lowermost window in the watchtower is his—the one that's lit." How she hoped he was all right.

"But why would anyone think there's a vampire about?"

"Eight men dead, all German soldiers, all with their throats torn open."

His mouth tightened into a grim line. "Still . . . a vampire?"

"There was also a matter of two corpses supposedly walking about. A vampire seems to be the only thing that could explain all that's happened in there. And after what I saw—"

"You saw him?" Glenn turned and leaned toward her, his eyes boring into hers, intent on her answer.

Magda retreated a step. "Yes."

"What did he look like?"

"Why do you want to know?" He was frightening her now. His words pounded at her as he leaned closer.

"Tell me! Was he dark? Was he pale? Handsome? Ugly? What?"

"I—I'm not even sure I can remember exactly. All I know is that he looked insane and . . . and unholy, if that makes any sense to you.''

He straightened. ''Yes. That says much. And I didn't mean to upset you.'' He paused briefly. ''What about his eyes?''

Magda felt her throat tighten. ''How did you know about his eyes?''

''I know nothing about his eyes,'' he said quickly, ''but it's said they are the windows to the soul.''

''If that's true,'' she said, her voice lowering of its own volition to a whisper, ''his soul is a bottomless pit.''

Neither of them spoke for a while, both watching the keep in silence. Magda wondered what Glenn was thinking. Finally, he spoke.

''One more thing: Do you know how it all began?''

''My father and I weren't here, but we were told that the first man died when he and a friend broke through a cellar wall.''

She watched him grimace and close his eyes, as if in pain; and as she had seen hours earlier, his lips again formed the word ''Fools'' without speaking it aloud.

He opened his eyes and suddenly pointed to the keep. ''What's happening in your father's room?''

Magda looked and saw nothing at first. Then terror clutched her. The light was fading. Without thinking, she started toward the causeway. But Glenn grabbed her by the wrist and pulled her back.

''Don't be a fool!'' he whispered harshly in her ear. ''The sentries will shoot you! And if by some chance they held their fire, they'd never let you in! There's nothing you can do!''

Magda barely heard him. Frantically, wordlessly, she struggled against him. She had to get away—she had to get to Papa! But Glenn was strong and refused to release her. His fingers dug into her arms, and the more she struggled, the tighter he held her.

Finally, his words sank in: She could not get to Papa. There was nothing she could do.

In helpless, agonized silence, she watched the light in Papa's room fade slowly, inexorably to black.

EIGHTEEN

Theodor Cuza had waited patiently, eagerly, knowing without knowing how he knew that the thing he had seen last night would return to him. He had spoken to it in the old tongue. It would return. Tonight.

Nothing else was certain tonight. He might unlock secrets sought by scholars for ages, or he might never see the morning. He trembled, as much with anticipation as with fear of the unknown.

Everything was ready. He sat at his table, the old books piled in a neat stack to his left, a small box full of traditional vampire banes within easy reach to his right, the ever-present cup of water directly before him. The only illumination was the cone of light from the hooded bulb directly overhead, the only sound his own breathing.

And suddenly he knew he was not alone.

Before he saw anything, he felt it—a malign presence,

beyond his field of vision, beyond his capacity to describe it. It was simply *there*. Then the darkness began. It was different this time. Last night it had pervaded the very air of the room, growing and spreading from everywhere. Tonight he watched it invade by a different route —slowly, insidiously seeping through the walls, blotting them from his view, closing in on him.

Cuza pressed his gloved palms against the tabletop to keep them from shaking. He could feel his heart thumping in his chest, so loud, so hard, he feared one of the chambers would rupture. The moment was here. This was it!

The walls were gone. Darkness surrounded him in an ebon dome that swallowed the glow from the overhead bulb—no light passed beyond the end of the table. It was cold, but not so cold as last night, and there was no wind.

"Where are you?" He spoke in Old Slavonic.

No reply. But in the darkness, beyond the point where light would not go, he sensed that something stood and waited, taking his measure.

"Show yourself—please!"

There was a lengthy pause, then a thickly accented voice spoke from the dark.

"I can speak a more modern form of our language." The words derived from a root version of the Daco-Romanian dialect spoken in this region at the time the keep was built.

The darkness on the far side of the little table began to recede. A shape took form out of the black. Cuza immediately recognized the face and the eyes from last night, and then the rest of the figure became visible. A giant of a man stood before him, at least six and a half feet tall, broad shouldered, standing proudly, defiantly, legs spread, hands on hips. A floor-length cloak, as black as his hair and eyes, was fastened about his neck with a clasp of jeweled gold. Beneath that Cuza could see a loose red blouse, possibly silk, loose black breeches that looked like jodhpurs, and high boots of rough brown leather.

It was all there—power, decadence, ruthlessness.

"How do you come to know the old tongue?" said the voice.

Cuza heard himself stammer. "I—I've studied it for years. Many years." He found his mind had gone numb, frozen. All the things he had wanted to say, the questions he had planned all afternoon to ask, all fled, all gone. Desperately, he verbalized the first thought that came into his head.

"I had almost expected you to be wearing evening clothes."

The thick eyebrows, growing so near to each other, touched as the visitor's brow furrowed. "I do not understand 'evening clothes.'"

Cuza gave himself a mental kick—amazing how a single novel, written half a century ago by an Englishman, could so alter one's perceptions of what was an essentially Romanian myth. He leaned forward in his wheelchair. "Who are you?"

"I am the Viscount Radu Molasar. This region of Wallachia was once mine."

He was saying that he was a feudal lord of his time. "A boyar?"

"Yes. One of the few who stayed with Vlad—the one they called *Tepes*, the Impaler—until his end outside Bucharest."

Even though he had expected such an answer, Cuza was still aghast. "That was in 1476! Almost five centuries ago! Are you that old?"

"I was there."

"But where have you been since the fifteenth century?"

"Here."

"But why?" Cuza's fear was vaporizing as he spoke, replaced by an intense excitement that sent his mind racing. He wanted to know everything—now!

"I was being pursued."

"By Turks?"

Molasar's eyes narrowed, leaving only the endless black of his pupils showing. "No. By . . . others . . . madmen who would pursue me across the world to destroy me. I knew I could not outrun them forever"—he smiled here, revealing long, tapered, slightly yellowed teeth, none of them particularly sharp, but all *strong*-looking—"so I decided to outwait them. I built this keep, arranged for its maintenance, and hid myself away."

"Are you . . ." There was a question Cuza had been burning to ask from the start but had dared not; now he could contain himself no longer. "Are you of the undead?"

Again the smile, cold, almost mocking. "Undead? Nosferatu? *Moroi?* Perhaps."

"But how did you—"

Molasar slashed a hand through the air. "*Enough!* Enough of your bothersome questions! I care not for your idle curiosity. I care not for you but that you are a countryman of mine and there are invaders in the land. Why are you with them? Do you betray Wallachia?"

"No!" Cuza felt the fear that had been washed away in the excitement of contact creep back into him as he saw Molasar's expression grow fierce. "They brought me here against my will!"

"*Why?*" The word was a jabbing knife.

"They thought I could find out what was killing the soldiers. And I guess I have . . . haven't I?"

"Yes. You have." Molasar underwent another mercurial shift of mood, smiling again. "I need them to restore my strength after my long repose. I will need them all before I am again at the peak of my powers."

"But you mustn't!" Cuza blurted without thinking.

Molasar flared again. "*Never* say to me what I must or must not do in my home! And never when invaders have taken it over! I saw to it that no Turk ever set foot in this pass while I was about, and now I am awakened to find my keep overrun with Germans!"

He was in a foaming rage, walking back and forth, swinging his fists wildly about to punctuate his words.

Cuza took the opportunity to lift the top off the box to his right and remove the fragment of broken mirror Magda had given him earlier in the day. As Molasar stormed about, lost in a rage, Cuza held up the mirror and tried to catch Molasar's reflection in it. He could glance to his left and see Molasar by the stack of books on the corner of the table, but when he looked in the mirror he could see only the books.

Molasar cast no reflection!

Suddenly, the mirror was snatched from Cuza's hand.

"Still curious?" He held up the mirror and looked into it. "Yes. The tales are true—I cast no reflection. Long ago I did." His eyes clouded for an instant. "But no more. What else have you in that box?"

"Garlic." Cuza reached under the cover and pulled out a clove. "It is said to ward away the undead."

Molasar held out his palm. There was hair growing at its center. "Give it to me." When Cuza complied, Molasar put the clove up to his mouth and took a bite, then tossed the rest into a corner. "I love garlic."

"And silver?" He pulled out a silver locket that Magda had left him.

Molasar did not hesitate to take it and rub it between his palms. "I could not very well have been a boyar if I had feared silver!" He seemed to be enjoying himself now.

"And this," Cuza said, reaching for the last item in the box, "is supposed to be the most potent of vampire banes." He pulled out the cross Captain Woermann had lent Magda.

With a sound that was part gasp and part growl, Molasar stepped away and averted his eyes. "Put it away!"

"It affects you?" Cuza was stunned. A heaviness grew in his chest as he watched Molasar cringe. "But why should it? How—"

"PUT IT AWAY!"

Cuza did so immediately, bulging the sides of the cardboard box as he pressed the lid down as tightly as he could over the offending object.

Molasar all but leaped upon him, baring his teeth and hissing his words through them. "I thought I might find an ally in you against the outlanders, but I see you are no different!"

"I want to see them gone, too!" Cuza said, terrified,

pressing himself back into the meager cushioning of his wheelchair. "More than you!"

"If that were true, you would never have brought that abomination into this room! And you would never have exposed it to me!"

"But I didn't know! It could have been another false folk tale like the garlic and the silver!" He had to convince him!

Molasar paused. "Perhaps." He whirled and stalked toward the darkness, his anger cooled, but minimally. "But I have doubts about you, Crippled One."

"Don't go! Please!"

Molasar stepped into the waiting dark and turned toward Cuza as it enveloped him. He said nothing.

"I'm on your side, Molasar!" Cuza cried. He couldn't leave now—not when there were so many unanswered questions! "Please believe me!"

Only pinpoint glints of light off the surfaces of Molasar's eyes remained. The rest of him had been swallowed up. Suddenly, a hand jabbed out of the blackness, pointing a finger at Cuza.

"I will watch you, Crippled One. And if I see you are to be trusted, I will speak with you another time. But if you betray our people, I shall end your days."

The hand disappeared. Then the eyes. But the words remained, hanging in the air. The darkness gradually receded, seeping back into the walls. Soon all was as it had been. The partially eaten clove of garlic that lay on the floor in the corner was the only evidence of Molasar's visit.

For a long while, Cuza did not move. Then he noticed how thick his tongue was in his mouth, and drier than usual. He picked up the cup of water and sipped from it; a mechanical exercise requiring no conscious thought. He swallowed with the usual difficulty, then reached for the box to his right. His hand rested on the lid awhile before lifting it. His numbed mind balked at facing what was within, but he knew he eventually must. Compressing his strictured mouth into a short, grim line, he lifted the lid, removed the cross, and laid it before him on the tabletop.

Such a little thing. Silver. Some ornate work at the ends of the upright and the crosspiece. No corpse affixed to it. Just a cross. If nothing else, a symbol of man's inhumanity to man.

From the millennia-old traditions and learning of his own faith that was so much a part of his daily life and culture, Cuza had always looked upon the wearing of crosses as a rather barbaric custom, a sure sign of immaturity in a religion. But then, Christianity was a relatively young offshoot of Judaism. It needed time. What had Molasar called the cross? An "abomination." No, it was not that; at least not to Cuza. Grotesque, yes, but never an abomination.

But now it took on new meaning, as did so many other things. The walls seemed to press in on him as he stared at the little cross, allowing it to become the focus of his attention. Crosses were so like the banes used by primitives to ward off evil spirits. Eastern Europeans, especially the Gypsies among them, had countless banes, from garlic to icons. He had lumped the cross in with the rest, seeing no reason why it should deserve more consideration than the rest.

Yet Molasar had been repulsed by the cross . . . could not even bear to look at it. Tradition gave it power over demons and vampires because it was supposedly the symbol of the ultimate triumph of good over evil. Cuza had always told himself that if the undead did exist, and the cross did have power over them, it was because of the innate faith of the person holding the object, not the object itself.

Yet he had just proved himself wrong.

Molasar was evil. That was given: Any entity that leaves a trail of corpses in order to continue its own existence is inherently evil. And when Cuza had held up the cross, Molasar had shrunk away. Cuza had no belief in the power of the cross, yet it had power over Molasar.

So it must be the cross itself which had the power, not its bearer.

His hands shook. He felt dizzy and lightheaded as his mind ran over all the implications. They were shattering.

NINETEEN

Two nights in a row without a death. Woermann found his mood edging into a sort of cautious jubilance as he buckled on his belt. He had actually slept last night, soundly and long, and was so much the better for it this morning.

The keep was no brighter or cheerier. There was still that indefinable sense of a malignant presence. No, it was he who had changed. For some reason he now felt there might be a real chance of his getting back to his home in Rathenow alive. For a while he had seriously come to doubt the possibility. But with the hearty breakfast he had eaten in his room perking through his intestines, and the knowledge that the men under his command numbered the same this morning as they had last night, all things seemed possible—perhaps even the departure of Erich Kaempffer and his uniformed hoodlums.

Even the painting failed to bother him this morning. The shadow to the left of the window still looked like a gibbeted corpse, but it no longer disturbed him as it had when Kaempffer had first pointed it out.

He descended the watchtower stairs and reached the first level in time to find Kaempffer approaching the professor's rooms from the courtyard, looking more supremely confident than usual, and with as little reason as ever.

"Good morning, dear Major!" Woermann called heartily, feeling he could forgo any overt venting of spleen this morning, considering the imminence of Kaempffer's departure. But a veiled jab was always in order. "I see we have the same idea: You've come to express your deepest thanks to Professor Cuza for the German lives he has saved again!"

"There's no evidence of his having done a damned thing!" Kaempffer said, his jauntiness disappearing in a snarl. "Even *he* makes no claim!"

"But the timing of the end of the murders with his arrival is rather suggestive of some cause-effect relationship, don't you think?"

"Coincidence! Nothing more!"

"Then why are you here?"

Kaempffer faltered for an instant. "To interrogate the Jew about what he has learned from the books, of course."

"Of course."

They entered the outer room, Kaempffer first. They found Cuza kneeling on the floor on his spread-out bedroll. He was not praying. He was trying to hoist himself back into the wheelchair. After the briefest glance in their direction as they walked in, he returned his full concentration to the task.

Woermann's initial impulse was to help the man—Cuza's hands appeared useless for gripping and his muscles seemed too weak to pull him up even if he could manage a firm grip. But he had asked for no aid, either with his eyes or with his voice. It was obviously a matter of pride for him to pull himself up into the chair unassisted. Woermann realized that beyond his daughter, the crippled man had little left in which to take any pride. He would not rob him of this small accomplishment.

Cuza seemed to know what he was doing. As Woermann watched from Kaempffer's side—he was sure the major was enjoying the spectacle—he could see that Cuza had braced the back of the wheelchair against the wall beside the fireplace, could see the pain on his face as he strained his weakened muscles to pull himself up, forcing his frozen joints to bend. Finally, with a groan that broke out beads of perspiration on his face, Cuza slid up onto the seat and slumped on his side, hanging over the armrest, panting and sweating. He still had to slide up a little farther and turn over fully onto his buttocks before he was completely in the chair, but the worst part was over.

"What do you want of me?" he said when he had caught his breath. Gone was that staid, overly polite manner that had typified his behavior since his arrival in the keep; gone, too, was the constant referral to them as "gentlemen." At the moment there appeared to be too much pain, too much exhaustion to cope with to allow him the luxury of sarcasm.

"What did you learn last night, Jew?" Kaempffer said.

Cuza heaved himself over onto his buttocks and leaned wearily against the back of the chair. He closed his eyes a moment, then reopened them, squinting at Kaempffer. He appeared to be almost blind without his glasses.

"Not much more. But there is evidence that the keep was built by a fifteenth-century boyar who was a contemporary of Vlad Tepes."

"Is that all? Two days of study and that is all?"

"*One* day, Major," the professor said, and Woermann sensed some of the old spark edging into the reply. "One day and two nights. That's not a long time when the reference materials are not in one's native tongue."

"I did not ask for excuses, Jew! I want results!"

"And have you got them?" The answer seemed important to Cuza.

Kaempffer straightened his shoulders and pulled himself up to his full height as he replied. "There have been two consecutive nights without a death, but I don't believe you have had anything to do with that." He rotated the upper half of his body and gave Woermann a haughty look. "It seems I have accomplished my mission here. But just for good measure, I'll stay one more night before continuing on my way."

"Ah! Another night of your company!" Woermann said, feeling his spirits soar. "Our cup runneth over!" He could put up with anything for one more night—even Kaempffer.

"I see no need for you to remain here even that long, Herr Major," Cuza said, visibly brightening. "I'm sure other countries have much greater need of your services."

Kaempffer's upper lip curled into a smile. "I shan't be leaving your beloved country, Jew. I go to Ploiesti from here."

"Ploiesti? Why Ploiesti?"

"You'll learn soon enough." He turned to Woermann. "I shall be ready to leave first thing tomorrow morning."

"I shall personally hold the gate open for you."

Kaempffer shot him an angry look, then strode from the room. Woermann watched him go. He sensed that nothing had been solved, that the killings had stopped of their own accord, and that they could begin again tonight, tomorrow night, or the next. It was only a brief hiatus they were enjoying, a moratorium; they had learned nothing, accomplished nothing. But he had not voiced his doubts to Kaempffer. He wanted the major out of the keep as much as the major wanted to be out. He would say nothing that might delay his departure.

"What did he mean about Ploiesti?" Cuza asked from behind him.

"You don't want to know." He looked from Cuza's ravaged, troubled face to the table. The silver cross his daughter had borrowed yesterday lay there next to the professor's spectacles.

"Please tell me, Captain. Why is that man going to Ploiesti?"

Woermann ignored the question. The professor had enough problems. Telling him that the Romanian equivalent of Auschwitz was in the offing would do him no good. "You may visit your daughter today if you wish. But you must go to her. She cannot come in."

He reached over and picked up the cross. "Did you find this useful in any way?"

Cuza glanced at the silver object for only an instant, then looked sharply away. "No. Not at all."

"Shall I take it back?"

"What? No—no! It still might come in handy. Leave it right there."

The sudden intensity in Cuza's voice struck Woermann. The man seemed subtly changed since yesterday, less sure of himself. Woermann could not put his finger on it, but it was there.

He tossed the cross onto the table and turned away. He had too many other things on his mind to worry about what was troubling the professor. If indeed Kaempffer were leaving, Woermann would have to decide what his next move would be. To stay or to go? One thing was certain: He now would have to arrange for shipment of the corpses back to Germany. They had waited long enough. At least with Kaempffer out of his hair he would be able to think straight again.

Preoccupied with his own concerns, he left the professor without saying good-bye. As he closed the door behind him, he noticed that Cuza had rolled his chair up to the table and fixed his spectacles over his eyes. He sat there holding the cross in his hand, staring at it.

At least he was alive.

Magda waited impatiently while one of the gate sentries went to get Papa. They had already kept her waiting a good hour before they opened the gates. She had rushed over at first light but they had ignored her pounding. A sleepless night had left her irritable and exhausted. But at least he was alive.

Her eyes roamed the courtyard. All quiet. There were piles of rubble strewn about the rear from the dismantling work, but no one was working now. All at breakfast, no doubt. What was taking so long? They should have let her go get him herself.

Against her will, her thoughts drifted. She thought of Glenn. He had saved her life last night. If he hadn't held her back when he had, she would have been shot to death by the German sentries. Luckily, he had been strong enough to hold her until she came to her senses. She kept remembering the feel of him as he had pressed her against him. No man had ever done that—had ever been close enough to do that. The memory of it was good. It had stirred something in her that refused to return to its former quiescent state.

She tried to concentrate on the keep and on Papa, forcing her thoughts away from Glenn . . .

. . . yet he had been kind to her, soothing her, convincing her to go back to her room and keep her vigil at the window. There was nothing to be done at the edge of the gorge. She had felt so utterly helpless, and he had understood. And when he had left her at her door, there had been a look in his eyes: sad, and something else. Guilt? But why should he feel guilty?

She noticed a movement within the entrance to the tower and stepped across the threshold. All the light and warmth of the morning drained away from her as she did—like stepping out of a warm house into a blustery winter night. She backed up immediately and felt the chill recede as soon as her feet were back on the causeway. There seemed to be a different set of rules at work within the keep. The soldiers didn't appear to notice; but she was an outsider. She could tell.

Papa and his wheelchair appeared, propelled from

behind by a reluctant sentry who seemed embarrassed by the task. As soon as she saw her father's face, Magda knew something was wrong. Something dreadful had happened last night. She wanted to run forward but knew they would not let her. The soldier pushed the wheelchair to the threshold and then let go, allowing it to roll to Magda unattended. Without letting it come to a complete halt, she swung around behind and pushed her father onto the causeway. When they were halfway across and he had yet to speak to her, even to say good morning, she felt she had to break the silence.

"What's wrong, Papa?"

"Nothing and everything."

"Did he come last night?"

"Wait until we're over by the inn and I'll tell you everything. We're too close here. Someone might overhear."

Anxious to learn what had disturbed him so, she hurriedly wheeled him around to the back of the inn where the morning sun shone brightly on the awakening grass and reflected off the white stucco of the building's wall.

Setting the chair facing north so the sun would warm him without shining in his eyes, she knelt and gripped both his gloved hands with her own. He didn't look well at all; worse than usual; and that caused her a deep pang of concern. He should be home in Bucharest. The strain here was too much for him.

"What happened, Papa? Tell me everything. He came again, didn't he?"

His voice was cold when he spoke, his eyes on the keep, not on her: "It's warm here. Not just warm for flesh and bone, but warm for the soul. A soul could wither away over there if it stayed too long."

"Papa—"

"His name is Molasar. He claims he was a boyar loyal to Vlad Tepes."

Magda gasped. "That would make him five hundred years old!"

"He's older, I'm sure, but he would not let me ask all my questions. He has his own interests, and primary among them is ridding the keep of all trespassers.''

''That includes you.''

''Not necessarily. He seems to think of me as a fellow Romanian—a 'Wallachian,' as he would say—and doesn't appear to be particularly bothered by my presence. It's the Germans—the thought of them in his keep has driven him almost insane with rage. You should have seen his face when he talked about them.''

''*His* keep?''

''Yes. He built it to protect himself after Vlad was killed.''

Hesitantly, Magda asked the all-important question: ''Is he a vampire?''

''Yes, I believe so,'' Papa said, looking at her and nodding. ''At least he is whatever the word 'vampire' is going to mean from now on. I doubt very much that many of the old traditions will hold true. We are going to have to redefine the word—no longer in terms of folklore, but in terms of Molasar.'' He closed his eyes. ''So *many* things will have to be redefined.''

With an effort, Magda pushed aside the primordial revulsion that welled up in her at the thought of vampires and tried to step back and analyze the situation objectively, allowing the long-trained, long-disciplined scholar within her to take over. ''A boyar under Vlad Tepes, was he? We should be able to trace that name.''

Papa was staring at the keep again. ''We may, and we may not. There were hundreds of boyars associated with Vlad throughout his three reigns, some friendly to him, some hostile . . . he impaled most of the hostile ones. You know what a chaotic, fragmented mess the records from that period are: If the Turks weren't invading Wallachia, someone else was. And even if we did find evidence of a Molasar who was a contemporary of Vlad's, what would it prove?''

''Nothing, I guess.'' She began filtering through her vast learning on the history of this region. A boyar, loyal to Vlad Tepes . . .

Magda had always thought of Vlad as a blood-red blot on Romanian history. As son of Vlad Dracul, the

Dragon, Prince Vlad was known as Vlad Dracula—Son of the Dragon. But he earned the name Vlad Tepes, which meant Vlad the Impaler, after his favorite method of disposing of prisoners of war, disloyal subjects, treacherous boyars, and virtually anyone else who displeased him. She remembered drawings she had seen depicting Vlad's St. Bartholomew's Day massacre at Amlas when 30,000 citizens of that unfortunate city were impaled on long wooden poles which were then thrust into the ground; the sufferers were left pierced through and suspended in the air until they died. There was occasionally a strategic purpose for impaling: In 1460 the sight of 20,000 impaled corpses of Turkish prisoners rotting in the sun outside Targoviste so horrified an invading army of Turks that they turned back and left Vlad's kingdom alone for a while.

"Imagine," she mused, "being loyal to Vlad Tepes."

"Don't forget that the world was very different then," Papa said. "Vlad was a product of his times; Molasar is a product of those same times. Vlad is still considered a national hero in these parts—he was Wallachia's scourge, but he was also its champion against the Turks."

"I'm sure this Molasar found nothing offensive in Vlad's behavior." Her stomach turned at the thought of all those men, women, and children impaled and left to die, slowly. "He probably found it entertaining."

"Who is to say? But you can see why one of the undead would gravitate to someone like Vlad: never a shortage of victims. He could slake his thirst on the dying and no one would ever guess that the victims had died from anything other than impalement. With no unexplained deaths around to raise questions, he could feast with no one suspecting his true nature."

"That does not make him any less a monster," she whispered.

"How can you judge him, Magda? One should be judged by one's peers. Who is Molasar's peer? Don't you realize what his existence means? Don't you see how many things it changes? How many cherished concepts assumed to be facts are going to wind up as so much garbage?''

Magda nodded slowly, the enormity of what they had found pressing on her with new weight. ''Yes. A form of immortality.''

''More than that! Much more! It's like a new form of life, a new mode of existence! No—that's not right. An *old* mode—but new as far as historical and scientific knowledge is concerned. And beyond the rational, look at the spiritual implications.'' His voice faltered. ''They're . . . devastating.''

''But how can it be true? *How?*'' Her mind still balked.

''I don't know. There's so much to learn and I had so little time with him. He feeds on the blood of the living—that seems self-evident from what I saw of the remains of the soldiers. They had all been exsanguinated through the neck. Last night I learned that he does *not* reflect in a mirror—that part of traditional vampire lore is true. But the fear of garlic and silver, those parts are false. He appears to be a creature of the night—he has struck only at night, and appeared only at night. However, I doubt very much that he spends the daylight hours asleep in anything so melodramatic as a coffin.''

''A vampire,'' Magda said softly, breathily. ''Sitting here with the sun overhead it seems so ludicrous, so—''

''Was it ludicrous two nights ago when he sucked the light from our room? Was his grip on your arm ludicrous?''

Magda rose to her feet, rubbing the spot above her right elbow, wondering if the marks were still there. She turned away from her father and pulled the sleeve up. Yes . . . still there . . . an oblong patch of gray-white, dead-looking skin. As she began to pull the sleeve back down, she noticed the mark begin to fade—the skin was returning to a pink healthy color under the direct light of the sun. As she watched, the mark disappeared completely.

Feeling suddenly weak, Magda staggered and had to clutch at the back of the wheelchair to steady herself.

Struggling to maintain a neutral expression, she turned back to Papa.

She needn't have bothered—he was again staring at the keep, unaware that she had turned away.

"He's somewhere in there now," he was saying, "waiting for tonight. I must speak to him again."

"Is he really a vampire, Papa? Could he really have been a boyar five hundred years ago? How do we know this isn't all a trick? Can he prove anything?"

"Prove?" he said, anger tingeing his voice. "Why should he prove anything? What does he care what you or I believe? He has his own concerns and he thinks I may be of use to him. 'An ally against the oulanders,' he said."

"You mustn't let him use you!"

"And why not? If he has need of an ally against the Germans who have invaded his keep, I just might go along with him—although I can't see what use I'd be. That's why I've told the Germans nothing."

Magda sensed that the Germans might not be the only ones; he was holding back from her as well. And that wasn't like him.

"Papa, you can't be serious!"

"We share a common enemy, Molasar and I, do we not?"

"For now, perhaps. But what about later?"

He ignored her question. "And don't forget that he can be of great use to me in my work. I must learn all about him. I must talk to him again. I must!" His gaze drifted back to the keep. "So much is changed now . . . have to rethink so many things . . ."

Magda tried but could not comprehend his mood.

"What's bothering you, Papa? For years you've said you thought there might be something to the vampire myth. You risked ridicule. Now that you're vindicated, you seem upset. You should be elated."

"Don't you understand anything? That was an intellectual exercise. It pleased me to play with the idea, to use it for self-stimulation and to stir up all those rock-bound minds in the History Department!"

"It was more than that and don't deny it."

"All right . . . but I never dreamed such a creature still existed. And I *never* thought I would actually meet him face to face!" His voice sank to a whisper. "And I in no way considered the possibility that he might really fear . . ."

Magda waited for him to finish, but he did not. He had turned inward, his right hand absently reaching into the breast pocket of his coat.

"Fear what, Papa? What does he fear?"

But he was rambling. His eyes had strayed again to the keep while his hand fumbled in his pocket. "He is patently evil, Magda. A parasite with supranormal powers feeding on human blood. Evil in the flesh. Evil made tangible. So if that is so, where then does good reside?"

"What are you talking about?" His disjointed thoughts were frightening her. "You're not making sense!"

He pulled his hand from his pocket and thrust something toward her face. "*This!* This is what I'm talking about!"

It was the silver cross she had borrowed from the captain. What did Papa mean? Why did he look that way, with his eyes so bright? "I don't understand."

"Molasar is terrified of it!"

What was wrong with Papa? "So? By tradition a vampire is supposed to—"

"*By tradition!* This is no tradition! This is real! And it *terrified* him! It nearly drove him from the room! *A cross!*"

Suddenly, Magda knew what had been so sorely troubling Papa all morning.

"*Ah!* Now you see, don't you," he said, nodding and smiling a small sad smile.

Poor Papa! To have spent all night with all that uncertainty. Magda's mind recoiled, refusing to accept the meaning of what she had been told.

"But you can't really mean—"

"We can't hide from a fact, Magda." He held up the

cross, watching the light glint off its worn, shiny surface. "It is part of our belief, *our* tradition, that Christ was not the Messiah. That the Messiah is yet to come. That Christ was merely a man and that his followers were generally goodhearted people but misguided. If that is true . . ." He seemed to be hypnotized by the cross. "If that is true . . . if Christ were just a man . . . why should a cross, the instrument of his death, so terrify a vampire? Why?"

"Papa, you're leaping to conclusions. There has to be more to this!"

"I'm sure there is. But think: It's been with us all along, in all the folk tales, the novels, and the moving pictures derived from those folk tales. Yet who of us has ever given it a second thought? The vampire fears the cross. Why? Because it's the symbol of human salvation. You see what that implies? It never even occurred to me until last night."

Can it be? she asked herself as Papa paused. *Can it really be?*

Papa spoke again, his voice dull and mechanical. "If a creature such as Molasar finds the symbol of Christianity so repulsive, the logical conclusion is that Christ must have been more than a man. If that is true, then our people, our traditions, our beliefs for two thousand years, have all been misguided. The Messiah did come and we failed to recognize him!"

"You can't say that! I refuse to believe it! There *has* to be another answer!"

"You weren't there. You didn't see the loathing on his face when I pulled out the cross. You didn't see how he shrank away in terror and cowered until I returned it to the box. *It has power over him!*"

It had to be true. It went against the most basic tenets of Magda's learning. But if Papa had said it, seen it, then it must be true. She yearned for something to say, something soothing, reassuring. But all that came out was a sad, simple, "Papa."

He smiled ruefully. "Don't worry, child. I'm not about to throw away my Torah and seek out a monastery. My faith goes deep. But this does give one pause, doesn't it? It does raise the question that we could be wrong . . . we all could have missed a boat that sailed twenty centuries ago."

He was trying to make light of it for her sake, but Magda knew he was being flayed alive in his mind.

She sank to the grass to think. And as she moved, she caught a flash of motion at the open window above. A glimpse of rust-colored hair. She clenched her fists as she realized that the window opened into Glenn's room. He must have heard everything.

Magda kept watch for the next few minutes, hoping to catch him eavesdropping, but saw nothing. She was about to give up when a voice startled her.

"Good morning!"

It was Glenn, rounding the southern corner of the inn, a small wooden ladderback chair in each hand.

"Who's there?" Papa asked, unable to twist around in his seat to see behind him.

"Someone I met yesterday. His name is Glenn. He has the room across the hall from me."

Glenn nodded cheerily to Magda as he walked around her and stood before Papa, towering over him like a giant. He wore woolen pants, climbing boots, and a loose-fitting shirt open at the neck. He set the two chairs down and thrust his hand toward her father.

"And good morning to you, sir. I've already met your daughter."

"Theodor Cuza," Papa replied hesitantly, with poorly veiled suspicion. He placed his gloved hand, stiff and gnarled, inside Glenn's. There followed a parody of a handshake, then Glenn indicated one of the chairs to Magda.

"Try this. The ground's still too damp to sit on."

Magda rose. "I'll stand, thank you," she said with all the haughtiness she could manage. She resented his eavesdropping, and she resented his intrusion into their company even more. "My father and I were just leaving anyway."

As Magda moved toward the back of the wheelchair,

Glenn laid a gentle hand on her arm.

"Please don't go yet. I awoke to the sound of two voices drifting through my window, discussing the keep and something about a vampire. Let's talk about it, shall we?" He smiled.

Magda found herself speechless, furious with the boldness of his intrusion and the casual presumption of his touching her. Yet she did not snatch her arm away. His touch made her tingle. It felt good.

Papa, however, had nothing to hold him back: "You must not mention one word of what you just heard to anyone! It could mean our lives!"

"Don't give yourself a moment's worry over that," Glenn said, his smile fading. "The Germans and I have nothing to say to each other." He looked back to Magda. "Won't you sit? I brought the chair for you."

She looked at her father. "Papa?"

He nodded resignedly. "I don't think we have too much choice."

Glenn's hand slipped away as Magda moved to seat herself, and she felt a small, unaccountable void within her. She watched him swing the other chair around and seat himself on it backwards, straddling the ladderback and resting his elbows on the top rung.

"Magda told me last night about the vampire in the keep," he said, "but I'm not sure I caught the name he gave you."

"Molasar," Papa said.

"Molasar," Glenn said slowly, rolling the name over on his tongue, his expression puzzled. "Mo . . . la . . . sar." Then he brightened, as if he had solved a puzzle. "Yes—Molasar. An odd name, don't you think?"

"Unfamiliar," Papa said, "but not so odd."

"And that," Glenn, said, gesturing to the cross still clutched in the twisted fingers. "Did I overhear you say that Molasar feared it?"

"Yes."

Magda noted that Papa was volunteering no information.

"You're a Jew, aren't you, Professor?"

A nod.

"Is it customary for Jews to carry crosses around?"

"My daughter borrowed it for me—a tool in an experiment."

Glenn turned to her. "Where did you get it?"

"From one of the officers at the keep." Where was all this leading?

"It was his own?"

"No. He said it came from one of the dead soldiers." She began to grasp the thread of deduction he seemed to be following.

"Strange," Glenn said, returning his attention to Papa, "that this cross did not save the soldier who first possessed it. One would think that a creature who feared the cross would pass up such a victim and search for another, one carrying no protective—what shall we call it?—charm."

"Perhaps the cross was stuffed inside his shirt," Papa said. "Or in his pocket. Or even back in his room."

Glenn smiled. "Perhaps. Perhaps."

"We didn't think of that, Papa," Magda said, eager to reinforce any idea that might bolster his sagging spirits.

"Question everything," Glenn said. "Always question everything. I should not have to remind a scholar of that."

"How do you know I'm a scholar?" Papa snapped, a spark of the old fire in his eyes. "Unless my daughter told you."

"Iuliu told me. But there's something else you've overlooked, and it's so obvious you're both going to feel foolish when I tell you."

"Make us feel foolish, then," Magda told him. *Please!*

"All right: Why would a vampire so afraid of the cross dwell in a structure whose walls are studded with them? Can you explain that?"

Magda stared at her father and found him staring back at her.

"You know," Papa said, smiling sheepishly. "I've

been in the keep so often, and I've puzzled over it for so long, I no longer even see the crosses!"

"That's understandable. I've been through there a few times myself, and after a while they do seem to blend in. But the question remains: Why does a being who finds the cross repulsive surround himself with countless crosses?" He rose and easily swung the chair onto his shoulder. "And now I think I'll go get some breakfast from Lidia and leave you two to figure out an answer. If there is one."

"But what's your interest in this?" Papa asked. "Why are you here?"

"Just a traveler," Glenn said. "I like this area and visit regularly."

"You seem to be more than a little interested in the keep. And quite knowledgeable about it."

Glenn shrugged. "I'm sure you know far more than I do."

"I wish I knew how to keep my father from going back over there tonight," Magda said.

"I must go back, my dear. I *must* face Molasar again."

Magda rubbed her hands together. They had gone cold at the thought of Papa's returning to the keep. "I just don't want them to find you with your throat torn open like the others."

"There are worse things that can happen to a man," Glenn said.

Struck by the change in his tone, Magda looked up and found all the sunniness and lightness gone from his face. He was staring at Papa. The tableau held for only a few seconds, then he smiled again.

"Breakfast awaits. I'm sure I'll see you again during our respective stays. But one more thing before I go."

He stepped around to the rear of the wheelchair and turned it in a 180-degree arc with his free hand.

"What are you doing?" Papa cried. Magda leaped to her feet.

"Just offering you a change of scenery, Professor. The keep is, after all, such a gloomy place. This is much too beautiful a day to dwell on it."

He pointed to the floor of the pass. "Look south and east instead of north. For all its severity, this is a most beautiful part of the world. See how the grass is greening up, how the wild flowers are starting to bloom in the crags. Forget the keep for a while."

For a moment he caught and held Magda's eyes with his own, then he was gone, turning the corner, the chair balanced on his shoulder.

"A strange sort, that one," she heard Papa say, a touch of a laugh in his voice.

"Yes. He most certainly is." But though she found Glenn strange, Magda felt she owed him a debt of gratitude. For reasons known only to him, he had intruded on their conversation and made it his own, lifting Papa's spirits from their lowest ebb, taking Papa's most painful doubts and casting doubt in turn upon them. He had handled it deftly and with telling effect. But why? What did he care about the inner torment of a crippled old Jew from Bucharest?

"He does raise some good points, though," Papa went on. "Some excellent points. How could they not have occurred to me?"

"Nor to me?"

"Of course," his tone was softly defensive, "he's not fresh from a personal encounter with a creature considered until now a mere figment of a gruesome imagination. It's easy for him to be more objective. By the way, how did you meet him?"

"Last night, when I was out by the edge of the gorge keeping watch on your window—"

"You shouldn't fret over me so! You forget that I helped raise *you*, not the other way around."

Magda ignored the interruption. "—he rode up on horseback, looking like he intended to charge right into the keep. But when he saw the lights and the Germans, he stopped."

Papa seemed to consider this briefly, then switched topics. "Speaking of Germans, I'd better be getting back before they come looking for me. I'd prefer to re-enter the keep on my own rather than at gunpoint."

"Isn't there a way we could—"

"Escape? Of course! You'll just wheel me down the ledge road, all the way to Campina! Or perhaps you could help me onto the back of a horse—that would certainly shorten the trip!" His tone grew more acid as he spoke. "Or best of all, why don't we go and ask that SS major for a loan of one of his lorries—just for an afternoon drive, we'll tell him! I'm sure he'll agree."

"There's no need to speak to me that way," she said, stung by his sarcasm.

"And there's no need for you to torture yourself with any hope of escape for the two of us! Those Germans aren't fools. They know *I* can't escape, and they don't think you'll leave without me. Although I want you to. At least *one* of us would be safe then."

"Even if you *could* get away, you'd return to the keep! Isn't that right, Papa?" Magda said. She was beginning to understand his attitude. "You *want* to go back there."

He would not meet her eyes. "We are trapped here, and I feel I must use the opportunity of a lifetime. I would be a traitor to my whole life's work if I let it slip away!"

"Even if a plane landed in the pass right now and the pilot offered to fly us to freedom, you wouldn't go, would you!"

"I *must* see him again, Magda! I must ask him about all those crosses on the walls! How he came to be what he is! And most of all, I must find out why he fears the cross. If I don't, I—I'll go mad!"

Neither spoke for the next few moments. Long moments. But Magda sensed more than silence between them. A widening gap. She felt Papa drawing away, drawing into himself, shutting her out. That had never happened before. They had always been able to discuss things. Now he seemed to want no discussion. He wanted only to get back to Molasar.

"Take me back," was all he said as the silence went on and on, becoming unbearable.

"Stay a little longer. You've been in the keep too much. I think it's affecting you."

"I'm perfectly fine, Magda. And I'll decide when I've been in the keep too long. Now, are you going to wheel me back or do I have to sit here and wait until the Nazis come and get me?"

Biting her lip in anger and dismay, Magda moved behind the chair and turned it toward the keep.

TWENTY

He seated himself a few feet back from the window where he could hear the rest of the conversation below yet remain out of sight should Magda chance to look up again. He had been careless earlier. In his eagerness to hear, he had leaned on the sill. Magda's unexpected upward glance had caught him. At that point he had decided that a frontal assault was in order and had gone downstairs to join them.

Now all talk seemed to have died. As he heard the creaky wheels of the professor's chair start to turn, he leaned forward and watched the pair move off, Magda pushing from behind, appearing calm despite the turmoil he knew to be raging within her. He poked his head out the window for one last look as she rounded the corner and passed from view.

On impulse, he dashed to his door and stepped out

into the empty hall; three long strides took him diagonally across to Magda's room. Her door opened at his touch and he went directly to the window. She was on the path to the causeway, pushing her father ahead of her.

He enjoyed watching her.

She had interested him from their first meeting on the gorge rim when she had faced him with such outward calm, yet all the while clutching a heavy stone in her hand. And later, when she had stood up to him in the foyer of the inn, refusing to give up her room, and he was seeing her then for the first time in the light with her eyes flashing, he had known that some of his defenses were softening. Deep-brown doe eyes, high-colored cheeks . . . he liked the way she looked, and she was lovely when she smiled. She had done that only once in his presence, crinkling her eyes at the corners and revealing white, even teeth. And her hair . . . the little wisps he had seen of it were a glossy brown . . . she would be striking with her hair down instead of hidden away.

But the attraction was more than physical. She was made of good stuff, that Magda. He watched her take her father to the gate and give him over to the guard there. The gate closed and she was left alone on the far end of the causeway. As she turned and walked back, he retreated to the middle of her room so he wouldn't be visible at the window. He watched her from there.

Look at her! How she walks away from the keep! She knows every pair of eyes on that wall is upon her, that at this very moment she is being stripped and ravished in half a dozen minds. Yet she walks with her shoulders back, her gait neither hurried nor dalliant. Perfectly composed, as if she's just made a routine delivery and is on her way to the next. And all the while she's cringing inside!

He shook his head in silent admiration. He had long ago learned to immerse himself in a sheath of impenetrable calm. It was a mechanism that kept him insulated, kept him one step removed from too intimate contact, reducing his chances for impulsive behavior. It allowed him a clear, serene, dispassionate view of everything and everyone around him, even when all was in chaos.

Magda, he realized, was one of those rare people with the power to penetrate his sheath, to cause turbulence in his calm. He felt attracted to her, and she had his respect—something he rarely awarded to anyone.

But he could not afford to get involved now. He must maintain his distance. Yet . . . he had been without a woman for so long, and she was awakening feelings he had thought gone forever. It was good to feel them again. She had slipped past his guard, and he sensed he was slipping past hers. It would be nice to—

No! You can't get involved. You can't afford to care. Not now. Of all times, not now! Only a fool—

And yet . . .

He sighed. Better to lock up his feelings again before things got out of hand. Otherwise, the result could be disastrous. For both of them.

She was almost to the inn. He left the room, carefully closing the door behind him, and returned to his own. He dropped onto the bed and lay with his hands behind his head, waiting for her tread on the stair. But it did not come.

To Magda's surprise, she found that the closer she got to the inn, the less she thought about Papa and the more she thought about Glenn. Guilt tugged at her. She had left her crippled father alone, surrounded by Nazis, to face one of the undead tonight, and her thoughts turned to a stranger. Strolling around to the rear of the inn, she experienced a light feeling in her chest and a quickening of her pulse at the thought of him.

Lack of food, she told herself. Should have had something to eat this morning.

There was no one there. The ladderback chair Glenn had brought for her sat empty and alone in the sunlight. She glanced up to his window. No one there, either.

Magda picked up the chair and carried it around to the front, telling herself it wasn't disappointment she felt, only hunger.

She remembered Glenn saying he intended to have breakfast. Perhaps he was still inside. She quickened her pace. Yes, she was hungry.

She stepped in and saw Iuliu sitting in the dining alcove to her right. He had sliced a large wedge from a wheel of cheese and was sipping some goat's milk. He seemed to eat at least six times a day.

He was alone.

"*Domnisoara* Cuza!" he called. "Would you like some cheese?"

Magda nodded and sat down. She now wasn't as hungry as she had thought, but she did need some food to keep going. Besides, there were a few questions she wanted to ask Iuliu.

"Your new guest," she said casually, taking a slice of white cheese off the flat of the knife blade, "he must have taken breakfast to his room."

Iuliu's brow furrowed. "Breakfast? He didn't have any breakfast here. But many travelers bring their own food with them."

Magda frowned. Why had he said he was going to see Lidia about breakfast? An excuse to get away?

"Tell me, Iuliu—you seemed to have calmed down since last night. What upset you so about this Glenn when he arrived?"

"It was nothing."

"Iuliu, you were trembling! I'd like to know why—especially since my room is across the hall from his. I deserve to know if you think he's dangerous."

The innkeeper concentrated hard on slicing the cheese. "You will think me a fool."

"No, I won't."

"Very well." He put the knife down and spoke in a

conspiratorial tone. "When I was a boy my father ran
the inn and, like me, paid the workers in the keep. There
came a time when some of the gold that had been
delivered was missing—stolen, my father said—and he
could not pay the keep workers their full amount. The
same thing happened after the next delivery; some of the
money disappeared. Then one night a stranger came and
began beating my father, punching him, hurling him
about the room as if he were made of straw, telling him
to find the money. 'Find the money! Find the
money!' " He puffed out his already ample cheeks.
"My father, I am ashamed to say, found the money. He
had taken some and hidden it. The stranger was furious.
Never have I seen such wrath in a man. He began
beating and kicking my father again, leaving him with
two broken arms."

"But what does this have to do—"

"You must understand," Iuliu said, leaning forward
and lowering his voice even further, "that my father
was an honest man and that the turn of the century was
a terrible time for this region. He only kept a little of the
gold as a means of being certain that we would eat
during the coming winter. He would have paid it back
when times were better. It was the only dishonest thing
he had done in an otherwise good and upright—"

"Iuliu!" Magda said, finally halting the flow of
words. "What has this to do with the man upstairs?"

"They look the *same*, *Domnisoara*. I was only ten
years old at the time, but I saw the man who beat my
father. I will never forget him. He had red hair and
looked so very much like this man. But," he laughed
softly, "the man who beat my father was perhaps in his
early thirties, just like this man, and that was forty years
ago. They couldn't be the same. But in the candlelight
last night, I—I thought he had come to beat me, too."

Magda raised her eyebrows questioningly, and he
hurried to explain.

"Not that there's any gold missing now, of course.
It's just that the workers have not been allowed to enter

the keep to do their work and I've been paying them anyway. Never let it be said that I kept any of the gold for myself. Never!''

"Of course not, Iuliu." She rose, taking another slice of cheese with her. "I think I'll go upstairs and rest awhile."

He smiled and nodded. "Supper will be at six."

Magda climbed the stairs quickly, but found herself slowing as she passed Glenn's door, her eyes drawing her head to the right and lingering there. She wondered what he was doing in there, or if he was there at all.

Her room was stuffy, so she left the door open to allow the breeze from the window to pass through. The porcelain water pitcher on her dresser had been filled. She poured some of the cool water into the bowl beside it and splashed her face. She was exhausted but knew sleep was impossible . . . too many thoughts swirling in her head to allow her to rest just yet.

A high pitched chorus of cheeps drew her to the window. Amid the budding branches of the tree that grew next to the north wall of the inn was a bird's nest. She could see four tiny chicks, their heads all eyes and gaping mouth, straining their scrawny necks upward for a piece of whatever the mother bird was feeding them. Magda knew nothing about birds. This one was gray with black markings along its wings. Had she been home in Bucharest she might have looked it up. But with all that had been happening, she found she couldn't care less.

Tense, restless, she wandered about the tiny room. She checked the flashlight she had brought with her. It still worked. Good. She would need it tonight. On her way back from the keep, she had reached a decision.

Her eyes fell on the mandolin propped in the corner by the window. She picked it up, seated herself on the bed and began to play. Tentatively at first, adjusting the tuning as she plucked out a simple melody, then with greater ease and fluidity as she relaxed into the instrument, segueing from one folk tune to another. As with many a proficient amateur, she achieved a form of transport with her instrument, fixing her eyes on a point in space, her hands playing by touch, humming inwardly as she jumped from song to song. Tensions eased away, replaced by an inner tranquillity. She played on, unaware of time.

A hint of movement at her open door jarred her back to reality. It was Glenn.

"You're very good," he said from the doorway.

She was glad it was he, glad he was smiling at her, and glad he had found pleasure in her playing.

She smiled shyly. "Not so good. I've gotten careless."

"Maybe. But the range of your repertoire is wonderful. I know of only one other person who can play so many songs with such accuracy."

"Who?"

"Me."

There it was again: smugness. Or was he just teasing her? Magda decided to call his bluff. She held out the mandolin.

"Prove it."

Grinning, Glenn stepped into the room, pulled the three-legged stool over to the bed, seated himself, and reached for the mandolin. After making a show of "properly" tuning the instrument, he began to play. Magda listened in awe. For such a big man with such large hands, his touch on the mandolin was astonishingly delicate. He was obviously showing off, playing many of the same tunes but in a more intricate style.

She studied him. She liked the way his blue shirt stretched across the width of his shoulders. His sleeves were rolled back to the elbows, and she watched the play of the muscles and tendons under the skin of his forearms as he worked the mandolin. There were scars on those arms, crisscrossing the wrists and trailing up to the point where the shirt hid the rest of him. She wanted to ask him about those scars but decided it was too personal a question.

However, she could certainly question him about how he played some of the songs.

"You played the last one wrong," she told him.

"Which one?"

"I call it 'The Bricklayer's Lady.' I know the lyrics vary from place to place, but the melody is always the same."

"Not always," Glenn said. "This was how it was originally played."

"How can you be so sure?" That irritating smugness again.

"Because the village *lauter* who taught me was ancient when we met, and she's now been dead many years."

"What village?" Magda felt indignation touch her. This was her area of expertise. Who was he to correct her?

"Kranich—near Suceava."

"Oh . . . Moldavian. That might explain the difference." She glanced up and caught him staring at her.

"Lonely without your father?"

Magda thought about that. She had missed Papa sorely at first and had felt at a loss as to what to do with herself without him. But at the moment she was very content to be sitting here with Glenn, listening to him play, and yes, even arguing with him. She should never have allowed him in her room, even with the door open, but he made her feel safe. And she liked his looks, especially his blue eyes, even though he seemed to be a master at preventing her from reading much in them.

"Yes," she said. "And no."

He laughed. "A straightforward answer—two of them!"

A silence grew between them, and Magda became aware that Glenn was very much a man, a long-boned man with flesh packed tightly to those bones. There was an aura of *maleness* about him that she had never noticed in anyone else. It had escaped her last night and this morning, but here in this tiny room it filled all the empty spaces. It caressed her, making her feel strange and special. A primitive sensation. She had heard of animal magnetism . . . was that what she was experiencing now in his presence? Or was it just that he seemed so alive? He fairly bristled with vitality.

"You have a husband?" he asked, his gaze resting on the gold band on her right ring finger—her mother's wedding band.

"No."

"A lover then?"

"Of course not."

"Why not?"

"Because . . ." Magda hesitated. She didn't dare tell him that except in her dreams she had given up on the possibility of life with a man. All the good men she had met in the past few years were married, and the unmarried ones would remain so for reasons of their own or because no self-respecting woman would have them. But certainly all the men she had ever met were stooped and pallid things compared with the one who sat across from her now. "Because I'm beyond the age when that sort of thing has any importance!" she said finally.

"You're a mere babe!"

"And you? Are you married?"

"Not at the moment."

"Have you been?"

"Many times."

"Play another song!" Magda said in exasperation. Glenn seemed to prefer teasing to giving her straight answers.

But after a while the playing stopped and the talking began. Their conversation ranged over a wide array of topics, but always as they related to her. Magda found herself talking about everything that interested her, starting with music and with the Gypsies and Romanian rural folk who were the source of the music she loved, and on to her hopes and dreams and opinions. The words trickled out fitfully at first, but swelled to a steady stream as Glenn encouraged her to go on. For one of the few times in her life, Magda was doing all the talking. And Glenn *listened.* He seemed genuinely interested in whatever she had to say, unlike so many other men who would listen only as far as the first opportunity to turn the conversation to themselves. Glenn kept turning the talk away from himself and back toward her.

Hours slipped by, until shadows began darkening the inn. Magda yawned.

"Excuse me," she said, "I think I'm boring myself. Enough of me. What about you? Where are you from?"

Glenn shrugged. "I grew up all over western Europe, but I guess you could say I'm British."

"You speak Romanian exceptionally well—almost like a native."

"I've visited often, even lived with some Romanian families here and there."

"But as a British subject, aren't you taking a chance being in Romania? Especially with the Nazis so close?"

Glenn hesitated. "Actually, I have no citizenship anywhere. I have papers from various countries proclaiming my citizenship, but I have no country. In these mountains, one doesn't need a country."

A man without a country? Magda had never heard of such a thing. To whom did he owe allegiance? "Be careful. There aren't too many red-haired Romanians."

"True." He smiled and ran a hand through his hair. "But the Germans are in the keep and the Iron Guard stays out of the mountains if it knows what's good for it. I'll keep to myself while I'm here, and I shouldn't be here that long."

Magda felt a stab of disappointment—she liked having him around.

"How long?" She felt she had asked the question too quickly, but it couldn't be helped. She wanted to know.

"Long enough for a last visit before Germany and Romania declare war on Russia."

"That's not—!"

"It's inevitable. And soon." He rose from the stool.

"Where are you going?"

"I'm going to let you rest. You need it."

Glenn leaned forward and pressed the mandolin back into her hands. For a moment their fingers touched and

Magda felt a sensation like an electric shock, jolting her, making her tingle all over. But she did not pull her hand away . . . Oh, no . . . because that would make the feeling stop, would halt the delicious warmth spreading throughout her body and down along her legs.

She could see that Glenn felt it, too, in his own way.

Then he broke contact and retreated to the door. The feeling ebbed, leaving her a trifle weak. Magda wanted to stop Glenn, to grasp his hand and tell him to stay. But she could not imagine herself doing such a thing and was shocked that she even wanted to. Uncertainty held her back, too. The emotions and sensations boiling within were new to her. How would she control them?

As the door closed behind him, she felt the warmth fade away, replaced by a hollow space deep within her. She sat quietly for a few moments, and then told herself that it was probably all for the best that he had left her alone now. She needed sleep; she needed to be rested and fully alert later on.

For she had decided that Papa would not face Molasar alone tonight.

TWENTY-ONE

Captain Woermann sat alone in his room. He had watched the shadows grow long across the keep until the sun was out of sight. His uneasiness had grown with them. The shadows shouldn't have disturbed him. After all, for two nights in a row there had been no deaths, and he saw no reason why tonight should be different. Yet there was this sense of foreboding.

The morale of the men had improved immensely. They had begun to act and feel like victors again. He could see it in their eyes, in their faces. They had been threatened, a few had died, but they had persisted and were still in command of the keep. With the girl out of sight, and with none of their fellows newly dead, there was a tacit truce between the men in gray uniforms and those in black. They didn't mingle, but there was a new sense of comradeship—they had all triumphed. Woermann found himself incapable of sharing their optimism.

He looked over to his painting. All desire to do further work on it had fled, and he had no wish to start another. He did not even have enough ambition to get out his pigments and blot out the shadow of the hanging corpse. His attention centered now on the shadow. Every time he looked it appeared more distinct. The shape looked darker today, and the head seemed to have more definition. He shook himself and looked away. Nonsense.

No . . . not quite nonsense. There was still something foul afoot in the keep. There had been no deaths for two nights, but the keep had not changed. The evil had not gone away, it was merely . . . resting. Resting? Was that the right word? Not really. Holding back was better. It certainly had not gone away. The walls still pressed in on him; the air continued to feel heavy and laden with menace. The men could slap one another on the back and talk one another out of it. But Woermann could not. He had only to look at his tainted painting and he knew with leaden certainty that there had been no real end to the killings, merely a pause, one that might last for days or might end tonight. Nothing had been overcome or driven out. Death was still here, waiting, ready to strike again when the occasion suited it.

He straightened his shoulders to ward off a growing chill. Something was going to happen soon. He could feel it in the core of his spine.

One more night . . . just give me one more night.

If death held off until tomorrow morning, Kaempffer would depart for Ploiesti. After that, Woermann could again make his own rules—without the SS. And he could move his men out of the keep immediately should trouble start again.

Kaempffer . . . he wondered what dear sweet Erich was doing. He hadn't seen him all afternoon.

SS-Sturmbannfuhrer Kaempffer sat hunched over the Ploiesti rail map spread out before him on his cot. Daylight was fading fast and his eyes ached from straining at the tiny interconnecting lines. Better to quit now than try to continue under one of the harsh electric bulbs.

Straightening, he rubbed his eyes with a thumb and forefinger. At least the day had not been a total loss. The new map of the rail nexus had yielded some useful information. He would be starting from scratch with the Romanians. Everything in the construction of the camp would be left to him, even choice of the site. He thought he had found a good one. There was a row of old warehouses on the eastern edge of the nexus. If they were not in use or not being put to any important use, they could act as the seed of the Ploiesti camp. Wire fences could be strung within a matter of days, and then the Iron Guard could get about the business of collecting Jews.

Kaempffer wanted to get started. He would let the Iron Guard gather up the first "guests" in whatever haphazard fashion they wished while he oversaw the design of the physical plant. Once that was under way he would devote more of his time to teaching the Romanians the SS's proven methods of corraling undesirables.

Folding the map, he found his thoughts turning to the immense profits to be earned from the camp, and of ways to keep most of those profits for himself. Get the prisoners' rings, watches, and jewelry immediately; gold teeth and the women's hair could be taken later. Commandants in Germany and in Poland were all becoming rich. Kaempffer saw no reason why he should be an exception.

And there would be more. In the near future, after he got the camp running like a well-oiled machine, there were certain to be opportunities to rent out some of the healthier inmates to Romanian industry. A growing practice at other camps, and very profitable. He might well be able to hire out large numbers of inmates,

especially with Operation Barbarossa soon to be
launched. The Romanian Army would be invading
Russia along with the Wehrmacht, draining off much of
the country's able-bodied work force. Yes, the factories
would be anxious for laborers. Their pay, of course,
would go to the camp commandant.

He knew the tricks. Hoess had taught him well at
Auschwitz. It was not often that a man was given an opportunity to serve his country, to improve the genetic
balance of the human race, and to enrich himself all at
once. He was a lucky man . . .

Except for this damnable keep. At least the problem
here seemed to be under control. If things held as they
were, he could leave tomorrow morning and report success back to Berlin. The report would look good:

He had arrived and had lost two men the first night
before he had been able to set up counteroffensive action; after that, there were no further killings. (He
would be vague as to how he had stopped the killings
but crystal clear as to whom the credit belonged.) After
three nights with no further deaths, he departed.
Mission accomplished. If the killings resumed after his
departure, it would be the fault of that bungler, Woermann. By then Kaempffer would be too involved with
setting up Camp Ploiesti. They would have to send
someone else to bail Woermann out.

Lidia's tap on the door to announce dinner startled
Magda out of her sleep. A few splashes of water from
the basin onto her face and she was fully awake. But not
hungry. Her stomach was so knotted she knew it would
be impossible to get down a bite of food.

She stood at the window. There were still traces of
daylight left in the sky, but none down in the pass.
Night had come to the keep, yet the bright courtyard
lights had not been turned on. There were windows il-

luminated here and there in the walls like eyes in the
dark, Papa's among them, but it was not yet lit up like
—what was it Glenn had called it that first night?—"a
cheap tourist attraction."

She wondered if Glenn was downstairs at the dinner
table now. Was he thinking of her? Waiting for her,
perhaps? Or was he intent solely on his meal? No
matter. She could not under any circumstances let him
see her. One look into her eyes and he would know what
she intended and might try to stop her.

Magda tried to concentrate on the keep. Why was she
thinking of Glenn? He obviously could take care of
himself. She should be thinking about Papa and her
mission tonight, not of Glenn.

And yet her thoughts persisted in turning to Glenn.
She had even dreamed of him during her nap. Details
were fuzzy now, but the impressions that lingered were
all warm and somehow erotic. What was happening to
her? She had never reacted to anyone this way, ever.
There had been times in her late teens when young men
had courted her. She had been flattered and briefly
charmed by two or three of them, but nothing more.
And even Mihail . . . they had been close, but she had
never desired him.

That was it: Magda realized with a shock that she
desired Glenn, wanted him near her, making her feel—

This was absurd! She was acting like a simple-minded
farm girl in heat upon meeting her first smooth-talking
man from the big city. No, she could not allow herself
to become involved with Glenn or with any man. Not
while Papa could not fend for himself. And especially
not while he was locked up in the keep with the Germans
and that *thing*. Papa came first. He had no one else, and
she would never desert him.

Ah, but Glenn . . . if only there were more men like
him. He made her feel important, as if being who she
was, was good, something to take pride in. She could
talk to him and not feel like the book-bound misfit
others seemed to see.

It was past ten o'clock when Magda left the inn. From

her window she had watched Glenn slink down the path and take up a position in the brush at the edge of the gorge. After waiting to make sure he had settled himself there, she tied her hair up in its kerchief, snatched her flashlight from the bureau, and left her room. She passed no one on her way down the stairs, through the foyer, and into the darkness outside.

Magda did not head for the causeway. Instead, she crossed the path and walked toward the towering shadows of the mountains, feeling her way in the dark. She could not use the flashlight until she was inside the keep; turning it on out here or in the gorge would risk giving her presence away to one of the sentries on the wall. She lifted her sweater and tucked the flashlight into the waistband of her skirt, feeling the cold of its metal against her skin.

She knew exactly where she was going. At the juncture of the gorge and the western wall of the pass was a large wedge-shaped pile of dirt, shale, and rocky rubble that had been sliding down the mountain and collecting there for ages. Its slope was gentle and the footing good—she had learned this years ago when she had embarked on her first trip into the gorge in search of the nonexistent cornerstone. She had made the climb numerous times since then, but always in sunlight. Tonight she would be hampered by darkness and by fog. There would not even be moonlight since the moon was not due to rise until after midnight. This was going to be risky, but Magda felt certain she could do it.

She reached the mountain wall where the gorge came to an abrupt halt. The wedge of rubble formed a half-cone, its base on the floor of the fog-filled gorge some sixty feet below and its point ending two paces from the site where she stood.

Setting her jaw and breathing deeply once, twice, Magda began the descent. She moved slowly, cautiously, testing each foothold before putting her full weight on it, holding on to the larger rocks for balance. She was in no great hurry. There was plenty of time. Caution was the key—caution and silence. One wrong move and she would begin to slide. The jagged rocks along the way would tear her flesh to shreds by the time she reached bottom. And even if she survived the fall, the rock slide she caused would alert the sentries on the wall. She had to be careful.

She made steady progress, all the while shutting out the thought that Molasar might well be waiting for her in the gorge below. There was one bad moment; it came after she had progressed below the gently undulating surface of the fog. For a moment she could not find any footing. She clung to a slab of rock with both legs dangling below her in a misty chasm, unable to make contact with anything. It was as if the whole world had fallen away, leaving her hanging from this jutting stone, alone, forever. But she fought off her panic and inched to her left until her questing feet found a bit of purchase.

The rest of the descent was easier. She reached the base of the wedge unharmed. More difficult terrain lay ahead, however. The floor of the gorge was a never-never land, a realm of jagged rocks and rank grasses, steeped in cloying fog that swirled around her as she moved, clutching at her with wispy tentacles. She moved slowly and with utmost care. The rocks were slick and treacherous, capable of causing a bone-breaking fall at her first unwary step. She was all but blind in the fog, but she kept moving. After an eternity, she passed her first landmark: a dim, dark strip of shadow overhead. She was under the causeway. The base of the tower would be ahead and to the left.

She knew she was almost there when her left foot suddenly sank ankle deep in icy water. She quickly drew back to remove her shoes, her heavy stockings, and to hike her skirt above her knees. Then she steeled herself. Teeth clenched, Magda waded ahead into the water, her breath escaping in a rush as cold spiked into her feet and lower legs, driving nails of pain into her marrow. Yet she kept her pace slow, even, determinedly suppressing the urge to splash over to the warmth and dryness of the far bank. Rushing would mean noise, and noise meant discovery.

She had walked a good dozen feet beyond the water's far edge before she realized she was out of it. Her feet were numb. Shivering, she sat on a rock and massaged her toes until sensation returned; then she stepped into her stockings and shoes again.

A few more steps took her to the outcropping of granite that formed the base on which the keep rested. Its rough surface was easy to follow to the spot where the leading edge of the tower stretched down to the floor of the gorge. There she felt the flat surfaces and right angles of man-made block begin.

She felt around until she found the oversized block she sought, and pushed. With a sigh and a barely audible scrape, the slab swung inward. A dark rectangle awaited her like a gaping mouth. Magda didn't let herself hesitate. Pulling the flashlight from her waistband, she stepped through.

The sensation of evil struck her like a blow as she entered, breaking her out in beads of icy perspiration, making her want to leap headlong back through the opening and into the fog. It was far worse than when she and Papa had passed through the gate Tuesday night, and worse, too, than this morning when she had stepped across the threshold at the gate. Had she become more sensitive to it, or had the evil grown stronger?

T

He drifted slowly, languidly, aimlessly, through the deepest recesses of the cavern that formed the keep's subcellar, moving from shadow to shadow, a part of the darkness, human in form but long drained of the essentials of humanness.

He stopped, sensing a new life that had not been present a moment ago. Someone had entered the keep. After a moment's concentration, he recognized the presence of the crippled one's daughter, the one he had touched two nights ago, the one so ripe with strength and goodness that his ever insatiable hunger quickened to a ravening need. He had been furious when the Germans had banished her from the keep.

Now she was back.

He began to drift again through the darkness, but his drifting was no longer languid, no longer aimless.

T

Magda stood in the stygian gloom, shaking and indecisive. Mold spores and dust motes, disturbed by her entry, irritated her throat and nose, choking her. She had to get out. This was a fool's errand. What could she possibly do to help Papa against one of the undead? What had she actually hoped to accomplish by coming here? Silly heroics like this got people killed! Who did she think she was, anyway? What made her think—

Stop!

A mental scream halted her terrified thoughts. She was thinking like a defeatist. This wasn't her way. She *could* do something for Papa! She did not know what, exactly, but at the very least she would be at his side to give moral support. She would go on.

Her original intention had been to close the hinged slab behind her. But she could not bring herself to do it. There would be comfort of a sort, scant comfort, in knowing her escape route lay open behind her.

She thought it safe to use the flashlight now, so she flicked it on. The beam struggled against the darkness, revealing the lower end of a long stone stairway that wound a spiral path up the inner surface of the tower's base. She flashed the beam upward but the light was completely swallowed by the darkness above.

She had no choice but to climb.

After her shaky descent and her trek through the fog-enshrouded gorge, stairs—even steep ones—were a luxury. She played the flashlight back and forth before her as she moved, assuring herself that each step was intact before she entrusted her weight to it. All was silence in the huge, dark cylinder of stone except for the echo of her footfalls and remained so until she had completed two of the three circuits that made up the stairway.

Then from off to her right she felt a draft. And heard a strange noise.

She stood motionless, frozen in the flow of cold air, listening to a soft, far-away scraping. It was irregular in pitch and in rhythm, but persistent. She quickly flashed the light to her right and saw a narrow opening almost six feet high in the stone. She had seen it there on her previous explorations but had never paid any attention to it. There had never been a draft flowing through it. Nor had she ever heard any noise within.

Aiming the beam through the hole, Magda peered into the darkness, hoping and at the same time not hoping to find the source of the scraping.

As long as it's not rats. Please, God, let there be no rats in there.

Inside she saw nothing but an empty expanse of dirt floor. The scraping seemed to come from deep within the cavity. Far off to the right, perhaps fifty feet away, she noticed a dim glow. Dousing the flashlight confirmed it: There was light back there, faint, coming from above. Magda squinted in the darkness and dimly perceived the outline of a stairway.

Abruptly, she realized where she was. She was looking into the subcellar from the east. Which meant that the light she saw to her right was seeping down through the ruptured cellar floor. Just two nights ago she had stood at the foot of those steps while Papa had examined the . . .

. . . corpses. If the steps were to her right, then off to her left lay the eight dead German soldiers. And still that noise continued, floating toward her from the far end of the subcellar—if it had an end.

Repressing a shudder, she turned her flashlight on again and continued her climb. There was one last turn to go. She shone the beam upward to the place where the steps disappeared into a dark niche at the edge of the ceiling. The sight of it spurred her on, for she knew that the buttressed ceiling of the stairwell was the floor of the tower's first level. Papa's level. And the niche lay within the dividing wall of his rooms.

Magda quickly completed the climb and eased into the space. She pressed her ear to the large stone on the right; it was hinged in a way similar to the entrance stone sixty feet below. No sound came through to her. Still she waited, forcing herself to listen longer. No footsteps, no voices. Papa was alone.

She pushed on the stone, expecting it to swing open easily. It didn't move. She leaned against it with all her weight and strength. No movement. Crouching, feeling locked in a tiny cave, Magda's mind raced over the possibilities. Something had happened. Five years ago, she had moved the stone with little effort. Had the keep settled in the intervening years, upsetting the delicate balance of the hinges?

She was tempted to rap the butt of her flashlight against the stone. That at least would alert Papa to her presence. But then what? He certainly couldn't help her move the stone. And what if the sound traveled up to one of the other levels and alerted a sentry or one of the officers? No—she could not rap on anything.

But she had to get into that room! She pushed once more, this time wedging her back against the stone and her feet against the opposing wall, straining all her muscles to their limit. Still no movement.

As she huddled there, angry, bitterly frustrated, a thought occurred to her. Perhaps there was another way—via the subcellar. If there were no guards there, she might make it to the courtyard; and if the bright courtyard lights were still off, she might be able to steal across the short distance to the tower and to Papa's room. So many *ifs* . . . but if at any time she found her way blocked, she could always turn back, couldn't she?

Quickly, she descended to the opening in the wall. The cold draft was still there, as were the far-off scraping sounds. She stepped through and began walking toward the stairs that would take her up to the cellar, making her way toward the light that filtered down from above. She played her flashlight beam down and just ahead of her, careful not to let it stray off to the left where she knew the corpses lay.

As she moved deeper into the subcellar, she found it increasingly difficult to keep up her pace. Her mind, her sense of duty, her love for her father—all the higher strata of her consciousness—were pushing her forward. But something else was dragging at her, slowing her. Some primal part of her brain was rebelling, trying to turn her around.

She pushed on, overriding all warnings. She would not be stopped now . . . although the way the shadows seemed to move and twist and shift about her was ghastly and unsettling. *A trick of the light*, she told herself. If she kept moving, she'd be all right.

Magda had almost reached the stairs when she saw something move within the shadow of the bottom step. She almost screamed when it hopped up into the light.

A rat!

It sat hunched on the step with its fat body partially encircled by a twitching tail as it licked its claws. Loathing welled up in her. She wanted to retch. She knew she could not take another step forward with that thing there. The rat looked up, glared at her, then scuttled off into the shadows. Magda didn't wait for it to change its mind and come back. She hurried halfway up the steps, then stopped and listened, waiting for her stomach to calm.

All was quiet above—not a word, not a cough, not a footstep. The only sound was the scraping, persistent, louder now that she was in the subcellar, but still far away in the recesses of the cavern. She tried to block it out. She could not imagine what it might be and did not want to try.

Again she flashed her light around to make sure no

more rats were about. Then she took the stairs, slowly, carefully, silently. Near the top, she peered cautiously over the edge of the hole in the floor. Through the ruptured wall to her right was the cellar's central corridor, alight with a string of incandescent bulbs, and apparently deserted. Three more steps brought her up to floor level, and another three took her to the ruined wall. Again she waited for the sound of guards. Hearing none, she peeked into the corridor: deserted.

Now came the truly risky part. She would have to travel the length of the corridor to the steps that led up to the courtyard. And then up those two short flights. And after that—

One step at a time, Magda told herself. _First the corridor. Conquer that before worrying about the stairs._

She waited, afraid to step out into the light. Until now she had moved in darkness and seclusion. Exposing herself under those bulbs would be like standing naked in the center of Bucharest at noon. But her only other alternative was to give up and go back.

She stepped forward into the light and moved quickly, silently, down the corridor. She was almost at the foot of the stairs when she heard a sound from above. Someone coming down. She had been ready to dart into one of the side rooms at the first sign of anyone approaching, and now she made that move.

Inside the doorway, Magda froze. She neither saw, heard, nor touched anyone, but she knew she was not alone. She had to get _out_! But that would expose her to whoever was coming down the steps. Suddenly, there was movement in the darkness behind her and an arm went around her throat.

"What have we here?" said a voice in German. A sentry had been in the room! He dragged her back toward the corridor. "Well, well! Let's have a look at you in the light!"

Magda's heart pounded with terror as she waited to see the color of her captor's uniform. If gray, she might have a chance, a slim one, but at least a chance. If it was black . . .

It was black. And there was another einsatz-kommando running toward them.

"It's the Jew girl!" said the first. His helmet was off and his eyes were bleary. He must have been dozing in the room when she slipped in.

"How'd she get in?" the second said as he came up.

Magda tried to shrink inside her clothes as they stared at her.

"I don't know," said the first, releasing her and pushing her toward the stairs to the courtyard, "but I think we'd better get her up to the major."

He leaned into the room to retrieve the helmet he had removed for his nap. As he did, the second SS man came alongside her. Magda acted without thinking. She pushed the first into the room and raced back toward the break in the wall. She did *not* want to face that major. If she could get below, she had a chance to reach safety, for only she knew the way.

The back of her scalp suddenly turned to fire and her feet almost left the ground as the second soldier yanked viciously on the fistful of hair and kerchief he had grabbed as she leaped past him. But he was not satisfied with that. As tears of pain sprang to her eyes, he pulled her toward him by her hair, placed a hand between her breasts, and slammed her against the wall.

Magda lost her breath and felt consciousness fade as her shoulders and the back of her head struck the stone with numbing force. The next few moments were a collage of blurs and disembodied voices:

"You didn't kill her, did you?"

"She'll be all right."

"Doesn't know her place, that one."

"Perhaps no one's ever taken the time to properly teach her."

A brief pause, then: *"In there."*

Still in a fog, her body numb, her vision blurred, Magda felt herself dragged by the arms along the cold

stone floor, pulled around a corner and out of the direct
light. She realized she was in one of the rooms. But
why? When they released her arms, she heard the door
close, saw the room go dark, felt them fall upon her,
fumbling over each other in their urgency, one trying to
pull her skirt down while the other tried to lift it up to
her waist to get at her undergarments.

She would have screamed but her voice was gone,
would have fought back but her arms and legs were
leaden and useless, would have been utterly terrified had
it not all seemed so far away and dreamlike. Over the
hunched shoulders of her assailants she could see the
lighted outline of the door to the corridor. She wanted
to be out there.

Then the outline of the door changed, as if a shadow
had moved across it. She sensed a presence outside the
door. Suddenly, there was a thundering crash. The door
split down the middle and smashed open, showering
them all with splinters and larger fragments of wood. A
form—huge, masculine—filled the doorway, blotting
out most of the light.

Glenn! she thought at first, but that hope was instantly doused by the wave of cold and malevolence
flooding in from the doorway.

The startled Germans cried out in terror as they rolled
away from her. The form seemed to swell as it leaped
forward. Magda felt herself kicked and jostled as the
two soldiers dove for the weapons they had lain aside.
But they were not quick enough. The newcomer was
upon them with blinding swiftness, bending down,
grasping each soldier by the throat and then straightening up again to his full height.

Magda's head began to clear as the horror of what she
was watching broke through to her. It was Molasar who
stood over her, a huge, black figure silhouetted in the
light from the corridor, two red points of fire where his
eyes should be, and in each hand a struggling, kicking,
choking, gagging einsatzkommando held out at arm's
length on either side of him. He held them until their
movements slowed and their strangled, agonized sounds

died away, until they both hung limp in his hands. He then shook them violently, so violently that Magda could hear the bones and cartilage in their necks snap, break, grind, and splinter. Then he threw them into a dark corner and disappeared after them.

Fighting her pain and weakness, Magda rolled over and struggled to a crouching position on her hands and knees. She still was not able to get to her feet. It would take a few more minutes before her legs would support her.

Then came a sound—a greedy, sibilant sucking noise that made her want to retch. It drove her to her feet and, after she leaned against the wall for an instant, propelled her out toward the light of the corridor.

She had to get out! Her father was forgotten in the wake of the unspeakable horror taking place in the room behind her. The corridor wavered as she stumbled toward the ruptured wall, but she determinedly held on to consciousness. She reached the opening without falling, but as she stepped through, she caught a movement out of the corner of her eye.

Molasar was coming, his long, purposeful stride bringing him swiftly, gracefully closer, his cloak billowing behind him, his eyes bright, his lips and chin smeared with blood.

With a small cry, Magda ducked inside the wall and ran for the steps to the subcellar. It did not seem even remotely possible that she could outrun him, yet she refused to give in. She sensed him close behind her but did not look around. Instead, she leaped for the steps.

As she landed, her heel skidded on slime and she began to fall. Strong arms, cold as the night, gripped her from behind, one slipping around her back, the other under her knees. She opened her mouth to scream out her terror and revulsion but her voice was locked. She felt herself lifted and carried downward. After one brief, horrified glance at the angular lines of Molasar's pale, blood-flecked face, his long, unkempt, stringy hair, the madness in his eyes, she was carried out of the light and into the subcellar and could no longer see

anything. Molasar turned. He was bearing her toward
the stairwell in the base of the watchtower. She tried to
fight him but his grip easily overcame her best efforts.
Finally she gave up. She would save her strength until
she saw a chance to escape.

As before, there was numbing cold where he touched
her, despite her multiple layers of clothing. There was a
heavy, stale odor about him. And although he did not
appear physically dirty, he seemed . . . unclean.

He carried her through the narrow opening into the
base of the tower.

"Where . . . ?" Her voice croaked out the first word
of her question before her terror strangled it.

There was no answer.

Magda had begun to shiver as they had moved
through the subcellar; now, on the stairwell, her teeth
were chattering. Contact with Molasar seemed to be
siphoning off her body heat.

All was dark around them, yet Molasar was taking
the steps two at a time with ease and confidence. After a
full circuit around the inner surface of the tower's base,
he stopped. Magda felt the sides of the niche within the
ceiling press around her, heard stone grate upon stone,
and then light poured in on her.

"Magda!"

It was Papa's voice. As her pupils adjusted to the
change in light, she felt herself placed on her feet and
released. She put a hand out toward the voice and felt it
contact the armrest of Papa's wheelchair. She grasped
it, clung to it like a drowning sailor clutching a floating
plank.

"What are you doing here?" he asked in a harsh,
shocked whisper.

"Soldiers . . ." was all she could say. As her vision
adjusted, she found Papa staring at her open mouthed.

"They abducted you from the inn?"

She shook her head. "No. I came in below."

"But why would you do such a foolish thing?"

"So you would not have to face *him* alone." Magda

did not make any gesture toward Molasar. Her meaning was clear.

The room had darkened noticeably since her arrival. She knew Molasar was standing somewhere behind her in the shadows by the hinged stone, but she could not bring herself to look in his direction.

She went on: "Two of the SS soldiers caught me. They pulled me into a room. They were going to . . ."

"What happened?" Papa asked, his eyes wide.

"I was . . ." Magda glanced briefly over her shoulder at the shadow . . . "saved."

Papa continued to stare at her, no longer with shock or concern, but with something else—disbelief.

"By Molasar?"

Magda nodded and finally found the strength to turn and face Molasar. "He killed them both!"

She stared at him. He stood in shadow by the open slab of stone, cloaked in darkness, a figure out of a nightmare, his face dimly seen but his eyes bright. The blood was gone from his face, as if it had been absorbed through the skin rather than wiped away. Magda shuddered.

"Now you've ruined everything!" Papa said, startling her with the anger in his voice. "Once the new bodies are found I'll be subjected to the full force of the major's wrath! And all because of you!"

"I came here to be with you," Magda said, stung. Why was he angry with her?

"I did not ask you to come! I did not want you here before, and I do not want you here now!"

"Papa, please!"

He pointed a gnarled finger at the opening in the wall. "Leave, Magda! I have too much to do and too little time in which to do it! The Nazis will soon be storming in here asking me why two more of their men are dead and I will have no answer! I must speak to Molasar before they arrive!"

"Papa—"

"Go!"

Magda stood and stared at him. How could he speak to her this way? She wanted to cry, wanted to plead, wanted to slap some sense into him. But she could not. She could not defy him, even before Molasar. He was her father, and although she knew he was being brutally unfair, she could not defy him.

Magda turned and rushed past the impassive Molasar into the opening. The slab swung closed behind her and she was again in darkness. She felt in her waistband for the flashlight—gone! It must have fallen out somewhere.

Magda had two alternatives: return to Papa's room and ask for a lamp or a candle, or descend in the dark. After only a few seconds she chose the latter. She could not face Papa again tonight. He had hurt her, more than she had ever known she could be hurt. A change had come over him. He was somehow losing his gentleness, and losing the empathy that had always been part of him. He had dismissed her tonight as though she were a stranger. And he hadn't even cared enough to be sure she had a light with her!

Magda bit back a sob. She would *not* cry! But what was there to do? She felt helpless. And worse, she felt betrayed.

The only thing left was to leave the keep. She began her descent, relying on touch alone. She could see nothing, but knew that if she kept her left hand against the wall and took each step slowly and carefully, she could make it to the bottom without falling to her death.

As she completed the first spiral, Magda half expected to hear that odd scraping sound through the opening into the subcellar. But it did not come. Instead, there was a new sound in the dark—louder, closer, heavier. She slowed her progress until her left hand slid off the stone of the wall and met the cool air flowing through the opening. The noise grew as she listened.

It was a scuffling sound, a dragging, fulsome, *shambling* sound that set her teeth on edge and dried her tongue so it stuck to the roof of her mouth. This could

not be rats . . . much too big. It seemed to come from
the deeper darkness to her left. Off to the right, dim
light still seeped down from the cellar above, but it did
not reach to the area where the sound was. Just as well.
Magda did not want to see what was over there.

She groped wildly across the opening, and for a mind-
numbing moment, could not find the far edge. Then her
hand contacted cold, wonderfully solid stone and she
continued downward, faster than before, dangerously
fast, her heart pounding, her breath coming in gulps. If
the thing in the subcellar was coming her way, she had
to be out of the keep by the time it reached the stairwell.

She kept going down and endlessly down, every so often looking back over her shoulder in an instinctive and
utterly fruitless attempt to see in the darkness. A dim
rectangle beckoned to her as she reached the bottom and
she stumbled toward it, through it and out into the fog.
She swung the slab closed and leaned against it, gasping
with relief.

After composing herself, Magda realized that she had
not escaped the malevolent atmosphere of the keep by
merely stepping outside its walls. This morning the
vileness that permeated the keep had stopped at the
threshold; now it extended beyond the walls. She began
to walk, to stumble through the darkness. It was not until she was almost to the stream that she felt she had
escaped the aura of evil.

Suddenly from above there came faint shouts, and the
fog brightened. The lights in the keep had been turned
up to maximum. Someone must have found the two
newly dead bodies.

Magda continued to move away from the keep. The
extra light was no threat, for none of it reached her. It
filtered down like sunshine viewed from the bottom of a
murky lake. The light was caught and held by the fog,
thickening it, whitening it, concealing her rather than
revealing her. She splashed carelessly across the stream
this time without pausing to remove her shoes and
stockings—she wanted to be away from the keep as
quickly as possible. The shadow of the causeway passed

overhead and soon she was at the base of the wedge of
rubble. After a brief rest to catch her breath, she began
to climb until she reached the upper level of the fog. It
almost completely filled the gorge now and there was
only a short distance to the top. A few seconds of exposure and she would be safe.

Magda pulled herself up over the rim and ran in a
half-crouch. As she felt the brush enfold her, her foot
caught on a root and she fell headlong, striking her left
knee on a stone. She hugged the knee to her chest and
began to cry, long, wracking sobs far out of proportion
to the pain. It was anguish for Papa, relief at being
safely away from the keep, a reaction to all she had seen
and heard there, to all that had been done to her, or
almost done to her.

"You've been to the keep."

It was Glenn. She could think of no one she wanted
more to see at this moment. Hurriedly drying her eyes
on her sleeve, she stood up—or tried to. Her injured
knee sent a knifing pain up her leg and Glenn put out a
hand to keep her from falling.

"Are you hurt?" His voice was gentle.

"Just a bruise."

She tried to take a step but the leg refused to bear her
weight. Without a word, Glenn scooped her up in his
arms and began carrying her back to the inn.

It was the second time tonight she had been carried
so. But this time was different. Glenn's arms were a
warm sanctuary, thawing all the cold left by Molasar's
touch. As she leaned against him she felt all the fear
ooze out of her. But how had he come up behind her
without her hearing him? Or had he been standing there
all along, waiting for her?

Magda let her head rest on his shoulder, feeling safe,
at peace. *If only I could feel this way forever.*

He carried her effortlessly through the front door of
the inn, through the empty foyer, up the stairs, and into
her room. After depositing her gently on the edge of the
bed, he knelt before her.

"Let's take a look at that knee."

Magda hesitated at first, then drew her skirt up over her left knee, leaving the right one covered and keeping the rest of the heavy fabric tight around her thighs. In the back of her mind was the thought that she should not be sitting here on a bed exposing her leg to a man she hardly knew. But somehow . . .

Her coarse, dark-blue stocking was torn, revealing a purpling bruise on the kneecap. The flesh was swollen, puffy. Glenn stepped over to the near side of the dresser and dipped a washcloth into the water pitcher, then brought the cloth over and placed it on her knee.

"That ought to help," he said.

"What's gone wrong with the keep?" she asked, staring at his red hair, trying to ignore, and yet reveling in, the tingling warmth that crept steadily up her thigh from where his hand held the cloth against her.

He looked up at her. "You were there tonight. Why don't you tell me?"

"I was there, but I can't explain—or perhaps I can't accept—what's happening. I do know that Molasar's awakening has changed the keep. I used to love that place. Now I fear it. There's a very definite . . . *wrongness* there. You don't have to see it or touch it to be aware of its presence, just as sometimes you don't have to look outside to know there's bad weather coming. It pervades the very air . . . seeps right into your pores."

"What kind of 'wrongness' do you sense in Molasar?"

"He's evil. I know that's vague, but I mean *evil*. Inherently evil. A monstrous, ancient evil who thrives on death, who values all that is noxious to the living, who hates and fears everything we cherish." She shrugged, embarrassed by the intensity of her words. "That's what I feel. Does it make any sense to you?"

Glenn watched her closely for a long moment before replying. "You must be extremely sensitive to have felt all that."

"And yet . . ."

"And yet what?"

"And yet tonight Molasar saved me from the hands of two fellow human beings who should have by all rights been allied with me against him."

The pupils in Glenn's blue eyes dilated. "Molasar *saved* you?"

"Yes. Killed two German soldiers"—she winced at the memory—"horribly . . . but didn't harm me. Strange, isn't it?"

"Very." Leaving the damp cloth in place, Glenn slid his hand off her knee and ran it through the red of his hair. Magda wanted him to put it back where it had been, but he seemed preoccupied. "You escaped him?"

"No. He delivered me to my father." She watched Glenn mull this, then nod as if it made some sort of sense to him. "And there was something else."

"About Molasar?"

"No. Something else in the keep. In the subcellar . . . something moving around in there. Maybe it was what had been making the scraping noise earlier."

"Scraping noise," Glenn repeated, his voice low.

"Rasping, scraping . . . from far back in the sub-cellar."

Without a word, Glenn rose and went to the window. Motionless, he stood staring out at the keep. "Tell me everything that happened to you tonight—from the moment you stepped into the keep until the moment you left. Spare no detail."

Magda told him everything she could remember up to the time Molasar deposited her in Papa's room. Then her voice choked off.

"What's wrong?"

"Nothing."

"How was your father?" Glenn asked. "Was he all right?"

Pain gathered in her throat. "Oh, he was fine." In spite of her brave smile, tears started in her eyes and began to spill onto her cheeks. Try as she might to will them back, they kept coming. "He told me to get out . . . to leave him alone with Molasar. Can you imagine that? After what I went through to reach him, he tells me to get out!''

The anguish in her voice must have penetrated Glenn's preoccupied state, for he turned away from the window and stared at her.

"He didn't care that I had been assaulted and almost raped by two Nazi brutes . . . didn't even ask if I was hurt! All he cared was that I had shortened his precious time with Molasar. I'm his daughter and he cares more about talking to that . . . that creature!''

Glenn stepped over to the bed and seated himself beside her. He put his arm around her back and gently pulled her against him.

"Your father's under a terrible strain. You must remember that.''

"And *he* should remember he's my father!''

"Yes,'' Glenn said softly. "Yes, he should.'' He swiveled half around and lay back on the bed, then tugged gently on Magda's shoulders. "Here. Lie down beside me and close your eyes. You'll be all right.''

With her heart pounding in her throat, Magda allowed herself to be drawn nearer to him. She ignored the pain in her knee as she swung her legs off the floor and turned to face him. They lay stretched out together on the narrow bed, Glenn with his arm under her, Magda with her head in the nook of his shoulder, her body almost touching his, her left hand pressed against the muscles of his chest. Thoughts of Papa and the hurt he had caused her washed away as waves of sensation crashed over and through her. She had never lain beside a man before. It was frightening and wonderful. The aura of his maleness engulfed her, making her mind spin. She tingled wherever they made contact, tiny electric shocks arcing through her clothing . . . clothing that was suffocating her.

On impulse, she lifted her head and kissed him on the lips. He responded ardently for a moment, then pulled back.

"Magda—''

She watched his eyes, seeing a mixture of desire, hesitation, and surprise there. He could be no more surprised than she. There had been no thought behind that kiss, only a newly awakened need, burning in its intensity. Her body was acting of its own accord, and she was not trying to stop it. This moment might never come again. It had to be now. She wanted to tell Glenn to make love to her but could not say it.

"Someday, Magda," he said, seeming to read her thoughts. He gently drew her head back down to his shoulder. "Someday. But not now. Not tonight."

He stroked her hair and told her to sleep. Strangely, the promise was enough. The heat seeped out of her, and with it all the trials of the night. Even worries about Papa and what he might be doing ebbed away. Occasional bubbles of concern still broke the surface of her spreading calm, but they became progressively fewer and farther between, their ripples smaller and more widely spaced. Questions about Glenn floated by: who he really was, and the wisdom, let alone the propriety, of allowing herself to be this close to him.

Glenn . . . he seemed to know more about the keep and about Molasar than he was admitting. She had found herself talking to him about the keep as if he were as intimately familiar with it as she; and he had not seemed surprised about the stairwell in the watchtower's base, or about the opening from the stairwell into the subcellar, despite her offhand references to them. To her mind there was only one reason for that: He already knew about them.

But these were niggling little qualms. If she had discovered the hidden entrance to the tower years ago, there was no reason why he could not have found it, too. The important thing now was that for the first time tonight she felt completely safe and warm and wanted.

She drifted off to sleep.

TWENTY-TWO

As soon as the stone slab swung shut behind his daughter, Cuza turned to Molasar and found the bottomless black of the creature's pupils already fixed on him from the shadows. All night he had waited to cross-examine Molasar, to penetrate the contradictions that had been pointed out by that odd red-haired stranger this morning. But then Molasar had appeared, holding Magda in his arms.

"Why did you do it?" Cuza asked, looking up from his wheelchair.

Molasar continued to stare at him, saying nothing.

"*Why?* I should think she'd be no more than another tempting morsel for you!"

"You try my patience, cripple!" Molasar's face grew whiter as he spoke. "I could no more stand by now and watch two Germans rape and defile a woman of my

country than I could stand idly by five hundred years
ago and watch the Turks do the same. That is why I
allied myself with Vlad Tepes! But tonight the Germans
went further than any Turk ever dared—they tried to
commit the act within the very walls of my home!"
Abruptly, he relaxed and smiled. "And I rather enjoyed
ending their miserable lives."

"As I am sure you rather enjoyed your alliance with
Vlad."

"His penchant for impalement left me with ample opportunities to satisfy my needs without attracting attention. Vlad came to trust me. At the end, I was one of
the few boyars he could truly count on."

"I don't understand you."

"You are not expected to. You are not capable of it. I
am beyond your experience."

Cuza tried to clear away the confusion that smudged
his thoughts. So many contradictions . . . nothing was
as it should be. And hanging over it all was the unsettling knowledge that he owed his daughter's safety,
and perhaps her life, to one of the undead.

"Nevertheless, I am in your debt."

Molasar made no reply.

Cuza hesitated, then began leading up to the question
he most wanted to ask. "Are there more like you?"

"You mean undead? *Moroi?* There used to be. I
don't know about now. Since awakening, I've sensed
such reluctance on the part of the living to accept my
existence that I must assume we were all killed off over
the last five hundred years."

"And were all the others so terrified of the cross?"

Molasar stiffened. "You don't have it with you, do
you? I warn you—"

"It's safely away. But I wonder at your fear of it."
Cuza gestured to the walls. "You've surrounded yourself with brass-and-nickel crosses, thousands of them,
and yet you panicked at the sight of the tiny silver one I
had last night."

Molasar stepped to the nearest cross and laid his hand
against it. "These are a ruse. See how high the cross-

piece is set? So high that it is almost no longer a cross. This configuration has no ill effect on me. I had thousands of them built into the walls of the keep to throw off my pursuers when I went into hiding. They could not conceive of one of my kind dwelling in a structure studded with 'crosses.' And as you will learn if I decide I can trust you, this particular configuration has special meaning for me.''

Cuza had desperately hoped to find a flaw in Molasar's fear of the cross; he felt that hope wither and die. A great heaviness settled on him. He had to think! And he had to keep Molasar here—talking! He couldn't let him go. Not yet.

''Who are 'they'? Who was pursuing you?''

''Does the name *Glaeken* mean anything to you?''

''No.''

Molasar stepped closer. ''Nothing at all?''

''I assure you I never heard the word before.'' Why was it so important?

''Then perhaps they are gone,'' Molasar muttered, more to himself than to Cuza.

''Please explain yourself. Who or what is a Glaeken?''

''The Glaeken were a fanatical sect that started as an arm of the Church in the Dark Ages. Its members enforced orthodoxy and were answerable only to the Pope at first; after a while, however, they became a law unto themselves. They sought to infiltrate all the seats of power, to bring all the royal families under their control in order to place the world under a single power—one religion, one rule.''

''Impossible! I am an authority on European history, especially this part of Europe, and there was never any such sect!''

Molasar leaned closer and bared his teeth. ''You dare call me a liar within the walls of my home? *Fool!* What do you know of history? What did you know of me—of my kind—before I revealed myself? What did you know of the history of the keep? *Nothing!* The Glaeken were a secret brotherhood. The royal families had never heard of them, and if the later Church knew of their continued existence, it never admitted it.''

Cuza turned away from the blood-stench of Molasar's breath. ''How did *you* learn of their existence?''

''At one time, there was little afoot in the world that the *moroi* were not privy to. And when we learned of the Glaeken's plans, we decided to take action.'' He straightened with obvious pride. ''The *moroi* opposed the Glaeken for centuries. It was clear that the successful culmination of their plans would be inimical to us, and so we repeatedly foiled their schemes by draining the life from anyone in power who came under their thrall.''

He began to roam the room.

''At first the Glaeken were not even sure we existed. But once they became convinced, they waged all-out war. One by one my brother *moroi* went down to true death. When I saw the circle tightening around me, I built the keep and locked myself away, determined to outlast the Glaeken and their plans for world dominion. Now it appears that I have succeeded.''

''Very clever,'' Cuza said. ''You surrounded yourself with ersatz crosses and went into hibernation. But I must ask you, and please answer me: Why do you fear the cross?''

''I cannot discuss it.''

''You must tell me! The Messiah—was Jesus Christ—?''

''No!'' Molasar staggered away and leaned against the wall, gagging.

''What's wrong?''

He glared at Cuza. ''If you were not a countryman, I would tear your tongue out here and now!''

Even the sound of Christ's name repels him! Cuza thought. ''But I never—''

''Never say it again! If you value whatever aid I can give you, never say that name again!''

''But it's only a word.''

''NEVER!'' Molasar had regained some of his composure. ''You have been warned. Never again or your

body will lie beside the Germans below."

Cuza felt as if he were drowning. He had to try something.

"What about these words? *Yitgadal veyitkadash shemei raba bealma divera chireutei, veyamlich—*"

"What is that meaningless jumble of sounds?" Molasar said. "Some sort of chant? An incantation? Are you trying to drive me off?" He took a step closer. "Have you sided with the Germans?"

"No!" It was all Cuza could say before his voice cracked and broke off. His mind reeled as if from a blow; he gripped the arms of his wheelchair with his crippled hands, waiting for the room to tilt and spill him out. It was a nightmare! This creature of the Dark cringed at the sight of a cross and retched at the mention of the name Jesus Christ. Yet the words of the Kaddish, the Hebrew prayer for the dead, were just so much meaningless noise. It could not be! And yet it was.

Molasar was speaking, oblivious to the painful maelstrom that swirled within his listener. Cuza tried to follow the words. They might be crucial to Magda's survival, and his own.

"My strength is growing steadily. I can feel it coming back to me. Before long—two nights at most—I shall have the power to rid my keep of all these oulanders."

Cuza tried to assimilate the meaning of the words: *strength . . . two more nights . . . rid my keep . . .* But other words kept rearing up in his consciousness, a persistent undertone . . . *Yitgadal veyitkadash shemei . . .* blocking their meaning.

And then came the sound of heavy boots running into the watchtower and pounding up the stone steps to the upper levels, the faint sound of human voices raised in anger and fear in the courtyard, the momentary dimming of the single bulb overhead, signaling a sudden draw on the power supply.

Molasar showed his teeth in a wolfish grin. "It seems they have found their two comrades-in-arms."

"And soon they will come here to place the blame on me," Cuza said, alarm pulling him from his torpor.

"You are a man of the mind," Molasar said, stepping to the wall and giving the hinged slab a casual shove. It swung open easily. "Use it."

Cuza watched Molasar blend and disappear into the deeper shadow of the opening, wishing he could follow. As the stone slab swung shut, Cuza wheeled his chair around to the table and leaned over the *Al Azif*, feigning study; waiting, trembling.

It was not a long wait.

Kaempffer burst into the room.

"Jew!" he shouted, jabbing an accusing finger at Cuza as he assumed a wide-legged stance he no doubt considered at once powerful and threatening. "You've failed, Jew! I should have expected no more!"

Cuza could only sit and stare dumbly at the major. What was he going to say? He had no strength left. He felt miserable, sick at heart as well as in body. Everything hurt him, every bone, every joint, every muscle. His mind was numb from his encounter with Molasar. He couldn't think. His mouth was parched, yet he dared not take any more water, for his bladder longed to empty itself at the very sight of Kaempffer.

He wasn't cut out for such stress. He was a teacher, a scholar, a man of letters. He was not equipped to deal with this strutting popinjay who had the power of life and death over him. He wanted desperately to strike back yet did not have the faintest hope of doing so. Was living through all this really worth the trouble?

How much more could he take?

And yet there was Magda. Somewhere along the line there must be hope for her.

Two nights . . . Molasar had said he would have sufficient strength two nights from now. Forty-eight hours. Cuza asked himself: Could he hold out that long? Yes, he would force himself to last until Saturday night. Saturday night . . . the Sabbath would be over . . . what did the Sabbath mean anymore? What did *anything* mean anymore?

"Did you hear me, Jew?" The major's voice was straining toward a scream.

Another voice spoke: "He doesn't even know what you're talking about."

The captain had entered the room. Cuza sensed a core of decency within Captain Woermann; a flawed nobility. Not a trait he expected to find in a German officer.

"Then he'll learn soon enough!" Two long strides took Kaempffer to Cuza's side. He leaned down and forward until his perfect Aryan face was only inches away.

"What's wrong, Major?" Cuza said, feigning ignorance, but allowing his genuine fear of the man to show on his face. "What have I done?"

"You've done *nothing*, Jew! And that's the problem. For two nights you've sat here with these moldering books, taking credit for the sudden halt in the deaths. But tonight—"

"I never—" Cuza began, but Kaempffer stopped him by slamming his fist on the table.

"*Silence!* Tonight two more of my men were found dead in the cellar, their throats torn out like the others!"

Cuza had a fleeting image of the two dead men. After viewing the other cadavers, it was easy to imagine their wounds. He visualized their gory throats with a certain relish. Those two had attempted to defile his daughter and deserved all they had suffered. Deserved worse. Molasar was welcome to their blood.

But it was he who was in danger now. The fury in the major's face made that clear. He must think of something or he would not live to see Saturday night.

"It's now evident that you deserve no credit for the last two nights of peace. There is no connection between your arrival and the two nights without a death—just lucky coincidence for you! But you led us to believe it was your doing. Which proves what we have learned in Germany: Never trust a Jew!"

"I never took credit for anything! I never even—"

"You're trying to detain me here, aren't you?" Kaempffer said, his eyes narrowing, his voice lowering to a menacing tone as he studied him. "You're doing your best to keep me from my mission at Ploiesti, aren't you?"

Cuza's mind reeled from the major's sudden change of tack. The man was mad . . . as mad as Abdul Alhazred must have been after writing the *Al Azif* . . . which lay before them on the table . . .

He had an idea.

"But Major! I've finally found something in one of the books!"

Captain Woermann stepped forward at this. "Found? What have you found?"

"He's found nothing!" Kaempffer snarled. "Just another Jew lie to let him go on living!"

How right you are, Major.

"Let him speak, for God's sake!" Woermann said. He turned to Cuza. "What does it say? Show me."

Cuza indicated the *Al Azif*, written in the original Arabic. The book dated from the eighth century and had absolutely nothing to do with the keep, or even Romania for that matter. But he hoped the two Germans would not know that.

Doubt furrowed Woermann's brow as he looked down at the scroll. "I can't read those chicken tracks."

"He's lying!" Kaempffer shouted.

"This book does not lie, Major," Cuza said. He paused an instant, praying that the Germans would not know the difference between Turkish and ancient Arabic, then plunged into his lie. "It was written by a Turk who invaded this region with Mohammed II. He says there was a small castle—his description of all the crosses can only mean he was in this keep—in which one of the old Wallachian lords had dwelt. The shade of the deceased lord would allow natives of the region to sleep unmolested in his keep, but should outlanders or invaders dare to pass through the portals of his former home, he would slay them at the rate of one per night for every night they stayed. Do you understand? The same thing that is happening here now happened to a unit of the Turkish Army half a millennium ago!"

Cuza watched the faces of the two officers as he finished. His own reaction was one of amazement at his facile fabrication from what he knew of Molasar and the region. There were holes in the story, but small ones, and they had a good chance of being overlooked.

Kaempffer sneered. "Utter nonsense!"

"Not necessarily," Woermann said. "Think about it: The Turks were always on the march back then. And count up our corpses—with the two new ones tonight, we have averaged one death a night since I arrived on April 22."

"It's still . . ." Kaempffer's voice trailed off as his confidence ebbed. He looked uncertainly at Cuza. "Then we're not the first?"

"No. At least not according to this."

It was working! The biggest lie Cuza had ever told in his life, composed on the spot, was working! They didn't know *what* to believe! He wanted to laugh.

"How did they finally solve the problem?" Woermann asked.

"They left."

Silence followed Cuza's simple reply.

Woermann finally turned to Kaempffer: "I've been telling you that for—"

"We *cannot* leave!" Kaempffer said, a hint of hysteria in his voice. "Not before Sunday." He turned to Cuza. "And if you do not come up with an answer for this problem by then, Jew, I shall see to it that you and your daughter personally accompany me to Ploiesti!"

"But why?"

"You'll find out when you get there." Kaempffer paused a moment, then seemed to come to a decision. "No, I believe I'll tell you now. Perhaps it will speed your efforts. You've heard of Auschwitz, no doubt? And Buchenwald?"

Cuza's stomach imploded. "Death camps."

"We prefer to call them 'Resettlement' camps. Romania lacks such a facility. It is my mission to correct that deficiency. Your kind, plus Gypsies and Freemasons and other human dross will be processed through the camp I will set up at Ploiesti. If you prove to be of service to me, I will see to it that your entry into the camp is delayed, perhaps even until your natural death. But if you impede me in any way, you and your daughter will have the honor of being our first residents."

Cuza sat helpless in his chair. He could feel his lips and tongue working, but he could not speak. His mind was too shocked, too appalled at what he had just heard. It was impossible! Yet the glee in Kaempffer's eyes told him it was true. Finally, a word escaped him.

"Beast!"

Kaempffer's smile broadened. "Strangely enough, I don't mind the sound of that word on a Jew's lips. It is proof positive that I am successfully discharging my duties." He strode to the door, then turned back. "So look well through your books, Jew. Work hard for me. Find me an answer. It's not just your own well-being that hangs on it, but your daughter's too." He turned and was gone.

Cuza looked at Woermann pleadingly. "Captain . . . ?"

"I can do nothing, *Herr* Professor," he replied in a low voice full of regret. "I can only suggest that you work at those books. You've found one reference to the keep; that means there's a good chance you can find another. And I might suggest that you tell your daughter to find a safer place of residence than the inn . . . perhaps somewhere in the hills."

He could not admit to the captain that he had lied about finding a reference to the keep, that there was *no* hope of ever finding one. And as for Magda: "My daughter is stubborn. She will stay at the inn."

"I thought as much. But beyond what I have just said, I am powerless. I am no longer in command of the keep." He grimaced. "I wonder if I ever was. Good evening."

"Wait!" Cuza clumsily fished the cross out of his pocket. "Take this. I have no use for it."

Woermann enclosed the cross in his fist and stared at him a moment. Then he, too, was gone.

Cuza sat in his wheelchair, enveloped in the blackest depression he had ever known. There was no way of winning here. If Molasar stopped killing the Germans, Kaempffer would leave for Ploiesti to begin the systematic extermination of Romanian Jewry. If Molasar persisted, Kaempffer would destroy the keep and drag him and Magda to Ploiesti as his first victims. He thought of Magda in their hands and truly understood the old cliché, a fate worse than death.

There had to be a way out. Far more than his own life and Magda's rested on what happened here. Hundreds of thousands—perhaps a million or more—lives were at stake. There had to be a way to stop Kaempffer. He had to be prevented from going off on his mission . . . it seemed of utmost importance to him to arrive in Ploiesti on Monday. Would he lose his position if delayed? If so, that might give the doomed a grace period.

What if Kaempffer *never* left the keep? What if he met with a fatal accident? But how? How to stop him?

He sobbed in his helplessness. He was a crippled Jew amid squads of German soldiers. He needed guidance. He needed an answer. And soon. He folded his stiff fingers and bowed his head.

O God. Help me, your humble servant, find the answer to the trials of your other servants. Help me help them. Help me find a way to preserve them . . .

The silent prayer trailed off into the oblivion of his despair. What was the use? How many of the countless thousands dying at the hands of the Germans had lifted their hearts and minds and voices in a similar plea? And where were they now? Dead! And where would he be if he waited for an answer to his own supplication? Dead. And worse for Magda.

He sat in quiet desperation . . .

There was still Molasar.

T

Woermann stood for a moment outside the professor's door after closing it. He had experienced a strange sensation while the old man was explaining what he had found in that indecipherable book, a feeling that Cuza was telling the truth, and yet lying at the same time. Odd. What was the professor's game?

He strolled out to the bright courtyard, catching the anxious expressions on the faces of the sentries. Ah, well, it had been too good to be true. Two nights without a casualty—too much to hope for three. Now they were all back to square one . . . except for the body count which continued to rise. Ten now. One per night for ten nights. A chilling statistic. If only the killer, Cuza's "Wallachian lord," had held off until tomorrow night. Kaempffer would have been gone by then and he could have marched his own men out. But as things looked now, they would all have to stay through the weekend. Friday, Saturday, and Sunday nights to go. A death potential of three. Maybe more.

Woermann turned right and walked the short distance to the cellar entrance. The interment detail should have the two fresh corpses down in the subcellar by now. He decided to see that they were laid out properly. Even einsatzkommandos should be accorded a modicum of dignity in death.

In the cellar he glanced into the room in which the two bodies had been found; their throats had not only been torn open but their heads had lolled at obscene angles. The killer had broken their necks for some reason. That was a new atrocity. The room was empty now except for pieces of the shattered door. What had happened here? The dead men's weapons had been found unfired. Had they tried to save themselves by locking the door against their attacker? Why had no one heard their shouts? Or hadn't they shouted?

He walked farther down the central corridor to the broached wall and heard voices coming from below. On the way down the stairs he met the interment detail coming up, blowing into their chilled hands. He directed them back down the stairs.

"Let's go see what sort of job you did."

In the subcellar the glow from flashlights and hand-held kerosene lamps glimmered dully off the ten white-sheeted figures on the ground.

"We neatened them up a bit, sir," said a private in gray. "Some of the sheets needed straightening."

Woermann surveyed the scene. Everything seemed in order. He was going to have to come to a decision on disposition of the bodies. He would have to ship them out soon. But how?

He clapped his hands together. Of course—Kaempffer! The major was planning to leave Sunday evening no matter what. *He* could transport the corpses to Ploiesti, and from there they could be flown back to Germany. Perfect . . . and fitting.

He noticed that the left foot of the third corpse from the end was sticking out from under its sheet. As he stooped to adjust the cover, he saw that the boot was filthy. It almost looked as if the wearer had been dragged to his resting place by the arms. Both boots were caked with dirt.

Woermann felt a surge of anger, then let it slip away. What did it really matter? The dead were dead. Why make a fuss over a muddy pair of boots? Last week it would have seemed important. Now it was no more than a quibble. A trifle. Yet the dirty boots bothered him. He could not say why, exactly. But they did bother him.

"Let's go, men," he said, turning away and letting his breath fog past him as he moved. The men readily complied. It was cold down there.

Woermann paused at the foot of the steps and looked back. The corpses were barely visible in the receding light. Those boots . . . he thought of those dirty, muddy boots again. Then he followed the others up to the cellar.

From his quarters at the rear of the keep, Kaempffer stood at his window and looked out over the courtyard. He had watched Woermann go down to the cellar and return. And still he stood. He should have felt relatively safe, at least for the rest of the night. Not because of the guards all around, but because the thing that killed his men at will had done its work for the night and would not strike again.

Instead, his terror was at a peak.

For a particularly horrifying thought had occurred to him. It derived from the fact that so far all the victims had been enlisted men. The officers had remained untouched. Why? It could be due purely to chance since enlisted men outnumbered officers by better than twenty to one in the keep. But deep within Kaempffer was a gnawing suspicion that he and Woermann were being held in reserve for something especially ghastly.

He didn't know why he felt this way, but he could not escape the dreadful certainty of it. If he could tell someone—anyone—about it, he would at least be partially freed of the burden. Perhaps then he could sleep.

But there was no one.

And so he would stand here at this window until dawn, not daring to close his eyes until the sun filled the sky with light.

TWENTY-THREE

Magda waited at the gate, anxiously shifting her weight from one foot to the other. Despite the morning sun, she was cold. The soul-chilling sensation of evil that had been confined to the keep before seemed to be leaking out into the pass. Last night it had followed her almost as far as the stream below; this morning it had struck her as soon as she had set foot on the causeway.

The high wooden gates had been swung inward and now rested against the stone sides of the short, tunnellike entry arch. Magda's eyes roamed from the tower entrance from which she expected Papa to emerge, to the dark opening directly across the courtyard that led down to the cellar, to the rear section of the keep. There soldiers were at work, hacking away at the stones. Whereas yesterday their movements had been lackadai-

sical, today they were frantic. They worked liked madmen—frightened madmen.

Why don't they just leave? She couldn't understand
why they remained here night after night waiting for
more of their number to die. It didn't make sense.

She had been feverish with concern for Papa. What
had they done to him last night after finding the bodies
of her two would-be rapists? As he had approached on
the causeway, the awful thought that they might have
executed him filled her mind. But that fear had been
negated by the sentry's quick agreement to her request
to see her father. And now that the initial anxiety had
been relieved, her thoughts began to drift.

The cheeping of the hungry baby birds outside her
window and the dull throb of pain in her left knee had
awakened her this morning. She had found herself alone
in her bed, fully clothed, under the covers. She had been
so terribly vulnerable last night, and Glenn easily could
have taken advantage of that. But he hadn't, even when
it had been so obvious that she had wanted him.

Magda cringed inside, unable to comprehend what
had come over her, shocked by the memory of her own
brazenness. Fortunately, Glenn had rejected her . . . no,
that was too strong a word . . . demurred was a better
way to put it. She wondered at that, glad he had held
back, and yet slighted that he had found her so easy to
refuse.

Why should she feel slighted? She had never valued
herself in terms of her ability to seduce a man. And yet,
there was that nasty whisper in a far corner of her mind
hinting that she lacked something.

But maybe it had nothing to do with her. It could be
he was one of those . . . those men who could not love a
woman, only another man. But that, she knew, was not
the case. She remembered their one kiss—even now it
caused a wave of welcome heat to brush over her—and
remembered the response she had felt on his part.

Just as well. Just as well he had not accepted her offer. How would she have faced him again if he had?
Mortified by her wantonness, she would be forced to

avoid him, and that would mean depriving herself of his company. And she so wanted his company.

Last night had been an aberration. A chance combination of circumstances that would not repeat itself. She realized now what had happened: Physical and emotional exhaustion, the near escape from the soldiers, the rescue by Molasar, Papa's rejection of her offer to stay by his side—all had combined to leave her temporarily deranged. That had not been Magda Cuza lying next to Glenn on the bed last night; it had been someone else, someone she did not know. It would *not* happen again.

She had passed his room this morning, limping from the pain in her knee. She had been tempted to knock on his door to thank him for his aid and to apologize for her behavior. But after listening a minute and hearing no sound, she hadn't wanted to wake him.

She had come directly to the keep, not solely to see that Papa was well, but to tell him how much he had hurt her, how he had no right to treat her in such a manner, and how she had a good mind to heed his advice and leave the Dinu Pass. The last was an empty threat, but she wanted to strike back at him in some way, to make him react, or at least apologize for his callous behavior. She had rehearsed exactly what she was going to say and exactly the tone of voice in which she would say it. She was ready.

Then Papa appeared at the entrance to the tower with a soldier pushing his chair from behind. One look at his ravaged face and all the anger and hurt went out of her. He looked terrible; he seemed to have aged twenty years overnight. She hadn't thought it possible, but he looked more feeble.

How he has suffered! More than any man should. Pitted against his countrymen, his own body, and now the German Army. I can't side against him, too.

The soldier pushing him this morning was more courteous than the one who had wheeled him yesterday. He brought the wheelchair to a halt before Magda, then turned away. Wordlessly, she moved behind and began to push Papa across the causeway. They had not gone a dozen feet when he held up his hand.

"Stop here, Magda."

"What's wrong?" She didn't want to stop. She could still feel the keep here. Papa didn't seem to notice.

"I didn't sleep at all last night."

"Did they keep you up?" she asked, coming around to crouch before him, her fierce protective instincts kindling anger within her. "They didn't hurt you, did they?"

His eyes were rheumy as they looked into hers. "They didn't touch me, but they hurt me."

"How?"

He began speaking in the Gypsy dialect they both knew: "Listen to me, Magda. I've found out why the SS men are here. This is just a stop along their way to Ploiesti where that major is going to set up a death camp—for our people."

Magda felt a wave of nausea. "Oh, no! That's not true! The government would never let Germans come in and—"

"They are already here! You know the Germans have been building fortifications around the Ploiesti refineries; they've been training Romanian soldiers to fight. If they're doing all that, why is it so hard to believe that they intend to start teaching Romanians how to kill Jews? From what I can gather, the major is experienced in killing. He loves his work. He will make a good teacher. I can tell."

It couldn't be! And yet hadn't she also said that Molasar couldn't be? There had been stories in Bucharest about the death camps, whispered tales of the atrocities, of the countless dead; tales which at first no one believed, but as testimony piled upon testimony, even the most skeptical Jew had to accept. The Gentiles did not believe. They were not threatened. It was not in their interest—in fact it could well prove to their detriment—to believe.

"An excellent location," Papa said in a tired voice devoid of emotion. "Easy to get us there. And should

one of their enemies try to bomb the oil fields, the
resulting inferno would do the Nazis' job for them. And
who knows? Perhaps the knowledge of the camp's existence might even cause an enemy to hesitate to bomb
the fields, although I doubt it.''

He paused, winded. Then: ''Kaempffer must be
stopped.''

Magda shot to her feet, wincing at the pain in her
knee. ''You don't think *you* can stop him, do you?
You'd be dead a dozen times over before you could even
scratch him!''

''I must find a way. It's no longer just your life I
worry about. Now it's thousands. And they all hang on
Kaempffer.''

''But even if something does . . . stop him, they'll
only send another in his place!''

''Yes. But that will take time, and any delay is in our
favor. Perhaps in the interval Russia will attack the Germans, or vice versa. I can't see two mad dogs like Hitler
and Stalin keeping away from each other's throats for
too long. And in the ensuing conflict perhaps the
Ploiesti Camp will be forgotten.''

''But how can the major be stopped?'' She had to
make Papa think, make him see how crazy this was.

''Perhaps Molasar.''

Magda was unwilling to believe what she had just
heard. ''Papa, no!''

He held up a cotton-gloved hand. ''Wait, now.
Molasar has hinted that he might use me as an
ally against the Germans. I don't know how I
could be of service to him, but tonight I'll find
out. And in return I'll ask that he be sure to put a
stop to Major Kaempffer.''

''But you can't deal with something like Molasar!
You can't trust him not to kill *you* in the end!''

''I don't care for my own life. I told you, there's more
at stake here. And besides, I detect a certain rough
honor in Molasar. You judge him too harshly, I think.
You react to him as a woman and not as a scholar. He is
a product of his times, and they were bloodthirsty times.

Yet he has a sense of national pride that has been deeply offended by the very presence of the Germans. I may be able to use that. He thinks of us as fellow Wallachians and is better disposed toward us. Didn't he save you from the two Germans you blundered into last night? He could just as easily have made you a third victim. We *must* try to use him! There's no alternative."

Magda stood before him and searched for another option. She could not find one. And although she was repelled by it, Papa's scheme did offer a glimmer of hope. Was she being too hard on Molasar? Did he seem so evil because he was so different, so implacably other? Could he be more of an elemental force than something consciously evil? Wasn't Major Kaempffer a better example of a truly evil being? She had no answers. She was groping.

"I don't like it, Papa," was all she could say.

"No one said you should like it. No one promised us an easy solution—or any solution at all, for that matter." He tried to stifle a yawn, but lost the battle. "And now I'd like to go back to my room. I need sleep for tonight's encounter. I'll require all my wits about me if I'm to strike a bargain with Molasar."

"A deal with the devil," Magda said, her voice falling to a quavering whisper. She was more frightened than ever for her father.

"No, my dear. The devil in the keep wears a black uniform with a silver Death's Head on his cap, and calls himself a *Sturmbannführer.*"

T

Magda reluctantly had returned him to the gate, then had watched until he had been wheeled back into the tower. She hurried back toward the inn in a state of confusion. Everything was moving too quickly for her. Her life until now had been filled with books and research, melodies and black music notes on white paper. She was not cut out for intrigue. Her head still spun with the monstrous implications of what she had been told.

She hoped Papa knew what he was doing. Instinctively, she had opposed his planned liaison with Molasar until she had seen that look on Papa's face. A spark of hope had glimmered there, a shining fragment of the old zest that had once made his company such a pleasure. It was a chance for Papa to *do* something rather than just sit in his wheelchair and have things done to him. He desperately needed to feel he could be of some use to his people . . . to anybody. She could not rob him of that.

As she approached the inn, Magda felt the chill of the keep finally slip away. She strolled around the building in search of Glenn, thinking he might be taking the morning sun at the rear. He was not outside, nor was he in the dining alcove when she passed. She went upstairs and stopped at his door, listening. There was still no sound from within. He hadn't struck her as a late riser; perhaps he was reading.

She raised her hand to knock, then lowered it. Better to run into him around the inn than come looking for him—he might think she was chasing him.

Back in her room she heard the plaintive cheeping of the baby birds and went to the window to look at the nest. She could see their four tiny heads straining up from the nest, but the mother wasn't there. Magda hoped she hurried back—her babies sounded terribly hungry.

She picked up her mandolin but after a few chords put it down again. She was edgy, and the constant noise of the baby birds was making her more so. With a sudden surge of determination, she strode out into the hall.

She rapped twice on the wooden door to Glenn's room. No answer, no sound of movement within. She hesitated, then gave way to impulse and lifted the latch. The door swung open.

"Glenn?"

The room was empty. It was identical to her own; in fact she had stayed in this room on the last trip she and Papa had made to the keep. Something was wrong, though. She studied the walls. The mirror—the mirror over the bureau was gone. A rectangle of whiter stucco marked its former spot on the wall. It must have been broken since her last visit and never replaced.

Magda stepped inside and walked in a slow circle. This was where he stayed, and here was the unmade bed where he slept. She felt excited, wondering what she would say if he came back now. How could she explain her presence? She couldn't. She decided she'd better leave.

As she turned to go, she saw that the closet door was ajar. Something glittered from within. It was pressing her luck, but how much could a quick peek hurt? She pulled the door open all the way.

The mirror that was supposed to hang over the bureau lay propped up in the corner of the closet. Why would Glenn take down the mirror? Maybe he hadn't. Maybe it had fallen off the wall and Iuliu had yet to rehang it. There were a few items of clothing in the closet and something else: A long case of some sort, nearly as long as she was tall, stood in the other corner.

Curious, Magda knelt and touched the leather of the case—rough, warped, puckered. It was either very old or poorly cared for. She could not imagine what could be in it. A quick look over her shoulder assured her that the room was still empty, the door still open, and all quiet in the hallway. It would take only a second to release the catches on the case, peek inside, reclose it, then be on her way. She had to know. Feeling the delicious apprehension of a naughty, inquisitive child exploring a forbidden area of the house, she reached for the brass clasps; there were three of them and they grated as she opened them, as if there were sand in their works. The hinges made a similar sound as she swung the cover open.

At first Magda did not know what it was. The color was blue, a deep, dark, steely blue; the object was metal, but what type of metal she could not say. Its shape was that of an elongated wedge—a long, tapering piece of metal, pointed at the top and very sharp along

both its beveled edges. Like a sword. That was it! A
sword! A broadsword. Only there was no hilt to this
sword, only a thick, six-inch spike at its squared-off
lower end, which looked like it was designed to fit into
the top of a hilt. What a huge, fearsome weapon this
would make when attached to its hilt!

Her eyes were drawn to the markings on the blade—it
was covered with odd symbols. These were not merely
etched into the shiny blue surface of the metal, they
were *carved* into in. She could slip the tip of her little
finger along the grooves. The symbols were runes, but
not like any runes she had ever seen. She was familiar
with Germanic and Scandinavian runes, which went
back to the Dark Ages, back as far as the third century.
But these were older. Much older. They possessed a
quality of eldritch antiquity that disturbed her, seeming
to shift and move as she studied them. This broadsword
blade was *old*—so old she wondered who or what had
made it.

The door to the room slammed closed.

"Find what you're looking for?"

Magda jumped at the sound, causing the lid of the
case to snap closed over the blade. She leaped to her feet
and turned around to face Glenn, her heart thumping
with surprise—and guilt.

"Glenn, I—"

He looked furious. "I thought I could trust you!
What did you hope to find in here?"

"Nothing . . .I came looking for you." She did not
understand the intensity of his anger. He had a right to
be annoyed, but this—

"Did you think you'd find me in the closet?"

"No! I . . ." Why try to explain it away? It would
only sound lame. She had no business being here. She
was in the wrong, she knew it, and she felt terribly guilty
standing here after being caught in the act. But it wasn't
as if she had come here to steal from him. As she felt her
own anger begin to grow at the way he was overreacting,
she found the will to meet his glare with her own. "I'm
curious about you. I came in to talk with you. I—I like

to be with you, and yet I know nothing about you.'' She
tossed her head. ''It won't happen again.''

She moved toward the hall, intending to leave him
with his precious privacy, but she never reached the
door. As she passed between Glenn and the bureau, he
reached out and gripped her shoulders, gently but with a
firmness that was not to be denied. He turned her
toward him. Their eyes locked.

''Magda . . .'' he began, then he was pulling her to
him, pressing his lips against hers, crushing her against
him. Magda experienced a fleeting urge to resist, to
pound her fists against him and pull away, but this was
mere reflex and was gone before she could recognize it,
engulfed by the heat of desire that surged over her. She
slipped her arms around Glenn's neck and pulled closer
to him, losing herself in the glow that enveloped her.
His tongue pushed through to hers, shocking her with
its audacity—she hadn't known anyone kissed like
this—and jolting her with the pleasure it gave. Glenn's
hands began to roam her body, caressing her buttocks
through the layers of her clothes, moving over her com-
pressed breasts, leaving tingling trails of warmth
wherever they went. They rose to her neck, untied her
kerchief and hurled it away, then came to rest on the
buttons of her sweater and began opening them. She
didn't stop him. Her clothes had shrunken on her and
the room had grown so hot . . . she had to be rid of
them.

There was a brief moment then when she could have
stopped it, could have pulled back and retreated. With
the parting of the front of her sweater a small voice
cried out in her mind—*Is this me? What's happening to
me? This is insane!* It was the voice of the old Magda,
the Magda who had faced the world since her mother's
death. But that voice was swept away by another
Magda, a stranger, a Magda who had slowly grown
amid the ruins of everything the old Magda had believed
in. A new Magda, awakened by the vital force that
burned white hot within the man who now held her. The
past, tradition, and propriety had lost all meaning;

tomorrow was a faraway place she might never see. There was only now. And Glenn.

The sweater slipped from her shoulders, then the white blouse. Magda felt fire where her hair brushed the bare skin of her upper back and shoulders. Glenn pushed the tight bandeau down to her waist, allowing her breasts to spring free. Still holding his lips to hers, he ran his fingertips lightly over each breast, zeroing in on the taut nipples and tracing tiny circles that caused her to moan deep in her throat. His lips finally broke from hers, sliding along her throat to the valley between her breasts, from there to her nipples, each in turn, his tongue making little wet circles over the dry ones his fingers had drawn. With a small cry she clutched the back of his head and arched her breasts against his face, shuddering as waves of ecstasy began to pulsate from deep within her pelvis.

He lifted her and carried her to the bed, removing the rest of her clothes while his lips continued to pleasure her. Then his own clothes were off and he was leaning over her. Magda's hands had taken on a life of their own, running over him as if to be sure that he was real. And then he was on her and slipping into her, and after the first jab of pain he was there and it was wonderful.

Oh, God! she thought as spasms of pleasure shot through her. Is this what it's like? Is this what I've been missing all these years? Can this be the awful act I've heard the married women talking about? It can't be! This is too wonderful! And I haven't been missing anything because it never could be like this with any man but Glenn.

He began to move inside her and she matched his rhythm. The pleasure increased, doubling and redoubling until she was sure her flesh would melt. She felt Glenn's body begin to stiffen as she felt the inevitability within herself, too. It happened. With her back arched, her ankles hooked on either side of the narrow mattress, and her knees wide in the air, Magda Cuza saw the world swell, crack, and come apart in a blazing burst of flame.

And after a while, to the accompaniment of her spent body's labored breathing, she watched it fall together again through the lids of her closed eyes.

They spent the day on that narrow little bed, whispering, laughing, talking, exploring each other. Glenn knew so much, taught her so much, it was as if he were introducing her to her own body. He was gentle and patient and tender, bringing her to peaks of pleasure time and time again. He was her first—she didn't say so; she didn't have to. She was far from his first; that, too, required no comment, and Magda found it didn't matter. Yet she sensed a great release within him, as if he had denied himself for a long time.

His body fascinated her. The male physique was *terra incognita* to Magda. She wondered if all men's muscles were so hard and so close to the skin. All of Glenn's hair was red, and there were so many scars on his chest and abdomen; old scars, thin and white on his olive skin. When she asked about them, he told her they were from accidents. Then he quieted her questions by making love to her again.

After the sun had dipped behind the western ridge, they dressed and went for a walk, arm in arm, stretching their limbs, stopping every so often to embrace and kiss. When they returned to the inn, Lidia was putting supper on the table. Magda realized she was famished and so they both sat down and helped themselves, Magda trying to do her best to keep her eyes off Glenn and concentrate on the food, feeding one hunger while another grew. A whole new world had been opened to her today and she was eager to explore it further.

They ate hurriedly and excused themselves the instant they were finished, like schoolchildren hurrying out to play before dark. From the table it was a race to the second floor, Magda ahead, laughing, leading Glenn to *her* room this time. *Her* bed. As soon as the door closed behind them they were pulling at each other's clothes, throwing them in all directions, then clutching each other in the growing dark.

As she lay in his arms hours later, fully spent, at peace

with herself and the world as she had never been before, Magda knew she was in love. Magda Cuza, the spinster bookworm, in love. Never, anywhere, at any time, had there been another man like Glenn. And he *wanted* her. She loved him. She hadn't said so, and neither had he. She felt she should wait until he said it first. It might not be for a while, but that was all right. She could tell he felt it, too, and that was enough.

She snuggled more closely against him. Today alone was enough for the rest of her life. It was almost gluttonous to look forward to tomorrow. Yet she did. Avidly. Surely no one had ever derived so much pleasure from body and emotions as she had today. No one. Tonight she went to sleep a different Magda Cuza than the one who had awakened in this very bed this morning. It seemed so long ago . . . a lifetime ago. And that other Magda seemed like such a stranger now. A sleepwalker, really. The new Magda was wide awake and in love. Everything was going to be all right.

Magda closed her eyes. Faintly, she heard the cheeping of the baby birds ourside the window. Their peeps were fainter than this morning and seemed to have taken on a desperate quality. But before she could wonder about what might be wrong, she was asleep.

⊤

He looked at Magda's face in the dark. Peaceful and innocent. The face of a sleeping child. He tightened his arms around her, afraid she might slip away.

He should have kept his distance; he had known that all along. But he had been drawn to her. He had let her stir the ashes of feelings he had thought long dead and gone, and she had found live coals beneath. And then this morning, in the heat of his anger at finding her snooping through his closet, the coals had burst into flame.

It was almost like fate. Like kismet. He had seen and

experienced far too much to believe that anything was truly ordained to be. There were, however, certain . . . inevitabilities. The difference was subtle, yet most important.

Still, it was wrong to let her care when he didn't even know if he would be walking away from here. Perhaps that was why he had been driven to be with her. If he died here, at least the taste of her would be fresh upon him. He couldn't afford to care now. Caring could distract him, further reducing his chances of surviving the coming battle. And yet if he did manage to survive, would Magda want anything to do with him when she knew the truth about him?

He drew the cover over her bare shoulder. He did not want to lose her. If there were any way to keep her after all this was over, he would do everything he could to find it.

TWENTY-FOUR

Captain Woermann sat before his easel. It had been his intention to force himself to blot out that shadow of the hanging corpse. But now, with his palette in his left hand and a tube of pigment in his right, he found himself unwilling to change it. Let the shadow remain. It didn't matter. He would leave the painting behind anyway. He wanted no reminders of this place when he departed. *If* he departed.

Outside, the keep lights were on full force, the men on guard in pairs, armed to the teeth and ready to shoot at the slightest provocation. Woermann's own weapon lay on his bedroll, holstered and forgotten.

He had developed his own theory about the keep, not one he took seriously, but one that fit most of the facts and explained most of the mysteries. The keep was alive. That would explain why no one had even seen what killed the men, and why no one could track it down, and why no one had been able to find its hiding place despite all the walls they had torn down. It was the keep itself doing the killing.

One fact was left dangling by this explanation, however. A major fact. The keep had not been malevolent when they had entered, at least not in a way one could sense. True, birds seemed to avoid nesting here, but Woermann had felt nothing *wrong* until that first night when the cellar wall had been broached. The keep had changed then. It had become bloodthirsty.

No one had fully explored the subcellar. There really didn't seem to be any reason to. Men had been on guard in the cellar while a comrade had been murdered above them, and they had seen nothing coming or going through the break in the floor. Maybe they should explore the subcellar. Perhaps the keep's heart lay buried in those caverns. That's where they should search. No . . . that could take forever. Those caverns could extend for miles, and frankly, no one really wanted to search them. It was always night down there. And night had become a dread enemy. Only the corpses were willing to stay.

The corpses . . . with their dirty boots and smudged shrouds. They still bothered Woermann at the oddest times. Like now. And all day long, ever since he had overseen the placement of the last two dead soldiers, those dirty boots had trudged unbidden into his thoughts, scattering them, smearing them with mud.

Those dirty, muddy boots. They made him uncomfortable in a way he could not pin down.

He continued to sit and stare at the painting.

Kaempffer sat cross-legged on his cot, a Schmeisser across his knees. A shiver rippled over him. He tried to still it but didn't have strength. He had never realized how exhausting constant fear could be.

He had to get *out* of here!

Blow up the keep tomorrow—that's what he should do! Set the charges and reduce it to gravel after lunch. That way he could spend Saturday night in Ploiesti in a bunk with a real mattress and not worry about every sound, every vagrant current of air. No more would he have to sit and shake and sweat and wonder what might be making its way down the hall to his door.

But tomorrow was too soon. It wouldn't look good on his record. He wasn't due in Ploiesti until Monday and would be expected to use up all the available time until then to solve the problem here. Blowing up the keep was the last resort, to be considered only when all else failed. The High Command had ordered that this pass be watched and had designated the keep as the chosen watchpoint. Destruction had to be the last resort.

He heard the measured treads of a pair of ein-satzkommandos pass his locked door. The hallway out there was doubly guarded. He had made sure of that. Not that there was the slightest chance a stream of lead from a Schmeisser could actually stop whatever was behind the killings here—he simply hoped the guards would be taken first, thereby sparing him another night. And those guards had better stay awake and on duty, no matter how tired they were! He had driven the men hard today to dismantle the rear section of the keep, con-centrating their efforts on the area around his quarters. They had opened every wall within fifty feet of where he now huddled, and had found nothing. There were no secret passages leading to his room, no hiding places anywhere.

He shivered again.

The cold and the darkness came as they had before,

but Cuza was feeling too weak and sick tonight to turn his chair around and face Molasar. He was out of codeine and the pain in his joints was a steady agony.

"How do you enter and leave this room?" he asked for want of anything better to say. He had been facing the hinged slab that opened into the base of the watchtower, assuming Molasar would arrive through there. But Molasar had somehow appeared behind him.

"I have my own means of moving about which does not require doors or secret passages. A method quite beyond your comprehension."

"Along with many other things," Cuza said, unable to keep the despair from his voice.

It had been a bad day. Beyond the unremitting pain was the sick realization that this morning's glimmer of hope for a reprieve for his people had been a chimera, a useless pipe dream. He had planned to bargain with Molasar, to strike a deal. But for what? The end of the major? Magda had been right this morning: Stopping Kaempffer would only delay the inevitable; his death might even make the situation worse. There would most certainly be vicious reprisals on Romanian Jews if an SS officer sent to set up a death camp were brutally murdered. And the SS would merely send another officer to Ploiesti, maybe next week, maybe next month. What did it matter? The Germans had plenty of time. They were winning every battle, overrunning one country after another. There did not seem to be any way of stopping them. And when they finally held the seats of power in all the countries they wanted, they could pursue their insane leader's goals of racial purity at their leisure.

In the long run there was nothing a crippled history professor could do that would make the least bit of difference.

And worsening it all was the insistent knowledge that Molasar feared the cross . . . *feared the cross!*

Molasar glided around into his field of vision and stood there studying him. *Strange*, Cuza thought. *Either I've immersed myself in such a morass of self-pity that*

I'm insulated from him, or I'm getting used to Molasar. Tonight he did not feel the crawling sensation that always accompanied Molasar's presence. Maybe he just didn't care anymore.

"I think you may die," Molasar said without preamble.

The bluntness of the words jolted Cuza. "At your hands?"

"No. At your own."

Could Molasar read minds? Cuza's thoughts had dwelt on that very subject for most of the afternoon. Ending his life would solve so many problems. It would set Magda free. Without him to hold her back, she could flee into the hills and escape Kaempffer, the Iron Guard, and all the rest. Yes, the idea had occurred to him. But he still lacked the means . . . and the resolve.

Cuza averted his gaze. "Perhaps. But if not by my own doing, then soon in Major Kaempffer's death camp."

"Death camp?" Molasar leaned forward into the light, his brow furrowed in curiosity. "A place where people gather to die?"

"No. A place where people are dragged off to be murdered. The major will be setting up one such camp not far south of here."

"To kill Wallachians?" Sudden fury drew Molasar's lips back from his abnormally long teeth. "A German is here to kill *my* people?"

"They are not your people," Cuza said, unable to shake his despondency. The more he thought about it, the worse he felt. "They are Jews. Not the sort you would concern yourself with."

"I shall decide what concerns me! But Jews? There are no Jews in Wallachia—at least not enough to matter."

"When you built the keep that was true. But in the following century we were driven here from Spain and the rest of western Europe. Most settled in Turkey, but many strayed into Poland and Hungary and Wallachia."

" 'We?' '' Molasar looked puzzled. "You are a Jew?"

Cuza nodded, half expecting a blast of anti-Semitism from the ancient boyar. Instead, Molasar said, "But you are a Wallachian, too."

"Wallachia was joined with Moldavia into what is now called Romania."

"Names change. Were *you* born here? Were these other Jews who are destined for the death camps?"

"Yes, but—"

"Then they are Wallachians!"

Cuza sensed Molasar's patience growing short, yet he had to speak: "But their ancestors were immigrants."

"It matters not! My grandfather came from Hungary. Am I, who was born on this soil, any less a Wallachian for that?"

"No, of course not." This was a senseless conversation. Let it end.

"Then neither are these Jews you speak of. They are Wallachians, and as such they are my countrymen!" Molasar straightened up and threw back his shoulders. "No German may come into my country and kill my countrymen!"

Typical! Cuza thought. *I bet he never objected to his fellow boyars' depredations among the Wallachian peasants during his day. And he obviously never objected to Vlad's impalements. It was all right for the Wallachian nobility to decimate the populace, but don't let a foreigner dare!*

Molasar had retreated to the shadows outside the bulb's cone of light. "Tell me about these death camps."

"I'd rather not. It's too—"

"Tell me!"

Cuza sighed. "I'll tell you what I know. The first one was set up in Buchenwald, or perhaps Dachau, around eight years ago. There are others: Flossenburg, Ravensbruck, Natzweiler, Auschwitz, and many others I've probably never heard of. Soon there will be one in Romania—Wallachia, as you would have it—and maybe more within a year or two. The camps serve one purpose: the collection of certain types of people, millions of them, for torture, debasement, forced labor, and eventual extermination."

"Millions?"

Cuza could not read Molasar's tone completely, but there was no doubt that he was having trouble believing what he had been told. Molasar was a shadow among the shadows, his movements agitated, almost frantic.

"Millions," Cuza said firmly.

"I will kill this German major!"

"That won't help. There are thousands like him, and they will come one after another. You may kill a few and you may kill many, but eventually they will learn to kill you."

"Who sends them?"

"Their leader is a man named Hitler who—"

"A king? A prince?"

"No . . ." Cuza fumbled for the word. "I guess *voevod* would be the closest word you have for it."

"Ah! A warlord! Then I shall kill him and he shall send no more!"

Molasar had spoken so matter-of-factly that the full meaning of his words was slow to penetrate the shroud of gloom over Cuza's mind. When it did:

"What did you say?"

"Lord Hitler—when I've regained my full strength I'll drink his life!"

Cuza felt as if he had spent the whole day struggling upward from the floor of the deepest part of the ocean with no hope of reaching air. With Molasar's words he broke surface and gulped life. Yet it would be easy to sink again.

"But you can't! He's well protected! And he's in Berlin!"

Molasar came forward into the light again. His teeth were bared, this time in a rough approximation of a smile.

"Lord Hitler's protection will be no more effective than all the measures taken by his lackeys here in my keep. No matter how many locked doors and armed men protect him, I shall take him if I wish. And no matter how far away he is, I shall reach him when I have the strength.''

Cuza could barely contain his excitement. Here at last was hope—a greater hope than he had ever dreamed possible. ''When will that be? When can you go to Berlin?''

''I shall be ready tomorrow night. I shall be strong enough then, especially after I kill all the invaders.''

''Then I'm glad they didn't heed me when I told them the best thing they could do was to evacuate the keep.''

''*You what?*'' It was a shout.

Cuza could not take his eyes off Molasar's hands— they clutched at him, ready to tear into him, restrained only by their owner's will.

''I'm sorry!'' he said, pressing himself back in his chair. ''I thought that's what you wanted!''

''I want their *lives*!'' The hands retreated. ''When I want anything else I will tell you what it is, and you will do exactly as I say!''

''Of course! Of course!'' Cuza could never fully and truly agree to that, but he was in no position to put on a show of resistance. He reminded himself that he must never forget what sort of a being he was dealing with. Molasar would not tolerate being thwarted in any way; he had no thought other than having his own way. Nothing else was acceptable or even conceivable to him.

''Good. For I have need of mortal aid. It has always been so. Limited as I am to the dark hours, I need someone who can move about in the day to prepare the way for me, to make certain arrangements that can only be made in the day. It was so when I built this keep and arranged for its upkeep, and it is so now. In the past I have made use of human outcasts, men with appetites different from mine but no more acceptable to their fellows. I bought their services by providing them the means to sate those appetites. But you—your price, I feel, will be in accord with my own desires. We share a common cause for now.''

Cuza looked down at his twisted hands. "I fear you could have a better agent than I."

"The task I will require of you tomorrow night is a simple one: An object precious to me must be removed from the keep and hidden in a secure place in the hills. With that safe I shall feel free to pursue and destroy those who wish to kill our countrymen."

Cuza experienced a strange floating sensation, a new emotional buoyancy as he imagined Hitler and Himmler cowering before Molasar, and then their torn and lifeless—better yet, headless—bodies strung up for viewing at the entrance to an empty death camp. It would mean an end to the war and the salvation of his people; not merely Romanian Jewry, but his entire race! It promised a tomorrow for Magda. It meant an end to Antonescu and the Iron Guard. It might even mean reinstatement at the university.

But then reality brought him back down from those heights, back down to his wheelchair. How could he carry anything from the keep? How could he hide it in the hills when his strength could barely wheel him through the door?

"You will need a whole man," he said to Molasar in a voice that threatened to break. "A cripple like me is useless to you."

He sensed rather than saw Molasar move around the table to his side. He felt light pressure on his right shoulder—Molasar's hand. He looked up to see Molasar looking down at him. Smiling.

"You have much to learn about the scope of my powers."

TWENTY-FIVE

Joy.

That's what it was. Magda had never imagined how wonderful it could be to awaken in the morning and find herself wrapped in the arms of someone she loved. Such a peaceful feeling, a safe feeling. It made the prospect of the coming day so much brighter to know that there would be Glenn to share it with.

Glenn lay on his side, she on hers, the two of them face to face. He was still asleep, and although Magda did not want to wake him, she found she could not keep her hands off him. Gently, she ran her palm over his shoulder, fingered the scars on his chest, smoothed the red tumble of his hair. She moved her bare leg against his. It was so sensuously warm under covers, skin to skin, pore to pore. Desire began to add its own kind of heat to her skin. She wished he would wake up.

Magda watched his face as she waited for him to stir. So much to learn about this man. Where exactly was he from? What had his childhood been like? What was he doing here? Why did he have that sword blade with him? Why was he so wonderful? She was like a schoolgirl. She was thrilled with herself. She could not remember being happier.

She wanted Papa to know him. The two of them would get along marvelously. But she wondered how Papa would react to their relationship. Glenn was not Jewish . . . she didn't know what he was, but he was certainly not Jewish. Not that it made any difference to her, but such matters had always been important to Papa.

Papa . . .

A sudden wave of guilt doused her burgeoning desire. While she had been snuggling in Glenn's arms, safe and secure between bouts of thrashing ecstasy, Papa had sat cold and alone in a stone room, surrounded by human devils while he awaited an audience with a creature from Hell. She should be ashamed!

And yet, why shouldn't she have stolen a little pleasure for herself? She had not deserted Papa. She was still here at the inn. He had driven her away from the keep the night before and had refused to leave it at all yesterday. And now that she thought of it, if Papa had come back to the inn with her yesterday morning she would not have entered Glenn's room, and they would not be together this morning.

Strange, how things worked.

But yesterday and last night don't really change things, she told herself. *I'm* changed, but our predicament remains unaltered. This morning Papa and I are at the mercy of the Germans, just as we were yesterday morning and the morning before that. We are still Jews. They are still Nazis.

Magda slipped from Glenn's side and rose to her feet, taking the thin bedspread with her. As she moved to the window she wrapped the fabric around her. Much had changed within her, many inhibitions had fallen away like scale from a buried bronze artifact, but still she could not stand naked at a window in broad daylight.

The keep—she could feel it before she reached the window. The sense of evil within it had stretched to the village during the night . . . almost as if Molasar were reaching out for her. Across the gorge it sat, gray stone under a gray, overcast sky, the last remnants of night fog receding around it. Sentries were still visible on its parapets; the front gate was open. And there was someone or something moving along the causeway toward the inn. Magda squinted in the morning light to see what it was.

It was a wheelchair. And in it . . . Papa. But no one was pushing him. He was propelling himself. With strong, rapid, rhythmic motions, Papa's hands were gripping the wheel rims and his arms were turning them, speeding him along the causeway.

It was impossible, but she was seeing it. And he was coming to the inn!

Calling to Glenn to wake up, she began to run around the room gathering her strewn-about garments and pulling them on. Glenn was up in an instant, laughing at her awkward movements and helping her find her clothes. Magda did not find the situation even slightly amusing. Frantically, she pulled her clothes on and ran from the room. She wanted to be downstairs when Papa arrived.

⊤

Theodor Cuza was finding his own kind of joy in the morning.

He had been cured. His hands were bare and open to the cool morning air as they gripped the wheels of his chair and rolled them along the causeway. All without pain, without stiffness. For the first time in longer than he wished to remember, Cuza had awakened without feeling as if someone had stolen in on him during the night and firmly splinted every one of his joints. His upper arms moved back and forth like well-oiled pistons, his head freely pivoted to either side without pain or protesting creaks. His tongue was moist—there was adequate saliva again to swallow, and it went down easily. His face had thawed so that he could once again smile in a way that did not cause others around him to wince and glance away.

And he was smiling now, grinning idiotically with the joy of mobility, of self-sufficiency, of being able once again to take an active physical role in the world around him.

Tears! There were tears on his cheeks. He had cried often since the disease had firmed its grip upon him, but the tears had long since dried up with the saliva. Now his eyes were wet and his cheeks were slick with them. He was crying, joyfully, unabashedly, as he wheeled himself toward the inn.

Cuza had not known what to expect as Molasar stood over him last night and placed a hand on his shoulder, but he had felt something change within him. He had not known what it was then, but Molasar had told him to go to sleep, that things would be different come morning. He had slept well, without the usual repeated awakenings during the night to grope for the water cup to wet his parched mouth and throat, and had risen later than usual.

Risen . . . that was the word for it. He had risen from a living death. On his first try he had been able to sit up, and then stand up without pain, without gripping the wall or the chair for support. He had known then that he would be able to help Molasar, and help him he would. Anything Molasar wanted him to do, he would do.

There had been some rough moments leaving the keep. He could not let anyone know he could walk, so he imitated his former infirmities as he wheeled himself toward the gate. The sentries had looked at him curiously as he rolled by, but they did not stop him—he had always been free to visit his daughter. Fortunately,

neither of the officers had been in the courtyard as he
had passed through.

And now, with the Germans behind and an unob-
structed causeway ahead, Professor Theodor Cuza spun
the wheels of his chair as fast as he could. He had to
show Magda. She had to see what Molasar had done for
him.

The wheelchair bounced off the end of the causeway
with a jolt that almost tipped him headfirst out of it, but
he kept rolling. It was rougher going in the dirt but he
didn't mind. It gave him a chance to stretch his muscles,
which felt unnaturally strong despite their years of
disuse. He rolled by the front door of the inn, then
turned left around its south side. There was only one
first floor window there, opening into the dining alcove.
He stopped after he passed that and wheeled up close to
the stucco wall. He was out of sight here—no one from
the inn or the keep could see him, and he simply had to
do it once more.

He faced the wall and locked the brakes on his chair.
A push against the armrests and there he was: standing
on his own two feet, supported by no one and nothing.
Alone. Standing. By himself. He was a man again. He
could look other men straight in the eyes instead of ever
up at them. No more a child's-eye view of existence
from down there, where he was always treated as a
child. Now he was up here . . . a man again!

"Papa!"

He turned to see Magda at the corner of the building,
gaping at him.

"Lovely morning, isn't it?" he said and opened his
arms to her. After a heartbeat's hesitation, she rushed
into them.

"Oh, Papa!" she said in a voice that was muffled by
the folds of his jacket as he crushed her against him.
"You can stand!"

"I can do more than that." He stepped away from
her and began to walk around the wheelchair, steadying
himself at first with a hand atop the backrest, then
releasing it as he realized he didn't need it. His legs

felt strong, even stronger than they had felt earlier this morning. He could walk! He felt as if he could run, dance. On impulse, he bent, turned, and spun around in a poor imitation of a step in the Gypsy *abulea*, almost falling over in the process. But he kept his balance and ended up at Magda's side, laughing at her astonished expression.

"Papa, what's happened? It's a miracle!"

Still gasping from laughter and exertion, he grasped her hands. "Yes, a miracle. A miracle in the truest sense of the word."

"But how—"

"Molasar did it. He cured me. I'm free of scleroderma—completely free of it! It's as if I never had it!"

He looked at Magda and saw how her face shone with happiness for him, how her eyes blinked to hold back tears of joy. She was truly sharing this moment with him. And as he looked more closely, he sensed that she was somehow different. There was another, deeper joy in her that he had never seen before. He felt he should probe for its source but could not be bothered with that now. He felt too good, too *alive*!

A movement caught the corner of his eye and he looked up. Magda followed his glance. Her eyes danced when she saw who it was.

"Glenn, look! Isn't it wonderful? Molasar has cured my father!"

The red-haired man with the strange olive skin said nothing as he stood by the corner of the inn. His pale-blue eyes bored into Cuza's own, making him feel as if his very soul were being examined. Magda kept talking excitedly, rushing over to Glenn and pulling him forward by the arm. She seemed almost drunk with happiness.

"It's a miracle! A true miracle! Now we'll be able to get away from here before—"

"What price have you paid?" Glenn said in a low voice that cut through Magda's chatter.

Cuza stiffened and tried to hold Glenn's gaze. He found he could not. There was no happiness for him in the cold blue eyes. Only sadness and disappointment.

"I've paid no price. Molasar did it for a fellow countryman."

"Nothing is free. Ever."

"Well, he did ask me to perform a few services for him, to help make arrangements for him after he leaves the keep since he cannot move about in the day."

"What, specifically?"

Cuza was becoming annoyed with this type of interrogation. Glenn had no right to an answer and he was determined not to give him one. "He didn't say."

"Odd, isn't it, to receive payment for a service you've not yet rendered, nor even agreed to render? You don't even know what will be required of you and yet you have already accepted payment."

"This is not payment," Cuza said with renewed confidence. "This merely enables me to help him. We've made no bargain for there is no need of one. Our bond is the common cause we share—the elimination of Germans from Romanian soil and the elimination of Hitler and Nazism from the world!"

Glenn's eyes widened and Cuza almost laughed at the expression on his face.

"He promised you that?"

"It was not a promise! Molasar was incensed when I told him of Kaempffer's plans for a death camp at Ploiesti. And when he learned that there was a man in Germany named Hitler who was behind it all, he vowed to destroy him as soon as he was strong enough to leave the keep. There was no need of a deal or a bargain or payment—*we have a common cause*!"

He must have been shouting because he noticed that Magda took a step away from him as he finished, a concerned look on her face. She clutched Glenn's arm and leaned against him. Cuza felt himself go cold. He tried to keep his voice calm as he spoke.

"And what have you been doing with yourself since we parted yesterday morning, child?"

"Oh, I—I've been with Glenn most of the time."

She needed to say no more. He knew. Yes, she had

been with Glenn. Cuza looked at his daughter, clinging to the stranger with a wanton familiarity, her head bare, her hair blowing in the wind. She had been *with* Glenn. It angered him. Out of his sight less than two days and she had given herself to this heathen. He would put a stop to *that*! But not now. Soon. There were too many other important matters at hand. As soon as he and Molasar had finished their business in Berlin, he would see to it that this Glenn character with the accusing eyes was taken care of, too.

. . . *taken care of* . . . ? He didn't even know what he meant by that. He wondered at the scope of his hostility toward Glenn.

"But don't you see what this means?" Magda was saying, obviously trying to soothe him. "We can leave, Papa! We can escape down into the pass and get away from here. You don't have to go back to the keep again! And Glenn will help us, won't you, Glenn?"

"Of course. But I think you'd better ask your father first if he *wants* to leave."

Damn him! Cuza thought as Magda turned wondering eyes on him. *Thinks he knows everything!*

"Papa . . . ?" she began, but the look on his face must have told her what the answer would be.

"I must go back," he told her. "Not for myself. I don't matter anymore. It's for our people. Our culture. For the world. Tonight he will be strong enough to put an end to Kaempffer and the rest of the Germans here. After that, I just have to perform a few simple tasks for him and we can walk away from here without worrying about hiding from search parties. And after Molasar kills Hitler—!"

"Can he really do that?" Magda asked, her expression questioning the enormity of the possibility he was describing.

"I asked myself that very question. And then I thought about how he has so terrified these Germans until they are ready to shoot at each other, and has eluded them in that tiny keep for a week and a half, killing them at will." He held up his hands bare to the

wind and watched with a renewed sense of awe as
the fingers flexed and extended easily, painlessly. "And
after what he has done for me, I've come to the conclusion that there is very little he cannot do."

"Can you trust him?" Magda asked.

Cuza stared at her. This Glenn had apparently tainted
her with his suspicious nature. He was no good for her.

"Can I afford *not* to?" he said after a pause. "My
child, don't you see that this will mean a return to nor-
malcy for us all? Our friends the Gypsies will no longer
be hunted down, sterilized, and put to work as slaves.
We Jews will not be driven from our homes and our
jobs, our property will no longer be confiscated, and we
will no longer face the certain extinction of our race.
How can I do anything else *but* trust Molasar?"

His daughter was silent. There was no rebuttal forth-
coming, for no rebuttal existed.

"And for me," he continued, "it will mean a return
to the university."

"Yes . . . your work." Magda seemed to be in a sort
of daze.

"My work was my first thought, yes. But now that I
am fit again, I don't see why I should not be made chan-
cellor."

Magda glanced up sharply. "You never wanted to be
in administration before."

She was right. He never had. But things were different now.

"That was before. This is now. And if I help rid
Romania of the fascists ruining it, don't you think I
should deserve some sort of recognition?"

"You will also have set Molasar loose upon the
world," Glenn said, breaking his prolonged silence.
"That may earn you a kind of recognition you don't
want."

Cuza felt his jaw muscles bunch in anger. Why didn't
this outsider just go away? "He's *already* loose! I'll
merely be channeling his power. There must be a way we
can come to some sort of an . . . arrangement with him.
We can learn so much from a being such as Molasar,

and he can offer so much. Who knows what other supposedly 'incurable' diseases he can remedy? We will owe him an enormous debt for ridding us of Nazism. I would consider it a moral obligation to find some way of coming to terms with him.''

''Terms?'' Glenn said. ''What kind of terms are you prepared to offer him?''

''Something can be arranged.''

''What, specifically?''

''I don't know—we can offer him the Nazis who started this war and who run the death camps. That's a good start.''

''And after they're gone? Who next? Remember, Molasar will go on and on. You will have to provide sustenance forever. Who next?''

''I will not be interrogated like this!'' Cuza shouted as his temper frayed to the breaking point. ''Something will be worked out! If an entire nation can accommodate itself to Adolf Hitler, surely we can find a way to coexist with Molasar!''

''There can be no coexistence with monsters,'' Glenn said, ''be they Nazis or Nosferatu. Excuse me.''

He turned and strode away. Magda stood still and quiet, staring after him. And Cuza in turn stared at his daughter, knowing that although she had not run after the stranger in body, she had done so in spirit. He had lost his daughter.

The realization should have hurt, should have cut him to the bone and made him bleed. Yet he felt no pain or sense of loss. Only anger. He felt two steps removed from all emotions except rage at the man who had taken his daughter away from him.

Why didn't he hurt?

After watching Glenn until he had rounded the corner of the inn, Magda turned back to her father. She studied his angry face, trying to understand what was going on inside him, trying to sort out her own confused feelings.

Papa had been cured, and that was wonderful. But at what price? He had changed so—not just in body, but in mind, in personality even. There was a note of arrogance in his voice she had never heard before. And his defensiveness about Molasar was totally out of character. It was as if Papa had been fragmented and then put back together with fine wire . . . but with some of the pieces missing.

"And you?" Papa asked. "Are you going to walk away from me, too?"

Magda studied him before answering. He was almost a stranger. "Of course not," she said, hoping her voice did not show how much she ached to be with Glenn right now. "But . . ."

" 'But' what?" His voice cut her like a whip.

"Have you really thought about what dealing with a creature like Molasar means?"

The contortions of Papa's newly mobilized face as he replied shocked her. His lips writhed as he grimaced with fury.

"*So!* Your lover has managed to turn you against your own father and against your own people, has he?" His words struck like blows. He barked a harsh, bitter laugh. "How easily you are swayed, my child! A pair of blue eyes, some muscles, and you're ready to turn your back on your people as they are about to be slaughtered!"

Magda swayed on her feet as if buffeted by a gale. This could not be Papa talking! He had never been cruel to her or to anyone, and yet now he was utterly vicious! But she refused to let him see how much he had just hurt her.

"My only concern was for you," she said through tight lips that would have quivered had she allowed them to. "You don't know that you can *trust* Molasar!"

"And you don't know that I *can't*! You've never spoken with him, never heard him out, never seen the look in his eyes when he talks of the Germans who have invaded his keep and his country.''

"I've felt his touch," Magda said, shivering despite the sunlight. "Twice. There was nothing there to convince me that he could care a bit for the Jews—or for any living thing."

"I've felt his touch, too," Papa said, raising his arms and walking in a quick circle around the empty wheelchair. "See for yourself what that touch has done for me! As for Molasar saving our people, I have no delusions. He doesn't care about Jews in other lands; only in his own. Only Romanian Jews. The key word is *Romanian*! He was a nobleman in this land, and he still considers it *his* land. Call it nationalism or patriotism or whatever—it doesn't matter. The fact is that he wants all Germans off what he calls 'Wallachian soil' and he intends to do something about it. Our people will benefit. And I intend to do anything I can to help him!''

The words rang true. Magda couldn't help but admit that. They were logical, plausible. And it could be a noble thing Papa was doing. Right now he could run off and save himself and her; instead, he was committing himself to return to the keep to try to save more than two lives. He was risking his own life for a greater goal. Maybe it was the right thing to do. Magda so wanted to believe that.

But she could not. The numbing cold of Molasar's touch had left her with a permanent rime of mistrust. And there was something else, too: the look in Papa's eyes as he spoke to her now. A wild look. Tainted . . .

"I only want you safe." It was all she could say.

"And I want *you* safe," he told her.

She noted a softening in his eyes and in his voice. He was more like his old self for a moment.

"I also want you to stay away from that Glenn," he said. "He's no good for you."

Magda looked away, downward to the floor of the pass. She would never agree to give up Glenn. "He's the best thing that ever happened to me."

"Is that so?"

She sensed the hardness creeping back into Papa's tone.

"Yes." Her voice sank to a whisper. "He's made me see that I've never really known the meaning of living until now."

"How touching! How melodramatic!" Papa said, his voice dripping scorn. "But he's not a Jew!"

Magda had been expecting this. "I don't care!" she said, facing him. And somehow she knew that Papa no longer cared either—it was just another objection to fling at her. "He's a good man. And if and when we get out of here, I'll stay with him, if he'll have me!"

"We'll see about that!" There was menace in his expression. "But for now I can see that we have no more to discuss!" He threw himself into the wheelchair.

"Papa?"

"Push me back to the keep!"

Anger flared in Magda. "Push yourself back!" She regretted her words immediately. She had never spoken to her father that way in her entire life. What was worse: Papa did not seem to notice. Either that, or he had noticed and did not care enough to react.

"It was foolish of me to wheel myself over this morning," he said as if she had not spoken at all. "But I could not wait around for you to come and get me. I must be more careful. I want no suspicions raised about the true state of my health. I want no extra watch on me. So get behind me and push."

Magda did so, reluctantly and resentfully. For once, she was glad to leave him at the gate and walk back alone.

Matei Stephanescu was angry. Rage burned in his chest like a glowing coal. He did not know why. He sat tense and rigid in the front room of his tiny house at the southern end of the village, a cup of tea and a loaf of

bread on the table before him. He thought of many
things. And his rage grew steadily hotter.

He thought of Alexandru and his sons and how it
wasn't right that they should get to work at the keep all
their lives and earn gold while he had to chase a herd of
goats up and down the pass until they grew big enough
to sell or barter for his needs. He had never envied
Alexandru before, but this morning it seemed that
Alexandru and his sons were at the core of all his ills.

Matei thought about his own sons. He needed them
here. He was forty-seven and already gray in the hair
and knobby in the joints. But where were his sons? They
had deserted him—gone to Bucharest two years ago to
seek their fortunes, leaving their father and mother
alone. They had not cared enough for their father to
stay near him and help him as he grew older. He hadn't
heard from either of them since they'd left. If he instead
of Alexandru had had the work at the keep, Matei was
sure his own sons would now be at his side and perhaps
Alexandru's would have run off to Bucharest.

It was a rotten world and getting rottener. Even his
own wife did not care enough about him to get out of
bed for him this morning. Ioan had always been anxious
to see that he got off with a good breakfast. But this
morning was different. She wasn't sick. She had merely
told him, "Go fix it yourself!" And so he had fixed his
own tea, which now sat cold and untasted before him.
He picked up the knife that lay next to the teacup and
cut a thick slice of bread. But after his first bite he spit it
out.

Stale!

Matei slammed his hand down on the table. He could
not take much more of this. With the knife still in his
hand he marched into the bedroom and stood over the
prone form of his wife still bundled under the covers.

"The bread's stale," he said.

"Then bake some fresh for yourself," came the muffled reply.

"You're a miserable wife!" he cried in a hoarse voice.
The handle of the knife was sweaty in his hand. His tem-

per was reaching the breaking point.

Ioan threw the covers off and rose to her knees on the bed, hands on hips, her black hair in wild disarray, her face puffy with sleep and fired with a rage that mirrored his own.

"And you are a poor excuse for a man!"

Matei stood and stared at his wife in shock. For a heartbeat he seemed to step outside himself to view the scene. It was not like Ioan to say such a thing. She loved him. And he loved her. But right now he wanted to kill her.

What was happening? It was as if there were something in the air they breathed that brought out the worst in them.

And then he was back behind his own eyes, boiling with insensate rage, driving the knife toward his wife. He felt the impact rattle up his arm as the blade rammed into Ioan's flesh, heard her scream in fear and pain. And then he turned and walked out, never turning back to see where the knife had struck, or whether Ioan was still alive or dead.

🜚

As Captain Woermann tightened the collar on his tunic before going down to the mess for lunch, he glanced out his window and saw the professor and his daughter approaching the keep on the causeway. He studied the pair, taking a certain grim satisfaction in the knowledge that his decision to make the girl stay at the inn rather than at the keep, and to allow the two of them to meet freely and confer during the day, had been a good one. There had been greater harmony among the men with her out of sight, and she had not bolted despite the fact that she had been left unguarded. He had made the proper assessment of her: loyal and devoted. As he watched, he saw that they were embroiled in a considerably animated discussion.

Something about the scene struck Woermann as wrong. He scrutinized them until he noticed that the old man's gloves were off. He had yet to see the professor's hands uncovered since his arrival. And Cuza seemed to be helping the chair along by pushing against the wheels.

Woermann shrugged. Perhaps the professor was just having a good day. He trotted down the steps, strapping on his belt and holster as he went. The courtyard was a shambles, a confusion of jeeps, lorries, generators, and granite block torn from the walls. The men on the work detail were in the mess in the rear having lunch. They did not seem to be working so hard today as they had been yesterday; but then, there had been no death last night to spur them on.

He heard voices raised from the gate and turned to look. It was the professor and the girl, arguing as the sentry stood by impassively. Woermann did not have to understand Romanian to know that there was contention between them. The girl seemed to be on the defensive but was holding her ground. Good for her. The old man seemed too much of a tyrant to Woermann, using his illness as a weapon against the girl.

But he seemed less ill today. His usually frail voice sounded strong and vibrant. The professor must be having a very good day indeed.

Woermann turned and began walking toward the mess area. After a few firm steps, however, his pace faltered and slowed as his gaze was drawn to the right where an open arch sat dark and still, giving access via its stone gullet to the cellar and beyond.

Those boots . . . those damned muddy boots . . .

They haunted him, taunted him . . . something nasty about them. He had to check them again. Just once.

He descended the steps quickly and hurried down the cellar hall. No need to prolong this. Just a quick look and then back up to the light. He snatched a lantern from the floor by the break in the wall, lit it, and then made his way down into the cold, silent night of the sub-cellar.

At the base of the steps were three large rats sniffing around in the slime and dirt. Grimacing with disgust, Woermann pawed for his Luger while the rats glared at him defiantly. By the time his weapon had been freed and a cartridge chambered, the rats had scurried away.

Keeping the pistol raised before him, Woermann hurried over to the row of sheeted cadavers. He saw no more rats on the way. The question of the muddy boots had been blotted from his mind. All he cared about now was the condition of the dead soldiers. If those rats had been at them he would never forgive himself for delaying shipment of the remains.

Nothing seemed amiss. The sheets were all in place. He lifted the covers one by one to inspect the dead faces, but there was no sign that the rats had been gnawing at them. He touched the flesh of one of the faces—cold . . . icy cold and hard. Probably not at all appetizing to a rat.

Still, he could take no chances now that he had seen rats here. The bodies would be shipped out first thing tomorrow morning. He had waited long enough. As he straightened up and turned to leave, he noticed a hand of one of the corpses sticking out from under its sheet. He bent again to tuck it back under the cover but snatched his hand away as it came in contact with the dead fingertips.

They were shredded.

Cursing the rats, he held the lamp closer to see how much damage they had done. A crawling sensation ran down his spine as he inspected the hand. It was filthy. The nails were shattered and caked with dirt, the flesh of each fingertip torn and shredded almost to the bone.

Woermann felt sick. He had seen hands like this once before. They had belonged to a soldier in the last war who had received a head wound and mistakenly had been pronounced dead. He had been buried alive. After awakening in his coffin he had clawed his way through a pine box and five or six feet of dirt. Despite his superhuman efforts, the poor fellow never made it to the surface. But before his lungs gave out, his hands had broken through to the air.

And those hands, both of them, had looked like this.

Shuddering, Woermann backed away toward the steps. He did not want to see the dead soldier's other hand. He did not want to see any more down here. Ever again.

He turned and ran for daylight.

Magda returned directly to her room, intending to spend a few hours alone there. So many things to think about; she needed time with herself. But she could not think. The room was too full of Glenn and of memories of last night. The rumpled bed in the corner was a continual distraction.

She wandered to the window, drawn as ever to the sight of the keep. The malaise that had once been confined within its walls now saturated the air she breathed, further frustrating her attempts at coherent thought. The keep sat out there on its stone perch like some slimy sea thing sending out tentacles of evil in all directions.

As she turned away, the bird's nest caught her eye. The chicks were strangely silent. After their insistent cheeping all yesterday and into the night, it was odd they should be so quiet now. Unless they had flown the nest. But that couldn't be. Magda did not know much about birds but she knew those tiny things had been far from ready for flight.

Concerned, she pulled the stool over to the window and stepped up for a view into the nest. The chicks were there: still, limp, fuzzy forms with open, silent mouths and huge, glassy, sightless eyes. Looking at them, Magda felt an unaccountable sense of loss. She jumped down from the stool and leaned against the windowsill, puzzled. No violence had been done to the baby birds.

They had simply died. Disease? Or had they starved to death? Had the mother fallen victim to one of the village cats? Or had she deserted them?

Magda didn't want to be alone anymore.

She crossed the hall and knocked on Glenn's door. When there was no reply she pushed it open and stepped inside. Empty. She went to the window and looked out to see if Glenn might be taking the sun at the rear of the building, but there was no one there.

Where could he be?

She went downstairs. The sight of dirty dishes left on the table in the alcove struck her. Magda had always known Lidia to be an immaculate housekeeper. The dishes reminded her that she had missed breakfast. It was almost lunchtime now and she was hungry.

Magda stepped through the front door and found Iuliu standing outside, looking toward the other end of the village.

"Good morning," she said. "Any chance of lunch being served early?"

Iuliu swiveled his bulk to look at her. The expression on his stubbly face was aloof and hostile, as if he could not imagine dignifying such a request with a reply. After a while he turned away again.

Magda followed his gaze down the road to a knot of people outside one of the village huts.

"What happened?" she asked.

"Nothing that would interest an outsider," Iuliu replied in a surly tone. Then he seemed to change his mind. "But perhaps you *should* know." There was a malicious slant to his smile. "Alexandru's boys have been fighting with each other. One is dead and the other badly hurt."

"How awful!" Magda said. She had met Alexandru and his sons, questioned them about the keep a number of times. They had all seemed so close. She was as shocked by the news of the death as she was by the pleasure Iuliu seemed to have taken in telling her.

"Not awful, *Domnisoara* Cuza. Alexandru and his

family have long thought themselves better than the rest of us. Serves them right!'' His eyes narrowed. ''And it serves as a lesson to outsiders who come here thinking themselves better than the people who live here.''

Magda backed away from the threat in Iuliu's voice. He had always been such a placid fellow. What had gotten into him?

She turned and walked around the inn. Now more than ever she needed to be with Glenn. But he was nowhere in sight. Nor was he at his usual spot in the brush where he watched the keep.

Glenn was gone.

Worried and despondent, Magda walked back to the inn. As she stepped up to the door she saw a hunched figure limping up from the village. It was a woman and she appeared to be hurt.

''Help me!''

Magda started toward her but Iuliu appeared at the doorway and pulled her back.

''You stay here!'' he told Magda gruffly, then turned toward the injured woman. ''Go away, Ioan!''

''I'm hurt!'' she cried. ''Matei stabbed me!''

Magda saw that the woman's left arm hung limp at her side and her clothing—it looked like a nightgown—was soaked with blood on the left side from shoulder to knee.

''Don't bring your troubles here,'' Iuliu told her. ''We have our own.''

The woman continued forward. ''Help me, please!''

Iuliu stepped away from the door and picked up an apple-sized rock.

''*No!*'' Magda cried and reached to stay his arm.

Iuliu elbowed her aside and threw the rock, grunting with the force he put behind it. Fortunately for the woman his aim was poor and the missile whizzed harmlessly past her head. But its message was not lost on her. With a sob, she turned and began hobbling away.

Magda started after her. ''Wait! I'll help you!''

But Iuliu grabbed her roughly by the arm and shoved her through the doorway into the inn. Magda stumbled and fell to the floor.

"You'll mind your business!" he shouted. "I don't need anyone bringing trouble to my house! Now get upstairs and stay there!"

"You can't—" Magda began, but then saw Iuliu step forward with bared teeth and a raised arm. Frightened, she leaped to her feet and retreated to the stairs.

What had come over Iuliu? He was a different person! The whole village seemed to have fallen under a vicious spell—stabbings, killings, and no one willing to give the slightest aid to a neighbor in need. What was happening here?

Once upstairs, Magda went directly to Glenn's room. It was unlikely he could have returned without her spotting him, but she had to check.

Still empty.

Where *was* he?

She wandered about the tiny room. She checked the closet and found everything as it had been yesterday—the clothes, the case with the hiltless sword blade in it, the mirror. The mirror bothered her. She looked over to the space above the bureau. The nail was still in the wall there. She reached behind the mirror and found the wire still intact. Which meant it hadn't fallen from the wall; someone had *taken* it down. Glenn? Why would he do that?

Uneasy, she closed the closet door and left the room. Papa's cruel words of the morning and Glenn's unexplained disappearance were combining, she decided, to make her suspicious of everything. She had to hold herself together. She had to believe that Papa would be all right, that Glenn would come back to her soon, and that the people in the village would return to their former gentle selves.

Glenn . . . where could he have gone? And why? Yesterday had been a time of complete togetherness for the two of them, and today she couldn't even find him. Had he used her? Had he taken his pleasure with her and now abandoned her? No, she couldn't believe that.

He had seemed greatly disturbed by what Papa had told him this morning. Glenn's absence might have something to do with that. Still, she felt he had deserted her.

As the sun sank closer to the mountaintops, Magda became almost frantic. She checked his room again—no change. Disconsolately, she wandered back to her own room and to the window facing the keep. Avoiding the silent nest, her eyes ranged the brush along the edge of the gorge, looking for something, anything that might lead her to Glenn.

And then she saw movement within the brush to the right of the causeway. Without waiting for a second look to be sure, Magda ran for the stairs. It had to be Glenn! It *had* to be!

Iuliu was nowhere about and she left the inn without any trouble. As she approached the brush, she spied his red hair among the leaves. Her heart leaped. Joy and relief flooded through her—along with a hint of resentment for the torment she had been through all day.

She found him perched on a rock, watching the keep from the cover of the branches. She wanted to throw her arms around him and laugh because he was safe, and she wanted to scream at him for disappearing without a word.

"Where have you been all day?" Magda asked as she came up behind him, trying her best to keep her voice calm.

He answered without turning around. "Walking. I had some thinking to do, so I took a walk along the floor of the pass. A long walk."

"I missed you."

"And I you." He turned and held out his arm. "There's room enough here for two." His smile was not as wide or as reassuring as it could have been. He seemed strangely subdued, preoccupied.

Magda ducked under his arm and hugged against him. Good . . . it felt good within the carapace of that arm. "What's worrying you?"

"A number of things. These leaves for instance." He grabbed a handful from the branches nearest him and crumbled them in his fist. "They're drying out. Dying. And it's only April. And the villagers . . ."

"It's the keep, isn't it?" Magda said.

"It seems that way, doesn't it? The longer the Germans stay in there, the more they chip away at the interior of the structure, the further the evil within spreads. Or so it seems."

"Or so it seems," Magda echoed him.

"And then there's your father . . ."

"He worries me, too. I don't want Molasar to turn on him and leave him"—she could not say it; her mind refused to picture it—"like the others."

"Worse things can happen to a man than having his blood drained."

The solemnity of Glenn's tone struck her. "You said that once before, on the first morning you met Papa. But what could be worse?"

"He could lose his self."

"Himself?"

"No. *Self*. His own self. What he is, what he has struggled all his life to be. That can be lost."

"Glenn, I don't understand." And she didn't. Or perhaps didn't want to. There was a faraway look in Glenn's eyes that disturbed her.

"Let's suppose something," he said. "Let's suppose that the vampire, or *moroi*, or undead, as he exists in legend—a spirit confined to the grave by day, rising at night to feed on the blood of the living—is nothing more than the legend you always thought it to be. Suppose instead that the vampire myth is the result of ancient tale-tellers' attempts to conceptualize something beyond their understanding; that the real basis for the legend is a being who thirsts for nothing so simple as blood, but who feeds instead on human weakness, who thrives on madness and pain, who steadily gains strength and power from human misery, fear, and degradation."

His voice, his tone, made her uncomfortable. "Glenn, don't talk like that. That's awful. How could anything feed on pain and misery? You're not saying that Molasar—"

"I'm just supposing."

"Well, you're wrong," she said with true conviction. "I know Molasar is evil, and perhaps insane. That's because of what he is. But he's not evil in the way you describe. He can't be! Before we arrived he saved the villagers the major had taken prisoner. And remember what he did for me when those two soldiers attacked me." Magda closed her eyes at the memory. "He saved me. And what could be more degrading than rape at the hands of two Nazis? Something that feeds on degradation could have had a small feast at my expense. But Molasar pulled them off me and killed them."

"Yes. Rather brutally, I believe, from what you told me."

Queasily, Magda remembered the soldiers' gurgling death rattles, the grinding of the bones in their necks as Molasar shook them. "So?"

"So he did not go completely unappeased."

"But he could have killed me, too, if that would have given him pleasure. But he didn't. He returned me to my father."

Glenn's eyes pierced her. "Exactly!"

Puzzled by Glenn's response, Magda faltered, then hurried on.

"And as for my father, he's spent the last few years in almost continual agony. Completely miserable. And now he's cured of his scleroderma. It's as if he never had it! If human misery nourishes Molasar, why has he not let my father remain ill and in pain and feed on that? Why cut off a source of 'nourishment' by healing my father?"

"Why indeed?"

"Oh, Glenn!" she said, clutching herself to him. "Don't frighten me any more than I already am! I don't want to argue with you—I've already had such an awful time with my father. I couldn't bear to be at odds with you, too!"

Glenn's arm tightened around her. "All right, then.

But think on this: Your father is healthier now in body than he has been for many years. But what of the man within? Is he the same man you came here with four days ago?"

That was a question that had plagued Magda all day—one she didn't know how to answer.

"Yes . . . No . . . I don't know! I think he's just as confused as I am right now. But I'm sure he'll be all right. He's just had a shock, that's all. Being suddenly cured of a supposedly incurable, steadily crippling disease would make anyone behave strangely for a while. But he'll get over it. You wait and see."

Glenn said nothing, and Magda was glad of that. It meant that he, too, wanted peace between them. She watched the fog form along the floor of the pass and start to rise as the sun ducked behind the peaks. Night was coming.

Night. Papa had said that Molasar would rid the keep of Germans tonight. That should have given her hope, but somehow it seemed terrible and ominous to her. Even the feel of Glenn's arm around her could not entirely allay her fear.

"Let's go back to the inn," she said at last.

Glenn shook his head. "No. I want to see what happens over there."

"It could be a long night."

"It might be the longest night ever," he said without looking at her. "Endless."

Magda glanced up and caught a look of terrible guilt passing over his face. What was tearing him up inside? Why wouldn't he share it with her?

TWENTY-SIX

"Are you ready?"

The words did not startle Cuza. After seeing the last dying rays of the sun fade from the sky, he had been anticipating Molasar's arrival. At the sound of the hollow voice, he rose from the wheelchair, proud and grateful to be able to do so. He had waited all day for the sun to go down, cursing it at times for being so slow in its course across the sky.

And now the moment was finally here. Tonight would be *his* night and no one else's. Cuza had waited for this. It was his. No one could take it from him.

"Ready!" he said, turning to find Molasar standing close behind him, barely visible in the glow of a single candle on the table. Cuza had unscrewed the electric bulb overhead. He found himself more comfortable in the wan flicker of the candle. More at ease. More at home. More at one with Molasar. "Thanks to you, I'm able to help."

Molasar's expression was neutral. "It took little to heal the wounds caused by your illness. Had I been stronger, I could have healed you in an instant; in my relatively weakened condition, however, it took all night."

"No doctor could have done it in a lifetime—*two* lifetimes!"

"Nothing!" Molasar said with a quick, deprecating gesture of his right hand. "I have great powers for bringing death, but also great powers for healing. There is always a balance. Always."

He thought Molasar's mood uncharacteristically philosophical. But Cuza had no time for philosophy tonight. "What do we do now?"

"We wait," Molasar said. "All is not yet ready."

"And after—what?" Cuza could barely contain his impatience. "What then?"

Molasar strolled to the window and looked out at the darkening mountains. After a long pause, he spoke in a low tone.

"Tonight I am going to entrust you with the source of my power. You must take it, remove it from the keep, and find a safe hiding place for it somewhere up in those crags. You must not let anyone stop you. You must *not* allow anyone to take it from you."

Cuza was baffled. "The source of your power?" He racked his memory. "I never heard of the undead having such a thing."

"That is because we never wished it to be known," Molasar said, turning and facing him. "My powers flow from it, but it is also the most vulnerable point in my defenses. It allows me to exist as I do, but in the wrong hands it can be used to end my existence. That is why I always keep it near me where I can protect it."

"What *is* it? Where—"

"A talisman, hidden now in the depths of the sub-cellar. If I am to depart the keep, I cannot leave it behind unprotected. Nor can I risk taking it with me to Germany. So I must give it over for safekeeping to someone I can trust." He moved closer.

Cuza felt a chill steal over his skin as the depthless black of Molasar's pupils fixed on him, but he forced himself to stand his ground.

"You can trust me. I'll hide it so well that even a mountain goat will be hard pressed to find it. I swear!"

"Do you?" Molasar moved even closer. Candlelight flickered off his waxy face. "It will be the most important task you have ever undertaken."

"I can do it—now," Cuza said, balling his fists and feeling strength rather than pain in the movement. "No one will take it away from me."

"It is unlikely that anyone will try. And even if someone does, it is doubtful anyone alive today would know how to use it against me. But on the other hand, it is made of gold and silver. Should someone find it and try to melt it down . . ."

A twinge of uncertainty plucked at Cuza. "Nothing can stay hidden forever."

"Forever is not necessary. Only until I have finished with Lord Hitler and his cohorts. It need remain safe only until I return. After that I shall again take charge of its protection."

"It *will* be safe!" Cuza's self-confidence flowed back into him. He could hide anything in these hills for a few days. "When you return it shall be waiting for you. Hitler gone—what a glorious day that will be! Freedom for Romania, for the Jews. And for me—vindication!"

"Vindication?"

"My daughter—she does not think I should trust you."

Molasar's eyes narrowed. "It was not wise to discuss this with anyone, even your own daughter."

"She is as anxious to see Hitler gone as I am. She simply finds it hard to believe that you are sincere. She's being influenced by the man I fear has become her lover."

"What man?"

Cuza thought he saw Molasar flinch, thought the pallid face had grown a shade paler. "I don't know much about him. His name is Glenn and he seems to have an interest in the keep. But as to—"

Cuza suddenly felt himself jerked forward and upward. In a blur of motion, Molasar's hands had shot out, grasped the fabric of his coat, and lifted him clear off the floor.

"What does he look like?" The words were harsh, forced through clenched teeth.

"He—he's tall!" Cuza blurted, terrified by the enormous strength in the cold hands just inches from his throat, and the long yellow teeth so near. "Almost as tall as you, and—"

"His hair! What about his hair?"

"Red!"

Molasar hurled him away through the air, sending him tumbling across the room, rolling and skidding helplessly, bruisingly along the floor. And as he did, a guttural sound escaped Molasar's throat, distorted by rage but recognizable to Cuza as—

"Glaeken!"

Cuza thudded against the far wall of the room and lay dazed for a moment. As his vision slowly cleared, he saw something he had never expected to see in Molasar's face: fear.

Glaeken? Cuza thought, crouching, afraid to speak. Wasn't that the name of the secret sect Molasar had mentioned two nights ago? The fanatics who used to pursue him? The ones he had built the keep to hide from? He watched Molasar go to the window and stare out toward the village, his expression unreadable. Finally, he turned again toward Cuza. His mouth was set in a tight, thin line.

"How long has he been here?"

"Three days—since Wednesday evening." Cuza felt compelled to add: "Why? What's wrong?"

Molasar did not answer immediately. He paced back

and forth in the growing darkness beyond the candlelight—three steps this way, three steps that way, deep in thought. And then he stopped.

"The Glaeken sect must still exist," he said in a hushed voice. "I should have known! They were always too tenacious, their zeal for world domination too fanatical for them to die out! These Nazis you speak of . . . this Hitler . . . it all makes sense now. Of course!"

Cuza felt it might be safe to rise. "What makes sense?"

"The Glaeken always chose to work behind the scenes, using popular movements to hide their identity and their true aims." Molasar stood there, a towering shadow, and raised his fists. "I see it now. Lord Hitler and his followers are just another façade for the Glaeken. I've been a fool! I should have recognized their methods when you first told me about the death camps. And then that twisted cross these Nazis have painted on everything—how obvious! The Glaeken were once an arm of the Church!"

"But Glenn—"

"He is one of them! Not one of their puppets like the Nazis, but one of the inner circle. A true member of the Glaeken—one of its assassins!"

Cuza felt his throat constrict. "But how can you be sure?"

"The Glaeken breed their assassins true to a certain form: always blue eyes, always faintly olive skin, always red hair. They are trained in every method of killing, including ways of killing the undead. This one who calls himself Glenn means to see that I never leave my keep!"

Cuza leaned against the wall, reeling at the thought of Magda in the arms of a man who was part of the real power behind Hitler. It was too fantastic to believe! And yet it all seemed to fit. That was the real horror of it—it all fit. No wonder Glenn had been so upset at hearing him say he was going to help Molasar rid the world of Hitler. It also explained Glenn's unceasing efforts to cast doubt on everything Molasar had told him.

And it explained, too, why Cuza had instinctively come to loathe the red-haired man. The monster was not Molasar—it was Glenn! And at this very moment Magda was no doubt with him! Something had to be done!

He steadied himself and looked at Molasar. Cuza could not allow himself to panic now. He needed answers before deciding what to do. "How can he possibly stop you?"

"He knows ways . . . ways perfected by his sect over centuries of conflict with my kind. He alone would be able to use my talisman against me. If he gains possession of it he will destroy me!"

"Destroy you . . ." Cuza stood in a daze. Glenn could ruin everything. If Glenn destroyed Molasar it would mean more death camps, more conquests by Hitler's armies . . . the eradication of the Jews as a people.

"He must be eliminated," Molasar said. "I cannot risk leaving my source of power here behind me while he is about."

"Then do it!" Cuza said. "Kill him like you killed the others!"

Molasar shook his head. "I am not yet strong enough to face one such as he—at least not outside these walls. I'm stronger in the keep. If there were some way to bring him here, I could deal with him. I could then see that he would never interfere with me—ever!"

"I have it!" The solution was suddenly clear in Cuza's brain, crystallizing even as he spoke. It was so simple. "We'll have him *brought* here."

Molasar's expression was dubious but interested. "By whom?"

"Major Kaempffer will be more than happy to do it!" Cuza heard himself laugh and was startled at the sound. But why not laugh? He could not suppress his glee at the idea of using an SS major to help rid the world of Nazism.

"Why should he want to do that?"

"Leave it to me!"

Cuza seated himself in the wheelchair and began rolling toward the door. His mind was working furiously. He would have to find the right way to bend the major to his way of thinking, to let Kaempffer reach the decision to bring Glenn over to the keep on his own. He wheeled himself out of the tower and into the courtyard.

"Guard! Guard!" he shouted. Sergeant Oster hurried over immediately, two other soldiers behind him. "Get the major!" he called, puffing with feigned exertion. "I must speak to him immediately!"

"I'll relay the message," the sergeant said, "but don't expect him to come running." The other two soldiers grinned at this.

"Tell him I've learned something important about the keep, something that must be acted upon tonight. Tomorrow may be too late!"

The sergeant looked at one of the privates and jerked his head toward the rear of the keep. "Move!" To the other, he gestured toward the wheelchair. "Let's see to it that Major Kaempffer doesn't have to walk too far to see what the professor has to say."

Cuza was wheeled as far across the courtyard as the rubble would allow, then left to wait. He sat quietly, composing what he would say. After many long minutes, Kaempffer appeared at the opening in the rear wall, his head bare. He was obviously annoyed.

"What do you have to tell me, Jew?" he called.

"It's of utmost importance, Major," Cuza replied, weakening his voice so Kaempffer would have to strain to hear. "And not for shouting."

As Major Kaempffer picked his way through the maze of fallen stone, his lips were moving, indubitably forming silent curses.

Cuza had not realized how much he would enjoy this little charade.

Kaempffer finally arrived at the wheelchair's side and waved the others away. "This had better be good, Jew. If you've brought me out here for nothing—"

"I believe I've discovered a new source of information about the keep," Cuza told him in a low, conspiratorial tone. "There's a stranger over at the inn. I met him today. He seems very interested in what is going on here—*too* interested. He questioned me very closely on it this morning.''

''Why should that interest me?''

''Well, he made a few statements which struck me as odd. So odd that I looked into the forbidden books when I returned and found references there which backed up his statements.''

''What statements?''

''They are unimportant in themselves. What *is* important is that they indicate that he knows more about the keep than he's telling. I think he may be connected in some way to the people who are paying for the keep's maintenance.''

Cuza paused to let this settle in. He didn't want to overburden the major with information. After sufficient time, he added:

''If I were you, Major, I would ask the gentleman to stop in tomorrow for a chat. Maybe he would be good enough to tell us something.''

Kaempffer sneered. ''You aren't me, Jew! I do not waste my time *asking* dolts to visit—and I don't wait until morning!'' He turned and gestured to Sergeant Oster. ''Get four of my troopers down here on the double!'' Then back to Cuza: ''You'll come along with us to assure we arrest the right man.''

Cuza hid his smile. It was all so simple—so hellishly simple.

T

''Another objection that my father has is that you're not a Jew,'' Magda said. The two of them were still seated amid the dying leaves, facing the keep. Dusk was deepening and the keep had all its lights on.

''He's right.''

''What *is* your religion?''

''I have none.''

"But you must have been born into one."

Glenn shrugged. "Perhaps. If so, I've long since forgotten it."

"How can you forget something like that?"

"Easy."

She was beginning to feel annoyed at his insistence on frustrating her curiosity.

"Do you believe in God, Glenn?"

He turned and flashed the smile that never failed to move her. "I believe in you . . . isn't that enough?"

Magda leaned against him. "Yes. I suppose it is."

What was she to do with this man who was so unlike her yet stirred her emotions so? He seemed well educated, even erudite, yet she could not imagine him ever opening a book. He exuded strength, yet with her he could be so gentle.

Glenn was a tangled mass of contradictions. Yet Magda felt she had found in him the man with whom she wanted to share her life. And the life she pictured with Glenn was nothing like anything she had ever imagined in the past. No cool lingering days of quiet scholarship in this future, but rather endless nights of tangled limbs and heated passion. If she were to have a life after the keep, she wanted it to be with Glenn.

She didn't understand how this man could affect her so. All she knew was how she felt . . . and she desperately wanted to be with him. Always. To cling to him through the night and bear his children and see him smile at her the way he had a moment ago.

But he wasn't smiling now. He was staring at the keep. Something was tormenting him terribly, eating away at him from the inside. Magda wanted to share that pain, ease it if she could. But she was helpless until he opened up to her. Perhaps now was the time to try . . .

"Glenn," she said softly. "Why are you *really* here?"

Instead of answering, he pointed to the keep. "Something's happening."

Magda looked. In the light that poured from the main gate as it opened, six figures could be seen on the causeway, one of them in a wheelchair.

"Where could they be going with Papa?" she asked, tension tightening her throat.

"To the inn, most likely. It's the only thing within walking distance."

"They've come for me," Magda said. It was the only explanation that occurred to her.

"No, I doubt that. They wouldn't have brought your father along if they meant to drag you back to the keep. They have something else in mind."

Chewing her lower lip uneasily, Magda watched the knot of dark figures move along the causeway over the rising river of fog, flashlights illuminating their way. They were passing not twenty feet away when Magda whispered to Glenn.

"Let's stay hidden until we know what they're after."

"If they don't find you they may think you've run off . . . and they may take their anger out on your father. If they decide to search for you, they'll find you—we're trapped between here and the edge of the gorge. Nowhere to go. Better to go out and meet them."

"And you?"

"I'll be here if you need me. But for now I think the less they see of me the better."

Reluctantly, Magda rose and pushed her way through the brush. The group had already passed by the time she reached the road. She watched them before speaking. There was something wrong here. She could not say what, but neither could she deny the feeling of danger that stole over her as she stood there on the side of the path. The SS major was there, and the troopers were SS, too; yet Papa appeared to be traveling with them willingly, even appeared to be making small talk. It must be all right.

"Papa?"

The soldiers, even the one assigned to pushing the wheelchair, spun around as one, weapons raised and leveled. Papa spoke to them in rapid German.

"Hold—please! That is my daughter! Let me speak to her."

Magda hurried to his side, skirting the menacing quintet of black uniformed shapes. When she spoke she used the Gypsy dialect.

"Why have they brought you here?"

He answered her in kind: "I'll explain later. Where's Glenn?"

"In the bushes behind me." She replied without hesitation. After all, it was Papa who was asking. "Why do you want to know?"

Papa immediately turned to the major and spoke in German. "Over there!" He was pointing to the very spot Magda had told him. The four troopers quickly fanned out into a semicircle and began moving into the brush.

Magda gaped in shock at her father. "Papa, what are you doing?" She instinctively moved toward the brush but he gripped her wrist.

"It's all right," he told her, reverting to the Gypsy dialect. "I learned only a few moments ago that Glenn is one of them!"

Magda heard her own voice speaking Romanian. She was too appalled by her father's treachery to reply in anything but her native tongue.

"No! That's—"

"He belongs to a group that directs the Nazis, that is using them for its own foul ends! He's *worse* than a Nazi!"

"That's a lie!" *Papa's gone mad!*

"No it's not! And I'm sorry to be the one to tell you. But better you hear it from me now than later when it's too late!"

"They'll kill him!" she cried as panic filled her. Frantically, she tried to pull away. But Papa held her tight with his newfound strength, all the time whispering to her, filling her ears with awful things:

"No! They'll never kill him. They'll just take him over for questioning, and that's when he'll be forced to reveal his link with Hitler so as to save his skin." Papa's eyes were bright, feverish, his voice intense as he spoke. "And that's when you'll thank me, Magda! That's when you'll know I did this for *you*!''

''You've done it for yourself!'' she screamed, still trying to twist free of his grip. ''You hate him because—''

There was shouting in the brush, some minor scuffling, and then Glenn was led out into the open at gunpoint by two of the troopers. He was soon surrounded by all four of them, each with an automatic weapon trained on Glenn's middle.

''Leave him alone!'' Magda cried, lunging toward the group. But Papa's grip on her wrist would not yield.

''Stay back, Magda,'' Glenn said, his expression grim in the dusky light as his eyes bored into Papa's. ''You'll accomplish nothing by getting yourself shot.''

''How gallant!'' Kaempffer said from behind her.

''And all a show!'' Papa whispered.

''Take him across and we'll find out what he knows.''

The troopers prodded Glenn toward the causeway with the muzzles of their weapons. He was just a dim figure now, backlit in the glow from the keep's open gate. He walked steadily until he reached the causeway, then appeared to stumble on its leading edge and fall forward. Magda gasped and then saw that he hadn't actually fallen—he was diving for the side of the causeway. What could he possibly—? She suddenly realized what he intended. He was going to swing over the side and try to hide beneath the causeway—perhaps even try to climb down the rocky wall of the gorge under protection of its overhang.

Magda began to run forward. *God, let him escape!* If he could just get under the causeway he would be lost in the fog and darkness. By the time the Germans could bring scaling ropes to go after him, Glenn might be able to reach the floor of the gorge and be on his way—if he didn't slip and fall to his death.

Magda was within a dozen feet of the scene when the first Schmeisser burped a spray of bullets at Glenn. Then the others chorused in, lighting the night with their muzzle flashes, deafening her with their prolonged roar as she skidded to a stop, watching in open-mouthed horror as the wooden planking of the causeway burst into countless flying splinters. Glenn was leaning over the edge of the causeway when the first bullets caught him. She saw his body twist and jerk as streams of lead stitched red perforations in lines across his legs and back, saw him twitch and spin around with the impact of the bullets, saw more red lines crisscross his chest and abdomen. He went limp. His body seemed to fold in on itself as he fell over the edge.

He was gone.

The next few moments were a nightmare as Magda stood paralyzed and temporarily blinded by the afterimages of the flashes. Glenn could not be dead—he *couldn't* be! It wasn't possible! He was too alive to be dead! It was all a bad dream and soon she would awaken in his arms. But for now she must play out the dream: She must force herself forward, screaming silently through air that had thickened to clear jelly.

Oh no! Oh-no-oh-no-oh-no!

She could only think the words—speech was utterly impossible.

The soldiers were at the rim of the gorge, flashing their hand lamps down into the fog when she reached them. She pushed through to the edge but saw nothing below. She fought an urge to leap after Glenn, turning instead on the soldiers and flailing her fists against the nearest one, striking him on the chest and face. His reaction was automatic, almost casual. With the slightest tightening of his lips as the only warning, he brought the short barrel of his Schmeisser around and slammed it against the side of her head.

The world spun as she went down. She lost her breath as she struck the ground. Papa's voice came from far off, calling her name. Blackness surged around her but she fought it off long enough to see him being wheeled onto the causeway and back toward the keep. He was twisted around in his chair, looking back at her, shouting.

"Magda! It will be all right—you'll see! Everything will work out for the best and then you'll understand!

Then you'll *thank* me! Don't hate me, Magda!"

But Magda did hate him. She swore to always hate him. That was her last thought before the world slipped away.

⊤

An unidentified man had been shot resisting arrest and had fallen into the gorge. Woermann had seen the smug faces of the einsatzkommandos as they marched back into the keep. And he had seen the distraught look on the professor's face. Both were understandable: The former had killed an unarmed man, the thing they did best; the latter for the first time in his life had witnessed a senseless killing.

But Woermann could not explain Kaempffer's angry, disappointed expression. He stopped him in the courtyard.

"One man? All that shooting for one man?"

"The men are edgy," Kaempffer said, obviously edgy himself. "He shouldn't have tried to get away."

"What did you want him for?"

"The Jew seemed to think he knew something about the keep."

"I don't suppose you told him that he was only wanted for questioning."

"He tried to escape."

"And the net result is that you now know no more than you did before. You probably frightened the poor man out of his wits. Of course he ran! And now he can't tell you anything! You and your kind will never learn."

Kaempffer turned toward his quarters without replying, leaving Woermann alone in the courtyard. The blaze of anger that Kaempffer usually provoked did not ignite this time. All he felt was cold resentment . . . and resignation.

He stood and watched the men who were not on guard duty shuffle dispiritedly back to their quarters.

Only moments ago when gunfire had erupted at the far
end of the causeway, he had called them all to battle
stations. But no battle had ensued and they were disappointed. He understood that. He, too, wished for a
flesh-and-blood enemy to fight, to see, to strike at, to
draw blood from. But the enemy remained unseen,
elusive.

Woermann turned toward the cellar stairway. He was
going to go down there again tonight. One final time.
Alone.

It had to be alone. He could not let anyone know
what he suspected. Not now—not after deciding to
resign his commission. It had been a difficult decision,
but he had made it: He would retire and have no more
to do with this war. It was what the Party members in
the High Command wanted from him. But if even a
whisper of what he thought he'd find in the subcellar
escaped, he would be discharged as a lunatic. He could
not let these Nazis smear his name with insanity.

. . . *muddied boots and shredded fingers . . . muddied
boots and shredded fingers* . . . a litany of lunacy
drawing him downward. Something foul and beyond all
reason was afoot in those depths. He thought he knew
what it might be but could not allow himself to vocalize
it, or even form a mental image of it. His mind shied
away from the image, leaving it blurred and murky, as if
viewed from a safe distance through field glasses that
refused to focus.

He crossed to the arched opening and went down the
steps.

He had turned his back too long waiting for what was
wrong with the Wehrmacht and the war it was fighting
to work itself out. But the problems were not going to
work themselves out. He could see that now. Finally he
could admit to himself that the atrocities following in
the wake of the fighting were no momentary aberra-
tions. He had been afraid to face the truth that *everything* had gone wrong with this war. Now he could, and
he was ashamed of having been a part of it.

The subcellar would be his place of redemption. He

would see with his own eyes what was happening there. He would face it alone and he would rectify it. There would be no peace for him until he did. Only after he had redeemed his honor would he be able to return to Rathenow and Helga. His mind would be satisfied, his guilt somewhat purged. He could then be a real father to Fritz . . . and would keep him out of the *Jugendführer* even if it meant breaking both his legs.

The guards assigned to the opening into the subcellar had not yet returned from their battle stations. All the better. Now he could enter unobserved and avoid offers of escort. He picked up one of the flashlights and stood uncertainly at the top of the stairway, looking down into the beckoning darkness.

It struck Woermann then that he must be mad. It would be insane to give up his commission! He had closed his eyes this long—why not keep them shut? Why not? He thought of the painting up in his room, the one with the shadow of the hanging corpse . . . a corpse that seemed to have developed a slight paunch when he had last looked at it. Yes, he must be mad. He didn't have to go down there. Not alone. And certainly not after sundown. Why not wait until morning?

. . . muddied boots and shredded fingers . . .

Now. It had to be now. He would not be venturing down there unarmed. He had his Luger, and he had the silver cross he had lent the professor. He started down.

He had descended half the steps when he heard the noise. He stopped to listen . . . soft, chaotic scraping sounds off to his right, toward the rear, at the very heart of the keep. Rats? He swiveled the beam of his flashlight around but could see none. The trio of vermin that had greeted him on these steps at noon were nowhere in sight. He completed his descent and hurried to where the corpses had been laid out, but came to a stumbling, shuddering halt as he reached the spot.

They were gone.

⊤

As soon as he wheeled into his darkened quarters and heard the door slam behind him, Cuza leaped from his chair and went to the window. He strained his eyes toward the causeway, looking for Magda. Even in the light of the moon that had just crested the mountains, he could not see clearly to the far side of the gorge. But Iuliu and Lidia must have seen what had happened. They would help her. He was sure of that.

It had been the ultimate test of his will to remain in his chair instead of running to her side when that German animal had knocked her down. But he had had to sit fast. Revealing his ability to walk then might have ruined everything he and Molasar had planned. And the plan now was more important than anything. The destruction of Hitler had to take precedence over the welfare of a single woman, even if she was his own daughter.

"Where is he?"

Cuza spun around at the sound of the voice behind him. There was menace in Molasar's tone as he spoke from the darkness. Had he just arrived or had he been waiting there all along?

"Dead," he said, searching for the source of the voice. He sensed Molasar moving closer.

"Impossible!"

"It's true. I saw it myself. He tried to get away and the Germans riddled him with bullets. He must have been desperate. I guess he realized what would happen to him if he were brought into the keep."

"Where's the body?"

"In the gorge."

"It must be found!" Molasar had moved close enough so that some of the moonlight from the window glinted off his face. "I must be absolutely certain!"

"He's *dead*. No one could have survived that many bullets. He suffered enough mortal wounds for a dozen men. He had to be dead even before he fell into the gorge. And the fall . . ." Cuza shook his head at the memory. At another time, in another place, under different circumstances, Cuza would have been aghast at what he had witnessed. Now . . . "He's doubly dead."

Molasar still appeared reluctant to accept this. "I needed to kill him myself, to feel the life go out of him by my own hand. Then and only then can I be sure he is out of my way. As it is, I am forced to rely on your judgment that he cannot have survived."

"Don't rely on me—see for yourself. His body is down in the gorge. Why don't you go find it and assure yourself?"

Molasar nodded slowly. "Yes . . . Yes, I believe I will do that . . . for I must be sure." He backed away and was swallowed by the darkness. "I will return for you when all is ready."

Cuza glanced once more out the window toward the inn, then returned to his wheelchair. Molasar's discovery that the Glaeken still existed seemed to have shaken him profoundly. Perhaps it was not going to be so easy to rid the world of Adolf Hitler. But still he had to try. He had to!

He sat in the dark without bothering to relight the candle, hoping Magda was all right.

His temples pounded and the flashlight wavered in his hand as Woermann stood in the chill stygian darkness and stared at the rumpled shrouds that covered nothing but the ground beneath them. Lutz's head was there, open-eyed, open-mouthed, lying on its left ear. All the rest were gone . . . just as Woermann had suspected. But the fact that he had half-expected to face this scene did nothing to blunt its mind-numbing impact.

Where were they?

And still, from far off to the right, came those scraping sounds.

Woermann knew he had to follow them to their source. Honor demanded it. But first . . . holstering the Luger, he dug into the breast pocket of his tunic and pulled out the silver cross. He felt it might give him more protection than a pistol.

With the cross held out before him, he started in the direction of the scraping. The subcellar cavern narrowed down to a low tunnel that wound a serpentine path toward the rear of the keep. As he moved, the sound grew louder. Nearer. Then he began seeing the rats. A few at first—big fat ones, perched on small outcroppings of rock and staring at him as he passed. Farther on there were more, hundreds of them, clinging to the walls, packed more and more tightly until the tunnel seemed to be lined with dull matted fur that squirmed and rippled and glared out at him with countless beady black eyes. Controlling his repugnance, he continued ahead. The rats on the floor scuttled out of his path but exhibited no real fear of him. He wished for a Schmeisser, yet it was unlikely any weapon could save him were they to pounce on him *en masse*.

Up ahead the tunnel turned sharply to the right, and Woermann stopped to listen. The scraping noises were louder still. So close he could almost imagine them originating around that next turn. Which meant he had to be very careful. He had to find a way of seeing what was going on without being seen.

He would have to turn his light off.

Woermann did not want to do that. The undulating layer of rats on the ground and on the walls made him fear the dark. Suppose the light were all that kept them at bay? Suppose . . . It didn't matter. He had to know what lay beyond. He estimated he could reach the turn in five long paces. He would go that far in the dark, then turn left and force himself to take another three paces. If by then he found nothing, he would turn the flashlight back on and continue ahead. For all he knew there might be nothing there. The nearness of the sounds could be an accoustical trick of the tunnel . . . he might have another hundred yards to go yet. Or he might not.

Bracing himself, Woermann flicked the flashlight off but kept his finger on the switch just in case something happened with the rats. He heard nothing, felt nothing. As he stood and waited for his eyes to adjust to the darkness, he noted that the noise had grown louder, as if amplified by the absence of light. *Utter* absence. There was no glow, not even a hint of illumination from around the bend. Whatever was making that noise had to have at least *some* light, didn't it? *Didn't it?*

He pushed himself forward, silently counting off the paces while every nerve in his body howled for him to turn and run. But he had to know! Where were those bodies? And what was making that noise? Maybe then the mysteries of the keep would be solved. It was his duty to learn. His duty . . .

Completing the fifth and final pace, he turned left and, in so doing, lost his balance. His left hand—the one with the flashlight—shot out reflexively to keep him from falling and came in contact with something furry that squealed and moved and bit with razor-sharp teeth. Pain knifed up his arm from the heel of his palm. He snatched his hand away and clamped his teeth on his lower lip until the pain subsided. It didn't take long, and he had managed to hold on to the flashlight.

The scraping noises sounded much louder now, and directly ahead. Yet there was no light. No matter how he strained his eyes, he could see nothing. He began to perspire as fear reached deep into his intestines and squeezed. There had to be light *somewhere* ahead.

He took one pace—not so long as the previous ones—and stopped.

The sounds now came from directly in front of him, ahead . . . and down . . . scraping, scratching, scrabbling.

Another pace.

Whatever the sounds were, they gave him the impression of concerted effort, yet he could hear no labored breathing accompanying them. Only his own ragged respirations and the sound of his blood pounding in his ears. That and the scratching.

One more pace and he would turn the light on again. He lifted his foot but found he could not move himself forward. Of its own volition, his body refused to take another step until he could see where he was going.

Woermann stood trembling. He wanted to go back. He didn't want to see what was ahead. Nothing sane or of this world could move and exist in this blackness. It was better not to know. But the bodies . . . he *had* to know.

He made a sound that was almost a whimper, and flicked the switch on the flashlight. It took a moment for his pupils to constrict in the sudden glare, and a much longer moment for his mind to register the horror of what the light revealed.

And then Woermann screamed . . . an agonized sound that started low and built in volume and pitch, echoing and re-echoing around him as he turned and fled back the way he had come. He rushed headlong past the staring rats and beyond. There were perhaps thirty more feet of tunnel to go when Woermann brought himself to a wavering halt.

There was someone up ahead.

He flashed his beam at the figure blocking his path. He saw the waxy face, the cape, the clothes, the lank hair, the twin pools of madness where the eyes should be. And he knew. Here was the master of the house.

Woermann stood and stared in horrified fascination for a moment, then marshaled his quarter-century of military training.

"Let me pass!" he said and directed the beam onto the cross in his right hand, confident that he held an effective weapon. "In the name of God, in the name of Jesus Christ, in the name of all that is holy, let me pass!"

Instead of retreating, the figure moved forward, closer to Woermann, close enough so that the light picked up his sallow features. He was smiling—a gloating vulpine grimace that weakened Woermann's knees and made his upheld hands shake violently.

His eyes . . . oh, God, his eyes . . . Woermann stood rooted to the spot, unable to retreat because of what he had seen behind him, and blocked from escape ahead.

He kept the quaking light trained on the silver
cross—*the cross! Vampires fear the cross!*—as he thrust
it forward, fighting fear as he had never known it.

Dear God, if you are my God, don't desert me!

Unseen, a hand slipped through the dark and
snatched the cross from Woermann's grasp. The creature held it between his thumb and forefinger and let
Woermann watch in horror and dismay as he began to
bend it, folding it until it was doubled over on itself.
Then he bent the crosspiece down until all that was left
was a misshapen lump of silver. This he flipped away
with no more thought than a soldier on leave would give
to a cigarette butt.

Woermann shouted in terror as he saw the same hand
dart toward him. He ducked away. But he was not quick
enough.

TWENTY-SEVEN

Magda drifted slowly back to consciousness, drawn by rough prodding at her clothing and by a painful pressure in her right hand. She opened her eyes. The stars were out. There was a dark shadow over her, pulling and pulling at her hand.

Where was she? And why did her head hurt so?

Images flashed through her mind—*Glenn . . . the causeway . . . gunfire . . . the gorge . . .*

Glenn was dead! It hadn't been a dream—*Glenn was dead!*

With a groan she sat up, causing whoever was pulling at her to scream in terror and run back toward the village. When the vertigo that rocked and spun the world about her subsided, she lifted her hand to the tender, swollen area near her right temple and winced in pain when she touched it.

She also became aware of a throbbing in her right ring finger. The flesh around her mother's wedding band was cut and swollen. Whoever had been leaning over her must have been trying to pull it off her finger! One of the villagers! He had probably thought her dead and had been terrified when she had moved.

Magda rose to her feet and again the world began to spin and tilt. When the ground had steadied, when her nausea had faded away and the roaring in her ears had dimmed to a steady thrum, she began to walk. Every step she took caused a stab of pain in her head but she kept going, crossing to the far side of the path and pushing into the brush. A half-moon drifted in a cloud-streaked sky. It hadn't been out before. How long had she been unconscious? She had to get to Glenn!

He's still alive, she told herself. *He has to be!* It was the only way she could imagine him. Yet how could he live? How could anyone survive all those bullets . . . and that fall into the gorge . . . ?

Magda began to sob, as much for Glenn as for her own overwhelming sense of loss. She despised herself for that selfishness, yet it would not be denied. Thoughts of all the things they would never do together rushed in on her. After thirty-one years she finally had found a man she could love. She had spent one full day at his side, an incredible twenty-four hours immersing herself in the true magnificence of life, only to have him torn from her and brutally murdered.

It's not fair!

She came to the rubble fall at the end of the gorge and paused to glare across the rising mist that filled it. Could you hate a stone building? She hated the keep. It held nothing but evil. Had she possessed the power she would have willed it to tumble into Hell, taking every-one inside—Yes! Even Papa!—with it.

But the keep floated, silent and implacable, on its sea of fog, lit from within, dark and glowering without, ignoring her.

She prepared to descend into the gorge as she had two nights ago. Two nights . . . it seemed like an age. The fog was right up to the rim, making the descent even more dangerous. It was insane to risk her life trying to find Glenn's body in the dark down there. But her life did not matter as much now as it had a few hours ago. She had to find him . . . had to touch his wounds, feel his still heart and cold skin. She had to know for certain he was beyond all help. There would be no rest for her until then.

As she began to swing her legs over the edge she heard some pebbles slide and bounce down the slope beneath her. At first she thought her weight had dislodged a clump of dirt from the edge. But an instant later she heard it again. She stopped and listened. There was another sound, too—labored breathing. Someone was climbing up through the fog!

Frightened, Magda backed away from the edge and waited in the brush, ready to run. She held her breath as she saw a hand rise out of the fog and claw the soft earth at the gorge's rim, followed by another hand, followed by a head. Magda instantly recognized the shape of that head.

"Glenn!"

He did not seem to hear, but continued struggling to pull himself over the edge. Magda ran to him. Gripping him under both arms and calling on reserves of strength she never knew she possessed, she pulled him up onto level ground where he lay face down, panting and groaning. She knelt over him, helpless and confused.

"Oh, Glenn, you're"—her hands were wet and glistened darkly in the moonlight—"bleeding!" It was inane, it was obvious, it was expected, but it was all she could say at the moment.

You should be dead! she thought but held back the words. If she didn't say it, maybe it wouldn't happen. Btut his clothing was soaked with blood oozing from dozens of mortal wounds. That he was still breathing was a miracle. That he had managed to pull himself out of the gorge was beyond belief! Yet here he was, prostrate before her . . . alive. If he had lasted this long, perhaps . . .

"I'll get a doctor!" Another stupid remark—a reflex. There was no doctor anywhere in the Dinu Pass. "I'll get Iuliu and Lidia! They'll help me get you back to the—"

Glenn mumbled something, Magda bent over him, touching her ear to his lips.

"Go to my room," he said in a weak, dry, tortured voice. The odor of blood was fresh on his breath. *He's bleeding inside!*

"I'll take you there as soon as I get Iuliu—" But would Iuliu help?

His fingers plucked at her sleeve. "Listen to me! Get the case . . . you saw it yesterday . . . the one with the blade in it."

"That's not going to help you now! You need medical care!"

"You *must*! Nothing else can save me!"

She straightened up, hesitated a moment, then jumped to her feet and ran. Her head started pounding again but now she found it easy to ignore the pain. Glenn wanted that sword blade. It didn't make sense, but his voice had been so full of conviction . . . urgency . . . need. She had to get it for him.

Magda did not slacken her pace as she entered the inn, taking the stairs up to the second floor two at a time, slowing only when she entered the darkness of Glenn's room. She felt her way to the closet and lifted the case. With a high-pitched creak it fell open—she hadn't closed the catches when Glenn had surprised her here yesterday! The blade slipped out of the case and fell against the mirror with a crash. The glass shattered and cascaded onto the floor. Magda bent and quickly replaced the blade in its case, found the catches, closed them, then lifted the case into her arms, groaning under its unexpected weight. As she turned to leave, she pulled the blanket from the bed, then hurried across to her room for a second blanket.

Iuliu and Lidia, alerted by the commotion she was making on the second floor, stood with startled expressions at the foot of the stairs as she descended.

"Don't try to stop me!" Magda said as she rushed by. Something in her voice must have warned them away, for they stepped aside and let her pass.

She stumbled back through the brush, the case and the blankets weighing her down, snagging on the branches, slowing her as she rushed toward Glenn, praying he was still alive. She found him lying on his back, weaker, his voice fainter.

"The blade," he whispered as she leaned over him. "Take it out of the case."

For an awful moment Magda feared he would ask for a *coup de grâce*. She would do anything for Glenn—anything but that. But would a man with his injuries make so desperate a climb out of the gorge just to ask for death? She opened the case. Two large pieces of the shattered mirror lay within. She brushed them aside and lifted the dark, cold blade with both her hands, feeling the shape of the runes carved in its surface press against her palms.

She passed it to his outstretched arms and almost dropped it when a faint blue glow, blue like a gas flame, leaped along its edges at his touch. As she released it to him, he sighed; his features relaxed, losing their pain, a look of contentment settling on them . . . the look of a man who has come home to a warm and familiar room after a long, arduous winter journey.

Glenn positioned the blade along the length of his battered, punctured, blood-soaked body, the point resting a few inches short of his ankles, the spike of the butt where the missing hilt should be almost to his chin. Folding his arms over the blade and across his chest, he closed his eyes.

"You shouldn't stay here," he said in a faint, slurred voice. "Come back later."

"I'm not leaving you."

He made no reply. His breathing became shallower and steadier. He appeared to be asleep. Magda watched him closely. The blue glow spread to his forearms, sheathing them in a faint patina of light. She covered him with a blanket, as much for warmth as to hide the glow from the keep. Then she moved away, wrapped the second blanket around her shoulders, and seated herself with her back against a rock. Myriad questions, held at bay until now, rushed in on her.

Who was he, really? What manner of man was this who suffered wounds enough to kill him many times over and then climbed a slope that would tax a strong man in perfect health? What manner of man hid his room's mirror in a closet along with an ancient sword with no hilt? Who now clasped that sword to his breast as he lay on the borderland of death? How could she entrust her love and her life to such a man? She knew *nothing* about him.

Then Papa's ranting came back to her: *He belongs to a group that directs the Nazis, that is using them for its own foul ends! He's worse than a Nazi!*

Could Papa be right? Could she be so blinded by her infatuation that she could not or would not see this? Glenn certainly was no ordinary man. And he did have secrets—he had been far from totally open with her. Was it possible that Glenn was the enemy and Molasar the ally?

She drew the blanket closer around her. All she could do was wait.

Magda's eyelids began to droop—the aftereffects of the concussion and the rhythmic sounds of Glenn's breathing lulled her. She struggled briefly, then succumbed . . . just for a moment . . . just to rest her eyes.

Klaus Woermann knew he was dead. And yet . . . not dead.

He clearly remembered his dying. He had been strangled with deliberate slowness here in the subcellar in darkness lit only by the feeble glow of his fallen flashlight. Icy fingers with incalculable strength had closed on his throat, choking off the air until his blood had thundered in his ears and blackness had closed in.

But not eternal blackness. Not yet.

He could not understand his continued awareness. He lay on his back, his eyes open and staring into the darkness. He did not know how long he had been this way. Time had lost all meaning. Except for his vision, he was cut off from the rest of his body. It was as if it belonged to someone else. He could feel nothing, not the rocky earth against his back or the cold air against his face. He could hear nothing. He was not breathing. He could not move—not even a finger. When a rat had crawled over his face, dragging its matted fur across his eyes, he could not even blink.

He was dead. And yet not dead.

Gone was all fear, all pain. He was devoid of all feeling except regret. He had ventured into the subcellar to find redemption and had found only horror and death—his own death.

Woermann suddenly realized that he was being moved. Although he could still feel nothing, he sensed he was being roughly dragged through the darkness by the back of his tunic, along a narrow passage, into a dark room—

—and into light.

Woermann's line of vision was along the limp length of his body. As he was dragged along a corridor strewn with granite rubble, his gaze swept across a wall he immediately recognized—a wall upon which words of an ancient tongue had been written in blood. The wall had been washed but brown smudges were still visible on the stone.

He was dropped to the floor. His field of vision was now limited to a section of the partially dismantled ceiling directly above him. At the periphery of his vision, moving about, was a dark shape. Woermann saw a length of heavy rope snake over an exposed ceiling beam, saw a loop of that same rope go over his face, and then he was moving again . . .

. . . upward . . .

. . . until his feet left the ground and his lifeless body

began to sway and swing and twist in the air. A shadowy figure melted into a doorway down the corridor and Woermann was left alone, hanging by his neck from a rope.

He wanted to scream a protest to God. For he now knew that the dark being who ruled the keep was waging war not only against the bodies of the soldiers who had entered his domain, but against their minds and their spirits as well.

And Woermann realized the role he was being forced to play in that war: a suicide. His men would think he had killed himself! It would completely demoralize them. Their officer, the man they looked to for leadership, had hanged himself—the ultimate cowardice, the ultimate desertion.

He could not allow that to happen. And yet he could do nothing to alter the course of events. He was dead.

Was this to be his penance for closing his eyes to the monstrousness of the war? If so, it was too much—too much to pay! To hang here and watch his own men and the einsatzkommandos come and gawk at him. And the final ignominy: to see Erich Kaempffer smiling up at him!

Was this why he had been left teetering on the edge of eternal oblivion? To witness his own humiliation as a suicide?

If only he could do *something*!

One final act to redeem his pride and—yes—his manhood. One last gesture to give meaning to his death.

Something!

Anything!

But all he could do was hang and sway and wait to be found.

Cuza looked up as a grating sound filled the room. The section of the wall that led into the base of the tower was swinging open. When it stopped moving, Molasar's voice came from the darkness beyond.

"All is ready."

At *last*! The wait had been almost unbearable. As the hours had edged by, Cuza had almost given up on seeing Molasar again tonight. Never had he been a patient man, but at no time could he remember being so consumed by an urgency such as he had known tonight. He had tried to distract himself by dredging up worries about how Magda was faring after that blow to the head . . . it was no use. The coming destruction of "Lord Hitler" banished all other considerations from his mind. Cuza had paced the length, breadth, and perimeters of both rooms again and again, obsessed by his fierce longing to get on with it and yet unable to do a thing until word came from Molasar.

And now Molasar was here. As Cuza ducked through the opening, leaving his wheelchair behind forever, he felt a cold metal cylinder pressed against the bare skin of his palm.

"What—?" It was a flashlight.

"You will need this."

Cuza switched the flashlight on. It was German Army issue. The lens was cracked. He wondered who—

"Follow me."

Molasar surefootedly led the way down the winding steps that clung to the inner surface of the tower wall. He did not seem to need any light to find his way. Cuza did. He stayed close behind Molasar, keeping the flashlight beam trained on the steps before him. He wished he could take a moment to look around. For a long time, he had desperately wanted to explore the base of the tower and until now had had to do so vicariously through Magda. But there was no time to drink in the details. When all this was over he promised himself to return here and do a thorough inspection on his own.

After a while they came to a narrow opening in the wall. He followed Molasar through and found himself in the subcellar. Molasar quickened his pace and Cuza had to strain to keep up. But he voiced no complaint, so

thankful was he to be able to walk at all, to brave the
cold without his hands losing their circulation or his ar-
thritic joints seizing up on him. He was actually working
up a sweat! Wonderful!

Off to his right he saw light filtering down the stairway up to the cellar. He flashed his lamp to the left. The
corpses were gone. The Germans must have shipped
them out. Strange, their leaving the shrouds in a pile
there.

Over the sound of his hurried footsteps Cuza began to
hear another noise. A faint scraping. As he followed
Molasar out of the large cavern that made up the subcellar and into a narrower, tunnellike passage, the
sound became progressively louder. He trailed Molasar
through various turns until, after one particularly sharp
left turn, Molasar stopped and beckoned Cuza to his
side. The scraping sound was loud, echoing all about
them.

"Prepare yourself," Molasar said, his expression
unreadable. "I have made certain use of the remains of
the dead soldiers. What you see next may offend you,
but it was necessary to retrieve my talisman. I could
have found another way, but this was convenient . . .
and fitting."

Cuza doubted there was much Molasar could do with
the bodies of German soldiers that would truly offend
him.

He then followed him into a large hemispherical
chamber with a roof of icy living rock and a dirt floor.
A deep excavation had been sunk into the middle of that
floor. And still the scraping, louder. Where was it
coming from? Cuza looked about, the beam from his
flashlight reflecting off the glistening walls and ceiling,
diffusing light throughout the chamber.

He noticed movement near his feet and all around the
periphery of the excavation. Small movements. He
gasped—rats! Hundreds of rats surrounded the pit,
squirming and jostling one another, agitated . . . expectant . . .

Cuza saw something much larger than a rat crawling up the wall of the excavation. He stepped forward and pointed the flashlight directly into the pit—and almost dropped it. It was like looking into one of the outer rings of Hell. Feeling suddenly weak, he lurched away from the edge and pressed his shoulder against the nearest wall to keep from toppling over. He closed his eyes and panted like a dog on a stifling August day, trying to calm himself, trying to hold down his rising gorge, trying to accept what he had seen.

There were dead men in the pit, ten of them, all in German uniforms of either gray or black, *all moving about*—even the one without the head!

Cuza opened his eyes again. In the hellish half-light that suffused the chamber he watched one of the corpses crawl crablike up the side of the pit and throw an armful of dirt over the far edge, then slide back down to the bottom.

Cuza pushed himself away from the wall and staggered to the edge for another look.

They appeared not to need their eyes, for they never looked at their hands as they dug in the cold hard earth. Their dead joints moved stiffly, awkwardly, as if resisting the power that impelled them, yet they worked tirelessly, in utter silence, surprisingly efficient despite their ataxic movements. The scuffling and shuffling of their boots, the scraping of their bare hands on the near-frozen soil as they deepened and widened the excavation . . . the noise rose and echoed off the walls and ceiling of the chamber, eerily amplified.

Suddenly, the noise stopped, gone as if it had never been. They had all halted their movements and now stood perfectly still.

Molasar spoke beside him. "My talisman lies buried beneath the last few inches of soil. You must remove it from the earth."

"Can't they—?" Cuza's stomach turned at the thought of going down there.

"They are too clumsy."

Looking pleadingly at Molasar, he asked, "Couldn't you unearth it yourself? I'll take it anywhere you want me to after that."

Molasar's eyes blazed with impatience. "It is part of your task! A simple one! With so much at stake do you balk now at dirtying your hands?"

"No! No, of course not! It's just . . ." He glanced again at the corpses.

Molasar followed his gaze. Although he said nothing, made no signal, the corpses began to move, turning simultaneously and crawling out of the pit. When they were all out, they stood in a ring along its edge. The rats crawled around and over their feet. Molasar's eyes swung back to Cuza.

Without waiting to be told again, Cuza eased himself over the edge and slid along the damp dirt to the bottom. He balanced the flashlight on a rock and began to scrape away the loose earth at the nadir point of the conical pit. The cold and the filth didn't bother his hands. After the initial revulsion at digging in the same spot as the corpses, he found he actually enjoyed being able to work with his hands again, even at so menial a task as this. And he owed it all to Molasar. It was good to sink his fingers into the earth and feel the soil come away in chunks. It exhilarated him and he increased his pace, working feverishly.

His hands soon contacted something other than dirt. He pulled at it and unearthed a square packet, perhaps a foot long on each side and a few inches thick. And heavy—very heavy. He pulled off the half-rotted cloth wrapper and then unfolded the coarse fabric that made up the inner packing.

Something bright, metallic, and heavy lay within. Cuza caught his breath—at first he thought it was a cross. But that couldn't be. It was an almost-cross, designed along the same eccentric lines as the thousands laid into the walls of the keep. Yet none of those could compare with this one. For here was the original, an inch thick all around, the template on which all the others had been modeled. The upright was rounded, almost cylindrical and, except for a deep slot in its top, appeared to be of solid gold. The crosspiece looked like silver. He studied it briefly through the lower lenses of his bifocals but could find no designs or inscriptions.

Molasar's talisman—the key to his power. It stirred Cuza with awe. There was power in it—he could feel the power surge into his hands as he held it. He lifted it for Molasar to see and thought he detected a glow around it—or was that merely a reflection of the flashlight beam off its bright surface?

"I've found it!"

He could not see Molasar above but noticed the animated corpses backing away as he lifted the crosslike object over his head.

"Molasar! Do you hear me?"

"Yes." The voice seemed to come from somewhere back in the tunnel. "My power now resides in your hands. Guard it carefully until you have hidden it where no one will find it."

Exhilarated, Cuza tightened his grip on the talisman.

"When do I leave? And how?"

"Within the hour—as soon as I have finished with the German interlopers. They must all pay now for invading my keep."

T

The pounding on the door was accompanied by someone's calling his name. It sounded like Sergeant Oster's voice . . . on the verge of hysteria. But Major Kaempffer was taking no chances. As he shook himself out of his bedroll, he grabbed his Luger.

"Who *is* it?" He let his annoyance show in his tone. This was the second time tonight he had been disturbed. The first for that fruitless sortie across the causeway with the Jew, and now this. He glanced at his watch:

almost four o'clock! It would be light soon. What could anyone want at this hour? Unless—someone else had been killed.

"It's Sergeant Oster, sir."

"What is it this time?" Kaempffer said, opening the door. One look at the sergeant's white face and he knew something was terribly wrong. More than just another death.

"It's the captain, sir . . . Captain Woermann—"

"It got him?" *Woermann? Murdered? An officer?*

"He killed himself, sir."

Kaempffer stared at the sergeant in mute shock, recovering only with great effort.

"Wait here." Kaempffer closed the door and hurriedly pulled on his trousers, slipped into his boots, and threw his uniform jacket over his undershirt without bothering to button it. Then he returned to the door. "Take me to where you found him."

As he followed Oster through the disassembled portions of the keep, Kaempffer realized that the thought of Klaus Woermann killing himself disturbed him more than if he had been killed like all the rest. It wasn't in Woermann's makeup. People do change, but Kaempffer could not imagine the teenager who had single-handedly sent a company of British soldiers running in the last war to be a man who would take his own life in this war, no matter what the circumstances.

Still . . . Woermann was dead. The only man who could point to him and say "Coward!" had been rendered forever mute. That was worth everything Kaempffer had endured since his arrival at this charnel house. And there was a special satisfaction to be gained from the manner of Woermann's death. The final report would hide nothing: Captain Klaus Woermann would go down on record as a suicide. A disgraceful death. Worse than desertion. Kaempffer would give much to see the look on the faces of the wife and the two boys Woermann had been so proud of—what would they think of their father, their *hero*, when they heard the news?

Instead of leading him across the courtyard to Woermann's quarters, Oster made a sharp right turn that led Kaempffer down the corridor to where he had imprisoned the villagers on the night of his arrival. The area had been partially dismantled during the past few days. They made the final turn and there was Woermann.

He hung by a thick rope, his body swaying gently as if in a breeze; but the air was still. The rope had been thrown over an exposed ceiling beam and tied to it. Kaempffer saw no stool and wondered how Woermann had got himself up there. Perhaps he had stood on one of the piles of stone block here and there . . .

. . . the eyes. Woermann's eyes bulged in their sockets. For an instant Kaempffer had the impression that the eyes shifted as he approached, then realized it was just a trick of the light from the bulbs along the ceiling.

He stopped before the dangling form of his fellow officer. Woermann's belt buckle swung two inches in front of Kaempffer's nose. He looked up at the engorged, puffed face, purple with stagnant blood.

. . . the eyes again. They seemed to be looking down at him. He glanced away and saw Woermann's shadow on the wall. Its outline was the same—exactly the same—as the shadow of the hanging corpse he had seen in Woermann's painting.

A chill ran over his skin.

Precognition? Had Woermann foreseen his death? Or had suicide been in the back of his mind all along?

Kaempffer's exultation began to die as he realized he was now the only officer in the keep. All the responsibility from this moment on rested solely on him. In fact, he himself might be marked for death next. What was he to—

—Gunfire sounded from the courtyard.

Startled, Kaempffer wheeled, saw Oster look down the corridor, then back to him. But the questioning look on the sergeant's face turned to one of wide-eyed horror as his gaze rose to a point above Kaempffer. The SS major was turning to see what could cause such a reaction when he felt thick, stone-cold fingers slip around his throat and begin to squeeze.

Kaempffer tried to leap away, tried to kick behind him at whoever it was, but his feet struck only air. He opened his mouth to scream but no more than a strangled gurgle escaped. Pulling, clawing at the fingers that were inexorably cutting off his life, he twisted frantically to see who was attacking him. He already knew—in a horror-dimmed corner of his mind he knew. But he had to *see!* He twisted further, saw his attacker's sleeve, gray, regular army gray, and he followed the sleeve back . . .up . . . to Woermann.

But he's dead!

In desperate terror, Kaempffer began to writhe and claw at the dead hands that encircled his throat. To no avail. He was being lifted into the air by his neck, slowly, steadily, until only his toes were touching the floor. Soon even they did not reach. He flung his arms out to Oster but the sergeant was useless. His face a mask of horror, Oster had flattened himself against the wall and was slowly inching himself away—*away!*—from him. He gave no sign that he even saw Kaempffer. His gaze was fixed higher, on his former commanding officer . . . dead . . . but committing murder.

Disjointed images flashed through Kaempffer's mind, a parade of sights and sounds becoming more blurred and garbled with each thump of his slowing heart.

. . . gunfire continuing to echo from the courtyard, mixing with screams of pain and terror . . . Oster inching away down the corridor, not seeing the two walking dead men rounding the corner, one of them recognizable as einsatzkommando Private Flick, dead since his first night in the keep . . . Oster seeing them too late and not knowing which way to run . . . more shooting from without, barrages of bullets . . . shooting from within as Oster emptied his Schmeisser at the approaching corpses, ripping up their uniforms, rocking them backward, but doing little to impede their progress

. . . screams from Oster as each of the corpses grabbed one of his arms to swing him headfirst toward the stone wall . . . the screams ending with a sickening thud as his skull cracked like an egg . . .

Kaempffer's vision dimmed . . . sounds became muted . . . a prayer formed in his mind:

O God! Please let me live! I'll do anything you ask if you'll just let me live!

A snap . . . a sudden fall to the floor . . . the hangman's rope had broken under the weight of two bodies . . . but no break in the pressure on his throat . . . a great lethargy settled upon him . . . in the fading light he saw Sergeant Oster's bloody-headed corpse rise and follow his two murderers out to the courtyard . . . and at the very end, in his terminal spasms, Kaempffer caught sight of Woermann's distorted features . . .

. . . and saw a smile there.

T

Chaos in the courtyard.

The walking corpses were everywhere, ravaging soldiers in their beds, at their posts. Bullets couldn't kill them—they were already dead. Their horrified former comrades pumped round after round into them but the dead kept coming. And worse—as soon as one of the living was killed, the fresh corpse rose to its feet and joined the ranks of the attackers.

Two desperate, black-uniformed soldiers pulled the bar from the gate and began to swing it open; but before they could squeeze through to safety, they were caught from behind and dragged to the ground. A moment later they were standing again, arrayed with other corpses before the open gate, making sure that none of their live comrades passed through.

Suddenly, all the lights went out as a wild burst of 9mm slugs slammed into the generators.

An SS corporal leaped into a jeep and started it up,

hoping to ram his way to freedom; but when he slipped the clutch too quickly, the cold engine stalled. He was pulled from the seat and strangled before he could get it started again.

A private, quaking and shivering under his cot, was smothered with his bedroll by the headless corpse he had once known as Lutz.

The gunfire soon began to die off. From a continuous barrage of overlapping fusillades it diminished to random bursts, then to isolated shots. The men's screaming faded to a lone voice wailing in the barracks. Then that, too, was cut off. Finally, silence. All quiet as the cadavers, fresh and old, stood scattered about the courtyard, motionless, as if waiting.

Suddenly, soundlessly, all but two of them fell to the courtyard floor and lay still. The remaining pair began to move, shuffling through the entry to the cellar, leaving a tall, dark figure standing alone in the center of the courtyard, undisputed master of the keep at last.

As the fog swirled in through the open gates, inching across the stone, layering the courtyard and the inert cadavers with an undulating carpet of haze, he turned and made his way down to the subcellar.

TWENTY-EIGHT

Magda awoke with a start at the sound of gunfire from the keep. At first she feared the Germans had learned of Papa's complicity and were executing him. But that hideous thought lasted only an instant. This was not the orderly sound of firing on command. This was the chaotic sound of a battle.

It was a short battle.

Huddled on the damp ground, Magda noted that the stars had faded in the graying sky. The echoes of gunfire were soon swallowed by the chill, predawn air. Someone or something had emerged victorious over there. Magda felt sure it was Molasar.

She rose and went to Glenn's side. His face was beaded with sweat and he was breathing rapidly. As she pulled back the blanket to check his wounds, a small cry escaped her: His body was bathed completely in the blue

glow from the blade. Cautiously, she touched him. The
glow didn't burn, but it did make her hand tingle with
warmth. Within the torn fabric of Glenn's shirt she felt
something hard, heavy, thimblelike. She pulled it out.

In the dim light it took her a moment to recognize the
object that rolled about in her palm. It was made of
lead. A bullet.

Magda ran her hands over Glenn again. There were
more of them—all over him. And his wounds—there
weren't nearly so many now. The majority had disappeared, leaving only dimpled scars instead of gaping
finger holes. She pulled the ripped and bloody shirt
away from his abdomen to expose an area where she felt
a lump beneath his skin. There to the right of the blade
he clutched so tightly to his chest was an open wound
with a hard lump just beneath its surface. As she
watched, the lump broke through. It was another bullet,
slowly, painfully extruding from the wound. It was as
wonderful as it was terrifying: The sword blade and its
glow were drawing the bullets from Glenn's body and
healing his wounds! Magda watched in awe.

The glow began to fade.

"Magda . . ."

She jumped at the sound. Glenn's voice was much
stronger than it had been when she had covered him.
She pulled the blanket back over him, tucking it around
his neck. His eyes were open, staring at the keep.

"Rest some more," she whispered.

"What's happening over there?"

"Some shooting before—a lot of it."

With a groan, Glenn tried to sit up. Magda pushed
him back easily. He was still very weak.

"Got to get to the keep . . . stop Rasalom."

"Who's Rasalom?"

"The one you and your father call Molasar. He reversed the letters of his name for you . . . real name is
Rasalom . . . got to stop him!"

He tried to rise again and again Magda pushed him
back.

"It's almost dawn. A vampire can't go anywhere after sunrise, so just—"

"He's no more afraid of sunlight than you are!"

"But a vampire—"

"He's *not* a vampire! Never was! If he were," Glenn said, a note of despair creeping into his voice, "I wouldn't bother trying to stop him."

Dread caressed her, a cold hand against the middle of her back. "Not a vampire?"

"He's the source of the vampire legends, but what he craves is nothing so simple as blood. That notion crept into the folk tales because people can see blood, and touch it. What Rasalom feeds on no one can see or touch."

"You mean what you were trying to tell me last night before the soldiers . . . came?" She did not want to remember last night.

"Yes. He draws strength from human pain, misery, and madness. He can feed on the agony of those who die by his hand but gains far more from man's inhumanity to other men."

"That's ridiculous! Nothing could live on such things. They're too . . . too insubstantial!"

"Is sunlight 'too insubstantial' for a flower to need for growth? Believe me: Rasalom feeds on things that cannot be seen or touched—all of them bad."

"You make him sound like the Serpent himself!"

"You mean Satan? The Devil?" Glenn smiled weakly. "Put aside every religion you've ever heard of. They mean nothing here. Rasalom predates them all."

"I can't believe—"

"He is a survivor of the First Age. He pretended to be a five-hundred-year-old vampire because that fit the history of the keep and the region. And because it generated fear so easily—another one of his delights. But he's much, much older. Everything he told your father—*everything*—was a lie . . . except for the part about being weak and having to build his strength."

"Everything? But what about saving me? What about

curing Papa? And what about those villagers the major took hostage? They would have been executed if he had not saved them!"

"He saved no one. You told me he killed the two soldiers guarding the villagers. But did *he* set the villagers free? No! He added insult to injury by marching the dead soldiers up to the major's quarters and making a fool out of him. Rasalom was trying to provoke the major into executing all the villagers on the spot. That's the sort of atrocity that swells his strength. And after half a millennium of imprisonment, he needed much strengthening. Fortunately, events conspired against him and the villagers survived."

"Imprisonment? But he told Papa . . ." Her voice trailed off. "Another lie?"

Glenn nodded. "Rasalom did not build the keep as he said. Nor was he hiding in it. The keep was built to trap and hold him . . . forever. Who could have foretold that it or anything else in the Dinu Pass might someday be considered of military value? Or that some fool would break the seal on his cell? Now, if he ever gets loose in the world—"

"But he's loose now."

"No. Not yet. That's another one of his lies. He wanted your father to believe he was free, but he's still confined to the keep by the other piece of this." He pulled the blanket down and showed her the butt end of the sword blade. "The hilt to this blade is the only thing on earth Rasalom fears. It's the only thing that has power over him. It can bind him. The hilt is the key. It locks him within the keep. The blade is useless without it, but the two joined together can destroy him."

Magda shook her head in an attempt to clear it. This was becoming more incredible every minute!

"But the hilt—where is it? What does it look like?"

"You've seen its image thousands of times in the walls of the keep."

"The crosses!" Magda's mind whirled. Then they weren't crosses after all! They were modeled on the hilt of a sword—no wonder the crosspiece was set so high!

She had been looking at them for years and had never even come close to guessing. And if Molasar—or should she start thinking of him as Rasalom now?—were truly the source of the vampire legends, she could see how his fear of the sword hilt might have been transmuted into a fear of the cross in the folk tales. "But where—"

"Buried deep in the subcellar. As long as the hilt remains within the walls of the keep, Rasalom is bound by them."

"But all he has to do is dig it up and dispose of it."

"He can't touch it, or even get too close to it."

"Then he's trapped forever!"

"No," Glenn said in a very low voice as he looked into Magda's eyes. "He has your father."

Magda wanted to be sick, to shout *No*! at the top of her lungs, but she could not. She had been turned to stone by Glenn's quiet words . . . words which for the life of her she could not deny.

"Let me tell you what I think has happened," he said into the lengthening silence. "Rasalom was released the first night the Germans moved into the keep. He had strength enough then to kill only one. After that he rested and took stock. His initial strategy, I think, was to kill them one at a time, to feed on that daily agony and on the fear that increased among the living each time he claimed one of them. He was careful not to kill too many at once, especially not the officers, for that might drive them all away. He probably hoped for one of three things to occur: The Germans would become so frustrated that they would blow up the keep, thereby freeing him; or they would bring in more and more reinforcements, affording him more lives to take, more fear to grow strong on; or that he might find among the men a corruptible innocent."

Magda could barely hear her own voice. "Papa."

"Or you. From what you told me, Rasalom's attention seemed to be centered on you when he first revealed himself. But the captain put you over here, out of reach. Therefore Rasalom had to concentrate on your father."

"But he could have used one of the soldiers!"

"He gains his greatest strength from the destruction of everything that is good in a person. The corruption of the values of a single decent human being enriches him more than a thousand murders. It's a *feast* for Rasalom! The soldiers were useless to him. Veterans of Poland and other campaigns, they had killed proudly for their Führer. Little of value in them for Rasalom. And their reinforcements—death camp troopers! Nothing left in those creatures to debase! So the only real use he's had for the Germans, besides the fear and death-agony gleaned from them, is as digging tools."

Magda couldn't imagine . . . "Digging?"

"To unearth the hilt. I suspect that the 'thing' you heard shuffling around in the subcellar after your father sent you away was a group of the dead soldiers returning to their shrouds."

Walking corpses . . . the thought was grotesque, too fantastic even to consider, and yet she remembered that story the major had told about the two dead soldiers who had walked from the place of their dying to his room.

"But if he has the power to make the dead walk, why can't he have one of them dispose of the hilt?"

"Impossible. The hilt negates his power. A corpse under his control would return to its inanimate state the instant it touched the hilt." He paused. "Your father will be the one to carry the hilt from the keep."

"But as soon as Papa touches the hilt, won't Rasalom lose control over him?"

Glenn shook his head sadly. "You must realize by now that he's helping Rasalom willingly . . . *enthusiastically*. Your father will be able to handle the hilt with ease because he'll be acting of his own free will."

Magda felt dead inside. "But Papa doesn't *know!* Why didn't you tell him?"

"Because it was *his* battle, not mine. And because I couldn't risk letting Rasalom know I was here. Your father wouldn't have believed me anyway—he preferred to hate me. Rasalom has done a masterful job on him, destroying his character by tiny increments, peeling away layer after layer of all the things he believed in, leaving only the base, venal aspects of his nature."

It was true. Magda had seen it happening and had been afraid to admit it, but it was *true*!

"You could have helped him!"

"Perhaps. But I doubt it. Your father's battle was against himself as much as against Rasalom. And in the end, evil must be faced alone. Your father made excuses for the evil he sensed within Rasalom, and soon he came to see Rasalom as the answer to all his problems. Rasalom started with your father's religion. He does *not* fear the cross, yet he pretended to, causing your father to question his entire heritage, undermining all the beliefs and values derived from that heritage. Then Rasalom rescued you from your would-be rapists—a testimony to the quickness and adaptability of his mind—putting your father deep in his debt. Rasalom went on to promise him a chance to destroy Nazism and save your people. And then, the final stroke—the elimination of all the symptoms of the disease your father has suffered with for years. Rasalom had a willing slave then, one who would do just about anything he asked. He has not only stripped away most of the man you called 'Papa,' but has fashioned him into an instrument that will effect the release of mankind's greatest enemy from the keep."

Glenn struggled to a sitting position. "I must stop Rasalom once and for all!"

"Let him go," Magda said through her misery as she contemplated what had happened to Papa—or rather, what Papa had allowed to happen to himself. She had to wonder: Would she or anybody else have been able to withstand such an assault on one's character? "Perhaps that will free my father from Rasalom's influence and we can go back to the way we were."

"You will have no lives to go about if Rasalom is set free!"

"In this world of Hitler and the Iron Guard, what can Rasalom do that hasn't been done already?"

"You haven't been listening!" Glenn said angrily. "Once free, Rasalom will make Hitler seem a suitable playmate for whatever children you might have planned on having."

"Nothing could be worse than Hitler!" Magda said. "Nothing!"

"Rasalom could. Don't you see, Magda, that with Hitler, as evil as he is, there is still hope? Hitler is but a man. He is mortal. He will die or be killed someday . . . maybe tomorrow, maybe thirty years from now, but he *will* die. He only controls a small part of the world. And although he appears invincible now, he has yet to deal with Russia. Britain still defies him. And there is America—if those Americans decide to turn their vitality and productive capacity to war, no country, not even Hitler's Germany, will be able to stand against them for long. So you see, there is still hope in this very dark hour."

Magda nodded slowly. What Glenn said paralleled her own feelings—she had never given up hope. "But Rasalom—"

"Rasalom, as I told you, feeds on human debasement. And never in the history of humankind has there been such a glut of it as there is today in eastern Europe. As long as the hilt remains within the keep walls, Rasalom is not only trapped, but is insulated from what goes on outside. Remove the hilt and it will all rush in on him at once—all the death, misery, and butchery of Buchenwald, Dachau, Auschwitz, and all the other death camps, all the monstrousness of modern war. He'll absorb it like a sponge, feast on it and grow incredibly strong. His power will balloon beyond all comprehension.

"But he'll not be satisfied. He'll want more. He'll move swiftly around the world, slaying heads of state, throwing governments into confusion, reducing nations to terrified mobs. What army could stand against the legions of the dead he is capable of raising against it?

"Soon all will be in chaos. And then the real horror will begin. Nothing worse than Hitler, you say? Think of the entire world as a death camp!''

Magda's mind rebelled at the vista Glenn was describing. "It couldn't happen!"

"Why not? Do you think there will be a shortage of volunteers to run Rasalom's death camps? The Nazis have shown that there are plenty of men more than willing to slaughter their fellows. But it will go far beyond that. You've seen what has happened to the villagers today, haven't you? All the worst in their natures has been drawn to the surface. Their responses to the world have been reduced to anger, hate, and violence.''

"But how?"

"Rasalom's influence. He has grown steadily stronger within the keep, feeding on the death and fear there, and on the slow disintegration of your father's character. And as he has gained strength, the walls of the keep have been weakened by the soldiers. Every day they tear down a little more of the internal structure, compromising its integrity. And every day the influence of Rasalom's presence extends farther beyond those walls.

"The keep was built to an ancient design, the images of the hilt placed in a specific pattern in the walls to cut Rasalom off from the world, to contain his power, to seal him in. Now that pattern has been tampered with and the villagers are paying the price. If Rasalom escapes and feeds on the death camps, the whole world will pay a similar price. For Rasalom will not be as selective as Hitler when it comes to victims: *Everyone* will be targeted. Race, religion, none of that will matter. Rasalom will be truly egalitarian. The rich will not be able to buy their way out, the pious will not be able to pray their way out, the crafty will not be able to sneak or lie their way out. Everyone will suffer. Women and children the most. People will be born into misery; they will spend their days in despair; they will die in agony. Generation after generation, all suffering to feed Rasalom.''

He paused for breath, then: "And the worst of it all,

Magda, is that there will be *no hope*. And no end to it!
Rasalom will be untouchable . . . invincible . . .
deathless. If he is freed now, there will be no stopping
him. Always in the past the sword has held him back.
But now . . . with the world as it is . . . he will grow too
strong for even this blade reunited with its hilt to stop
him. *He must never leave the keep!*"

Magda saw that Glenn meant to go into the keep.
"No!" she shouted, her arms reaching to hold him
back. She couldn't let him go. "He'll destroy you in
your condition! Isn't there anybody else?"

"Only me. No one else can do this. Like your father,
I have to face this alone. After all, it's really my fault
that Rasalom still exists at all."

"How can that be?"

Glenn didn't answer. Magda tried another approach.

"Where did Rasalom come from?"

"He was a man . . . once. But he gave himself over to
dark power and was forever changed by it."

Magda felt a catch in her throat. "But if Rasalom
serves a 'dark power,' who do *you* serve?"

"Another power."

She sensed his resistance, but she pressed on.

"A power for good?"

"Perhaps."

"For how long?"

"All my life."

"How can it be . . . ?" She was afraid of the answer.
"How can it be your fault, Glenn?"

He looked away. "My name isn't Glenn—it's
Glaeken. I'm as old as Rasalom. *I* built the keep."

Cuza had not seen Molasar since descending into the
pit to uncover the talisman. He had said something
about making the Germans pay for invading his keep,
then his voice had trailed off and he was gone. The

corpses had begun to move then, filing out behind the miraculous being who controlled them.

Cuza was left alone with the cold, the rats, and the talisman. He wished he could have gone along. But he supposed what really mattered was that soon they would all be dead, officers and enlisted men alike. Yet he would have enjoyed seeing Major Kaempffer die, seeing him suffer some of the agonies he had inflicted on countless innocent and helpless people.

But Molasar had said to wait here. And now, with the faint echoes of gunfire seeping down from above, Cuza knew why: Molasar had not wanted the man to whom he had entrusted his source of power to be endangered by any stray bullets. After a while the shooting stopped. Leaving the talisman behind, Cuza took his flashlight and climbed to the top of the pit where he stood among the clustered rats. They no longer bothered him; he was too intent on listening for Molasar's return.

Soon he heard it. Footsteps approaching. More than one pair. He flashed his light toward the entrance to the chamber and saw Major Kaempffer round the corner and approach him. A cry escaped Cuza and he almost fell over into the pit, but then he saw the glazed eyes, the slack expression, and realized that the SS major was dead. Woermann came filing in behind him, equally dead, a length of rope trailing from his neck.

"I thought you might like to see these two," Molasar said, following the dead officers into the chamber. "Especially the one who proposed to build the so-called death camp for our fellow Wallachians. Now I shall seek out this Hitler and dispose of him and his minions." He paused. "But first, my talisman. You must see to it that it is hidden securely in the hills. Only then can I devote my energies to ridding the world of our common foe."

"Yes!" Cuza said, feeling his pulse begin to race. "It's right here!"

He scrambled down into the pit and grabbed the talisman. As he tucked it under his arm and began to climb up again, he saw Molasar step back.

"Wrap it up," he said. "Its precious metals will attract unwanted attention should someone see them."

"Of course." Cuza reached for the wadded wrapper and packing. "I'll tie it up securely when I get into the better light upstairs. Don't worry. I'll see to it that it's all—"

"Cover it *now!*" The command echoed through the chamber.

Cuza halted, struck by Molasar's vehemence. He didn't think he should be spoken to in such a manner. But then, one had to make allowances for fifteenth-century boyars.

He sighed. "Very well." He squatted in the bottom of the pit and folded the coarse cloth packing over the talisman, then covered it all with the tattered wrapper.

"Good!" said the voice from above and behind him. Cuza looked up and saw that Molasar had moved to the other side of the pit, away from the entry. "Now hurry. The sooner I know the talisman is safe, the sooner I can depart for Germany."

Cuza hurried. He crawled from the pit as swiftly as he could and began to make his way through the tunnel to the steps that would take him upward to a new day, not only for himself and for his people, but for all the world.

"It's a long story, Magda . . . ages long. And I fear there's no time left to tell it to you."

His voice sounded to Magda as if it were coming from the far end of a long, dark tunnel. He had said Rasalom predated Judaism . . . and then he had said he was as old as Rasalom. But that couldn't be! The man who had loved her could not be some leftover from a forgotten age! He was real! He was human! Flesh and blood!

Movement caught her eye and brought her back to the here and now. Glenn was attempting to rise to his feet, using the sword blade for support. He managed to get to his knees but was too weak to rise farther.

"Who are you?" she said, staring at him, feeling as if she were seeing him for the first time. "And who is Rasalom?"

"The story starts long ago," he said, sweating and swaying, leaning on the hiltless blade. "Long before the time of the Pharaohs, before Babylonia, even before Mesopotamia. There was another civilization then, in another age."

" 'The First Age,' " Magda said. "You mentioned that before." It was not a new idea to her. She had run across the theory now and then in the historical and archeological journals she had read at various times while helping Papa with his research. The obscure theory contended that all of recorded history represented only the Second Age of Man; that long, long ago there had been a great civilization across Europe and Asia—some of its apologists even went so far as to include the island continents of Atlantis and Mu in this ancient world, a world they claimed had been destroyed in a global cataclysm. "It's a discredited idea," Magda said, a defensive quaver in her voice. "All historians and archeologists of any repute condemn it as lunacy."

"Yes, I know," Glenn said with a sardonic twist to his lips. "The same type of 'authorities' who scoffed at the possibility that Troy might have truly existed—and then Schliemann found it. But I'm not going to debate you. The First Age was real. I was born into it."

"But how—"

"Let me finish quickly. There isn't much time and I want you to understand a few things before I go to face Rasalom. Things were different in the First Age. This world was then a battleground between two . . ." He appeared to be groping for a word. "I don't want to say 'gods' because that would give you the impression that they had discrete identities and personalities. There were two vast, incomprehensible . . . forces . . . *Powers* abroad in the land then. One, the Dark Power, which was called Chaos, reveled in anything inimical to mankind. The other Power was . . ."

He paused again, and Magda could not help but prompt him.

"You mean the White Power . . . the power of Good?"

"It's not so simple as that. We merely called it Light. What mattered was that it opposed Chaos. The First Age eventually became divided into two camps: those who sought dominion through Chaos and those who resisted. Rasalom was a necromancer of his time, a brilliant adept to the Dark Power. He gave himself over to it completely and eventually became the champion of Chaos."

"And you chose to be champion of Light—of Good." She wanted him to say yes.

"No . . . I didn't exactly choose. And I can't say the Power I serve is all that good, or all that light. I was . . . conscripted, you might say. Circumstances too involved to explain now—circumstances that have long since lost any shred of meaning for me—led me to become involved with the armies of Light. I soon found it impossible to extricate myself, and before long I was at their forefront, leading them. I was given the sword. Its blade and hilt were forged by a race of small folk now long extinct. It was fashioned for one purpose; to destroy Rasalom. There came a final battle between the opposing forces—Armageddon, Ragnarök, all the doomsday battles rolled into one. The resulting cataclysm—earthquakes, fire storms, tidal waves—wiped out every trace of the First Age of Man. Only a few humans were left to begin all over again."

"But what of the Powers?"

Glenn shrugged. "They still exist, but their interest waned after the cataclysm. There was not much left for them in a ruined world whose inhabitants were reverting to savagery. They turned their attention elsewhere while Rasalom and I fought on across the world and across the ages, neither one gaining the upper hand for long, neither one sickening or aging. And somewhere along the way we lost something . . ."

He glanced down at a broken fragment of mirror that had fallen out of the blade case and now lay near his knees.

"Hold that up to my face," he told Magda.

Magda lifted the fragment and positioned it next to his cheek.

"How do I look in it?" he asked.

Magda glanced at the glass—and dropped it with a tiny scream. The mirror was empty! Just as Papa had said of Rasalom!

The man she loved cast no reflection!

"Our reflections were taken away by the Powers we serve, perhaps as a constant reminder to Rasalom and me that our lives were no longer our own."

His mind seemed to drift for a moment "It's strange not to see yourself in a mirror or a pool of water. You never get used to it." He smiled sadly. "I believe I've forgotten what I look like."

Magda's heart went out to him. "Glenn . . . ?"

"But I never stopped pursuing Rasalom," he said, shaking himself. "Wherever there was news of butchery and death, I would find him and drive him off. But as civilization gradually rebuilt itself, and people began to crowd together again, Rasalom became more ingenious in his methods. He was always spreading death and misery in any way he could, and in the fourteenth century, when he traveled from Constantinople throughout Europe, leaving plague-ridden rats in every city along his way—"

"The Black Death!"

"Yes. It would have been a minor epidemic without Rasalom, but as you know, it turned out to be one of the major catastrophes of the Middle Ages. That was when I knew I had to find a way to stop him before he devised something even more hideous. And if I'd done the job right, neither of us would be here right now."

"But how can you blame yourself? How can Rasalom's escape be your fault? The Germans let him loose."

"He should be *dead*! I could have killed him half a

millennium ago but I didn't. I came here looking for
Vlad the Impaler. I had heard of his atrocities and they
fit Rasalom's pattern. I expected to find him posing as
Vlad. But I was wrong. Vlad was just a madman under
Rasalom's influence, feeding Rasalom's strength by impaling thousands of innocents. But even at his worst,
Vlad could not match by one tenth what is happening
every day in today's death camps. I built the keep. I
tricked Rasalom by luring him inside. I bound him with
the power of the hilt and sealed him in the cellar wall
where he would stay forever." He sighed. "At least I
thought it would be forever. I could have killed him
then—I *should* have killed him then—but I didn't."

"Why not?"

Glenn closed his eyes and was quiet for a long time
before replying. "This isn't easy to say . . . but I was
afraid. You see, I've lived on as a counterbalance to
Rasalom. But what happens if I'm finally victorious and
kill him? When his threat is extinguished, what happens
to me? I've lived for what seems like eons, but I've
never grown tired of life. It may be hard to believe, but
there's always something new." He opened his eyes
again and looked squarely at Magda. "Always. But I
fear Rasalom and I are a pair, the continued existence of
one dependent on the other. I am Yang to his Yin. I'm
not ready to die yet."

Magda had to know: "*Can* you die?"

"Yes. It takes a lot to kill me, but I can die. The injuries I received tonight would have done me in had you
not brought the blade to me. I had gone as far as I could
. . . I would have died right here without you." His eyes
rested on her for a moment, then he looked over to the
keep. "Rasalom probably thinks I'm dead. That could
work to my advantage."

Magda wanted to throw her arms around him but
could not bring herself to touch him again just yet. At
least now she understood the guilt she had seen in his
face at unguarded moments.

"Don't go over there, Glenn."

"Call me Glaeken," he said softly. "It's been so long

since someone called me by my real name."

"All right . . . Glaeken." The word felt good on her tongue, as if saying his true name linked her more closely to him. But there were still so many unanswered questions. "What about those awful books? Who hid them there?"

"I did. They can be dangerous in the wrong hands, but I couldn't let them be destroyed. Knowledge of any kind—especially of evil—must be preserved."

There was another question, one which Magda hesitated to ask. She had come to realize as he spoke that it mattered little to her how old he was—it didn't change him from the man she had come to know. But how did he feel about her?

"What of me?" she said finally. "You never told me . . ." She wanted to ask him if she were just a stop along the way, another conquest. Was the love she had sensed in him and seen in his eyes just a trick he had learned? Was he even *capable* of love anymore? She couldn't voice the thoughts. Even thinking them was painful.

Glaeken seemed to read her mind. "Would you have believed me if I had told you?"

"But yesterday—"

"I love you, Magda," he said, reaching for her hand. "I've been closed off for so long. You reached me. No one has been able to do that for a long time. I may be older than anyone or anything you've ever imagined, but I'm still a man. That was never taken away from me."

Magda slowly put her arms around his shoulders, holding him gently but firmly. She wanted to hold him to this spot, root him here where he'd be safe outside the keep.

After a long moment he spoke into her ear. "Help me to my feet, Magda. I've got to stop your father."

Magda knew she had to help him, even though she feared for him. She gripped his arm and tried to lift him but his knees buckled repeatedly. Finally, he slumped to the ground and pounded it with a closed fist.

"I need more time!"

"I'll go," Magda said, half wondering where the
words came from. "I can meet my father at the gate."

"No! It's too dangerous!"

"I can talk to him. He'll listen to me."

"He's beyond all reason now. He'll listen only to
Rasalom."

"I have to try. Can you think of anything better?"

Glaeken was silent.

"Then I'll go." She wished she could have stood
there and tossed her head in defiance to show him she
wasn't afraid. But she was terrified.

"Don't cross the threshold," Glaeken warned her.
"Whatever you do, don't step across into the keep.
That's Rasalom's domain now!"

I know, Magda thought as she broke into a run
toward the causeway. *And I can't allow Papa to step
across to this side, either—at least not if he's holding the
hilt to a sword.*

Cuza had hoped to be done with the flashlight after
reaching the cellar level, but all the electric lights were
dead. He found, however, that the corridor was not
completely dark. There were glowing spots in the walls.
He looked more closely and saw that the images of the
crosslike talisman set in the stones were glowing softly.
They brightened as he neared and faded slowly after he
had passed, responding to the object he carried.

Theodor Cuza moved along the central corridor in a
state of awe. Never had the supernatural been so real to
him. Never would he be able to view the world or
existence itself as he had before. He thought about how
smug he had been, thinking he had seen it all, yet never
realizing the blinders that had limited his vision. Well,
now his blinders were off and there was a whole new
world all around him.

He hugged the wrapped talisman snugly against his

chest, feeling close to the supernatural . . . and yet far
from his God. But then, what had God done for his
Chosen People? How many thousands, millions, had
died in the past few years calling out his name, and had
never been answered?

Soon there would be an answer, and Theodor Cuza
was helping to bring it.

As he ascended toward the courtyard he felt a twinge
of uneasiness and paused halfway up. He watched
trailers of fog ooze down the steps like white honey
while his thoughts whirled.

His moment of personal triumph was at hand. He was
finally able to *do* something, to take an active role
against the Nazis. Why, then, this feeling that all was
not quite right? He had to admit to some nagging
doubts about Molasar, but nothing specific. All the
pieces fit . . .

Or did they? Cuza could not help but find the shape
of the talisman bothersome: It was too close to the
shape of the cross Molasar feared so. But perhaps that
was Molasar's way of protecting it—make it resemble a
holy object to throw his pursuers off the track, just as
he had done with the keep. But then there was Molasar's
seeming reluctance to handle the talisman himself, his
insistence that Cuza take charge of it immediately. If the
talisman were so important to Molasar, if it were truly
the source of all his power, why didn't he find a hiding
place for it himself?

Slowly, mechanically, Cuza took the final steps up to
the courtyard. At the top he squinted into the unaccustomed gray light of predawn and found the answer
to his questions: daylight. Of course! Molasar could not
move around in the day and he needed someone who
could! What a relief it was to erase those doubts—
daylight explained everything!

As Cuza's eyes adjusted to the growing light, he
looked across the foggy ruin of the courtyard to the gate
and saw a figure standing there, waiting. For a single
terrified moment he thought one of the sentries had
escaped the slaughter; then he saw that the figure was

too small and slim to be a German soldier.

It was Magda. Filled with joy, he hurried toward her.

⊤

From the threshold of the keep, Magda looked in on the courtyard; it was utterly silent and deserted but showed signs of battle everywhere: bullet holes in the fabric and the metal of the lorries, smashed windshields, pock marks in the stone blocks of the walls, smoke rising from the shattered ruins of the generators. Nothing moved. She wondered what gore lay beneath the fog that floated knee deep over the courtyard floor.

She also wondered what she was doing here shivering in the predawn chill, waiting for Papa, who might or might not be carrying the future of the world in his hands. Now that she had a quiet moment to think, to calmly consider all that Glenn—Glaeken—had told her, doubt began to insinuate its way into her mind. Words whispered in the dark lost their impact with the approach of day. It had been so easy to believe Glaeken while she was listening to his voice and looking into his eyes. But now that she was away from him, standing here alone, waiting . . . she felt unsure.

It was mad—immense, unseen, unknowable forces . . . Light . . . Chaos . . . in opposition for control of humanity! Absurd! It was the stuff of fantasy, the deranged dream of an opium eater!

And yet . . .

. . . there was Molasar—or Rasalom or whatever he was truly called. He was no dream, yet certainly more than human, certainly beyond anything she had ever experienced or wished to experience again. And certainly evil. She had known that from the first time he had touched her.

And then there was Glaeken—if *that* was his true name—who did not seem evil but who might well be mad. He was real, and he had a sword blade that glowed and healed wounds that were enough to kill a score of men. She had seen that with her own eyes. And he cast no reflection . . .

Perhaps it was she who was mad.

But oh, if she was *not* mad. If the world truly stood on the brink here in this remote mountain pass . . . whom was she to trust? Trust Rasalom, who by his own admission and confirmed by Glaeken had been locked away in some sort of limbo for five centuries and, now that he was free, was promising to put an end to Hitler and his atrocities? Or trust the red-haired man who had become the love of her life but had lied to her about so many things, even his name? Whom her own father accused of being an ally of the Nazis?

Why is it all coming to rest on me?

Why did *she* have to be the one to choose when everything was so confused? Whom to believe? The father she had trusted all her life, or the stranger who had unlocked a part of her being she never even knew existed? It wasn't fair!

She sighed. *But nobody ever said life was fair.*

She had to decide. And soon.

Glenn's parting words came back to her: *Whatever you do, don't step across into the keep. That's Rasalom's domain now.* But she knew she had to step across. The malignant aura around the keep had made it an effort merely to walk across the causeway. Now she had to feel what it was like inside. It would help her decide.

She edged her foot forward, then pulled it back. Perspiration had broken out all over her body. She didn't want to do this but circumstances left her little choice. Setting her jaw, she closed her eyes and stepped across the threshold.

The evil exploded against her, snatching her breath away, knotting her stomach, making her weave drunkenly about. It was more powerful, more intense than ever. She wavered in her resolve, wanting desperately to step back outside. But she fought this down, willing herself to weather the storm of malice she felt raging about her. The very air she was breathing confirmed what she had known all along: No good would ever come from within the keep.

And it was here inside the threshold where she would have to meet Papa. And stop him here if he carried the hilt to a sword.

A movement across the courtyard caught her eye. Papa had emerged from the cellar entry. He stood staring about for a moment, then spotted her and ran forward. After adjusting to the sight of her once-crippled father running, she noticed that his clothes were caked with dirt. He was carrying a package of some sort, something heavy and carelessly wrapped.

"Magda! I have it!" he called, panting as he stopped before her.

"What do you have, Papa?" The sound of her own voice was flat and wooden in her ears. She dreaded his answer.

"Molasar's talisman—the source of his power!"

"You've stolen it from him?"

"No. He gave it to me. I'm to find a safe hiding place for it while he goes to Germany."

Magda went cold inside. Papa was removing an object from the keep, just as Glaeken had said he would.

She had to know what it looked like. "Let me see it."

"There's no time for that now. I've got to—"

He stepped to the side to go around her, but Magda moved in front of him, blocking his way, keeping him within the boundary of the keep.

"Please?" she pleaded. "Show it to me?"

He hesitated, studying her face questioningly, then pulled off the wrapper and showed her what he had called "Molasar's talisman."

Magda heard her breath suck in at the sight of it. *Oh, God!* It was obviously heavy, and appeared to be gold and silver—exactly like the strange crosses throughout the keep. And there was even a slot in its top, the perfect size to accept the spike she had seen at the butt end of Glaeken's sword blade.

It was the hilt to Glaeken's sword. The hilt . . . the

key to the keep . . . the only thing that protected the world from Rasalom.

Magda stood and stared at it while her father said something she could not hear. The words would not reach her. All she could hear was Glaeken's description of what would become of the world should Rasalom be allowed to escape the keep. Everything within her revolted at the decision that faced her, but she had no choice. She had to stop her father—at any cost.

"Go back, Papa," she said, searching his eyes for some remnant of the man she had loved so dearly all her life. "Leave it in the keep. Molasar has been lying to you all along. That's not the source of his power—it's the only thing that can *withstand* his power! He's the enemy of everything good in this world! You can't set him free!"

"Ridiculous! He's already free! And he's an ally— look what he's done for me! I can walk!"

"But only as far as the other side of this gateway. Only far enough to remove that from the keep—he can't leave here as long as the hilt remains within the walls!"

"Lies! Molasar is going to kill Hitler and stop the death camps!"

"He'll *feed* on the death camps, Papa!" It was like talking to a deaf man. "For once in your life listen to *me*! Trust *me*! Do as *I* say! *Don't remove that thing from the keep!*"

He ignored her and pressed forward. "Let me by!"

Magda placed her hands against his chest, steeling herself to defy the man who had raised her, taught her so much, given her so much. "Listen to me, Papa!"

"No!"

Magda set her feet and shoved with all her strength, sending him stumbling backward. She hated herself for doing it but he had left her no alternative. She had to stop thinking of him as a cripple; he was well and strong now—and as determined as she.

"You strike your own father?" he said in a hoarse, hushed voice. Shock and anger roiled on his face. "Is this what a night of rutting with your red-headed lover has done to you? I am your father! I command you to let me pass!''

"No, Papa," she said, tears starting in her eyes. She had never dared to stand up to him before, but she had to see this through—for both their sakes and for all the world.

The sight of her tears seemed to disconcert him. For an instant his features softened and he was himself again. He opened his mouth to speak, then closed it with a snap. Snarling with fury, he leaped forward and swung the hilt at her head.

T

Rasalom stood waiting in the subterranean chamber, immersed in darkness, the silence broken only by the sound of the rats crawling over the cadavers of the two officers which he had allowed to tumble to the dirt after the crippled one had left with that accursed hilt. Soon it would be gone from the keep and he would be free again.

Soon his hunger would be appeased. If what the crippled one had told him was true—and what he had heard from some of the German soldiers during their stay seemed to confirm it—Europe had now become a sinkhole of human misery. It meant that after ages of struggling, after so many defeats at Glaeken's hands, his destiny at last was about to come to pass. He had feared all lost when Glaeken had trapped him in this stone prison, but in the end he had prevailed. Human greed had released him from the tiny cell that had held him for five centuries. Human hate and powerlust were about to give him the strength to become master of this globe.

He waited. And still his hunger remained untouched. The expected surge of power did not come. Something was wrong. The crippled one could have journeyed through that gate twice by now. Three times!

Something had gone wrong. He let his senses range

the keep until he detected the presence of the crippled one's daughter. It was she who must be the cause of the delay. But why? She couldn't know—

—unless Glaeken had told her about the hilt before he died.

Rasalom made a tiny gesture with his left hand, and behind him in the dark the corpses of Major Kaempffer and Captain Woermann began to struggle to their feet again, to stand stiffly erect, waiting.

In a cold rage, Rasalom strode from the chamber. The daughter would be easy to handle. The two corpses stumbled after him. And after them followed the army of rats.

Magda watched in dumb awe as the gold-and-silver hilt swung toward her head with crushing force. Never had it occurred to her that Papa might actually try to harm her. Yet he was aiming a killing blow at her skull. Only an instinctive reflex for self-preservation saved her—she stepped back at the last moment, then dove forward, knocking her father to the ground as he tried to recover his balance after the wild swing. She fell on top of him, clutching at the silver crosspiece, finally gripping it with one hand on each side and twisting the hilt out of his grasp.

He clawed at her like an animal, scratching the flesh of her arms, trying to pull her down again to the point where the hilt would be in reach, screaming:

"Give it to me! Give it to me! You're going to ruin everything!"

Magda regained her feet and backed away to the side of the gateway arch, holding the hilt with both hands by its golden handle. She was uncomfortably close to the threshold, but she had managed to retain the hilt within the bounds of the keep.

He struggled to his feet and ran at her with his head

down, his arms outstretched. Magda dodged the full
force of his charge but he managed to catch her elbow as
he went by, twisting her around. Then he was on her,
striking at her face and screeching incoherently.

"Stop it, Papa!" she cried, but he seemed not to
hear. He was like a wild beast. As his ragged dirty
fingernails raked toward her eyes, she swung the hilt at
him; she didn't think about what she was doing—it was
an automatic move. *"Stop it!"*

The sound of the heavy metal striking Papa's skull
sickened her. Stunned, she stood and watched as his
eyes rolled back behind his glasses and he slipped to the
ground and lay still, tendrils of fog drifting over him.

What have I done?

"Why did you make me hit you?" she screamed at his
unconscious form. "Couldn't you trust me just once?
Just once?"

She had to get him out—just a few feet beyond the
threshold would be enough. But first she had to dispose
of the hilt, put it somewhere well inside the keep. Then
she would try to drag Papa out to safety.

Across the courtyard lay the entrance to the cellar.
She could throw the hilt down there. She began running
toward the entrance but stopped halfway there.
Someone was coming up the steps.

Rasalom!

He seemed to float, rising from the cellar as a huge
dead fish might rise from the bottom of a stagnant
pond. At the sight of her, his eyes became twin spheres
of dark fury, assaulting her, stabbing her. He bared his
teeth as he seemed to glide through the mist toward her.

Magda held her ground. Glaeken had said the hilt had
the power to counter Rasalom. She felt strong. She
could face him.

There was movement behind Rasalom as he approached. Two other figures were emerging from the
subcellar, figures with slack, white faces that followed
Rasalom as he stalked forward. Magda recognized
them: the captain and that awful major. She did not
need a closer look to know that they were dead. Glaeken

had told her about the walking corpses and she had been half expecting to see them, but that did not keep her blood from running cold at the sight of them. Yet she felt strangely safe.

Rasalom stopped within a dozen feet of her and slowly raised his arms until they were spread out like wings. For a moment, nothing happened. Then Magda noticed stirrings in the fog that blanketed the courtyard and swirled about her knees. All around her, hands rose out of the mist, clutching at the air, followed by heads, and then torsos. Like loathsome fungal growths sprouting from moldy soil, the German soldiers who had occupied the keep were rising from the dead.

Magda saw their ravaged bodies, their torn throats, yet she stood firm. She had the hilt. Glaeken had said the hilt could negate Rasalom's animating power. She believed him. She had to!

The corpses arrayed themselves behind Rasalom and to his right and left. No one moved.

Maybe they're afraid of the hilt! Magda thought, her heart leaping. *Maybe they can't get any closer!*

Then she noticed a curious rippling in the fog around the corpses' feet. She looked down. Through gaps in the mist she glimpsed scuttling forms, gray and brown. Rats! Revulsion tightened her throat and swept over her skin. Magda began to back away. They were moving toward her, not in a solid front, but in a chaotic scramble of crisscrossing paths and squat, bustling bodies. She could face anything—even the walking dead—anything but rats.

She saw a smile spread over Rasalom's face and knew she was responding just as he had hoped—retreating from his final threat, edging ever closer to the gateway. She tried to stop, to will her legs to be still, but they kept backing her away from the rats.

Dark stone walls closed around her—she was back within the gate arch. Another yard or two and she would be over the threshold . . . and Rasalom would be set loose upon the world.

Magda closed her eyes and stopped moving.

This far will I go, she told herself. *This far and no farther . . . this far and no farther . . .* repeating it over and
over in her mind—until something brushed her ankle
and skittered away. Something small and furry.
Another. Then another. She bit her lip to keep from
screaming. The hilt wasn't working! The rats were attacking her! They'd be all over her soon.

In a panic, she opened her eyes. Rasalom was closer
now, his depthless eyes fixed on her through the misty
half-light, his legion of the dead fanned out behind him,
and the rats massed before him. He was driving the rats
forward, forcing them against her feet and ankles.
Magda knew she was going to break and run any second
now . . . she could feel the overpowering terror welling
up inside her, ready to drown and wash away all her
resolve . . . *the hilt isn't protecting me!* She started to
turn and then stopped. The rats were brushing against
her, but they didn't bite or claw her. They made contact
and then ran. It was the hilt! Because she held the hilt,
Rasalom lost control over the rats as soon as they
touched her. Magda took heart and calmed herself.

*They can't bite me. They can't touch me for more
than an instant.* Her greatest horror had been that they
might crawl up her legs. Now she knew they could not.
She stood firm again.

Rasalom must have sensed this. He scowled and made
a motion with his hands.

The corpses again began to move. They parted
around him, then rejoined into a near-solid moving wall
of dead flesh, scuffling, stumbling forward, crowding
up to where she stood, stopping within inches of her.
They gaped at her with slack, expressionless faces and
glazed, empty eyes. There was no malevolence in their
movements, no hatred, no real purpose. They were
merely dead flesh. *But they were so close!* Had they
been alive, their breath would have wafted against her
face. As it was, a few of them smelled as if they had
already begun to putrefy.

She closed her eyes again, fighting the loathing that
weakened her knees, hugging the hilt against her.

*. . . this far and no farther . . . this far and no farther
. . . for Glaeken, for me, for what's left of Papa, for
everyone . . . this far and no farther . . .*

Something heavy and cold slumped against her. She
staggered back, crying out in surprise and disgust. The
corpses nearest her had begun to go limp and fall
against her. Another one slammed into her and she was
rocked back again. She twisted to the side and let its
slack bulk slip by her. Magda realized what Rasalom
was doing—if he couldn't frighten her out of the keep,
then he would push her out by hurling the physical bulk
of his dead army against her. He was succeeding. There
were only inches left to her.

As more corpses pressed forward, Magda made a
desperate move. She grasped the gold handle of the hilt
firmly with both hands and swung it out in a wide arc,
dragging it against the dead flesh of those closest to her.

Bright flashes of light and sizzling noises erupted
upon contact with the bodies; wisps of acrid, yellow-
white smoke stung her nostrils . . . and the corpses—
they jerked spasmodically and fell away like marionettes
with severed strings. She stepped forward, waving the
hilt again, this time in a wider arc, and again the flashes,
the sizzle, the sudden limpness.

Even Rasalom retreated a step.

Magda allowed a small, grim smile to touch her lips.
Now at least she had breathing room. She had a weapon
and she was learning how to use it. She saw Rasalom's
gaze shift to her left and looked to see what had caught
his attention.

Papa! He had regained consciousness and was on his
feet, leaning against the wall of the gateway arch. It
sickened Magda to see the thin trickle of blood running
down the side of his face—blood from the blow she had
struck.

"You!" Rasalom said, pointing to Papa. "Take the
talisman from her! She has joined our enemies!"

Magda saw her father shake his head, and her heart
leaped with new hope.

"No!" Papa's voice was a feeble croak, yet it echoed

off the stone walls around them. "I've been watching! If what she holds is truly the source of your power, you do not need me to reclaim it. Take it yourself!"

Magda knew she had never been so proud of her father as at that moment when he stood up to the creature who had tried to plunder his soul. And had come so close to succeeding. She brushed away tears and smiled, taking strength from Papa and giving it back to him.

"Ingrate!" Rasalom hissed, his face contorted with rage. "You've failed me! Very well, then—welcome back your illness! Revel in your pain!"

Papa slumped to his knees with a stifled moan. He held his hands before him, watching them turn white and lock once again into the gnarled deformity that until yesterday had rendered them useless. His spine curved and he crumpled forward with a groan. Slowly, with agony seeping from every pore, his body curled in on itself. When it was over he lay whimpering in a twisted, tortured parody of the fetal position.

Magda stepped toward him, shouting through her horror. "Papa!" She could almost feel his pain herself.

Yet he suffered through it all with no plea for mercy. This seemed to incite Rasalom further. Amid a chorus of shrill squeaks, the rats started forward, a dun wave that sluiced around Papa, then swept over him, tearing at him with tiny razor teeth.

Magda forgot her loathing and rushed to his side, batting at the rats with the hilt, swatting them away with her free hand. But for every few she swept away, more sets of tiny jaws darted in to redden themselves on Papa's flesh. She cried, she sobbed, she called out to God in every language she knew.

The only answer came from Rasalom, a taunting whisper behind her. "Throw the hilt through the gate and you will save him! Remove that thing from these walls and he lives!"

Magda forced herself to ignore him, but deep within she sensed that Rasalom had won. She could not let this horror go on—Papa was being eaten alive by vermin!

And she seemed helpless to save him. She had lost. She would have to surrender.

But not yet. The rats were not biting her, only Papa.

She sprawled across her father, covering his body with her own, pressing the hilt between them.

"He will die!" the hated voice whispered. "He will die and there will be no one to blame but you! Your fault! All you—"

Rasalom's words suddenly broke off as his voice climbed to a screech—a sound full of rage, fear, and disbelief.

"YOU!"

Magda twisted her head upward and saw Glaeken—weak, pale, caked with dried blood, leaning against the keep's gate a few feet away. There was no one in the world she wanted more to see right now than him.

"I knew you would come."

But the way he looked, it seemed a miracle he had made it across the causeway. He could never stand up to Rasalom in his present condition.

And yet he was here. The sword blade was in one hand, the other he held out to her. No words were necessary. She knew what he had come for and knew what she must do. She lifted herself away from Papa and placed the hilt in Glaeken's hand.

Somewhere behind her, Rasalom was screaming, *"Nooooo!"*

Glaeken smiled weakly at her, then in a single motion, smooth and swift, he stood the blade point down and poised the top of the hilt over the butt spike. As it slid home with a solid rasping click, there came a flash of light brighter than the sun at summer solstice, intolerably bright, spreading in a ball from Glaeken and his sword to be caught and amplified by the images of the hilt inlaid throughout the keep.

The light struck Magda like a blast from a furnace, good and clean, dry and warm. Shadows disappeared as everything within sight was etched in blinding white light. The fog melted away as though it had never existed. The rats fled squealing in all directions. The light scythed through the standing corpses, toppling them like stalks of dry wheat. Even Rasalom reeled away with both arms covering his face.

The true master of the keep had returned.

The light faded slowly, drawing back into the sword, and a moment passed before Magda could see again. When she could, there stood Glaeken, his clothes still ripped and bloodied, but the man within renewed. All fatigue, all weakness, all injury, had been wiped away. He was a man made whole again, radiating awesome power and implacable resolve. And his eyes were so fierce, so terrible in their determination that she was glad he was a friend and not a foe. This was the man who led the forces of Light against Chaos ages ago . . . the man she loved.

Glaeken held the reassembled sword out before him, its runes swirling and cascading over the blade. His blue eyes shining, he turned to Magda and saluted her with it.

"Thank you, my Lady," he said softly. "I knew you had courage—I never dreamed how much."

Magda glowed in his praise. *My Lady . . . he called me his Lady.*

Glaeken gestured to Papa. "Take him through the gate. I'll stand guard until you're safe on the causeway."

Magda's knees wobbled as she stood up. A quick glance around showed a jumble of fallen corpses. Rasalom had disappeared. "Where—?"

"I'll find him," Glaeken said. "But first I must see you where I know you'll be safe."

Magda bent and grabbed Papa under the arms and dragged his pitifully light form the few feet that took them across the threshold and onto the causeway. His breathing was shallow. He was bleeding from a thousand tiny wounds. She began dabbing at them with her skirt.

"Good-bye, Magda."

It was Glaeken's voice and it held a terrible note of finality. She looked up to see him staring at her with a look of infinite sadness on his face.

"Good-bye? Where are you going?"

"To finish a war that should have been over ages ago." His voice faltered. "I wish . . ."

Dread gripped her. "You're coming back to me, aren't you?"

Glaeken turned and walked toward the courtyard.

"Glaeken?"

He disappeared into the maw of the tower. Her cry was half wail, half sob.

"Glaeken!"

TWENTY-NINE

There was darkness within the tower. More than mere shadow—it was the blackness that only Rasalom could spawn. It engulfed Glaeken, but he was not entirely helpless against it. His rune sword began to glow with a pale blue light as soon as he stepped through the tower entrance. The images of the hilt laid into the walls responded immediately to the presence of the original and lit with white-and-yellow fire that pulsated slowly, dimly, as if to the rhythm of a massive and faraway heart.

The sound of Magda's voice followed Glaeken within and he stood at the foot of the tower stairs trying to shut out the pain he heard as she called his name, knowing that if he listened he would weaken. He had to cut her off, just as he had to sever all other ties to the world outside the keep. There was only he and Rasalom now.

Their millennia of conflict would end here today. He would see to that.

He let the power of the glowing sword surge through him. It was good to hold it again—like being reunited with a lost part of his body. But even the power of the sword could not reach the growing knot of despair tangled deep within him.

He was not going to win today. Even if he succeeded in killing Rasalom, the victory would cost him everything . . . for victory would eliminate the purpose of his continued existence. He would no longer be of use to the Power he served.

If he could defeat Rasalom . . .

He pushed all that behind him. This was no way to enter battle. He had to set his mind to victory—that was the only way to win. And he *must* win.

He looked around. He sensed Rasalom somewhere above. Why? There was no escape that way.

Glaeken ran up the steps to the second-level landing and stood there, alert, wary, his senses bristling. He could still sense Rasalom far above him, yet the dark air here was thick with danger. The replicas of the hilts pulsed dully from the walls, cruciform beacons in a black fog. A short distance to his right he saw the dim outline of the steps to the third level. Nothing moved.

He started for the next set of steps, then stopped. Suddenly, there was movement all around him. As he watched, a crowd of dark shapes rose from the floor and the shadowed corners. Glaeken swiveled left and right, quickly counting a dozen German corpses.

So . . . Rasalom wasn't alone when he retreated.

As the corpses lurched toward him, Glaeken positioned himself with the next flight of stairs to his rear and prepared to meet them. They didn't frighten him—he knew the scope and limits of Rasalom's powers and was familiar with all his tricks. Those animated lumps of dead flesh could not hurt him.

But they did puzzle him. What did Rasalom hope to gain by this grisly diversion?

With no conscious effort on his part, Glaeken's body

set itself for battle—legs spread, the right slightly rearward of the left, sword held ready before him in a two-handed grip—as the corpses closed in. He did not have to do battle with them; he knew he could stroll through their ranks and make them fall away to all sides by merely touching them. But that was not enough for him. His warrior instinct demanded that he strike out at them. And Glaeken willingly gave in to that demand. He ached to slash at anything connected with Rasalom. These dead Germans would feed the fire he would need for his final confrontation with their master.

The corpses had gained momentum and were now a closing semicircle of dim forms rushing toward him, arms outstretched, hands set into claws. As the first came within reach, Glaeken began to swing the sword in short, slicing arcs, severing an arm to his right, lopping off a head to his left. There was a white flash along the length of the blade each time it made contact, a hiss and sizzle as it seared its way effortlessly through the dead flesh, and a rising curl of oily yellow smoke from the wound as each cadaver went limp and sank to the floor.

Glaeken spun and swung and spun again, his mouth twisting at the nightmarish quality of the scene around him. It was not the pale voids of the oncoming faces, gray in the muted light, that disconcerted him, or the stench of them. It was the *silence*. There were no commands from officers, no cries of pain or rage, no shouts of bloodlust. Only shuffling feet, the sound of his own breathing, and the sizzle of the sword as it did its work.

This was not battle, this was cutting meat. He was only adding to the carnage the Germans had wrought upon one another hours earlier. Still they pressed toward him, undaunted, undauntable, the ones behind pushing against those closest to Glaeken, ever tightening the ring.

With half of the cadavers piled at his feet, Glaeken took a step backward to give himself more room to swing. His heel caught on one of the fallen bodies and he began to stagger back, off balance. In that instant he sensed movement above and behind him. Startled, he glanced up to see two cadavers come hurtling down off the steps leading to the next level. There was no time to dodge. Their combined weight struck him with numbing force and bore him to the floor. Before he could throw them off, the remaining cadavers were upon him, piling on one another and pinning Glaeken under half a ton of dead flesh.

He remained calm, although he could barely breathe under the weight. The little air that did reach him reeked with a mixture of burnt flesh, dried blood, and excrement from those cadavers with gut wounds. Gagging, grunting, he marshaled all his strength and forced his body upward through the suffocating pile.

As he raised himself to his hands and knees, he felt the stone blocks of the floor beneath him begin to vibrate. He did not know what it meant or what was causing it—Glaeken knew only that he had to get away from here. With a final convulsive heave, he threw off the remaining bodies and leaped to the steps.

Behind him there came a loud grinding and scraping of stone upon stone. From the safety of the steps he turned and saw the section of the floor where he had been pinned disappear. It shattered and fell away, taking many of the cadavers with it. There was a muffled crash as the tumbling stone and flesh struck the first-floor landing directly below.

Shaken, Glaeken leaned against the wall to catch his breath and clear the stench of the cadavers from his nostrils. There was a reason behind these attempts to hinder his progress—Rasalom never acted without a purpose—but what? As Glaeken turned to make his way up to the third level, movement on the floor caught his eye. At the edge of the hole a severed arm from one of the corpses had begun dragging itself toward him, clawing its way along the floor with its fingers. Shaking his head in bafflement, Glaeken continued up the steps, his thoughts racing through what he knew of Rasalom, trying to guess what was going on in that twisted mind. Halfway up, he felt a trickle of falling dust brush against his face. Without looking up, he slammed himself flat against the wall just in time to avoid a stone block falling from above. It landed with a shattering crash on the spot he had occupied an instant before.

An upward glance showed that the stone had dislodged itself from the inner edge of the stairwell. Rasalom's doing again. Did Rasalom still harbor hopes of maiming or disabling him? Rasalom must know that he was only forestalling the inevitable confrontation.

But the outcome of that confrontation . . . that was anything but inevitable. In the powers each of them had been allotted, Rasalom had always had the upper hand. Chief among his powers were command over light and darkness, and the power to make animals and inanimate objects obey his will. Above all, Rasalom was invulnerable to trauma of any kind, from any weapon— save Glaeken's rune sword.

Glaeken was not so well armed. Although he never aged or sickened and had been imbued with a fierce vitality and supernal strength, he could succumb to catastrophic injury. He had come close to succumbing in the gorge. Never in all his millennia had he felt death's chill breath so close on the nape of his neck. He had managed to outrun it, but only with Magda's help.

The scales were nearly balanced now. The hilt and blade were reunited—the sword was intact in Glaeken's hands. Rasalom had his superior powers but was hemmed in by the walls of the keep; he could not retreat and plan to meet Glaeken another day. It had to be now. Now!

Glaeken approached the third level cautiously. It was deserted—nothing moving, nothing hiding in the dark. As he walked across the landing to the next flight of stairs, he felt the tower tremble. The landing shook, then cracked, then fell away, almost beneath his feet, leaving him pressed against a wall with his heels resting precariously on a tiny ledge. Peering over the toes of his boots, he saw the crumbling stone block of the floor crash down to the landing below in a choking cloud of dust.

Too close, he thought, allowing himself to breathe

again. *And yet, not close enough.*

He surveyed the wreckage. Only the landing had fallen away. The third-level rooms were still intact behind the wall against his back. He turned around and inched his way along the ledge toward the next set of steps. As he passed the door to the rooms, it was suddenly jerked open and Glaeken found himself facing the lunging forms of two more German cadavers. They flung themselves against him as one, going slack as soon as they made contact with him, but striking with enough force to knock him backwards. Only the fingertips of his free hand saved him from falling by catching and clinging to the doorjamb as he swung out in a wide arc over the yawning opening below.

The pair of corpses, unable to cling to anything, fell limp and silent through the darkness to the rubble below.

Glaeken pulled himself inside the doorway and rested. *Much too close.*

But he could now venture a guess as to what his ancient enemy had in mind: Had Rasalom hoped to push him into the opening and then collapse all or part of the tower's inner structure down on him? If the falling tons of rock did not kill Glaeken once and for all, they would at least trap him.

It could work, Glaeken thought, his eyes searching the shadows for more cadavers lying in wait. And if successful, Rasalom would be able to use the German corpses to remove just enough rubble to expose the sword. After that he would have to wait for some villager or traveler to happen by—someone he could induce to take the sword and carry it across the threshold. It might work, but Glaeken sensed that Rasalom had something else in mind.

Magda watched with dread and dismay as Glaeken disappeared into the tower. She yearned to run after him and pull him back, but Papa needed her—more now than at anytime before. She tore her heart and mind away from Glaeken and bent to the task of tending her father's wounds.

They were terrible wounds. Despite her best efforts to stanch its flow, Papa's blood was soon pooled around him, seeping between the timbers of the causeway and making the long fall to the stream that trickled below.

With a sudden flutter his eyes opened and looked at her from a mask that was ghastly in its whiteness.

"Magda," he said. She could barely hear him.

"Don't talk, Papa. Save your strength."

"There's none left to save . . . I'm sorry . . ."

"Shush!" She bit her lower lip. *He's not going to die—I won't let him!*

"I have to say it now. I won't have another chance."

"That's not—"

"Only wanted to make things right again. That was all. I meant you no harm. I want you to know—"

His voice was drowned out by a deep crashing rumble from within the keep. The causeway vibrated with the force of it. Magda saw clouds of dust billowing out of the second- and third-level windows of the tower. *Glaeken . . . ?*

"I've been a fool," Papa was saying, his voice even weaker than before. "I forsook our faith and everything else I believe in—even my own daughter—because of his lies. I even caused the man you loved to be killed."

"It's all right," she told him. "The man I love still lives! He's in the keep right now. He's going to put an end to this horror once and for all."

Papa tried to smile. "I can see in your eyes how you feel about him . . . if you have any sons . . ."

There was another rumble, much louder than the first. Magda saw dust gush out from all the levels of the tower this time. Someone was standing alone on the edge of the tower roof. When she turned back to Papa his eyes were glazed and his chest was still.

"Papa?" She shook him. She pounded his chest and shoulders, refusing to believe what all her senses and instincts told her. "Papa, wake up! *Wake up!*"

She remembered how she had hated him last night, how she had wished him dead. And now . . . now she wanted to take it all back, to have him listen to her for just a single minute, to have him hear her say she had forgiven him, that she loved and revered him and that nothing had really changed. Papa couldn't leave without letting her tell him that!

Glaeken! Glaeken would know what to do! She looked up at the tower and saw that there were now two figures facing each other on the parapet.

Glaeken sprinted up the next two flights to the fifth level, dodging falling stone, skirting sudden holes in the floors. From there it was a quick vertical climb out of the darkness to the tower roof.

He found Rasalom standing on the parapet at the far side of the roof, his cloak hanging limp in the expectant hush before sunrise. Below and behind Rasalom lay the mist-choked Dinu Pass; and beyond that, the high eastern wall of the pass, its crest etched in fire by the awakening sun, as yet unseen.

As he started forward, Glaeken wondered why Rasalom waited so calmly in such a precarious position. When the roof suddenly began to crumble and fall away beneath his feet, he knew. In a purely reflexive move, Glaeken made a headlong lunge to his right and managed to fling his free arm over the parapet. By the time he had pulled himself up to a crouching position, the roof and all the inner structure of the third, fourth, and fifth levels had fallen away to crash onto and break through the second level with an impact that shook the remaining structure of the tower. The tons of debris came to rest on the first level, leaving Glaeken and Rasalom balanced on the rim of a giant hollow cylinder of stone. But Rasalom could do nothing more to the tower. The images of the hilt laid into the outer walls made them proof against his powers.

Glaeken moved counterclockwise around the rim, expecting Rasalom to back away.

He did not. Instead, he spoke in the Forgotten Tongue.

"So, barbarian, it's down to the two of us again, isn't it?"

Glaeken did not reply. He was feeding his hatred, stoking the fires of rage with thoughts of what Magda had endured at Rasalom's hands. Glaeken needed that rage to strike the final blow. He couldn't allow himself to think or listen or reason or hesitate. He had to strike. He had weakened five centuries ago when he had imprisoned Rasalom instead of slaying him. He would not weaken now. This conflict had to find its end.

"Come now, Glaeken," Rasalom said in a soft, conciliatory tone. "Isn't it time we put an end to this war of ours?"

"Yes!" Glaeken said through clenched teeth. He glanced down at the causeway and saw the miniature figure of Magda bending over her stricken father. The old berserker fury reared up in him, pushing him to run the last four paces with his sword poised for a two-handed decapitating blow.

"Truce!" Rasalom screamed and cowered back, his composure shattered at last.

"No truce!"

"Half a world! I offer you half a world, Glaeken! We'll divide it evenly and you can keep whomever you wish with you! The other half will be mine."

Glaeken slowed, then raised the sword again. "No! No half measures this time!"

Rasalom ferreted out Glaeken's worst fear and flung it at him. "Kill me and you seal your own doom!"

"Where is that written?" Despite all his prior resolve, Glaeken could not help but hesitate.

"It doesn't need to be written! It's obvious! You continue to exist only to oppose me. Eliminate me and you eliminate your reason for being. Kill me and you kill yourself."

It *was* obvious. Glaeken had dreaded this moment since that night in Tavira when he had first become aware of Rasalom's release from the cell. Yet all the while, in the back of his mind, there had been a tiny hope that killing Rasalom would not be a suicidal act.

But it was a futile hope. He had to face that. The choice was clear: Strike now and end it all or consider a truce.

Why not a truce? Half a world was better than death. At least he would be alive . . . and he could have Magda at his side.

Rasalom must have guessed his thoughts.

"You seem to like the girl," Rasalom said, looking down toward the causeway. "You could keep her with you. You wouldn't have to lose her. She's a brave little insect, isn't she?"

"That's all we are to you? Insects?"

" 'We'? Are you such a romantic that you still count yourself among *them*? We are above and beyond anything they could ever hope to be—as close to gods as they'll ever see! We should unite and act the part instead of warring as we do."

"I've never set myself apart from them. I've tried all along to live as a normal man."

"But you're *not* a normal man and you can't live as one! They die while you go on living! You *can't* be one of them. Don't try! Be what you are—their superior! Join me and we'll rule them. Kill me and we'll *both* die!"

Glaeken wavered. If only he could have a little more time to decide. He wanted to be rid of Rasalom once and for all. But he didn't want to die. Especially not now after he had just found Magda. He couldn't bear the thought of leaving her behind. He needed more time with her.

Magda . . . Glaeken dared not look, but he could feel her eyes on him at this very moment. A great heaviness settled in his chest. Only moments ago she had risked

everything to hold Rasalom in the keep and give him
time. Could he do any less and still deserve her? He
remembered her glowing eyes as she had handed him the
hilt: *"I knew you would come."*

He had lowered his sword while battling with himself.
Seeing this, Rasalom smiled. And that smile was the
final impetus.

For Magda! Glaeken thought and lifted the point. At
that moment the sun topped the eastern ridge and
poured into his eyes. Through the glare he saw Rasalom
diving toward him.

Glaeken realized in that instant why Rasalom had
been so talkative, why he had tried so many seemingly
fruitless delaying tactics, and why Rasalom had allowed
him to approach within striking range of the sword: He
had been waiting for the sun to crest the mountains
behind him and momentarily blind Glaeken. And now
Rasalom was making his move, a last, desperate attempt
to remove Glaeken and the hilt from the keep by
pushing them both over the edge of the tower.

He came in low under the point of Glaeken's sword,
his arms outstretched. There was no room for Glaeken
to maneuver—he could not sidestep, nor could he safely
retreat. All he could do was brace himself and lift the
sword higher, dangerously high until his arms were
almost straight up over his head. Glaeken knew it raised
his center of gravity to a precarious level, but he was no
less desperate than Rasalom. It had to end here and
now.

When the impact came—Rasalom's hands ramming
against his lower rib cage with numbing force—Glaeken
felt himself driven backwards. He concentrated on the
sword, driving the point down into Rasalom's exposed
back, piercing him through. With a scream of rage and
agony, Rasalom tried to straighten up, but Glaeken held
on to the sword as he continued to fall backwards.

Together they toppled over the edge and plummeted
down.

Glaeken found himself unnaturally calm as they
seemed to drift through the air toward the gorge below,

locked in combat to the very end. He had won.

And he had lost.

Rasalom's scream wavered to a halt. His black, incredulous eyes bulged toward Glaeken, refusing to believe even now that he was dying. And then he began to shrivel—the rune sword was devouring him body and essence as they fell. Rasalom's skin began to dry, peel, crack, flake off, and fly away. Before Glaeken's eyes, his ancient enemy crumbled into dust.

As he approached the level of the fog, Glaeken looked away. He caught a glimpse of Magda's horrified expression as she watched from the causeway. He began to lift his hand in farewell but the fog engulfed him too soon.

All that remained now was the shattering impact with the stones invisible below.

Ŧ

Magda stared at the two figures atop the tower parapet. They were close, almost touching. She saw the red of Glaeken's hair turn to fire as it caught the light of the rising sun, saw a flash of metal, and then the two figures grappled. They twisted and teetered on the edge. Then they fell as one.

Her own scream rose to join the fading wail from one of the struggling pair as their intertwined forms fell into the ebbing mist and were lost from sight.

For a long frozen moment time stood still for Magda. She did not move, did not breathe. Glaeken and Rasalom had fallen together, and had been swallowed up by the fog in the gorge. *Glaeken had fallen!* She had watched helplessly as he plunged to certain death.

Dazed, she stepped to the edge of the causeway and looked down at the spot where this man who had come to mean everything to her had disappeared. Her mind and body were completely numb. Darkness encroached on the periphery of her vision, threatening to overwhelm her. With a start she shook off the awful lethargy, the creeping desire to lean farther and farther over the edge until she, too, toppled forward and joined Glaeken below. She turned and began to run along the causeway.

It can't be! she thought as her feet pounded the timbers. *Not both of them! First Papa and now Glaeken —not the two of them at once!*

Off the causeway, she ran to the right toward the closed end of the gorge. Glaeken had survived one fall into the gorge—he could survive two! *Please, yes!* But this fall was so much farther! She scrambled down the wedge of rocky debris, unmindful of the scrapes and bruises she collected along the way. The sun, although not high enough yet to shine directly into the gorge, was warming the air in the pass and thinning the mist. She made her way swiftly across the floor of the gorge, stumbling, falling, picking herself up and pushing on, as close to a run as the broken, rutted terrain permitted. Passing under the causeway, she blotted out the thought of Papa's body lying up there alone, unattended. She splashed across the stream to the base of the tower.

Panting, Magda stopped and turned in a slow circle, her frantic eyes searching among the boulders and rocks for some sign of life. She saw no one . . . nothing.

"Glaeken?" Her voice sounded weak and raspy. She called again, "Glaeken?"

No answer.

He has to be here!

Something glittered not far away. Magda ran over to look. It was the sword . . . what was left of it. The blade had shattered into countless fragments; and among the fragments lay the hilt, bereft of its glossy gold and silver hues. An immeasurable sense of loss settled over Magda as she lifted the hilt and ran her hands over its dull-gray surface. A reverse alchemy had occurred; it had turned to lead. Magda fought against the conclusion, but deep within her she knew that the hilt had served the purpose for which it had been designed.

Rasalom was dead, therefore the sword was no longer

necessary. Neither was the man who had wielded it.

There would be no miracle this time.

Magda cried out in anguish, a formless sound that escaped her lips involuntarily and continued for as long and as loud as her lungs and voice could sustain it. A sound full of loss and despair, reverberating off the walls of the keep and the gorge, echoing away into the pass.

And when the last trace of it had died away, she stood with bowed head and slumped shoulders, wanting to cry but all cried out; wanting to strike out at whoever or whatever was to blame for this, but knowing everyone—everyone but her—was dead; wanting to scream and rage at the blind injustice of it all but too dead inside to do anything more than give way to deep, dry, wracking sobs from the very core of her being.

Magda stood there for what seemed like a long time and tried to find a reason to go on living. There was nothing left. Every single thing she had cherished in life had been torn from her. She could not think of one reason to go on . . .

And yet there had to be. Glaeken had lived so long and had never run out of reasons to go on living. He had admired her courage. Would it be an act of courage now to give up everything?

No. Glaeken would have wanted her to live. Everything he was, everything he did, had been for life. Even his death had been for life.

She hugged the hilt against her until the sobs stopped, then turned and began walking away, not knowing where she would go or what she would do, but knowing she would somehow find a way and a reason to keep going.

And she would keep the hilt. It was all she had left.

EPILOGUE

I'm alive.

He sat in the darkness, touching his body to reassure himself that he still existed. Rasalom was gone, reduced to a handful of dust flung into the air. At last, after ages, Rasalom was no more.

Yet I live on. Why?

He had plummeted through the fog, landing on the rocks with force enough to shatter every bone in his body. The blade had broken, the hilt had changed.

Yet he lived on.

At the moment of impact he had felt something go out of him and he had lain there waiting to die.

Yet he hadn't.

His right leg hurt terribly. But he could see, he could feel, breathe, move. And he could hear. When he had picked up the sound of Magda approaching across the floor of the gorge, he had dragged himself to the hinged stone at the base of the tower, opened it, and crawled within. He had waited in silence as she called out his name, covering his ears to shut out the pain and bewilderment in her voice, longing to answer her, yet unable to. Not yet. Not until he was sure.

And now he heard her splashing away through the stream. He swung the stone open all the way and tried to stand. His right leg wouldn't support him. Was it broken?—he had never had a broken bone before. Unable to walk, he crawled down to the water. He had to look. He had to know before he did another thing.

At the edge of the stream he hesitated. He could see the growing blue of the sky in the rippled surface of the water. Would he see anything else when he leaned over it?

Please, he said in his mind to the Power he had served, the Power that might no longer be listening. *Please let this be the end of it. Let me live out the rest of my allotted years like a normal man. Let me have this woman to grow old with instead of watching her wither away while I remain young. Let this be the end of it. I have completed the task. Set me free!*

Setting his jaw, he thrust his head over the water. A weary red-haired man with blue eyes and an olive complexion stared back. His image was there! He could see himself! His reflection had been returned to him!

Joy and relief flooded through Glaeken. *It's over! It's finally over!*

He lifted his head and looked across the gorge to the slowly receding figure of the woman he loved like no other woman in all his long life.

"Magda!" He tried to stand but the damn leg still wouldn't hold him up. He was going to have to let it heal like anybody else. "Magda!"

She turned and stood immobile for an eternity. He waved both his arms over his head. He would have sobbed aloud had he remembered how. Among other things, he would have to learn how to cry again.

"Magda!"

Something fell from her hands, something that looked like the hilt to his sword. Then she was running toward him, running as fast as her long legs would carry her, her expression a mixture of joy and doubt, as if she wanted him to be there more than anything in the world but could not allow herself to believe until she had touched him.

Glaeken was there, waiting to be touched.

And far above, a blue-winged bird with a beak full of straw fluttered to a gentle perch on a window ledge of the keep in search of a place to build a nest.